Meet the Sha

This Is
"A delight for readers…a classic love story."
—*RT Book Reviews*, 4 Stars

"Well-written and uniquely appealing… Recommend Chase to fans of Susan Elizabeth Phillips."
—*Booklist*

"Chase has crafted another successful love match that readers will embrace."
—*Publishers Weekly*

Always My Girl
"Vivid descriptions, endearing yet flawed characters, and a steady pace add vibrancy to the well-developed plot."
—*Publishers Weekly*, Starred Review

"The Shaughnessys' return is welcome, as always… This is another winner in a series that is true to life."
—*RT Book Reviews*, 4 Stars

"Spectacular characters with loads of depth…so much more than just a romance. I can't wait to read more about the Shaughnessy family."
—*Night Owl Reviews*

"Chase excels in weaving humor and poignancy into her stories, and she does not disappoint with this one."
—*The Romance Dish*

Also by Samantha Chase

A Sky Full of Stars

SAMANTHA CHASE

sourcebooks
casablanca

Published by Sourcebooks Casablanca, an imprint of Sourcebooks, Inc.
P.O. Box 4410, Naperville, Illinois 60567-4410
(630) 961-3900
Fax: (630) 961-2168
www.sourcebooks.com

Printed and bound in Canada.
MBP 10 9 8 7 6 5 4 3 2 1

Prologue

THE SKY WAS FULL OF STARS. LOOKING UP AT THEM HAD Owen Shaughnessy feeling peace for the first time in days.

He had snuck out of the house and was currently standing on the small hill in the far corner of the yard, far away from the lights and noise. Part of the reasoning was so he could get a better glimpse of the night sky, but the rest was because he couldn't bear to be around the crowd of people inside.

Today had been his mother's funeral.

Even thinking of it made him want to cry again. And now he could do it without an audience.

Taking in the darkened sky, Owen let out a shaky sigh. His heart hurt. Everyone said it was normal, but for once, that didn't make him feel better.

Owen knew he was different—no one ever called him or referred to him as being normal. He was smarter and far more serious than other kids, and that made him a target for bullies and those who were mean-spirited. His only saving grace was a twin brother who was popular and didn't mind coming to Owen's rescue on a daily basis.

Yes, he was fortunate to have Riley, and now with their mother gone, Owen knew he was going to need his brother more than ever. If the steady flow of tears didn't start to let up, Owen figured he would get picked on at school for being a crybaby on top of everything else.

His three older brothers would look out for him too, but they were in different schools and had their own grief to deal with. Another shuddery sigh came out as he looked up and saw one star shining brighter than the others. Logically, Owen knew it to be Sirius, but his heart tried to tell him it was his mother looking down and smiling at him.

Fresh tears threatened to fall.

This was something they used to do together—stargazing. It had been his mother who bought him his first telescope, and it had been his mother who would sit out here with him on clear nights and let him talk all about the cosmos.

"Tell me what we see tonight," Lillian Shaughnessy said.

At six years of age, Owen had already begun studying the solar system in earnest, and his mother let him teach her on their nightly explorations. "You see that star over there?" he asked, pointing at the sky.

Beside him, his mother chuckled. "You'll have to be more specific, Owen. It looks like there are a million stars out tonight."

It was true—the sky was particularly clear tonight. "The really bright one," he replied seriously. "If you look to the side of the moon, you can see it."

"Ah," she began. "Now I see it. It definitely seems bigger and brighter than the rest of them."

"It is. I'm going to ask Mrs. Peters if she can find me a book on the stars tomorrow at school."

Lillian smiled. "I thought you had one of those already."

He shook his head. "All of my books have been about the planets. I'm going to talk about Jupiter tomorrow for show-and-tell."

"Tell me something about Jupiter," she prompted, her tone just as solemn as his. "What are you going to share with the class?"

"You can see four of Jupiter's moons with a pair of binoculars at night. Also, Jupiter spins fast. It only takes ten hours to go from night to day on Jupiter. And because of that, its middle has been stretched out. So instead of being round like the other planets, it's short and fat, kind of like when someone spins pizza dough fast to stretch it out. This shape is called an oblate spheroid."

Lillian looked down at Owen and smiled. "Wow! Very impressive. And I like the way you used the analogy of the pizza dough. Very clever. You gave a good visual to understand."

He shrugged. "It won't matter. They'll still make fun of me for it."

She frowned. "Why do you say that?"

Another shrug. "They all bring in stuff like frogs or their remote-control cars for show-and-tell. I'm the only one who talks about science." He paused. "Maybe I should just bring in one of my toys or something."

"Maybe you can bring in your telescope," she suggested.

Owen's eyes lit up. "Really? You'd let me do that?"

Lillian nodded. "Absolutely."

"But...but what if something happens to it? What if someone touches it or breaks it?"

"Hmm...that is a possibility," she said thoughtfully.

"What if I brought it up to the school and dropped it off right before show-and-tell and then took it home?"

Owen studied her for a moment. "No one else's mom brings their stuff. I'll get picked on for that too."

Lillian crouched down beside him. "Owen Shaughnessy, you listen to me. There is nothing wrong with you. Do you understand me?" Her tone was gentle, but her eyes were a little fierce. "You are an amazing young man with a brilliant mind. I don't want you living your life in fear of what other people do or think. You can't control that. You can only be the best person you can be, and if they don't like it, then that's their problem."

"But, Mom—"

"I'll tell you what," she quickly interrupted. "I'll bring your telescope to the office and have them call you to come and pick it up. And when you're done, you can bring it back to the office and I'll take it home. How does that sound?"

He nodded solemnly. "Thanks, Mom."

She smiled. "One day, Owen, you're going to realize how amazing you are. And people are going to flock to you because of it. You're going to make a big difference in this world. Believe me."

Somehow he doubted it, but it was nice of her to say it. Rather than respond, he looked back up at the sky. "Did you know that Jupiter is the largest planet in our solar system? Earth could fit inside Jupiter more than a thousand times."

Without a word, Lillian stood back up and put her arm around him and listened as he told her more about what he had learned about Jupiter.

Who was going to stand out here and listen to him talk about astronomy now? It was something only the two of them did together—it was their special time.

Walking over to the shed, Owen went inside, pulled out his telescope, and set it up. Maybe he'd be able to get a better look at Sirius tonight and convince his heart that it really was just a star he was seeing and not his mother looking down on him.

Although, for the first time in his life, Owen Shaughnessy wanted to prove science wrong. As much as he hated to admit it, he secretly hoped that when he looked through the lens, it wasn't a binary star system he would see but the smiling, understanding, and loving gaze of his mother.

Chapter 1

THERE WAS A GIRL IN OWEN SHAUGHNESSY'S CLASS.

A. Girl.

Okay, a woman. And she wasn't a scientist and she wasn't awkward. She was…pretty. Beautiful, actually. Though he had no idea if she was awkward or not. She had walked into the lecture hall minutes ago, and there were only five minutes left in his talk, so…why was she here? Maybe she was the girlfriend of one of his students?

Looking around the room, he ruled that out. He seemed to be the only one taking note of her presence. He chanced another glance her way, and she smiled. He felt a nervous flutter in the region of his belly, and as he continued to look at her, her smile grew.

And now Owen felt like he was going to throw up.

He immediately forced his gaze away and looked at the notes in front of him. "Next time we'll be discussing dust trails and dust tails, which represent large and small dust particles, respectively. Please refer to your syllabus for the required reading material." Lifting his head, Owen scanned the large lecture hall and noted the almost universally bored expressions staring back at him.

Except for her. She was still smiling.

He cleared his throat before adding, "Class dismissed."

There was a collective sigh of relief in the room as everyone stood and began collecting their belongings.

As the students began to file past him, Owen did his best to keep his eyes down and not react to the words he was hearing.

Geek. Nerd. Weird. Awkward.

Yeah, Owen not only heard the words being murmured but knew they were being used to describe him. It was even worse considering the students in the room were all interested in the same subject he was—astronomy. So even in a group of his peers, he was still the odd man out. He shrugged. He'd learned not to let the hurtful words land—to fester—but sometimes they stung a little.

Okay, a lot.

Packing up his satchel, he kept his head down as the class of two hundred students made their way out. Or escaped. Maybe that was the better word for it. He didn't make eye contact with any of them—he simply went about his task of collecting his papers and belongings so the next instructor could come in and set up on time. He was nothing if not polite and conscientious.

His phone beeped to indicate a new text, and he couldn't help but smile when he pulled out his phone and saw it was from his twin brother, Riley.

Skype. Tonight. 8 your time.

Refusing to acknowledge how once again he and his brother were in sync with one another—Riley loved to say it was because they were twins—Owen was at the very least grateful for the timing. There were just times when he needed to talk to someone—or, more specifically, Riley—and there he was.

And the more he commented on it, the more Riley would go on about twin telepathy.

It was ridiculous.

As a man of science, there was no way Owen could accept the phenomenon as fact. Coincidence? Yes. Fact? No. His phone beeped again with a second text from Riley.

Whatever you're stressing about, we'll discuss.

He read the text and chuckled. "Nope," he murmured. "It was just a coincidence."

The last of the students exited the lecture hall as he slipped the phone back into his satchel, and Owen relished the silence. This was how he preferred things—quiet. Peaceful. He enjoyed his solitude, and if it were at all possible, he'd stick to speaking at strictly a few select conferences and then spend the rest of the day doing research and mapping the night sky.

"Excuse me," a soft, feminine voice said.

His entire body froze, and he felt his mouth go dry. Looking up, Owen saw her. Up close, she was even more beautiful. Long blond hair, cornflower-blue eyes, and a smile that lit up her entire face. And that light was shining directly at him.

She wore a long, gauzy skirt with a white tank top. There was a large portfolio case hanging over her shoulder, along with the sweater she'd obviously chosen to do without in the too-warm classroom, and multiple bangle bracelets on her arm.

Gypsy.

No. That wasn't the right word. Gypsies were more

of the dark-haired variety and wore a lot of makeup. This woman was too soft and delicate and feminine to meet that description.

Nymph.

Yes. That was definitely more fitting, and if he were the kind of man who believed there were such things, that's what he would have categorized her as.

He couldn't form a single word.

Her expression turned slightly curious. "Hi. Um... Dr. Shaughnessy?"

She was looking for him? Seriously? Swallowing hard, Owen tried to speak—he really did—but all he could do was nod.

The easy smile was back. Her hand fluttered up to her chest as she let out a sigh of relief. "I'm so sorry for showing up so close to the end of your class. It was inconsiderate of me. I meant to be here earlier. Well, I was supposed to be here for the entire lecture, but I lost track of time talking to Mr. Kennedy." She looked at him as if expecting him to know who she was talking about. "He's the head of the art department," she clarified.

Again, all he could do was nod. He cleared his throat too, but it didn't help.

"Anyway, I'm supposed to meet my uncle here— Howard Shields. He suggested I come and listen to you speak. He thinks very highly of you and thought I'd enjoy your lecture."

Seriously? Howard Shields thought someone would *enjoy* hearing him talk about meteor showers? That wasn't the normal reaction Owen received from his talks. Informative? Educational? Yes. Enjoyable? Never.

Not sure how he should respond, he offered her a

small smile and felt a flush cover him from the tips of his toes to the roots of his hair. She was probably regretting listening to her uncle. As it was, she was looking at him expectantly.

"Anyway," she said, her voice still pleasant and friendly, "Uncle Howard talks about you all the time, and when he told me you were in Chicago guest lecturing, I knew I had to come and meet you. My uncle really respects your work."

Owen finally met her gaze head-on because her words struck him. It was no secret that Owen looked up to Howard—he'd been a mentor to Owen for as long as he could remember—but to hear it wasn't all one-sided? Well, it meant the world to him.

Most people in his field looked at Owen a little oddly. It wasn't because he didn't know what he was talking about or that he wasn't respected; it was because of his social skills. Or lack thereof. It seemed to overshadow all of his fieldwork, research, and teachings. He was more well-known for being painfully shy than anything else. He was filled with a sense of relief—and pride—to know that Howard had said something nice about him.

And now he also knew he was going to have to speak.

"Um…thank you," he said softly, feeling like his mouth was full of marbles. When he saw her smile broaden, it made him want to smile too.

So he did.

But he had a feeling it wasn't nearly as bright or as at ease as hers.

"Ah, there you are!" They both turned and saw Howard walk into the room, his white lab coat flowing slightly behind him. "I was on my way here and was sidetracked talking with Dr. Lauria about the waiting list for the telescope." He shook his head. "Students are up in arms over the lack of availability."

Owen nodded but remained silent.

"I see you've met my niece, Brooke," Howard said before leaning over and kissing her on the cheek.

"We haven't been formally introduced," she said shyly, turning back to Owen.

"Well, let's rectify that," Howard said, grinning. "Owen Shaughnessy, I'd like you to meet my niece, Brooke Matthews. Brooke, this is Dr. Owen Shaughnessy."

Her smile looked so genuine as she held out her hand to Owen. "Feel free to make fun," she said.

Owen looked at her oddly. "Fun?"

Her head tilted slightly. "Yeah…you know. Because of my name."

Now he was confused. "I'm sorry," he said nervously, "is there something funny about the name *Brooke*?"

Howard laughed out loud and clapped Owen on the shoulder again as he shook his head. "Don't mind him, Brookie. He doesn't get pop culture references."

Pop culture references? Owen looked back and forth between the two of them for some sort of explanation. Then he realized Brooke's hand was still outstretched, waiting for him to take it. Quickly wiping his palm on his slacks, he took her hand in his and gave it a brief shake. He murmured an apology and averted his gaze before stepping back.

Tucking her hair behind her ear, she nodded. "My parents named me after Brooke Matthews, the model." When he still didn't react, she added, "She's also an actress." Still nothing. Looking at her uncle, she shrugged and let out a nervous chuckle. "Well, anyway…um, Uncle Howard, I'm afraid I was late to Dr. Shaughnessy's class."

Howard placed an arm around her and hugged her. "I knew pointing you in the direction of the art department was going to be a problem." He chuckled and turned to Owen. "Brooke is an artist and looking to either intern here at the university or maybe get a lead on a gallery where she can work and perhaps get her paintings looked at." He smiled lovingly at her. "She teaches painting classes during the summer semester at the community college, but she's far too talented to keep doing it."

"Uncle Howard," she said shyly.

"What? It's true!"

Owen still couldn't quite figure out why Brooke was here or why Howard had thought she should come to hear him lecture. He was just about to voice the question when Howard looked at him.

"Brooke's specialty is painting the night sky."

For a moment, Owen wasn't sure how to respond.

Brooke blushed and then looked at Owen to explain. "I know most people would say the night sky is simply dark—or black—with some stars, but I don't see it that way. I see the way the stars reflect off one another and how it causes different hues in the sky." She gave a small shrug. "Most of the time my work is a little more… Well, it's not abstract, but it's more whimsical than a true portrait."

"Don't just tell him about it," Howard suggested. "You have your portfolio with you. Why don't you show him?"

"Oh!" Brooke turned and took the leather case from her shoulder and laid it on the desk in front of her.

Owen watched in fascination as she worked, noting her slender arms and the music that came from her wrists as her bracelets gently clattered together. Her long hair fell over one shoulder, and it was almost impossible to take his eyes off her.

"I hope we're not keeping you, Owen," Howard said, stepping closer. "I probably should have asked you earlier about your schedule before we both sort of bombarded you like this."

He shook his head. "I…I don't have anything else scheduled for this afternoon. I had planned on heading back to the hotel and doing some reading before dinner. I'll talk with Riley later." Howard and Owen had known each other for so long that he didn't need to specify anything regarding his family—Howard knew all about them.

"How's he doing? Is he back in the studio yet?"

"Not yet. He didn't want to do another solo project, but getting the band back together isn't going as smoothly as he'd hoped."

Hands in his pockets, Howard nodded. "That's too bad. Still…I'm sure the time off is enjoyable. How is Savannah doing?"

Owen smiled at the mention of his sister-in-law. "She's doing well. She found an agent, and she's submitting proposals for a book she's been working on."

"Wonderful! Is it based on her work interviewing rock stars?"

Beside them, Brooke straightened and gasped.

"Are you okay, my dear?" Howard asked.

But Brooke was looking directly at Owen. "You're Riley Shaughnessy's brother," she said. It wasn't a question but a simple statement of fact.

A weary sigh was Owen's immediate response. This was how it normally went—not that it happened very often. At least not to him. But he heard from his other brothers what usually occurred when a woman found out they were related to Riley. And it wasn't as if Owen knew Brooke or was involved with her, but he braced himself for the disappointment of knowing that from this point on, she was probably only going to want to talk about his famous brother.

And for the first time in a long time—possibly since high school—he resented his twin.

Might as well get it over with.

Clearing his throat, Owen nodded. "Um…yes. Riley's my brother."

Brooke nodded, her smile just as sweet as it had been since she walked into the lecture hall. "How fascinating! I mean, I think it is, anyway, to see such diversity in a family."

And here it comes, he thought.

"You're both so talented but in such different occupations. Your parents must be incredibly proud of you both!" Then she turned and straightened her pictures.

Wait…that was it? She wasn't going to obsess or go on and on about how talented Riley was or how much she loved his latest song?

"So let me ask you," she began as she turned to face him, and Owen braced himself again. Now she was going to do it. Now she was going to gush. "What colors do you see when you look up at the night sky? Do you just see black, or do you see different shades of blue?"

He stared at Brooke.

Hard.

And his jaw was quite possibly on the floor.

"Owen?" Howard asked, stepping forward. "Are you all right?"

He shook his head as if to clear it and then focused on Brooke and said the first thing that came to mind. "Why aren't you talking about Riley?"

She looked at him as if he were a little bit crazy and then turned to her uncle before looking at Owen again, shrugging. "I'm sorry. Did you want to talk about him? I thought I was going to show you some examples of my paintings."

He blinked, still unable to believe what he was hearing. Glancing at Howard, he saw the older man smirking as if he knew exactly what was going on in Owen's mind. People always wanted to talk about Riley. He was big news. People liked celebrities, and he was far more interesting than most. Certainly more interesting than Owen.

"Oh...um. Yes. Yes. You were going to show me your paintings," he said nervously, and he stepped forward to take a look.

And was rendered speechless.

Not that it was hard to do—Owen was already a man of few words—but the canvases Brooke had strewn across the desk were nothing like he was expecting.

The colors were bold and bright, and made with large brushstrokes. He thought of Van Gogh's painting *The Starry Night* and admired how she had layered the paint.

He stepped closer to the desk, picked up the closest painting, and studied it. This one was darker—it portrayed gravitational waves—and Brooke had managed to capture all of the light and the colors, and make it feel as if you could reach into the painting and touch the stars. It was brilliant. It was compelling. It was… He put it down and picked up the next one. A shooting star. It was a little more whimsical than the previous one, but the colors were just as vibrant, and looking at it made Owen feel as if he were looking through his telescope and watching the stars fly across the night sky.

"So what do you…?"

He placed the painting down—ignoring Brooke's attempt at a question—and picked up the third painting. This was the one that reminded him of Van Gogh. This had depth, texture. Owen wasn't in the least bit artistic, but he knew what he was looking at was amazing. Gently he ran his hand over the canvas, taking in the feel of the paint, and was mesmerized. How many times had he wished he could reach out and touch the sky, to feel the heat of a star and study its contours? And standing here now, that was exactly what he felt he was doing. Unable to help himself, he looked at Brooke with wonder. "This is…amazing." And then he wanted to curse himself because that description didn't do her work justice.

And yet she looked pleased.

Relieved.

Her hand fluttered up over her chest as she let out a happy sigh. "Thank you. I know they're all different. I'm trying to find the style that calls to me the most and reflects how I'm feeling, but they all do. It sort of depends on the night. Does that make sense?"

Owen had no idea if it did or it didn't—he certainly had never tried this medium, so who was he to judge? But he was still confused. What did her artwork have to do with him? And again, as if reading his mind, Howard spoke.

"Brooke's favorite subject is nature—particularly the night sky and sunsets, that sort of thing. She's been talking about wanting to go out to the desert and paint, and I immediately thought of you and the Nevada project."

It still didn't make sense to him. "The Nevada project?" Owen parroted. "But…that's to watch the meteor shower, and it's for students and undergrads. I…I don't understand."

Beside them, Brooke cleared her throat and began collecting her paintings. "I should probably let the two of you talk," she murmured. "I thought it was already—"

Howard cut her off. "I meant to discuss this with Owen sooner, but our schedules haven't quite matched up. You don't need to leave, Brooke. It's good that you're here and we can go over it together."

Nodding, she continued to put her things away and then stood back silently while her uncle explained his idea.

"I fully support Brooke's work and her desire to experience different places to paint. But her heading off to the desert alone just isn't practical or safe. Her mother has some…issues, and Brooke is willing to respect them for the moment. So she needs to go with a group."

Nodding in agreement, Owen offered a suggestion. "Perhaps she could find painters interested in doing the same thing. Make it an artist's retreat." That was a thing, wasn't it?

"I want you to hear me out, Owen. I have a proposition for you."

Dread sank like a lead weight in his belly.

"You and I both know you're going to need help on your upcoming trip to Red Rock. An assistant. Someone to help you manage your time and keep you on task."

"I don't have a problem with staying on task, Howard," Owen argued lightly. "I have excellent time-management skills—"

"No, what you have is excellent social-avoidance skills. You get too wrapped up in reading and studying, and you forget there are people around you are supposed to be interacting with. This project is going to require you to lead a group of twenty, and that means you have to be accessible to them and able to communicate with them without having a panic attack."

All Owen wanted at the moment was to hide— especially from Brooke. While Owen knew of his own shortcomings, he didn't appreciate them being pointed out to an audience.

Howard placed a reassuring hand on Owen's shoulder and squeezed. "You are an amazing teacher and scientist, Owen. But your people skills could use a little... help. There's nothing wrong with admitting that."

Easy for him to say, Owen thought. The man was one of the most personable professors and scientists he'd ever worked with. "Howard—"

"Brooke is at ease in front of a class and working with people. She's friendly and personable and very sociable. She would be an asset to your team and would free you up to concentrate on the science aspects. And while she's in the desert with you, she could paint. It's a win-win."

"But..." And how did he put this without it coming off as arrogant or a put-down to Brooke? "She's not a scientist, Howard," he said softly, hoping to cushion his words. "I think it's important to have someone working with me who understands the project and what we're doing so if anyone has questions and I'm not available, that person can answer them."

"Owen—"

"No, it's okay, Uncle Howard," Brooke said, her voice soft and not sounding at all offended. "I understand what Dr. Shaughnessy is saying." Then she turned to Owen. "I know I'm not someone you would normally consider having as an assistant, especially here on campus or in the normal scope of your work. What my uncle is proposing is just for the time you're working on this trip to Red Rock. I do have excellent organizational skills, and I'm comfortable working in an office environment and am proficient with all the computer programs you may need to get information ready for this trip. I can make phone calls and set up schedules for you and your group. And once we arrive in Red Rock, I'll be there to help you with the group on a...social level. If that even makes sense."

It did. It seriously did. But Owen wasn't sure he was comfortable with it.

Brooke must have sensed his hesitation because she smiled and then looked at her watch. "I'll tell you what, why don't you think about it and let Uncle Howard know? I have an appointment to get to." She held out her hand to Owen, and this time he didn't hesitate quite so long to shake it. With a quick wave to Owen, she gave her uncle a hug and wished them both a good day.

Owen watched her leave and immediately felt as if the sun had gone behind the clouds. The lecture hall felt dark and quiet and…lonely. He stood and watched the empty doorway for several minutes until Howard cleared his throat.

Damn.

He looked over at his mentor and hoped he didn't look like some sort of lovesick puppy.

"Think about it, Owen. I believe Brooke is the perfect person for you." He paused. "And for this project."

And then he was gone too and Owen was completely alone and left wondering if Howard's words were somehow a double entendre.

Brooke slipped into the first empty lecture hall she could find, feeling completely defeated.

Not sure what to do with herself, she walked over to the first row of desks and took a seat. A long, slow sigh came out as she sat there and replayed the last several minutes. It wasn't as if she had been expecting Owen Shaughnessy to jump at the chance to have her work with him, but she still couldn't help but feel…disappointed.

It shouldn't have come as a surprise. She looked down at herself and shook her head. What serious scientist would want someone who looked like her to help him on such a prestigious event? She looked like some sort of bohemian. Why hadn't she thought of that sooner?

Dress for the job you want, not the job you have.

Ugh. How many times had *that* phrase been thrown at her? Too many. And honestly, the job she wanted was to be an artist. Well…to be taken seriously as an artist. But so far, no such luck. Sure, Uncle Howard supported her, but he was the only one. Which was why she had relocated to Chicago from Long Island—because her parents just didn't get it. And they never would.

In their minds, Brooke was wasting her time and energy by pursuing her love of painting. Not that they had high expectations for her in general, but they certainly had been vocal about her need to find a suitable husband from a "good family."

Not interested.

The thought of settling into the type of marriage her parents had was beyond unappealing. The last thing Brooke wanted to do was get married—especially to someone chosen because he looked good on paper and would impress the country club set. It almost made her shudder with revulsion. And her parents were getting even more vocal about their desire to have grandchildren. Right. Like she wanted to inflict the kind of relationship she'd had with her brother on kids of her own.

Again, not interested.

Growing up, she hadn't been particularly nice to her brother—as a matter of fact, she had been out-and-out bitchy. While she had been popular in school and seemed to make friends wherever she went, Neal had been the object of teasing and bullying because he was a computer geek. A nerd. Completely unpopular. While Brooke had been winning beauty pageants, Neal had been tucked away with his nose stuck in a book. It was both comical and sad how their parents had pushed them toward such typical—and outdated—gender roles. The beauty queen and the brainiac.

Just the thought of it made her entire body tense up.

It wasn't until recently that she'd had the epiphany about how unjustly her parents had treated them. It was more than the roles she and Neal had been put in; it was the way they were taught to view one another. She was never allowed to focus on her education, mainly because her mother was busy entering her in pageants. And Neal? Well, he had been encouraged to study hard and make something of himself since he was old enough to read.

Which was at age three.

Her brother was a genius—no one could doubt that— but for the longest time, he had been a major social outcast, and even though he was older, Brooke and her friends had teased him about his social status mercilessly.

Not her finest time in life.

As an adult, things had changed, and Brooke came to realize how being the captain of the cheerleading squad and waving to a crowd while wearing a sash and tiara were only enviable when you were in high school. Out in the real world and dealing with everyday life, her former status didn't benefit her in any way, shape, or form. Yeah. Reality had hit her hard when she went to college and found out there were dozens of girls on campus who had the exact same titles. There was no one to *ooh* and *aah* over her. There was no special treatment from her professors.

And no one was impressed.

As her star was fading, Neal's had started to shine. He'd finally hit his stride, had stopped looking like he was a young boy and grown into a man. He'd gained confidence, and all the people who had once scorned him were now praising him. And while her brother had been making a name for himself, Brooke had been floundering.

Was still floundering.

When her uncle had offered her the chance to come and stay with him in Chicago to look for work, she had grabbed it like a lifeline. Out of all of her relatives, he had always been the one to see how she was more than just a shallow, spoiled girl with a pretty face. She couldn't remember a time when he'd even talked to her about her pageants. He'd always talked to her about school and things that made her think.

It hadn't been easy to ask him to help her get a meeting with the head of the art department here at the university—she didn't want to take advantage of his generosity. It was one thing to encourage her to find work. It was quite another for him to actually have to get personally involved and risk looking foolish to a colleague if she wasn't any good.

Stop thinking so little of yourself!

But here was the thing—it wasn't as if she were asking him to actually *get* her a job. She just needed a little help making some connections. If Brooke was completely honest with herself, she wasn't even sure why she was seeking his help. Hell, she wasn't even sure what job she was looking for or what she hoped to achieve by coming here. She loved painting and drawing, and had an appreciation for art history, but she wasn't quite sure if teaching was her thing. Or if she was even qualified to teach beyond the community college level. Night school, essentially. She didn't have a degree in teaching. She didn't have a degree in anything.

So why am I here?

Good question.

In her typical pattern of over-researching everything,

she'd found that the head of the art department was truly talented and had done very well in multiple showings and galleries. More than anything, Brooke wanted to pick his brain—and maybe see if he could give her some direction on how and where to focus her time and energy to get her own name out there, as well as her work.

Over the last week, Uncle Howard had pretty much been in cheerleader mode, encouraging her choice of trying to make art her career. She wished she shared his optimism. But she wasn't like him. Uncle Howard had known since he was eight that he wanted to be an astrophysicist. He'd been fascinated by the solar system his entire life, and he had turned that love into a respected career, teaching and traveling to different colleges and universities to give lectures. There wasn't a doubt in Brooke's mind that, even if she poured all of her energy into her art, it was unlikely she'd have a career as successful as her uncle's. There were thousands of artists out there, and she was quickly becoming familiar with the phrase *starving artist*. If she didn't find work soon, she'd be able to drop the *artist* part of that statement.

It was tiring to keep searching for creative ways to pay the bills—working part-time jobs at galleries—and doing her best to network with people who could help her and also have time to travel when she found a lead. And though she appreciated her uncle taking her in for the next couple of months, she just hoped it wasn't all for nothing.

When he'd mentioned working with Owen Shaughnessy out in Red Rock three days ago, it seemed almost too good to be true. The chance to paint in the desert and have someone so highly respected take her on as an assistant? It had seemed like the perfect opportunity. And even though Brooke initially felt excited about it, it didn't take long for her own insecurities to come to the surface.

In a lot of ways, Owen reminded her of Neal—quiet, shy, and scary smart. When they were younger, Brooke took great pleasure in making fun of him because he was socially inept. She'd outgrown it, had apologized for it, but she'd never been able to forget it. And she certainly never received his forgiveness. And now...

She stopped the train of thought and sighed. She had a feeling Owen had probably experienced a lot of the same bullying Neal had—and probably at the hands of people just like her. It would serve her right if he didn't want her to work with him. As a former "mean girl," she knew she didn't deserve anyone's forgiveness for her behavior. No mercy. Which was exactly how she used to view those she deemed to be socially beneath her.

Maybe someday she'd be able to forgive herself.

But she doubted it.

Taking a deep breath, she stood and knew she needed to get going. There was no way she could stay here in this empty lecture hall and hide out all day—no matter how much she wanted to. Securing her portfolio strap over her shoulder, Brooke made her way to the door and pulled it open. There were several people in the hallway, but luckily none of them were her uncle or Owen Shaughnessy.

She looked around at the display cases as she made her way toward the exit. The science department wasn't a place where she was comfortable. Even though she loved painting the night sky and the cosmos, she certainly didn't know anything about them. And without anyone having said a word to her, she felt inferior. With every step she took, she could hear voices mocking her, telling her she wasn't smart enough to be there. Wasn't smart enough to assist someone as brilliant as Owen Shaughnessy.

Another sigh escaped before she could help it.

He had seemed nice. Sweet. His shyness had been endearing, and when he looked at her—well, when he had finally looked at her and met her gaze—she felt something she'd never felt before.

A connection.

Maybe she was crazy. Maybe she was imagining things. But as soon as Owen's dark eyes had met hers, she'd felt…well, everything.

He was younger than she had expected—not that her uncle had said too much about him, but for some reason, she had pictured Owen Shaughnessy to be older. After meeting him, she figured him to be in his early thirties, and he was tall but not overly so, with thick, dark-brown hair that probably could have used a haircut but on him looked good. Mussed. A little bit wild.

A giggle came out before she could stop it. She was sure no one would look at Owen and think "wild," but she certainly did. That wasn't to say he didn't have his nerdy vibe going on—because he did—but there was something about him that called to her. And not in a professional "let's work together" kind of way, but as a man.

She swallowed hard and tried to calm her thoughts, which were now starting to wander toward how wise it would be to work with him if she was already feeling like this.

Giddy.

Fluttery.

Totally crushing on a man who'd said maybe five words to her.

Yeah. Maybe this wasn't such a good idea.

Pushing through the heavy exit door, Brooke stepped out into the crisp and cold Chicago air and cursed the fact that she had forgotten to put on her sweater. Shaking her head, she stopped and quickly slipped it on before walking down the steps to the parking lot at a fairly quick pace and making her way to her car. Just as she was opening the door, she saw him off in the distance.

Owen.

He must be through for the day too, she thought, and watched him walk toward what she assumed to be his own car. Why she stood and watched, she couldn't say. She found she enjoyed watching him. He was so different from almost every man she knew, and part of her longed to walk over and talk to him some more.

He seemed lonely.

Her uncle had mentioned how Owen wasn't based out of Chicago but was doing a short-term lecture series here before going to Nevada to prepare for the meteor shower project. And after that, who knew where he was going to go? From what she could tell, Owen Shaughnessy hadn't settled anywhere. He traveled too much. She almost envied him for it and then immediately took the thought back.

No wonder he was lonely.

Brooke wondered if he had any family other than his brother, Riley. Was it just the two of them? Did Owen have anyone he connected with when he wasn't working?

Was he involved with someone? That thought stopped her cold—it bothered her. Here she was just meeting him, yet the thought of feeling the connection she'd felt and then finding out he was involved with—or married to—someone else upset her more than it should have.

Maybe she'd talk to her uncle a little more at dinner tonight.

Maybe she'd have to do some investigating of her own.

Either way, whether she got to work with Owen Shaughnessy or not, Brooke knew today couldn't be their only interaction.

Relief.

It was Owen's immediate reaction when he had returned to his hotel room and closed the door. The entire drive had been spent thinking about Brooke Matthews.

And that reminded him—he needed to do a Google search and figure out who she was talking about because he had a feeling it was a pop culture reference he should know. Of course, it was too late to undo the awkwardness of not knowing it already, but that couldn't be helped. She seemed to recover from his faux pas, so at least there was that.

Right now, all Owen wanted was some peace and quiet to unwind. Maybe read the copy of *Sky & Telescope* he'd picked up just this morning—that would be a great way to relax and forget about the possibility of having a beautiful woman working as his assistant.

Right. As if he was going to forget *that* anytime soon.

Things like that didn't happen to him. Ever. Not that

he didn't date attractive women—he had, but... Wait a minute. He wasn't dating Brooke; he was going to work with Brooke. Maybe. Sighing, he put his satchel and laptop case on the desk and took off his jacket. And whether the assistant was Brooke or somebody else, Howard was right. He needed the help. Badly. As it was, Owen had been warned, repeatedly, that he needed to hone his social skills because his students weren't connecting with him.

If he wasn't on this lecture circuit, Owen knew he wouldn't have to deal with things like this—with the constant stream of people wanting to socialize with him and talk about what he was doing. If he had stayed the course of his original plans, he'd be enjoying quiet time safely ensconced in his research.

Unfortunately, his career had taken a slight detour, and because of his inability to say no, he was stuck doing short-term guest lectures at universities all over the country. If he'd only been able to decline the very first time he'd been asked, Owen had no doubt he'd be happily situated in an office of his choosing right now.

He just wasn't sure where that office would be.

The thought of working close to his family in North Carolina was appealing. More so now that he'd been away for so long. It seemed as if everyone was slowly making their way back to their childhood hometown, and he had to admit he was a little envious, but it wasn't in the cards for him yet. Maybe in another year or so he'd be able to reevaluate his schedule and dictate where he wanted to be, but for now he had commitments he needed to honor, and that meant more time away.

Later that evening, he would have time to Skype with

Riley. Just the thought of his brother made Owen smile. They hadn't had a whole lot of time together in person in the past couple of months—mainly because his brother was on tour, promoting his new solo album—but they always tried to make time to talk via Skype. And lately Owen had felt the need for the connection.

Maybe he was feeling homesick, or maybe he was at a crossroads in his life because his brothers were all settling down and starting families and Owen just didn't see that as a possibility for himself. He didn't have much of a social life, and even though he dated occasionally, Owen had never felt a connection with a woman in a way that mattered. He dated other scientists, and even when they were on dates, they talked about…science.

And the more he learned about his brothers and their wives, the more Owen realized that solid relationships—the kind where you fell in love and formed a bond and wanted a future together—weren't always based on common interests.

Like work.

His eldest brother, Aidan, had met and fallen in love with his wife, Zoe, when she had started working for him. But even though they did have their work in common, they were opposite in a lot of ways. Zoe had been all about starting her life over and forging a new path, while Aidan had been so deeply entrenched in living his life in the past. But it hadn't taken long for his control freak of a brother to let his guard down and learn to accept—and enjoy—their differences.

All the women around Owen were exactly like him.

It was no different with his brother Hugh. Hugh had been emotionally cut off and seemed unlikely to ever settle down in a relationship that was based on love. There had been a time when Owen had actually been able to relate to Hugh the easiest because of that outlook. But after working with the carefree Aubrey, Hugh too had taken the plunge. Hell, last Owen had heard, they'd been on a trip to Belize and were teaching their young son, Connor, to snorkel and swim with the dolphins. And Owen could only listen with a bit of envy because Hugh had come out of his self-imposed emotional exile and was finally living his life.

At the last big convention Owen had gone to, no one had even wanted to get within ten feet of the hotel pool, let alone swim with a dolphin.

And then there was Quinn, the ultimate middle child. He'd been the love-'em-and-leave-'em type for so long that Owen never thought Quinn would settle down either. And for the most part, everyone accepted how that was just the way Quinn was. But through it all, Anna had been there—playing the part of the best friend even though she was secretly in love with Quinn. Then—and this part still made Owen chuckle—Quinn had seen Anna in a bikini and suddenly realized his best friend was a beautiful woman. The entire Shaughnessy family had been happy to see him wake up and notice what had been right in front of him for years.

Having been too shy to even talk to girls when he was younger, Owen had no female friends, let alone any harboring a crush on him, or vice versa.

Riley. His twin. His other half. They were fraternal twins, and it wasn't only their looks that were completely different. Everything about them was. Things came easily to Riley, especially women. And when he met Savannah and she blatantly told him she didn't like him—and hadn't for some time—it had come as quite a shock. Yeah, that was another story that made Owen laugh, imagining his rock-star brother being told there was a female alive who wasn't in love with him. Of course, Riley had changed Savannah's mind, and now they were happily married, but other than their love of rock and roll, they'd had to work hard to overcome some of their differences.

There wasn't even anyone Owen knew of who he'd be able to try to overcome differences with. And there was no way he was going to seek out any kind of relationship advice from Darcy. She might be his sister, but she was so much younger than him. He chuckled to himself. Although she probably had a hell of a lot more experience than he did. Then he shook his head. No. Darcy still scared the hell out of him just because she was so…different from him.

A sigh came out before he could stop it. He definitely needed this time with Riley tonight. Not so long ago, Owen had helped his twin when he was at a crossroad. Now he was hoping Riley would return the favor. The only problem was that Riley had known—sort of—what his problem was. He'd had writer's block and couldn't complete the album he'd been working on. Not that Owen wasn't oversimplifying Riley's issue, but at least there had been a definitive problem for them to work on. Owen couldn't define his problem. He had an overall feeling of discontent in his life, and no amount of looking up at the sky and watching the stars was helping.

And it used to always help.

No matter what was going on.

Hell, when his mother had died, Owen had…

The alarm on his phone beeped, reminding him of his upcoming time to Skype with Riley. Not that he was going to forget it. He was looking forward to the call. Needed it. He might even call his brother early.

He opened up his satchel and went about the task of emptying it out and organizing everything neatly on the desk — his laptop, his phone, his chargers, his notes, and his magazine. Looking at the clock, he confirmed the amount of time he had until Riley's call — two hours and thirty-seven minutes — and frowned.

With nothing left to do, he quickly called and ordered room service — a turkey club sandwich and french fries — and then started up his laptop. He was intent on finding out all he could about Brooke Matthews.

The model-slash-actress *and* the beautiful artist he'd met today.

Chapter 2

"ARE YOU SITTING DOWN?"

"Of course I am. What else would I be doing?"

Riley laughed. "You could be pacing. I had a feeling you were pacing."

"Don't be ridiculous. You can't *feel* like someone's pacing."

"It's a twin thing," Riley said seriously and then started laughing again. "Sometimes you make it too easy, Owen!"

"Ha-ha," Owen replied dryly. "If you remember correctly, we're supposed to be Skyping. Why aren't we Skyping? And for that matter, why does it matter if I'm pacing or sitting?"

"First of all, something's up with the computer. Savannah's looking at it now, so maybe we'll be able to switch over in a few minutes."

"Oh."

"Maybe I should wait until we are…"

"Are what?" Owen asked, not following his brother's train of thought.

"Skyping."

"Ah…no. We'll be fine talking until then. What's going on?"

"I have some news."

"Okay."

"Savannah's pregnant. We're having a baby! Can you believe it?" Riley asked excitedly.

Could he believe it? Yes. Biology was relatively clear, and Owen had no doubt his brother and his wife were... Well, that wasn't important, and he didn't think Riley wanted to hear what he remembered from biology class about how babies were made.

"Um...Owen? You still there?"

"Oh, yeah. Sorry. Congratulations!" he said happily and realized he really was excited about this news. His brothers were all getting married and having babies, but...this was Riley. His twin. This baby just meant a little...more. "So...have you started picking baby names yet?"

Riley chuckled. "It's a bit soon for that, but—"

"I know you. You already have names in mind. You're probably going to make Savannah crazy over the next nine months with them."

"I wouldn't say crazy...but yeah. I've already got a list of names going."

"How is Savannah feeling? Is she okay? Has she had any morning sickness?"

"Not yet, but it's still real early in the pregnancy. She's only six weeks along. Her doctor said it could hit at any time or not at all. There's no way of knowing if she'll get sick or not. Of course, we're hoping she doesn't, but that doesn't mean anything."

"Seventy-five percent of pregnant women experience morning sickness," Owen replied. "It's most common in the first twelve weeks, or the first trimester, but some women have it throughout their entire pregnancy. And it's not just limited to the morning, you know."

"Well, that settles it."

"Settles what?"

"You're not allowed to talk to Savannah yet. You'll freak her out if you start talking statistics like that to her. She's feeling good, and she's optimistic about the whole pregnancy thing, and I want her to stay that way."

Owen felt terrible. It wasn't something he even thought about—sharing statistics and scientific facts about the things he knew. But this was the first time he realized how sometimes those statements could upset the people around him. And he certainly didn't want to upset Savannah.

"I…I'm sorry. I won't say anything like that again," he stammered. "I promise. Please don't let me freak her out. I wasn't thinking."

"Dude, all you do is think," Riley said, but he said it with humor. "It's one of the things we all love about you. But right now Savannah's emotions are…well… they're all over the place, and I never know what's going to set her off. She's cries a lot lately—like at the drop of a hat. I came home today and found her on our closet floor crying."

"What happened? Was she hurt?"

"Nope. She was putting laundry away and realized our hangers didn't all match." He gave a small chuckle. "I mean…who cares about matching hangers?"

"Obviously, your wife does," Owen reasoned.

"This is what I'm saying—she's emotional. I'm not used to seeing her like this—she's normally very calm and levelheaded, and to see her crying all the time? It's killing me. And we've still got, like…months to go!"

"Thirty-four weeks."

"You're not helping, Owen!"

"Sorry." He took a minute to collect his thoughts. "Okay, so…you're having a baby. You're going to be a dad. Are you freaking out?"

"I love how you don't beat around the bush."

"Oh, come on. You can't tell me Quinn, Hugh, and Aidan haven't said the same thing to you already."

"They haven't," Riley said evenly.

"Really? They haven't? Why not?"

"Because I haven't told them yet."

"What?" Owen cried.

"You're the first to know. I haven't even told Dad yet."

"But…but…why?"

"Are you seriously asking me that? Owen…you and me? We're like…one. This is the biggest thing to ever happen to me. Of course you're the first one I'm going to tell."

A lump the size of a golf ball lodged itself in Owen's throat. More than anything he wished he were in the same room with his brother so he could hug him. "I…I'm honored."

They were silent for a moment. "I am scared," Riley said softly.

And now even more, Owen wished they were together. "Why?"

"Savannah grew up as an only child, and we grew up in relative chaos. I know we were a little bit older when Darcy was born, so being around babies doesn't freak me out, but…it's just so much, you know?"

Owen didn't, but he figured he'd let his brother speak.

"Dad worked so much when we were growing up,

and he missed a lot. I don't want to do that. I want to be there for everything. I don't want it to be on Savannah's shoulders to do all the parenting like it was for Mom for so long."

"So you'll be there," Owen said reasonably. "You can control your schedule, Ry. That's the beauty in what you do. Your family can come on tour with you. And think of all the amazing things you'll be able to show him…or her."

Riley sighed loudly. "Yeah, I know, but…but what if something happened?"

"What do you mean?"

"Like with Mom," he said, and Owen could feel the sadness his brother was feeling. "What if something were to happen to Savannah, and then it was just me and the baby?"

"You can't think like that, Riley," Owen said carefully. "You just can't."

"It's kind of hard not to. I mean, I get it. I know we have no control over things like that. Accidents happen all the time, but… I don't know. Maybe Savannah's not the only one who's emotional right now. Maybe this is sympathy emotions. Is that even a thing?" he asked with a nervous chuckle.

"Probably not," Owen replied, laughing a little.

"Okay, so…distract me. Tell me what's going on with you. How are your lectures going?"

"They're okay."

Riley sighed loudly again. "Owen…"

"What?"

"What is going on with you? You sound even more…I don't know…disenchanted than you usually do."

"I usually sound disenchanted? Since when? When did that start? Why haven't you mentioned it before?"

"Okay, maybe that's not the right word, but…you sound different. What's up?"

The last thing Owen wanted to do was burden his brother, especially now, but maybe talking about his situation would help him.

"A beautiful woman wants to go to the desert with me," Owen blurted out before he could stop himself.

"Holy shit! What?" Riley cried. "Wait, wait, wait. Start at the beginning and go slow. I have a feeling you've left out some key information here." He paused, and Owen could hear his brother murmuring something to Savannah. "Hold on."

It was Owen's turn to sigh, and the next thing he knew, his laptop was beeping with an incoming Skype call. Great. Now Riley would not only get to hear how freaked out he was, but he'd be able to see it too. Clicking on the icon, Owen accepted the call and couldn't help but smile when his brother's face filled the screen. "I take it Savannah figured out the problem?"

Riley chuckled. "Um…yeah. Apparently, I forgot to plug the damn thing in earlier, so it was dead. And then we couldn't find the charger because I left it down in the studio. So basically it was all my fault." He laughed again. "As usual. I hate all this electronic crap. It's hard to keep track of it all."

"Not really. If you keep a universal charger in key areas of your home, then you won't have to—"

"Stop trying to change the subject and go back to the beautiful woman in the desert!"

"Oh…right," Owen mumbled and then went on to

tell Riley about his meeting with Howard and Brooke. Owen hadn't spoken long when Riley interrupted him.

"I have to stop you right there. Are you telling me her name is Brooke Matthews? Seriously?"

Owen sagged with a bit of embarrassment. "So you know who this famous Brooke is too?"

"Dude, everyone knows who she is. She used to be one of the biggest models in the world, and she's a great actress and a spokesperson for several big companies. You have to know who she is."

"I had to use Google."

Riley groaned lightly. "I know you watch television, Owen."

"I do, but…it's normally documentaries or the History Channel. I don't watch a lot of what's popular on television. Besides, it's not a crime for me not to know the name of a model."

"Have you seen her?" he teased. "Yes, it is."

"Can we move on from this? I was explaining to you about how this Brooke Matthews is Howard's niece and why he thought she and I should work together."

"You're right, you're right. Sorry. Go on."

Owen went on to describe their conversation and how Brooke was an artist.

"So…wait. She's an artist, and she wants to paint in the desert?" Riley asked.

Owen nodded.

"But Howard thinks she'd make a good assistant? How? Why? I mean, I get the whole two birds with one stone thing, but if she's just interested in painting, what good is she going to be to you?"

"She claims she's also good at organizing things,

and Howard feels…" He paused, shaking his head. He hated to have to admit this again—even to Riley. "He feels I need someone to help me learn how to be better at social interaction."

He expected his brother to laugh—or at the very least grin.

But he didn't.

If anything, Riley looked fierce and pissed off.

"I hope you told them both to go to hell," Riley said firmly.

"Excuse me?"

"You heard me." Then he stopped and took a calming breath. "Owen, there isn't a damn thing wrong with you. You're an amazing scientist, and you love what you do. That's all that should matter. Who cares if you can make social chitchat with people? The truth is you talk about the things that are important to you. And, if memory serves, this whole project out in Nevada is about teaching people about the meteors. So…why are they harping on this social skills thing? You know how to talk about meteors and the planets and the stars! That's what they're paying you to go there and talk about, not about pop culture or whatever current event people are gossiping about!" He cursed. "That's just bullshit!"

If there was one thing Owen loved about his brother, it was how, no matter what, Riley was fiercely defensive of him. No matter what the situation was, Riley had Owen's back, and it was at times like this that Owen was grateful.

"It's not so bad. Really. I…I do need to work on my social skills. Maybe then I'd be a little less of a—"

"Don't say it."

Owen frowned and looked at his brother. "Not saying it doesn't make it any less true, Ry. I'm a freak— socially. I'm not comfortable around people."

"You do fine around us."

"That's family, and it's different, and even then… you guys all make fun of me from time to time. I know it, and I'm okay with it."

"We don't make fun," Riley said with a hint of defensiveness. "You're just very overwhelming. You make the rest of us feel like idiots."

"That's not my intention. Ever. I…I have so much going on in my brain, and sometimes stuff comes out before I can stop it. It usually isn't until after I've said something that I realize how ridiculous it sounds. I mean…no one wants to hear random statistics spouted out at them all the time. I wish I could change it, I do, but I don't know how!"

"Okay," Riley said, sounding calmer. "Then maybe this Brooke person isn't such a bad idea."

"That just sounds…wrong."

"Hear me out—if Howard recommended her, then you know you can trust her. I know how close you and Howard are, and you know he wouldn't steer you wrong, right?"

"*Steer me?* He's not driving me anywhere."

"Figure of speech, Bro. Try to keep up," Riley teased. "All I'm saying is if you need an assistant on this trip, and it seems like you do, then maybe you should take her up on the offer. And you said she's beautiful, right?"

Owen nodded. "I'm not sure what that has to do with anything."

Riley rolled his eyes. "Do you have something against beautiful women?"

"Not exactly."

That fierce look was back on Riley's face. "Was she mean to you? Did she say anything to upset you? And for that matter, do you think Howard would even suggest this working scenario to you if she was going to make you uncomfortable?"

"All women make me uncomfortable," Owen reminded him.

"You do better than you think. You're totally at ease with Savannah, Zoe, Aubrey, Anna, and Darcy."

"That's because they're all family now—and Darcy's our sister! It's not the same thing."

"It's exactly the same thing!"

"So you're saying I should look at Brooke like she's my sister?" He gave a mirthless yet nervous laugh. "I don't think that's even possible."

"Ah…so you do find her attractive!"

Ugh. He always hated talking about women with his brother—any of his brothers. They were all so at ease with the opposite sex while Owen was…not. He could actually feel his face turning red and suddenly wished they had stuck to just talking on the phone.

"Tell me about her," Riley prompted, and Owen knew he wasn't going to be able to avoid doing so.

"She's beautiful," he started. "When she walked into the lecture hall, I was… I don't even know how to describe it. Honestly, no more than the sight of her left me speechless. Besides the fact that women like her don't normally take my classes or come to hear me speak, she walked in and…the entire room was brighter."

A slow grin tugged at Riley's lips, but he stayed silent.

"When she approached me after class and then I was close to her, I realized she was more than beautiful—that word seemed too small to describe her. She smiled, and her entire face glowed," he said with awe. "Fair skin, light-blue eyes, and she has this amazing long blond hair. You just know it would feel soft."

Riley's smile grew, but Owen wasn't paying attention; he was too lost in remembering everything about Brooke.

"And she talked to me like…you know…like I was normal. She seemed excited to work with me." He paused and remembered the sweet sound of her voice as she talked about her skills. "And then there's her art. Her paintings. Riley, they were… I've never seen anything like them before. Maybe in a museum, but…" Owen trailed off, unable to find the right words.

By now Riley was grinning like a loon.

"When I picked them up, I felt like I was actually touching the sky—the entire universe! She has this way of making the colors draw you in, and then there're the textures, and the way she sees them is almost…magical."

Riley's face came close to the screen. "*Magical?* Did you seriously just use the term *magical*?"

"Um—"

"You, Owen Shaughnessy, don't believe in things like that. You've never looked at anything that way. You're a man of science. Of practicality. Even with the most whimsical of things, you tend to look at them in a logical and pragmatic way. And you're sitting here telling me Brooke's work is magical?"

Owen hung his head. "I know. This is a terrible idea, right? I shouldn't even be considering it."

"Hold on." This came from Savannah, who was pushing her husband aside so she could be seen on the screen. "Owen? Look at me."

Her tone was sweet but firm, and knowing she was a little fragile at the moment, Owen did as she asked without arguing.

"Do not listen to your brother." She playfully slapped Riley on the back of the head. "If you think her work is magical, then I think that's great! And if you had that strong of a reaction to it, then she is truly talented. Don't feel bad about how you feel!"

"I...I wasn't. I know Riley was teasing. And he's right. I never look at anything that way, but when Brooke walked into the room in her flowy skirt and bracelets, she reminded me of..." He stopped and shook his head. "Never mind."

"Oh, no," Riley said. "You can't get out of it that easy. Finish the sentence."

"Riley," Savannah sighed, bumping her husband's shoulder. "Leave him alone."

"Hell no. Do you know this has never happened?" He looked at his wife with a big grin still in place. "Owen never gets like this over a girl. Never."

"Well..." Owen stammered.

Riley sighed and gave another exaggerated eye roll. "Okay, he was mildly intrigued by you when he first met you, and he was the one to convince me to stop being such an ass around you, but still. This is different." He turned back to the screen and leaned in close again. "Out with it. What did she remind you of?"

"A fairy. A gypsy. A nymph," he said, his face flaming. "It… I…I never—"

"Okay, okay," Riley said, sitting back and looking satisfied. "We get it. You're totally crushing on her right now. Which makes this whole situation perfect."

"Oh, this I must hear," Savannah said, grinning.

"Hear me out—again. If you let Brooke help you on this project and you find you're comfortable around her, then it's a game changer."

Owen wasn't following.

"If you can sit and comfortably talk with a beautiful woman—have conversations with her that aren't just you spouting encyclopedia passages—then it's going to completely change your world, Bro."

"I think you're oversimplifying this."

Riley shook his head. "Nuh-uh. No way. Trust me on this. Girls make you nervous in general. Pretty girls make you more than a little uncomfortable. Beautiful women practically render you catatonic. Now, according to your theory, you can get over it when you're related to them—like all of your sisters-in-law—but not any other way. Maybe by spending time with Brooke, you'll relax and see she's just like everyone else."

"Somehow I doubt that."

"Owen, you just met her, and from what you described, it lasted all of fifteen minutes. Don't write her off yet."

"I'm not writing her off," Owen said defensively and then huffed with agitation. Why did he have to keep explaining himself over and over and over? "I like Brooke. A lot. And spending time with her? Um…

it's not going to do anything but make me even more attracted to her!"

Once again Savannah slapped Riley on the back of the head. "Stop giving your brother bad advice." She shook her head and looked into the camera. "Owen, the decision has to be yours, and you need to be comfortable. While Riley might be onto something, the fact remains you have an important event you're prepping for, and you have to decide if you need the distraction."

"Distraction?" he questioned.

"Brooke."

"Ah."

"Personally, I don't think you're so bad with the opposite sex," she said with a wink.

"Hey!" Riley cried with a bit of outrage. "What the hell does that mean?"

"It means," she said with an exaggerated sigh, "the first time Owen and I met, he did just fine putting me in my place. He was uncomfortable, but I think it had more to do with what was going on between you and me. So I say he doesn't need to do some sort of crazy social experiment with Brooke. If he wants her with him on this project, it should be because she'll be an asset to him professionally. Not personally."

Riley shook his head and scooted his wife out of the camera frame. "Now who's offering bad advice?" he teased before looking back at Owen. "If you ask me, I think she sounds perfect all the way around."

"But…what if she…you know…doesn't like me?"

A look of understanding crossed Riley's face. "It's a chance we all have to take at one time or another, Owen. No one likes it, and, let's be honest, rejection sucks. But…not everyone gets rejected. And for all you know, she might be crushing on you a little bit too."

Somehow Owen greatly doubted that, but rather than argue about the subject, he decided to let it go.

"So, Savannah…talk to me about baby names."

—⁓—

"I don't think he's going to call."

"He never said he would."

Brooke sat and watched as her uncle contemplated his next chess move. They were out in his yard, a small piece of land with a tiny garden and an all-season game table where he loved to play chess. It wasn't a particular favorite of hers, but he enjoyed it, so she indulged him. Chess had been her brother's game. He and Howard would play for hours. Even now she could still picture the two of them sitting out here playing.

"But…how am I supposed to know if he's going to hire me?"

Sighing, Howard reached across the table and patted his niece's hand. "Patience. Owen Shaughnessy doesn't make decisions lightly. Or quickly. We've planted the seed, and now…we wait."

Her eyes went a little wide, and she shivered in the cool afternoon breeze. There was an outdoor heater beside them, but for the life of her, she wished they could just go inside. "For how long?"

Howard shrugged. "As long as he needs."

This was *not* the news she had been hoping for. Brooke felt as if she was on the cusp of doing something great, and the thought of having to sit around and wait until she knew if she was finally going to get to paint in the desert—safely and with her family's blessing—was making her crazy.

"Can't you...you know...call him? Prompt him? Make sure he's even considering it? Because if he's not, then I'd like to start looking at other options."

"Brooke, sometimes you need to be a little less impulsive. Waiting another day or two isn't a big deal." He looked at her, saw her shiver again. "You want a heavier sweater?"

Ignoring his question, she went back to the topic they were already on. "But it's already been a week, and you just said it could take a while," she reminded.

"No, what I said is Owen doesn't make decisions quickly."

"Same difference."

"Hardly."

Now it was her turn to sigh. "Okay. Fine. What do you suggest I do? Do I go to see him tomorrow? Maybe just pop in and remind him of our conversation?"

Howard thoughtfully considered her for a moment and then started to smile. "Actually, I think that is a marvelous idea."

Relief washed over her. "You do? Seriously? Because I was thinking of bringing him my résumé and telling him about all of the work I did on committees back in college and how that experience would come in handy for this trip. And—"

Howard stood, shook his head, and reached down to move his bishop. "That won't do. What you need is to stop in and say hello. No pressure. No sales pitch. Maybe sit in on the entire lecture this time."

She blushed at the reminder of her showing up late. "What good will that do?"

"Like I said, Owen doesn't make decisions lightly. And he certainly doesn't do well under pressure, so if you go in there at full throttle, trying to convince him to hire you, you'll more than likely scare him off. Trust me on this one. I've known him for a very long time."

Brooke watched as her uncle turned to walk into the house. "What if he doesn't want me?" she blurted out and then realized how that sounded. "I mean…what if he doesn't want to hire me?" She hated the desperation in her voice.

Her uncle smiled at her—a smile that was part sympathy, part pleasure. "It's good to see you believe this isn't going to be handed to you."

Sometimes she hated when his comments came out sounding like Yoda's. "What does that even mean?"

"It means there was a time when you thought the world owed you everything, that you didn't have to earn it or work for it. Sort of like a game of chess. It makes you think. It's not just about skipping around the board, you have to put a lot of effort into every move. Your brother used to love it."

She rubbed her temple at her uncle's lengthy statement. "And this has to do with Dr. Shaughnessy…how?"

"Go see him tomorrow. For the entire class. Take notes. Learn a little about what he's doing."

"But…"

But Howard had already gone inside.

Sighing, Brooke sat and rested her face in her hands. Patience wasn't her thing. She was more of a get-it-done kind of girl, and that meant always being on the move and in action, not waiting around for the phone to ring. True, it had only been a week, but she had thought she and Howard had presented a great opportunity to Owen Shaughnessy.

Owen.

Or was she supposed to refer to him as Dr. Shaughnessy? Professor Shaughnessy?

Her immediate impulse was to call him Owen—it was more personal, and she had a feeling he would probably prefer that to the stuffy title. How she knew, Brooke wasn't sure, but she just…did.

Weird.

Deep down, Brooke felt confident she could be an asset to…Owen. She smiled. They would be assets to one another—she would help him feel more at ease with his students on this trip, and she would get to paint in the one place she was dying to with everyone's blessings.

Why was it so important to get her family's permission to take this trip? Well, she owed them. Her parents had become more and more protective of her over the past several years—and with good reason—and the last thing she wanted to do was cause them any more undue stress. So if that meant not going to the desert without a strong support system around her, then she'd wait.

Sometimes it was hard to do what was right. The old her—the girl who used to be selfish and frivolous and uncaring of other people's feelings—wanted to come out and stomp her foot and demand to be heard. And sometimes it was hard to push that girl aside and remember who she was now—who she needed to be and why. Not that she didn't like the woman she had grown into.

She did. On every level, Brooke was proud of who she was now.

She just hated remembering the person she had been.

That was one of the reasons this position with Owen Shaughnessy was so damn important. She'd get to paint and…she'd get to help him. Swallowing the painful lump of emotion that instantly clogged her throat, Brooke wandered back to the guest room her uncle had transformed into a temporary studio for her.

Blank canvases lined the walls, and there were several easels collapsed in the corner and one set up on a tarp in the middle of the room. She'd been here for almost three weeks and hadn't picked up a paintbrush yet.

That was about to change.

With a long stretch to help herself relax, Brooke started making her way around the room to set up. Within minutes she had her hair pulled back and her favorite smock on to protect her clothes. Her paints were organized on her palette, and Taylor Swift's *1989* was playing on her iPod.

Stepping up to the canvas, Brooke dipped her brush into the blue paint and was about to touch it to the canvas when she stopped. As she'd been setting up, in her mind, she knew she was going to paint the desert— the way she'd seen it in pictures—but with her own twist on it. But now that the brush was in her hand and the canvas was in front of her, her subject changed. Turning, she put the palette down, rinsed her brush, and wiped her hands on her smock as her heart began to pound.

It had been so long since she'd painted anything other than the skies and landscapes that she was almost afraid to get started, afraid that once the first stroke of paint was on the canvas, she'd realize she'd made a mistake. But rather than letting that twinge of fear stop her, Brooke took a deep breath and picked the brush back up again.

She took in her palette with the primary colors— yellow, blue, red—and began to mix them together. With a hint of white, she continued to blend until she refined the colors to her liking. When she glanced up at her canvas, it wasn't blank. There, before her eyes, she could see what she was going to paint, what she was going to create, and it made her smile.

Her hand began to move, color began to cover the surface, and her subject began to take form. In the background, Taylor Swift sang of wildest dreams, while in front of her, Brooke's was taking shape.

It was amazing—how fluid it all felt, how confident her strokes were. Her shoulder began to cramp, but she refused to stop—couldn't have even if she had wanted to. So she worked through the discomfort, refusing to call it pain. Every so often, she would step back and critique what she'd done, but immediately she'd return to the canvas with more color.

Every time Brooke had picked up her brush in the past, she had been inspired. She loved what she did and received great pleasure from the art she was able to create. But this? This wasn't simply inspiration that had her painting like a woman possessed.

This was art on an emotional level she didn't know existed.

This was coming from a place within that had yet to be defined.

And as silence filled the room after Taylor's last breath, Brooke stepped back and stared in wonder at the painting before her.

And looked into the eyes of Owen Shaughnessy.

The next day, Brooke made her way to the lecture hall and checked her watch to ensure she was early. It wasn't enough to be on time; she had to get to the room, get inside, and find a seat so she could observe Owen in a way she hadn't on her previous visit.

Of course, he was there already, standing at the front of the room, behind the podium, and reading his notes. At least, she guessed that was what he was doing. There were several students already seated, and as Brooke made her way up the aisle to a higher seat, she stopped and turned to look at him.

And found him looking right back at her.

Heat flooded her cheeks, and she was thankful to be standing so far away. Smiling, she gave a small wave and then turned to find a seat—which wasn't what she wanted to do at all. Nope. Her first instinct was to turn, walk back down the steps, go over, and say hello to him.

If you go in there at full throttle trying to convince him to hire you, you'll more than likely scare him off. Trust me on this one. I've known him for a very long time.

Her uncle's words came back to her, and Brooke knew she was doing the right thing. No matter how wrong it felt. She finally chose a seat right on the center aisle, so she could see Owen clearly, and pulled out her notebook. Looking around, she noticed how all of the other students in the room had laptops or tablets, but—call her crazy—she still liked the feel of putting pen to paper. And besides, it wasn't as if she were *taking* the class. The only notes would have to do with topics that might come up on the Nevada trip.

Meteor showers, right?

All of a sudden, she couldn't remember what, specifically, the purpose of the trip was other than going to watch the meteor shower. *Damn it!* Maybe she should have brought her laptop with her. *Ugh*.

At the front of the hall, Owen cleared his throat to get everyone's attention, and Brooke instantly sat up straighter.

"Good afternoon," he said, his voice loud but not overly confident. "Today we're going to continue on our topic with the discussion of dust tails and dust trails. As you should know, there are two types of comet tails: dust and gas ion." He looked up to make sure no one had any questions so far, and then he returned to the notes in front of him.

"A dust tail contains small, solid particles that are approximately the same size as those found in cigarette smoke. This tail forms because sunlight pushes on these small particles, gently shoving them away from the comet's nucleus. Because the pressure from sunlight is relatively weak, the dust particles end up forming a diffuse, curved tail."

Behind Owen, a screen diagrammed everything he was saying, and Brooke found herself fascinated. She studied the picture and wondered how she could replicate it with acrylics. When he started speaking again, she forced herself to stop looking at the screen and focus on him.

"Gas ion tails form when ultraviolet sunlight rips one

or more electrons from gas atoms in the coma, making them into ions in a process called…" He looked up to see if anyone could fill in the blanks.

"Ionization?" someone called out.

"Exactly," Owen replied with a small smile. And Brooke felt a fluttering in her belly.

She was in serious trouble here.

Stuff like this didn't happen to her. She didn't get crushes—certainly not at her age—and she was beginning to feel utterly ridiculous at her schoolgirl reaction to Owen Shaughnessy. Brooke was comfortable with the amount of men she'd dated in her twenty-eight years of life, and even though most of them were shallow jocks who were full of flash, she'd never reacted to any of them the way she was right now to this shy and quiet astrophysicist.

"And at that point, the solar wind will carry those ions straight outward away from the sun. The resulting tail is straight and narrow. However, both types of tails may extend millions of kilometers into space." Owen lifted his head and scanned the room again, and when his gaze landed on Brooke, she smiled. And when he smiled back, she felt like she had been given a gift.

Maybe her uncle was right. Maybe being here in the lecture hall and observing Owen teaching a class and listening to what he was saying was the smarter way to go. If she had gone to him when she arrived in the classroom earlier, she may have spooked him—crazy as it sounded—and could have possibly ruined her chances to work with him. Maybe if he saw how she was taking this seriously, it would make him feel a little more at ease with her.

response, but she had a feeling a little humor or a smile couldn't hurt. He had patience. The last student to stop to talk to him had been the one who had asked the meteorite-versus-meteor question and a list of others over the course of the class. She had to wonder why he was even taking the class if there was so much he didn't seem to understand.

Then she wanted to smack herself for being judgmental. Not everyone learned at the same pace, and as long as he was willing to ask the questions and Owen was willing to answer them, who was she to judge? Feeling like she was being rude for staring at them, she began putting her notebook and pen away, and organizing her purse while she waited for them to be done.

"Thanks, Dr. Shaughnessy," she heard the student say. "I appreciate the help. See you next week."

Brooke stood up, straightened her skirt, and fidgeted with her hair for a moment before she made her way down the stairs toward Owen. He watched her descend warily. When she reached the bottom, she smiled. "Hi."

"Oh…um…hi. Brooke," he stammered.

She stepped closer to the podium and saw him take a small step back. "So I figured I'd come for an entire class today," she teased lightly and immediately realized he didn't quite get the joke. "You know…since I showed up late for the last one."

"Ah," he replied with a nod. "It wasn't necessary. It's not like I'm taking attendance on you."

Brooke immediately relaxed. In his own way, she knew, he was making a joke, so she chuckled. "It's a good thing because showing up late for my first class would not look good on my record."

And this time, when she laughed, Owen laughed with her.

"I…I haven't come to a decision about the position yet," he said, his gaze focused on the floor and not on Brooke.

"Oh, that's okay," she said, quickly trying to put him at ease. "I just came to hear today's lecture. I felt awful about the other day, and…well…I was kind of curious about those dust trails and tails."

His head snapped up, and he looked at her with a hint of disbelief. "Really?"

Brooke nodded and then smiled as Owen began to relax. "I have to admit, I had no idea what you were talking about half the time, so I was kind of happy that one student asked so many questions. It made me feel a little less…stupid." She meant it to be a silly put-down, but the look on Owen's face told her he didn't see it quite the same way.

At all.

"Of course you don't understand what we're talking about. This is a basic astronomy class. Mr. Kelly may have been the only one to ask the questions, but I can almost guarantee you that everyone in the room benefited from them." He shook his head and began stuffing his papers into his satchel. He ignored her for a few moments before he stopped and looked at her. "You shouldn't put yourself down because you don't understand something like this class. There's nothing wrong with you, and you most certainly aren't stupid." On the last word, he shoved the last of his papers in the bag and then seemed at a loss for something to do with his hands.

And Brooke was at a loss for something to say.

So they stood there in awkward silence for several minutes before Brooke figured she needed to be the one to speak. "I…I appreciate your saying that. I don't think I'm stupid most of the time. But the level of intelligence in this room was kind of intimidating."

"If you're going to work with me, then you'll need to get used to it," Owen said and then seemed surprised by the statement, as if he hadn't even thought it through.

Brooke gasped and had to fight the urge to hug him and thank him. Instead, she went for a very calm approach to be sure she didn't spook him—her uncle's words, not hers. She cleared her throat and smiled. "I believe I'll have no problem adjusting. After all, if I'm going to be surrounded by scientists and students all day for several days, I'll be sure to do some studying beforehand, so I can better understand them."

Wow. She even impressed herself with how professional she sounded.

"I…I still haven't decided—for sure—that this is going to be feasible. For either of us," he quickly added. "I don't think you fully understand what you'd be dealing with. They're all very smart and socially awkward. Like me."

Her smile was meant to reassure him, but she wasn't sure he got it. "Dr. Shaughnessy…Owen…do you want my honest opinion?"

Brooke saw him swallow hard before he nodded.

"I don't think you're as socially awkward as you think." When he went to correct her, she held up a hand to stop him. "It's true. I don't think you're comfortable in social settings, but here you are, talking to me, defending me, and you're doing fine. I'm sorry if I make you nervous. I hope the more time we spend together, the more relaxed you'll become."

"Umm…maybe," he murmured.

Brooke looked over her shoulder at the clock on the wall before turning back toward Owen. "Would you like to grab a cup of coffee with me?" He looked like he was ready to bolt—or at least turn her down—so she quickly added, "We don't have to talk about the job. I just would like to get to know you."

He frowned. "Why?"

She laughed. An honest-to-goodness laugh. "Why? Because my uncle does nothing but sing your praises. Because I enjoyed listening to you teach. Because I think what you do is fascinating." She gave him her most confident look. "Are those good enough reasons?"

And she knew she had him. There was no way he could possibly doubt her reasons for wanting to spend time with him.

Owen looked at the clock and seemed to be weighing his options. "I need to go back to my office and take care of some notes and return a call first. Maybe I can meet you in an hour at the cafeteria?"

It wasn't hard to see what he was doing—he wanted to stay in a neutral zone and was giving himself a clear out if he needed it. His work. Well, she'd just see about that.

"How about this—you take care of what you need to, and I'll grab drinks and bring them to your office. That way we can sit someplace a little quieter and less chaotic. What do you say?"

Clearly she'd thrown him for a loop because his mouth seemed to move but no words came out. "Um—"

"I'm not a huge fan of the coffee in any cafeteria," she said pleasantly. "There's a Starbucks up the block, so I can go there and grab us a couple of cups of coffee and maybe a slice or two of cake or some cookies. Although they do have fabulous brownies. Do you have a preference? I'm a bit of a chocoholic, but I know it's not the case for everyone. The marble pound cake is a good choice too—it gives me the chocolate I crave while balancing it out with the yellow cake. Of course, there are scones if that's more your thing."

"You talk a lot," he stated very matter-of-factly.

And that had her laughing again. She liked his bluntness. "I know. Sometimes it works for me, sometimes it doesn't. I tend to chatter more when I'm nervous. Most of the time I don't even realize I'm doing it. The words just keep coming, and I'll end up flowing from one topic to another with no end in sight."

"You mean like now?"

Brooke immediately stopped talking and considered him. "Oh. I guess I was kind of yammering on there."

"Why are you nervous?"

Was he kidding? She shrugged and twisted the shoulder strap of her purse. "You make me that way."

Owen's eyes went wide. "Me?" he asked incredulously. "I make you nervous?"

She nodded. "You're a little intimidating."

"Me?" his voice came out almost as a squeak.

Brooke nodded again. "You are a highly respected man, Owen. I'm sure you're used to sitting around and talking with people who are more on your level. I'm afraid of saying something ridiculous and putting my foot in my mouth."

"Brooke, I…I don't even know how to respond to that. I'm intimidated by you."

She already knew that by how her uncle had prepared her, but she was curious about how he saw himself. "Why?"

"I may be respected here on campus or in my field of study, but…that's it. Outside of the lab and away from the telescope, I'm fairly invisible."

"I find that hard to believe."

He gave a mirthless laugh. "Trust me. As you learned the other day, my brother is one of the most popular rock stars in the world. Do you think anyone sees me when he's around?"

In that instant, she wanted to reach out and hug him.

"I have five siblings including Riley—four brothers and one sister," he said, not meeting her gaze. "They all have impressive jobs and wonderful lives. All of my brothers are married and have kids. Well, Riley and Savannah just found out they're pregnant, so…" He stopped abruptly, and this time he looked directly at her. "Forget you heard that," he said quickly. "No one is supposed to know! Dang it."

And that was totally adorable—he didn't even curse.

Unable to help herself, Brooke reached out and placed a hand on his arm. They both seemed a little shocked by the contact. He was…muscular. Much more so than she would have imagined. Forcing herself to not focus on that, she gave him a reassuring smile. "You don't have to worry. Their secret is safe with me."

Owen nodded and gave her a small smile. "Thank you."

She felt like they were having a moment.

And she didn't really want it to end.

Patience…

"Okay," she finally said, taking a step back. "Tell me what I can get you from Starbucks, and I'll meet you in your office in an hour."

Chapter 3

IT WAS QUITE POSSIBLE THAT OWEN WOULD PASS OUT before he made it back to his office.

Doing his best to recite the names of all the planets and constellations as he walked, he almost sagged with relief when his doorway came into view. He quickly made his way inside, pulled his phone out of his satchel, and immediately called Riley's number.

It went to voice mail.

Cursing, he put the phone down without leaving a message and tried to figure out what he was supposed to do. He didn't have any notes to make or papers to grade or any scheduled calls. No. He had said that to Brooke to buy himself a little bit of time. Most things that came out of Owen's mouth were carefully considered, and in one conversation with her he had managed to blurt out that he was more than likely going to hire her and then lied about his plans.

Who the heck was he?

He sat down in his chair and tried to consider his options. By his own calculations, Brooke would be knocking on his door in around fifty-three minutes. He could probably come up with a reasonable excuse why he had to leave before she returned and just text her his apology.

But he didn't have her number, and he didn't like the idea of lying.

Again.

And just because Riley wasn't available didn't mean he couldn't call one of his other brothers. Owen knew if he picked up the phone and called any one of them, they'd help him out. Okay, there was his solution.

He called Aidan first. But he was in the middle of an inspection on one of the new homes he was building, and after a quick apology and a promise to call later, he was gone.

No big deal—he was going to remain hopeful.

Next he called Hugh. Unfortunately—according to his wife, Aubrey, who had answered his phone—his brother was getting ready to cut the ribbon on the new property they were breaking ground on. And with another quick apology and a promise to call, she was gone.

Great.

That left Quinn. And as much as he knew Quinn would make the time to talk, if he could, Owen felt the most intimidated by him. Quinn was always the most confident and cocky brother, and somehow that wasn't what Owen needed at the moment. He needed a little… sympathy. That wasn't Quinn's strong suit.

But desperate times called for desperate measures, so he dialed.

"What's up, Bro?" Quinn asked by way of greeting.

"Oh…um…I was wondering if you had a few minutes to talk. I need advice."

Silence.

"Um…Quinn?"

"Yeah, yeah…give me a minute. I'm trying to process that. You, the brainiac of the family, want advice from me, the guy who almost flunked out of school. Wow."

Owen couldn't help but huff with irritation. Why couldn't anyone look at him like he was just a man? Why did everything come back to IQ and intelligence? It was beyond frustrating!

"Okay, I'm ready," Quinn said, interrupting Owen's thoughts. "Lay it on me."

Taking a steadying breath, Owen quickly went over the situation with Brooke and how she was coming to his office for coffee. "So what do I do?"

"You mean other than drink the coffee and talk to her?"

"Quinn," he said, "there's more to it. At least there is for me, and you know it! She's different. She's not a colleague, and she's not shy like me, and I have a feeling that by having her come here to the office where there are no distractions, it's going to be like there's a spotlight on me or something and all of my…awkwardness is going to be on full display."

"And what if it is?" Quinn countered. "Dude, we've all been saying it for years—there is nothing wrong with you. Hell, there's nothing wrong with being smart or quiet or shy or…just different! And if anyone makes you feel that way, then it's their problem, not yours. If this woman says anything to make you feel that way, then she can leave. Don't hire her. Don't talk to her, and tell her uncle you don't appreciate his interference."

"Wait, wait, wait," Owen replied. "Brooke hasn't said or done anything to make me feel uncomfortable. This is about me. This is how I feel. All the time."

"Oh."

"Yeah…oh. So what do I do? How do I stop feeling this way? She's going to be here in…" He stopped and looked at his watch. "Thirty-seven minutes. How do I act, what do I say to guarantee I'm not going to have a panic attack?"

"Owen," Quinn began seriously, "there is no way you can change how you feel or how you respond in that amount of time."

"I wish Riley had answered the phone," Owen grumbled.

"Hey! I take offense to that!"

"Sorry."

"Look, I get it. You and Riley—the twin thing—I get it. But there isn't anything he could do or say to make you transform into a different person who is full of witty conversation skills and confidence in the next thirty minutes."

"Thirty-six."

"Whatever!" Quinn snapped. "There's no quick fix here, Owen. You need to believe in yourself. You think you're the only one who gets nervous around a beautiful woman? Well…you're not."

"I bet you never were."

"Are you kidding me?" he laughed. "Holy crap…I was always nervous, but I knew how to hide it. Call it false bravado or whatever, but I was insecure. And even though Anna and I knew each other for practically our entire lives? She scared the hell out of me when we first started dating. My feelings for her kind of terrified me. And on top of that, I suddenly felt insecure and clueless."

"I remember," Owen said, recalling a conversation the two of them had had when Quinn and Anna began dating.

"So you're not alone, Owen. It's not just you. And you know what? It's not a bad thing to be a little bit nervous around a woman." He paused. "I think the difference is…when it's the right woman, those nerves make you want to be a better person, a better man. And being that you've never freaked out over a woman before like this, I'm thinking Brooke has to mean something to you."

"How is that possible? I just met her. I barely know her." But even as Owen was saying the words, he knew. He'd dated women—not as much as his brothers, but he'd dated enough to realize Brooke was different.

"It's not about how long you know someone. Look at me and Anna."

"You were friends since you were five. This is hardly the same thing."

"And yet it took me over twenty years to realize she was the one!" Quinn chuckled. "Then look at Hugh. He fell for Aubrey. Fast."

"Well—"

"Or Aidan. It took him a while to admit it, but you know he fell for Zoe at first sight. But he was too uptight to do anything about it."

"I guess—"

"And then there's Riley and Savannah. He fell hard and fast, and they pretty much ran to the altar!"

"I'm not looking to run—"

"I'm only trying to point out how there is no set-in-stone timeline for how long it takes to fall for someone. And besides that, it's totally okay to like this woman and she doesn't end up being the one. Not every girl you date is going to be. You know what I mean?"

Actually, he did. Go figure. "I do."

"Okay. Whew," Quinn said with relief. "So I helped, right? I totally stepped up and was the one to talk you down from the ledge."

"I wasn't planning on climbing out on one."

Quinn laughed. "Not an actual… You know what? Never mind. Listen, I have to go. I'm under this Mustang, and now I need both hands to get this pipe down."

"You've been under a car this whole time?"

"Well…yeah. Why?"

"Why didn't you simply tell me you were busy?"

"Because you said you needed advice. You never call me for advice. There was no way I was going to blow you off. This is just a pipe. It will be here until I'm ready to remove it. You're my brother, and you're more important."

Well, damn, Owen thought. And then he felt bad he hadn't wanted to call Quinn.

"I know I tease you a lot," Quinn said, "and I'm pretty sure I was your last resort."

"I didn't call Darcy."

"Well, at least there's that," Quinn laughed. "But, Owen? I'm glad you called. And I want you to promise me you're going to call me back tonight and let me know how it went."

"You mean…call and tell you about my conversation with Brooke?"

"No…I mean to tell me about your *date* with Brooke."

"But…it's not a date," he quickly stammered. "It's… coffee. We're merely going to talk. It's not a big deal."

"Owen?"

"Yeah?"

"Consider it an informal date, and be happy about it.

A beautiful woman asked to have a coffee date with you. That's a good thing."

"But—"

"I have to go. You're going to be fine. Just remember…a good thing." And then he hung up.

Owen wasn't so sure he believed his brother because now that he was looking at Brooke's coming to his office as a date, he felt even more nervous than he had before he'd picked up the phone! But, on the flip side, he'd bonded with the one brother he normally had nothing in common with. And that made him feel better.

About everything.

If his overly confident and cocky brother believed in him, why couldn't he believe in himself? Brooke wanted to have coffee with him. She seemed to enjoy talking to him, and, if he thought about it, he felt like the ice had been broken between them. If he looked at this as an informal job interview rather than a date, he'd be fine.

Because at the bottom of all of this, that was what Brooke was doing. She wanted to come and work with him in Nevada for her own personal reasons. He was the means to an end. And Owen was okay with it. It wasn't as if she were interested in him as a man. If anything, this knowledge would make social interaction with her easier. This was strictly a business relationship, and as long as he remembered that, he would be fine.

He kept up that line of mental reasoning as he went about straightening his desk and going over his schedule for the following week. For a minute, he even managed to let himself imagine how his schedule would change if he had Brooke working with him. He tried to figure out how much of his time would be spent on training her on the things she'd need to know about the meteor shower and the rules in place for the students. Then he tried to imagine them switching places while Brooke taught him how to be more at ease leading such a small group.

He had a feeling her job would be tougher.

And before he could second-guess that thought, there was a soft knock on the door. He took a steadying breath, turned around, and faced her.

And forgot to be nervous.

———

Beside her, Brooke's cell phone rang, and she almost couldn't hear it over the sound of laughter.

Hers and Owen's.

He had been telling her about one of his first attempts at teaching, and it had been a comedy of errors—something he could laugh about now but at the time had been pretty traumatic.

"Excuse me," she said, trying to contain her lingering giggles. Looking at the screen she saw it was her uncle. "Hey, Uncle Howard!"

"Hey there!" he replied. "I was wondering if I'm supposed to be holding dinner for you."

She frowned. "What do you mean?"

"Well, it's after six, and you and I normally are sitting down to eat at this time. When you didn't call or text, I figured maybe you were sidetracked at the art department again," he teased.

"What? Oh...no," she said, chuckling. "Owen and I are having coffee and talking, and I guess I lost track of time. I'm so sorry. Please go ahead and eat without me. I'll probably just grab something on the way home."

"Are you sure? I was only going to do some soup and sandwiches tonight, but...like I said, I wanted to make sure you were all right and that you didn't want me to wait for you."

"I'm so sorry I didn't call. It was very rude of me."

"Nonsense. I'm glad you're spending time getting to know Owen. Remind him that I have those applications for next year if he's interested."

"Applications for what?"

"For him, if he wants to come back next year to teach again."

"Oh."

"Anyway, enjoy yourself, and I'll see you when you get home."

"Okay, Uncle Howard. Thanks!"

"Oh...and, Brooke?"

"Yes?"

"I noticed the studio door was shut. Does this mean you started painting?"

She blushed and looked over at Owen, who was watching her with curiosity. "Um...yes. I started it yesterday and finished it today. I didn't realize I had shut the door." Actually, she had. She still was coming to grips with the fact that she had painted Owen. She wasn't ready to explain that choice to her uncle yet.

"Wonderful! Well, I can't wait to see it."

"Um—"

"No, no, no...I understand. You'll show me when you're ready. I'm just glad you're putting the room to good use."

"I am, I am," she replied and smiled. "Thank you for setting it up for me. It was nice to be able to just go in there and paint when the mood struck and to have such wonderful equipment ready for me. It was very thoughtful of you."

"Nonsense. You're my favorite niece."

"I'm your only niece," she reminded him playfully—it was a game they'd been playing with one another since she was a little girl. "Go have your soup, and I'll see you when I get home."

Brooke hung up, placed her phone back down on the desk, and smiled at Owen.

"Is everything all right?" he asked.

"Everything's fine. He was just concerned because I wasn't home yet and he was making dinner." And then she started to giggle again.

"What? What's so funny?"

"I guess I can't believe we lost track of time. I mean…I can believe I did. You've witnessed me doing that already. But I guess I thought you'd be watching the clock to see how fast you could get rid of me." Then she smiled at him. "I'm kind of glad you didn't. I've enjoyed talking with you, Owen."

He dipped his head as if trying to hide the slight flush of his cheeks, but it was too late. She thought it was very sweet.

With a happy sigh, Brooke stood, cleaned up the wrappers from the brownie and marble pound cake they'd eaten, and then threw away their empty coffee cups. Owen stood as well and straightened the chairs.

"I enjoyed talking with you too," he said softly, and Brooke heard the uncertainty in his voice and had to fight the urge—again—to just wrap her arms around him and hug him. She was that kind of person, a hugger, and she couldn't help it. But she also knew Owen probably wouldn't be comfortable with her doing that.

"I'm glad," she replied and gripped her hands together to keep from touching him.

He cleared his throat. "I'm sorry you missed dinner with Howard."

She chuckled and shook her head. "Don't be. It was only soup-and-sandwich night, and I got to have a brownie."

Confusion was written all over his face. "That's not your dinner, is it?"

Brooke shrugged. "I'm not sure. Maybe. Probably not. It seems like enough right now, but I have a feeling once I get home and relax, I'll regret not eating more. There are some great takeout places I pass on the way home. Maybe I'll grab a salad or something."

What she really wanted was pizza but figured that wouldn't sound very flattering—even though she just admitted to being satisfied with a brownie for dinner.

Owen nodded. "I'm probably going to grab some pizza. I still haven't gotten used to the whole Chicago deep-dish thing, but it's growing on me."

She could only stare at him.

"Um…what? Did I say something wrong?" he asked after a moment.

Shaking her head to clear it, she nodded. "I…" She stopped and laughed at herself. "I was actually sitting here thinking I probably wasn't going to get a salad because I wanted pizza. But I was afraid to admit it."

He frowned. "Why?"

"I thought it would make me look bad," she murmured and looked away, feeling a little ridiculous.

"Being honest will make you look bad? I don't…I don't understand that."

Brooke rolled her eyes and looked at him. "No woman wants to admit that a brownie is her dream dinner with pizza for dessert, Owen. We're trained to say things like we would love a salad for dinner when really what we want is a bacon double cheeseburger with fries and a milkshake."

"I thought you wanted pizza?"

And then she couldn't help it—and she didn't even want to.

She hugged him.

Hugged him hard as she laughed.

When she pulled back, she saw he still looked confused. "In a perfect world, we'd be able to eat them all at one sitting and never gain weight and never be judged. I'm just saying society has taught us that women aren't supposed to love food—even though we do. So," she stated as she stood up straight, "I'm going to stand here and tell you that I love food. All kinds of food. Junk food. Healthy food. Foreign food. All of it."

"But you do like pizza," he said. It wasn't a question.

She nodded.

"Good," he said with a quick nod of his head. "Would you like to go and grab some deep-dish pizza with me?"

Brooke readily agreed.

Maybe hugging him hadn't been such a bad decision after all.

—◦◦◦—

It was after ten when Brooke tiptoed down the hall toward her bedroom. She knew her uncle well enough to know he had gone to his bedroom at nine and was probably reading, and as much as she wanted to talk to him about her night, Brooke figured it could wait until the morning. For now she'd just—

"Brooke? Is that you, sweetheart?"

Busted.

Walking over to his door, she gently knocked and waited for him to invite her in. She stepped into the room and smiled. "I hope you weren't waiting up."

"I may be getting old, but I believe I can handle staying up past ten o'clock at night," he said with a chuckle and then held up the latest James Patterson novel. "I think this one is going to keep me up much later than usual. I'm having a hard time putting it down."

"That's the sign of a good book."

"It is, it is." He sat up straighter. "So…how was your night?"

She wasn't even going to try to pretend she didn't know what he was asking. Instead, Brooke walked over and sat on the corner of his bed, her smile broadening. "I had a lovely evening."

Howard's eyes widened slightly as his own smile grew. "A lovely evening? I don't think I've ever heard you use that phrase before."

"That's because I've never had a lovely evening before," she said reasonably. "After you and I talked on the phone, Owen and I grabbed some pizza."

He nodded approvingly.

"The place was loud and crowded, and it didn't take long for me to realize Owen wasn't enjoying himself. And, to be honest, I wasn't either."

"So what did you do?"

"The restaurant was close to campus, so once we were done eating, we walked back and just sort of wandered around."

"So you walked the entire time?"

She laughed. "No, silly. We eventually found a quiet spot near the library and then just…talked."

"That does sound lovely," he said. "Did you find it hard to listen to him talk about astronomy?"

"Actually, we didn't talk about astronomy."

Howard's eyes went wide. "Really?"

She nodded. "I don't know if it was a conscious decision on his part, but we spent a lot of time talking about painting. He was very curious about what kind of paints I use and why and what kind of brushes and canvases…" She looked at her uncle and gave a happy little shrug. "And when we exhausted that topic, we talked about artists we both like and admire, we covered some current events, and it was just—"

"Lovely?" he teased.

Brooke nodded and then her expression turned serious. "Uncle Howard…I know we've talked about this before, not judging a book by its cover, but never has that hit home more than tonight."

"Really?" he said and then relaxed a bit against his pillows. "Do tell."

"I think it's fair to say that at first glance, Owen comes across as being quiet and shy. He's not comfortable in his own skin, it seems."

"Sounds accurate."

"But it's so wrong," she said. "I think he spends so much of his time surrounded by his peers that he tends to be in work mode more than anything else, and he's comfortable with it, but once he relaxes and you get him out of that environment?" Pausing, Brooke tried to think of the perfect phrasing to describe Owen. "He's…he's charming. And funny—even though I don't think he's trying to be most of the time, but he is. He knows so much about so many things, and I could have stayed and talked to him all night!"

"So why didn't you?" Howard asked with a hint of humor.

Brooke made a face at him. "You did not just ask me that."

"I believe I did."

Sighing, she reached down and took her shoes off. "For starters, it wouldn't have been appropriate."

"Brooke, I'm not a prude. I know your generation isn't quite as concerned with propriety anymore. No one's old-fashioned like they were in my time, and I didn't say you were going to be doing anything you would be ashamed of. I was merely pointing out if you were truly enjoying your time talking with Owen, then you should have stayed out later. You don't have a curfew here."

"I know, and I probably would have stayed out later, but he said he needed to leave." And now she wondered if he'd had to or if he was done talking to her. Well, that took a little of the wind out of her sails.

"I can hear you thinking from here," Howard said, chuckling. "Don't overthink this. If Owen said he needed to leave, then he needed to leave. Personally, I'm surprised you got him to spend so much time with you today. Between the class and coffee and then dinner—"

"Well, to be fair, I don't think he counted the class as spending time with me."

Howard gave her a look that said he didn't agree, but he said nothing.

Pasting a smile she didn't quite feel on her face, she stood up and gave her uncle a kiss on the cheek. "Anyway, I enjoyed myself. And even if Owen decides he doesn't need or want an assistant on this project, I'm very happy to have met him. I can see why you think so highly of him." She straightened and yawned. "I'll let you get back to your book. Good night."

She closed the door behind her and made her way to the guest room at the end of the hall. Flipping on the light, she walked in, placed her shoes by the closet, and went to close the blinds.

It *had* been a lovely night. And spending hours talking to Owen Shaughnessy had left an impression on her. From the things her uncle had said to her and the very few comments Owen had made about himself, she had the impression he didn't often engage in casual conversations—not because he didn't want to, but because most of the people he surrounded himself with didn't.

She knew the feeling. The frustration.

She'd been a local pageant queen and cheerleader for so many years that people naturally assumed she wasn't smart. And because of that, so many conversations bored her to tears because she felt as if they were being dumbed down.

And far be it from her to correct anyone.

Maybe she should have, but when? Was there ever a good time to look someone in the eye and say, "Hello? I have an IQ of 136! I'm not completely clueless!" As much as she hated to admit it, Brooke knew she probably could have tried harder to make people take her seriously.

But Neal had been the smart one, and she was the pretty one, and that was the way things always seemed to be. For whatever reason, it made her family…work.

Until it didn't.

Sighing, she wandered around the room, collecting pajamas and a hair clip, and then walked into the en suite bathroom and closed the door. This was her routine—change into pajamas, pull her hair back, wash her face, brush her teeth, floss, apply moisturizer, and stare at her reflection. Brooke knew who, and what, she saw looking back at her, but tonight she couldn't help but wonder what other people saw.

Okay, that was a lie. She knew what most people saw—the pretty girl with a nice smile, a pointless hobby, and no real direction for her future.

But what did Owen see when he looked at her? Did he make that same blanket assumption, or was he able to see more? He was the first person—other than her uncle—who seemed to take a real interest in her painting. And not just about her love of it—he wanted to know about the actual mechanics of it and why she chose the materials she did. He seemed to want to delve deeper and get beneath the surface.

And he listened when she spoke.

"Ugh," she groaned as she walked back into the bedroom. Within minutes she was propped up against a pile of pillows and had her Kindle on. As much as she loved reading, tonight she just wasn't in the mood. Tonight she felt… Well, she didn't feel the need to escape. Not really. Normally a good book was the perfect way to end the day, to put all of her worries behind her and clear her mind.

But tonight she didn't want her mind cleared. She

wanted to remember everything that had happened today. Tapping the Scrabble app on the screen, she booted up a game against the computer.

And smiled as she spelled out her first word.

Lovely.

———

"Dude, it's like eleven o'clock. What the hell? Are you all right?"

Owen immediately regretted calling Quinn. By the sound of his brother's voice, he was half-asleep and had forgotten he was the one who had asked for the phone call. "Um…you told me to call."

"I… Wait, what?" Quinn paused. "Oh. Oh yeah." He yawned. "Sorry. So? How did it go?"

For ten minutes, Owen spoke—almost without stopping for breath—about his night with Brooke. Even as he relayed all of the things they'd talked about, Owen could still hear her voice in his mind as she said them and wished he was still sitting, talking with her rather than sitting alone on the phone with Quinn.

"Okay!" Quinn said excitedly. "So it sounds like you had a good night. Are you just getting home?"

"No. I got home about an hour ago."

"Oh."

"Oh? What does that mean?"

"It's just kind of early. Did she need to get home?"

"Well…no."

"So whose idea was it to end the night?"

"Uh…mine."

"Owen!" Quinn snapped. "Why? Why would you do that?"

"I...I, um...I thought maybe it was time to call it a night. Maybe she goes to bed early. I know I enjoy going to bed early. Not that this is early, but when I'm not on the telescope, I'm in bed by ten thirty. You need a solid seven to eight hours of sleep a night to replenish your body and give it the rest it deserves. Studies have shown—"

"Studies have shown that this is why you used to get wedgies," Quinn said with a huff. "When you are out with a beautiful woman to whom you are attracted, the last thing you should be thinking of is whether you're going to get seven to eight hours of *sleep*!"

"Really?"

"Yeah, really," Quinn said with an irritated sigh. "So when are you seeing her again? Did you make plans for the weekend?"

"Uh..."

"Please tell me you asked to see her again," Quinn said slowly, and Owen could tell he was fighting hard not to clench his teeth.

"Uh..."

"You've dated women before, right? I mean, I *know* you've dated other women! How on earth did you get anyone to go out with you a second time?"

Part of Owen wanted to just hang up the phone in total embarrassment, but suddenly another part was clamoring to be heard—the offended part. The angry part. "Hey!" he snapped. "You know what? I get it that you're disappointed in me, as usual, but I don't need to sit here and be insulted. Yes, looking back, I should have asked her out again. But I didn't. And you know what? That's okay."

"Owen—"

"And do you want to know why?" he asked, completely ignoring the fact that Quinn was trying to speak. "Because I am going to see her again. I have her number, and I'll call her. Not everyone has to do things like you, Quinn. Not everyone has been fortunate enough to never have to work at getting a woman's attention."

"Owen, look—"

"And you know what? For a guy who seems to have all the answers, need I remind you how you were completely clueless for years about how Anna was in love with you and you were the one who looked like a… a…jerk!"

Wow, did that feel good!

There was silence on the other end of the phone, and Owen wasn't sure if he had gone too far. He was just about to speak when Quinn cleared his throat.

"Are you done?"

Owen let out a breath and said, "I believe I am."

"Good."

More silence. Was he supposed to say something next?

"I'm not disappointed in you, Owen," Quinn began, his voice softer and calmer than it had been a minute ago. "Not really. I just…I was excited for you. And it was cool how you called and asked for my advice."

"Probably won't be doing *that* again," Owen muttered.

"Yeah, yeah, yeah… And I don't blame you. My first instinct is to get mad when something doesn't go the way I think it should, and then I realize what an ass I sound like. Anna reminds me of it all the time."

"She's right."

"Okay, so somebody's coming into their own," Quinn chuckled. "It's about damn time."

"Wait…what? What are you talking about?"

"You! Do you realize you just stood up to me? You never do that! Ever!" A hearty laugh interrupted his praising. "Normally you're quick to apologize, or you just sort of…I don't know…disappear. And yet today you took a stand. And you know what? I am proud of you."

"You are?" Owen asked hesitantly and immediately hated that he needed—and wanted—the validation.

"Dude, I think you are at a crossroads here."

"How?"

"How did it feel to tell me off?"

"Honestly? It felt…good," Owen said with a laugh.

"I know it had to," Quinn agreed. "And how did it feel to go out with Brooke and not talk about your work?"

Owen thought for a minute. "That felt kind of good too."

"You've been on this path, dude, for so long. Everything has been about your education and your job and how smart you are and all that. So let me ask you— are you happy with your job?"

"Yes. No. Maybe"

"Right. That was clear," Quinn murmured. "Let me rephrase that. Are you…aspiring for something more?"

"Not particularly."

"So? Maybe it's time for you to put some focus on another part of life. Like your personal life."

Could that be it? Could his brother be *that* insightful? Again? Twice in one day? Maybe…

"Listen…I am glad you called, and I'm glad we had

the chance to talk. But Anna hasn't been feeling well, and neither of us have been getting much sleep, so…can we talk over the weekend?"

"Why didn't you say anything sooner? Is she okay? Has she gone to the doctor?"

Quinn chuckled. "Yeah. And you know what the doctor told us?"

"No. What?"

"That Anna's eight months pregnant."

"And?"

"And that's it. That's what's wrong. The baby is growing, and so she can't get comfortable, and it means she doesn't sleep well, and then being on her feet all day at the pub…"

"Maybe she should start her maternity leave early."

"Dude, don't even think of telling her that. She will bite your head off."

"I don't understand."

Quinn sighed. "She loves that place, and she loves her independence and thinks she's superwoman. Honestly, I cannot wait for the baby to be here so she'll be forced to take it easy." And then he yawned loudly. "So…can I call you this weekend?"

"I'd like that." Owen hung up after saying good-bye and roamed around his hotel room. It was more like a suite—it had a small kitchenette and a sitting area along with the bedroom and bathroom, and it suited him for these short-term guest lectures. Could he even call them that? Technically he was teaching, but no matter how he looked at his situation, it wasn't permanent. That was something else he needed to focus on—finding something permanent. Traveling so much and staying in hotels was starting to get old. Hell, if he had his way, he'd back out of the Red Rock project and go home to his father's house for a while to try to figure out where he wanted to concentrate his job search.

Then you wouldn't need to spend time with Brooke.

And that's when Owen knew he was in trouble. Clearly, he was infatuated with her. Other than when he was back in middle school and thought he could overcome his shyness, Owen hadn't allowed himself to feel this way about a woman. He had learned to be practical, and while, yes, he had been involved seriously with several women over the years, none had made him feel quite like this.

Happy.

Carefree.

Hopeful.

He snorted with disgust. It had been only eight days since he'd first met her. How was it even possible he was feeling such a strong pull toward her? It wasn't logical. It certainly wasn't practical. And no matter what Quinn had said earlier in the day about how he and his brothers had all fallen in love at different rates—from first sight to over twenty years—it did little to comfort Owen.

Why? Because Owen didn't do...first sight. Didn't believe in it.

Even as it was trying to stare him in the face.

It's not that Owen didn't believe in falling in love. He did. He knew it was possible but...more so for other people. Like his brothers. They were normal. No one ever looked at any of them and called them strange or weird or...awkward. Yeah. Those were all reserved for him. How was it possible in such a large family that they could all be so different from one another and yet he was the only one who managed to be different in such an off way?

He sighed.

How many times had his mother held him close and told him there was nothing wrong with being different? That he should embrace it because it made him special? Too many times to count.

And that was saying something for him—a man who had a knack for counting everything.

But when Lillian Shaughnessy died, there was no one there to remind him that it was okay to be different. Or that he was going to make a difference in the world. Not that his father hadn't tried. But with six kids, he had been more than a little overwhelmed and didn't seem to know how to do and say all the things his wife had.

Emotion clogged his throat, and Owen tried to will it away. It had been a long time since the memory of his mother had brought him to tears. And as he sat on the upholstered chair in the corner of the room, he felt overwhelmed. And confused.

With his head thrown back, Owen tried to focus on the logical—he knew his father and his siblings would all offer him any encouragement he needed. That had been proven over and over again. And even though it wasn't the same as hearing it from him mother, he was still extremely grateful for his family. But he also knew that this—how he was feeling about Brooke—was something he would have to deal with alone. It was too difficult to explain his insecurities to his brothers. After all, none of them ever struggled the way he had with insecurity. And, really, he was glad that they hadn't.

He wouldn't have wished this on his worst enemy.

So where did that leave him?

Right where he knew he was—back at square one. Women like Brooke didn't go for men like him. She was sweet and friendly…and nice to him because she wanted the position as his assistant. He needed to remember that. He'd seen it before—people sucking up to him in order to get a job or a recommendation. It was just that this time he had allowed himself to develop feelings for the person doing it.

Was he going to see her again like he'd just told his brother he would?

No.

Was he going to offer her the job?

No.

As much as Owen appreciated Howard's attempt at helping him, he wasn't going to take him up on the offer. Owen was who he was, and no matter how much the faculty and the administration hounded him about learning to be less "stiff" with his students, he wasn't going to change. He couldn't.

Or wouldn't.

He knew he was a damn fine astrophysicist, and at the end of the day, that's all that mattered. He could tour every college campus with a telescope and teach and share his wisdom. It wasn't a particularly fun subject— the creation of the cosmos was serious business. And if Owen chose to take it seriously and treat it with the respect it deserved, then why was everyone having an issue with that? There was no need for an assistant or someone to help him be less…awkward.

Damn it, he was beginning to hate that word.

Standing up, he stalked over to his closet, kicked off his shoes, and started to get ready for bed. His mind made up, he quickly decided he would seek out Howard in the morning and explain that he wouldn't be hiring his niece. It was the coward's way out—Owen was aware of that—but it was the best way to handle it.

Was he disappointed?

Yes.

But better to be disappointed now than to get even more attached to or involved with Brooke and then have all of his suspicions confirmed—that she had only been nice to him so she could get the job and do her painting. Which still seemed a little weird to him. She was a grown woman. Why did she need her family's permission to paint in the desert? If she felt that strongly about her painting, there must be other ways for her to go about getting there. He understood the need for safety, but it seemed like she was going through an awful lot of trouble to appease her family.

Even sucking up to a socially awkward scientist like him.

Chapter 4

To his credit, Howard Shields didn't outwardly react to Owen's news. He sat behind his desk and continued to look at Owen with a serene smile on his face.

Which bothered Owen. He wished the man would stand up and reprimand him for being unreasonable and selfish and rude.

All the things he'd been telling himself all morning.

Clearing his throat, he went on, "So you see, it would be pointless to hire an assistant. I have the entire event outlined already, and I've looked at the roster of the students who will be accompanying me, and they've all worked with me before. They're familiar with my teaching style, so there isn't going to be an issue." He paused. "Please thank your niece for me."

He couldn't even bring himself to say her name.

After neither of them had spoken after a minute, Owen stood. "Well, I, um…I should be going," he said, not meeting Howard's gaze. "Have a good weekend." Owen was almost out the door when Howard called his name. He dreaded turning around.

"I have those contracts for you," Howard began. "I've been meaning to bring them by, but it kept slipping my mind." He chuckled. "Just another symptom of getting old. Forgetfulness."

Relief swamped Owen. "I'm actually not sure if I'm going to need them."

Howard arched a graying brow at him. "Is that so?"

Nodding, Owen stepped back toward the desk. "I've been giving this some thought, and…I'm a little worn out from all the traveling. I think I'm at a point where I'd like to find one specific university to work for and maybe do very limited speaking engagements. Although, to be honest, I could use a break from those as well."

"I know you haven't been particularly happy about the way things have gone in the past year…"

"If I could, I would even back out of the Red Rock project." Owen paused and shrugged. "I knew it was done as a lottery with the professors, I just didn't realize it was a mandatory one."

"They do like to be fair," Howard reminded him.

"That's all fine and well when all of the participants who are being considered actually *want* to be participating!" he cried and then immediately stepped back in embarrassment for raising his voice to his mentor. "What I mean is—"

"I know what you mean, Owen. And I understand." He studied Owen for a moment. "I think you've been looking at this project as some sort of punishment. It's not meant to be that way. Viewing the meteor shower in Red Rock is an amazing experience! I think if you stopped focusing on the parts of it you are dreading, you'll find there are many great things about it you will enjoy."

Sighing, Owen pulled out a chair and sat back down. "Howard, you know I love what I do. But there are people who are just better at that aspect of the job than I am. I enjoy working alone in a lab. I love doing research on my own. I work better alone." He emphasized those last words.

"It's not good to be alone all the time, Owen."

"I grew up in a big family," Owen replied with a hint of defensiveness. "I was never alone. Now, as an adult, I don't mind it. And either way, it should be my decision to make and mine alone. I don't believe a committee should have the right to tell me I need to hone my social skills and force me to participate in heading up events when there are more qualified interested parties!"

"Some would disagree."

Owen took a steadying breath. "How much more enjoyable and educational would it be for a group of students to participate in an exciting event that was being led by someone who is passionate about being there? I believe what is happening now—forcing me to take this on—will be a disservice to those students. So is it worth it? For the university, for the faculty, to try to prove a point no one asked them to prove?"

Owen's heart was racing, and he knew he was sweating, but he didn't care. It felt wonderful to get his feelings off his chest. Even if they didn't change a damn thing, Owen felt better just saying the words out loud. Maybe talking to Quinn was better for him than he could have imagined.

Swallowing hard, Owen looked at Howard and expected to see disappointment—or at the very least a hint of anger for his tirade—but what he saw was compassion. Sympathy. And understanding. Howard stood and walked around to the front of the desk until he was standing beside Owen.

"I had no idea you felt like this," he said softly.

"I've been telling people I didn't want to go on the trip ever since I was appointed," Owen reminded him.

"Yes, but…I think we all felt it was because you were just uncomfortable with the expectations. No one suspected—at least I didn't—that you felt this strongly about going."

Owen met his gaze almost defiantly. "Well, I do."

Howard nodded. "I can see that."

"So what happens now?"

Crossing his arms, Howard sighed. "Unfortunately, it's not for me to decide. I can put in a recommendation to see about someone replacing you, but—"

"But what?"

"It's not my place," Howard said.

"What's not your place?"

"Owen, I know it took a lot for you to come here today and tell me all of this. And I respect you for doing so. But I also know I'm a pretty safe bet."

Safe bet? What did that even mean? "I'm confused."

"You know you can come to me at any time and I'm going to listen to you and try to help in any way I can. We're not just colleagues, we're friends, right?"

Owen nodded.

"You know I'm not going to judge you, and I'm certainly not going to get angry with you for speaking your mind, right?"

Another nod.

"Then, as your friend, I feel you should know that if you want out of this project—if you honestly believe you cannot do it to the *best* of your ability—then you need to plead your own case."

Owen jumped to his feet. "Excuse me?"

"You heard me. If you can stand here and express how you feel about the project and the entire process, then you should be able to go to the faculty and talk to them as well. It will mean more coming directly from you. Although…"

Great. Now what? "Although what?" Owen asked.

Waving him off, Howard walked back around his desk and sat down. "It's nothing. Just promise me you'll think about it."

He was dumbfounded. When did the world suddenly decide to go topsy-turvy? Quinn was giving good advice, and Howard was giving bad? How was that even possible? This had to be a bad dream because, for the life of him, Owen couldn't make a damn bit of sense out of any of it.

Okay, maybe he could. It wasn't as if Howard was giving bad advice, per se. He just wasn't giving the advice Owen wanted to hear.

Unable to make himself leave, he stared at his friend, his mentor, and frowned. "So you're saying you're not going to help me with this."

"If you're looking for someone to be a sounding board for you, I'm here. If you're looking for someone to do your dirty work for you…" He paused. "Well, that isn't me."

Unfortunately, he knew Howard had a point. It wasn't fair for Owen to ask Howard to fight his battles—no matter how badly he wanted to. With nothing left to say, Owen gave a curt nod and turned to leave. "I understand." He was at the door once again when Howard said his name. "Yes?" Owen replied softly, almost afraid to turn around.

"I'm sorry."

And so was Owen. He nodded again with a murmured word of thanks.

"About everything," Howard added. When Owen didn't move except to place a hand on the doorframe, Howard added, "I never should have pushed you on this. I hope you can forgive me."

"I do," Owen said as he walked out the door.

―――――

Brooke happily made her way down the hall toward the faculty offices for her lunch date with her uncle. Between her classes and painting, she had been doing a lot of research on the meteor shower and thinking of ways she could assist Owen on the trip—should he ever ask her—that she had missed spending time with Howard. So, that morning, she had suggested getting together for lunch as he was leaving for work. Part of her wondered if Owen was lecturing today, and she considered taking a slight detour past his classroom but opted to go to see her uncle first.

Maybe she'd stop and surprise Owen after lunch and see if he wanted to go to a gallery with her tonight. She had texted him a couple of times over the past week— just saying hi or asking how his day was—and she had sat in on two more of his classes, but they hadn't spent any time alone since the previous week. And she found she missed him.

"Knock, knock," she sang as she tapped on her uncle's office door. He looked up at her with a smile, but she could instantly tell something was wrong. "Hey, is everything okay?"

Howard stood up and came around the desk to hug her. "I'm fine." He paused and then stepped back. "So where should we go for lunch?"

"Uncle Howard," she admonished. "I can tell something's the matter. It might make you feel better to talk about it."

He took her hand and squeezed it. "We'll talk at lunch. For now, why don't you tell me about your day?"

She knew a diversion when she heard one but decided not to fight him on it. "Considering it's only a little after noon, there's not much to tell." She paused. "That's not true. I actually did quite a bit."

They were walking down the hall, and Howard chuckled. "Okay, now I'm intrigued. Did you paint something spectacular?"

Blushing, she shook her head and laughed with him. "Hardly. I spent the morning doing some research on the Eta Aquarid meteor shower."

"Really? And what brought that on?"

Brooke nudged him with her shoulder playfully. "Well, if I do end up going to Red Rock with Owen, it would be beneficial to know more about it. I've been reading up on it quite a bit. My mind wanders a lot, so I'm a slow study. And I know it's important, not only so I can talk to the students, but also so I can also start thinking about my paintings and what I might expect. It never hurts to study beforehand and hope it leads to inspiration."

Howard smiled as they continued to walk out of the building and toward the parking lot.

"I thought we'd just walk to lunch," Brooke suggested. "There are a lot of places close by. That is, if you don't mind walking."

"Not at all," he said, still seeming distracted. "The fresh air will do me good."

Okay, she thought, something was definitely up. Maybe she could cheer him up with a little astronomy talk. Or at least her weak attempt at it.

"So…you want to hear what my research taught me today?" she asked playfully.

"Absolutely," he replied, his smile never wavering.

"Okay, but just remember, I'm not as eloquent with it as you and Owen are. I memorized just the basic facts."

He nodded.

They made their way across campus, and Brooke decided she'd give him a quick overview and then they'd choose where they wanted to eat. "Well, the Eta Aquarids is an above-average shower, and it can produce up to sixty meteors per hour at its peak. The best place to view it is in the Southern Hemisphere. Well, that's actually where you'll see more activity. Not necessarily better viewings, just more."

Howard nodded and said, "That's right."

He didn't seem quite as impressed as she'd hoped, but she went on. "However, you can see up to thirty meteors an hour in the Northern Hemisphere. This particular shower is from the dust particles left behind by Halley's Comet. This is an annual event seen from mid-April to mid-May. The best way to view the shower is from a dark location after midnight."

Howard chuckled as they crossed the street. "Well done, Brooke. You weren't kidding when you said you memorized some facts."

"Wait…I have one more," she said proudly. "Although the meteors can be seen anywhere in the sky, they actually radiate from Aquarius." She stopped and took a small bow. "And now I'm done."

Laughing, Howard stood beside her and clapped. "You did a great job." They continued walking along with the throngs of people.

"Thank you. Not that I'm ready to hold my own with a group of astrophysicists, but I have to admit it might be nice to have at least a basic level of understanding of what's going on and a couple of facts tucked away to pull out if needed."

When her uncle didn't respond, Brooke got a sinking sensation in her belly.

She wasn't going to Red Rock.

Don't cry. Don't cry. Don't cry, she chanted to herself.

Softly, she cleared her throat and willed away the tears as she looked around. "So…um…how about that hot dog place you've been bragging about?"

Howard came to an abrupt halt. "You want hot dogs for lunch? You're always telling me you don't like them and all the reasons why I shouldn't eat them."

Shrugging, she did her best to smile. "Sometimes a girl just wants some junk food. Are you saying you don't want them?"

"Huh? Uh…no. No. That's not what I'm saying at all. I was just trying to give you an out if you want it."

"I'm good."

They walked in silence for the two blocks to Howard's favorite lunch haunt. At the counter, Brooke told her uncle to get her whatever he was having while she went and grabbed a booth for them. To be honest, she was happy to have a few minutes to herself. As she sat, she realized she was shaking. Damn it.

What happened? For days Brooke had been marveling at how great she and Owen had gotten along, how they'd just…clicked. How could she have possibly been so wrong?

Deep breaths, she reminded herself. There was a chance she was misreading the situation—the current one with her uncle. Maybe he wasn't going to tell her she wasn't going to work with Owen at Red Rock. Maybe something else was bothering him.

Then she immediately shook that off. Other than her parents, there was no one she was closer to than her uncle. And just like she could never hide anything from him, there wasn't anything he could hide from her. At least he never had before.

And she kind of hoped this time was going to be the first.

"Okay," Howard said as he slid into the booth across from her, "you are in for a treat. I got you a traditional Chicago-style hot dog, a side of fries, and a Coke." He placed the plate of food in front of her along with her drink and then set up his own food before sliding the plastic tray to the side.

Brooke studied the mess of food in front of her with a combination of dread and curiosity. "Um…what exactly am I eating?" she asked with a nervous chuckle.

"That, my dear, is a classic Chicago-style hot dog— also known as a Chicago dog or Chicago red hot. It's an all-beef frankfurter on a poppy seed bun, and it originated right here in the city of Chicago. Hence the name. It's topped with yellow mustard, chopped white onions, sweet pickle relish, a dill pickle spear, tomato wedges, pickled sport peppers, and a dash of celery salt. Trust me when I say it is a feast for your taste buds."

Somehow she doubted that. "Um…back home we do it with sauerkraut, spicy brown mustard, and onions in red sauce. I'm not sure how I'm supposed to eat this. Do I cut it up or…?"

"Watch and learn," he said, picking up his hot dog and taking a giant bite out of it. The look of pure joy on his face made Brooke smile. When he finished chewing, he motioned for Brooke to pick hers up. "Go ahead. Try it!"

To say that she had made a huge error in suggesting this place for lunch was an understatement. Other than the hot dog and bun, there wasn't anything else on there Brooke would eat—at least not together like this. Looking up she saw that her uncle was watching her expectantly, and she figured he wasn't going to take another bite of his own lunch until she tried hers.

"Okay," she said hesitantly. "Here goes nothing." The hot dog was awkward to handle, and she took a minute to figure out how she was going to even take one complete bite because the damn thing was so big and cluttered with toppings. Finally, she thought, *Screw it,* took a bite, and… "Holy crap! That's good!"

Howard laughed out loud with pleasure. "I knew it! I knew you'd like it!" Then he took another bite of his own, and all was quiet until they were done. He was wiping his hands with a paper napkin when he spoke again. "Now that I've introduced you to some of Chicago's finest cuisine, is it fair to say we can come here again?"

"We definitely can," she agreed. "I cannot believe how much I enjoyed that. It's certainly not an easy thing to eat—it's incredibly messy but well worth it."

"Excellent! I knew if you gave it a chance you'd like it. Now don't get me wrong. I enjoy a New York hot dog just like everyone else, but there is something about a Chicago dog that is…well, it's more like an experience than just a meal."

Brooke laughed. "I don't know if I'd go that far, but it was very good." She took a sip of her drink before growing serious. "So what's going on, Uncle Howard? You looked a little…distracted when I arrived at your office earlier. Is everything all right?"

And right before her eyes, his expression seemed to close. Gone was the happiness of moments ago, and his shoulders slumped.

"I had a visit from Owen this morning."

Damn it. For once it didn't feel good to be right. Fiddling with her napkin, she let her gaze drop to the table. "Oh? Did you give him those contracts you mentioned the other day?" It seemed like a good way to let him break the news to her gently. Although maybe it would have been better to rip the Band-Aid off quickly.

"He doesn't want to look at the contracts," he replied sadly.

Brooke looked up at his tone.

Howard shrugged. "Owen seems to feel like he's done traveling so much. He wants to find one university to teach and study and work at and cut back on the lecture tours."

"And that's upsetting to you…why?" she asked curiously.

It took a moment for Howard to speak again. "I see a lot of myself in Owen. When I was his age, I was an extreme introvert."

Brooke couldn't help but smile. "I still can't picture that. You were never like that around us."

"You're family. Family is like a safe zone. It's comforting and familiar and easy to relax around them. But once I was at work and back here in Chicago, I was a different person. I wasn't comfortable in my own skin." He chuckled. "Isn't that how you described Owen?"

She nodded.

"Anyway, I remember going to a conference in California. San Diego. I didn't want to go and did everything I could to get out of it. I argued with all of my colleagues about the validity of making a conference mandatory. After months of carrying on, I finally accepted the assignment. But in my mind, I knew I was going to hate it—every moment of it."

"What was the conference about?"

"It was on theoretical astrophysics," he replied.

Brooke just nodded because she had a feeling the description would be way over her head. "And you didn't think it was necessary?"

"Of course not!" he laughed. "I thought I knew it all. I still do sometimes." He shrugged. "The thought of going across the country and having to stay at a hotel with a bunch of people I didn't know was beyond unappealing. But in the end I went."

"And you hated it?"

He shook his head. "On the contrary, I loved it. That conference changed my life."

Her eyes went wide. "It did? How?"

"That's where I met your Aunt Marie."

"Really? I didn't know she was a scientist too."

"She wasn't," he said, his voice turning a little

whimsical. "She worked at the hotel where the conference was being held. Her job was assisting the event coordinator. She spent a lot of time walking around the convention center and checking on the rooms and making sure everything was stocked and clean. Those first few days I was there, I always found a room that wasn't in use in between my workshops and just sort of sat by myself to decompress a little."

She didn't push him to say more, knowing he was getting lost in his own memories.

"The first time I talked to her, I was kind of a jerk. I was so prepared for her to tell me to get out of the room that I sort of went on the attack first." He shook his head and let out a small chuckle. "When she said she completely understood my need to hide out for a bit, I relaxed. So I went back to that room the next day in hopes of seeing her again."

"And did you?" Brooke asked, finding herself getting engrossed in his story.

He nodded. "She came in, and this time I helped her move chairs around. We talked about her job, and she asked about mine and if I was enjoying the conference. At that point, I hadn't done much, but I told her it was okay."

"Did you go back there again the next day?"

Howard grinned. "I did. And this time I brought snacks and drinks for us to share. We had a picnic."

"That sounds nice…very sweet."

"It was. I asked her to dinner that night, and she said yes. Believe it or not, she was the first woman I ever asked out who wasn't a colleague." He smiled and shook his head. "I was so damn nervous. We ate at a restaurant right across the street from the hotel because I didn't rent a car and I didn't want her to drive us anywhere—I'm old-fashioned that way. And we stayed out all night talking. When the restaurant closed, we just went back across the street to the hotel and sat outside by the pool until the sun came up."

Brooke gasped. "That's amazing!"

"It certainly was. Luckily she didn't have to work that day. I had lectures to go to, and when she left to go home, she said she'd see me later. Imagine my surprise when she showed up at our room during my break."

"Wow," Brooke sighed. "I love that."

"But I lived in Chicago, and she lived in San Diego, and I knew at the end of the week I'd be leaving."

"So what did you do? I mean…I know she eventually came to Chicago, but how long did it take?"

"She flew home with me that weekend."

"No!"

Howard smiled broadly. "Yes," he said. "It was something we both felt strongly about. Neither of us wanted a long-distance relationship."

"But…how? I mean…you barely knew each other!"

"Scandalous, right?" he teased. "Actually, the hotel set up a transfer for her to one of its properties here. The manager wasn't happy to do it on such short notice, but her supervisor was a friend and pulled some strings. And up until that point, Marie had been staying with a friend because her apartment lease ended the month before and she hadn't found anything new. It was perfect timing."

"Aww…I still can't believe you moved in together so quickly!"

"Oh, Marie didn't move in with me."

"She didn't?"

He shook his head. "I paid for her to stay at the hotel for a week, and we found her a small apartment close to mine. And once she was settled in, she sort of…drew me out of my shell. She forced me to get out and socialize. I started making friends with people I didn't work with. We traveled. We went to plays and movies and galleries, and for the first time in my life, I was living."

Her heart squeezed in her chest because of how passionately he spoke.

"Your aunt? She was an amazing woman. And if I hadn't gone to that conference, I never would have known her. I never would have experienced the greatest love of my life." He sighed and looked at Brooke with a sad smile. "And it doesn't matter that we only had ten years together. I wouldn't change a thing. She made me a better person."

Tears stung Brooke's eyes as she reached out and squeezed one of his hands. "You were very lucky to have found each other."

They sat in silence for several long moments before Howard straightened in his seat. "And that's why I see myself in Owen. He's choosing to close himself off, and I hate to see that for him. He's young, and he's in a bit of a rut. I know he travels on these lecture tours, but even when he goes someplace new, he's not…he's not connecting. He's not interacting."

"You can't force him to," she heard herself say, even though it was exactly what she wanted to do for Owen herself.

"I know I can't." He looked up at her pleadingly. "But it's hard to stand back and watch someone make the same mistakes I did, you know? I was hoping with a little nudge in the right direction, he'd see that there's another way."

"I know you meant well—"

"I shouldn't have involved you. I'm sorry for that."

She shook her head. "It's all right. I understand why you did."

He gave a mirthless laugh. "Do you? Because I'm a little ashamed of myself. I got your hopes up about the job and I was trying to play God with a friend." He shook his head again. "I don't know what I was thinking."

"You were looking out for people you love. There's nothing wrong with that."

"Normally I would agree, but in this case I hurt the both of you."

For a minute, Brooke wanted to linger on how Owen was feeling, but she didn't. She couldn't. Not yet. "I'm fine. Really. I just have to start looking at other ways to get to the desert that make everyone comfortable."

The smile he gave her was sad. "You know there's going to come a time when you can't please everyone, right? You're going to have to start living for *you*."

"I know," she said, nodding. "But not on this."

Howard's phone beeped with an alarm, reminding him of a faculty meeting. "Where does the time go?" he wondered as he stood up. "If I were stuck in my office for lunch, the time would be dragging, but now that I'm out and enjoying a meal with a delightful girl, it flies by."

Brooke chuckled as she stood and joined him, linking her arm through his. "I'm glad we did this." She rested her head on his shoulder as they started to walk. "And thank you for introducing me to this culinary delight."

That made him laugh out loud. "It was my pleasure,

Brookie." He kissed the top of her head, and they walked out into the sunshine and began to make their way back toward the campus.

Neither spoke on the walk back other than to comment on the weather or the sights, and Brooke was good with that. It had been a bit of an emotional lunch, so the relative silence was a blessing, though it did leave her mind free to wander toward thoughts of Owen and why he didn't tell her himself about not wanting to hire her as his assistant—and not wanting to go on the trip, period. She had thought they'd crossed that hurdle from strangers to friends, and being that he knew how much she had riding on the position, it would have been polite to tell her to her face.

Rather than having her uncle break the news to her.

Once they were back at the entrance to the faculty building, they stopped, and Howard hugged her. "What are your plans for the rest of the day? Anything exciting?"

"There's a showing at a gallery Dr. Kennedy told me about that opens tonight. I'm planning on checking it out."

"Wonderful! What time are you heading out?"

"If it's all right with you, I think I'm going to go home and relax for a bit and then come back this way and grab a bite to eat before going to the gallery. So I'm afraid you're on your own for dinner again."

He smiled. "No worries there. I'm quite used to it. Although I'll admit I've been enjoying sharing meals with you since you arrived."

That warmed her heart. "I have too. I'm just in the mood to explore the city a bit tonight and see what other shops or shows I can find."

"Is anyone going with you?" he asked, concern lacing his voice.

As much as she hated for anyone to worry, this was going to be one of those times she was doing something purely for herself. "Nope. Just me, playing the bohemian tourist."

Howard frowned.

"Wasn't it just you a few minutes ago—"

He held up a hand to stop her. "You're right, you're right. Go and enjoy yourself." He kissed her on the forehead before turning to walk into the building.

Brooke stood there for several minutes as she tried to decide what to do first—go straight home and make some calls or go straight to Owen's classroom and demand he talk to her. With a steadying breath, she turned to go when her phone rang. Rummaging through her purse, she pulled her cell phone out and sighed. Swiping the screen, she lifted the phone to her ear and put on her cheeriest voice.

"Hi, Mom!"

―――

All day Owen felt ill at ease, like he was waiting for something bad to happen.

Maybe an angry mob would hunt him down or something.

Actually, that would be preferable to the ways he was torturing himself.

After leaving Howard's office, he had felt anxious and a combination of angry and sad. All of which were pretty much out of the ordinary for him. Not the anxiousness—he felt that sometimes on a daily basis—but the anger and sadness definitely weren't part of the norm.

It wasn't as if he expected Howard to fight his battles for him. He didn't. But in this particular case, Owen had hoped his friend would take pity on him and help him out of a difficult situation.

Wasn't that what he was already doing with Brooke?

Damn. Owen hated it when his subconscious had a point.

Okay, so he left Howard to break the news to Brooke about not coming on the trip with him. It was the coward's way out, and Owen knew it, but there was no way he could have done it himself. One look into her blue eyes, and he would have caved, just so he'd have the opportunity to spend time with her.

He scrolled through the text messages on his phone — the ones she had sent him over the last week. Smiley faces, friendly greetings, and a picture of a starry night from several days ago. Each one of them had made him smile. Most of the time he hadn't responded. Didn't know how. There wasn't anyone in his life he just... texted with for no reason. It was a common form of communication — he was aware of that — but normally that communication had a purpose.

So did hers. She was reaching out to you!

And he'd felt unsure of what the proper etiquette was for responding back or how to respond without sounding uncomfortable.

The constant seesawing he was doing where she was concerned was giving him motion sickness, and it had to stop. Class was over, and the rest of his day was free, as was his weekend, and that meant he was able to go

back to his hotel and find something to do to distract
him. Collecting his things, Owen left the lecture hall and
made his way out to the parking lot to his car.

Friday afternoon traffic was fairly brutal, but he
wasn't in a rush. His hotel wasn't that far from the
campus—a couple of miles tops—but right now it could
have been ten miles away. The roads were pretty much
like a parking lot, which left him time to think.

What do do…what to do…

There were several books he had planned to read.
Maybe he could download them to his tablet and settle
in for a night of relative escapism. Boring but still a
viable option. He didn't have to be back at the campus
until Tuesday, so he had three and half days to himself.
Maybe he'd look into taking a flight home to see his
family. He shook his head. Too much time wasted in
travel to make it more than a rushed event.

He inched along in traffic and sighed. You'd think
in such a busy city he wouldn't have any trouble trying
to come up with something to do. But that's what happened, he supposed, when you weren't the outgoing and
social type.

You could be…

Yeah, yeah, yeah. He'd had the option, and he'd
thrown it away. It was self-preservation. At least…that's
what Owen was telling himself. There was no way he
could take on going to Red Rock and spending time with
Brooke—time he knew was going to do nothing for him
but make him want her more—and then watch her walk
away when they were done. He was many things, but a
masochist wasn't one of them.

He turned off the main road and felt relief when the

hotel came into sight. Within minutes he had parked and was walking through the lobby toward the elevators. While waiting for the elevator to arrive, Owen realized he was no closer to having something to do for the weekend. He walked back toward the concierge desk, intent on getting some suggestions for things to do outside of the hotel.

He could read anytime.

"Excuse me," he said softly and then cleared his throat and spoke a little louder. "I was wondering if you could recommend something to do this weekend."

The young man behind the desk had a ready smile. "Absolutely! Tell me what you're looking for—museums, shopping, restaurants, tourist attractions, something off the beaten path...we've got everything!"

He was too upbeat and perky for Owen's taste, but Owen could mildly appreciate his enthusiasm for his job. "I'm thinking more along the lines of museums or something equally quiet."

"Ah, give me just one minute."

And sure enough, a minute later Owen had a handful of brochures and literature about a local history museum, an art museum, a natural history museum, and even a nature museum.

"As you can see, we have quite a few museums to choose from," the concierge said. Then he handed Owen a map of the area. "This map specifically details how to get from the hotel to each of the museums. Several are within walking distance." He stopped and chuckled. "Or at least a somewhat reasonable walking distance. It's easier than dealing with the traffic."

Owen nodded.

"Is there anything else I can do for you?"

"No, but thank you. I appreciate the information."

"Anytime. And enjoy your weekend, sir."

After another murmured thank-you, Owen made his way back to the elevators and went up to his room. All of this information he could have easily found himself online, but he was trying to make himself interact with people more. And honestly it hadn't been...terrible. Huh. How about that?

Once inside his room, he got comfortable and sat down to look at all of the brochures. He was a fan of museums—any museum, really. It was very satisfying to spend the day immersed in history or learning something new, and suddenly Owen felt some excitement for the weekend.

His plan was to relax for the night—order some room service and do some reading—and then spend the next three days touring the Field Museum, the Chicago History Museum, and then the Museum of Science and Industry. With that decision made, he spent a few minutes ordering and downloading the books he had wanted, and when he looked at the clock, he saw it was almost six.

"Dinner," he said and reached for the room service menu. Scanning it, he quickly realized nothing was appealing—at least not tonight. A BLT was always an option because...well...bacon. And even though it would have been fine, it wasn't what he wanted. Owen wasn't sure what specifically he was in the mood for, but it wasn't on this particular menu. There went his perfectly planned evening. But rather than letting that stress him out, he decided to try to go with flow. A quick walk around the block to find something interesting to eat would not only kill some time, but it would also give him an opportunity to enjoy more of the great spring weather.

When he stepped out onto the sidewalk a few minutes later, he took in the sights and smells of the city, something Owen didn't normally take the time to do. But he was trying something new, trying to break out of his little comfort zone and see what else was out in the world for him to experience.

So far? He wasn't overly impressed. There were a lot of traffic and a ton of people walking all around him, and it felt a little chaotic and crowded. He shuddered with discomfort but decided he was going to deal with it. He needed dinner, and if this was how he had to go about getting it, then so be it.

The first block didn't have anything that piqued his interest. The second block either. Next thing Owen knew, he was almost to Grant Park, which he knew was almost a mile from his hotel! His stomach was growling, and he couldn't believe he'd walked so far and hadn't found a single place where he wanted to eat. He stopped on the corner, looked around, and decided he was going to pick a place right then.

A diner.

There, on the opposite side of the street, was a diner. Most diners had hundreds of selections on their menus, so Owen had no doubt he'd find the perfect dinner and be back in his room enjoying his book in no time.

He crossed the street with a pep in his step, and even though there was a crowd of people waiting, he wasn't deterred. He was a single person, and if there was a counter, he'd be more than happy to sit there. Maneuvering his way through the crowd, he made his way up to the podium and waited for the hostess to come back and take his name.

"Owen?"

He froze. It couldn't be.

Slowly he turned around, and there were those eyes—those blue eyes that had captured him from the start and had been haunting him for weeks.

Except they were looking at him now with a whole lot of negativity, anger, and disappointment.

Next time he'd order the BLT in his room and be done with it.

"Hi, Brooke," he murmured and looked over his shoulder to see if the hostess was back so he'd have an excuse to get his thoughts together. But no such luck. Turning back around, he faced Brooke. "What brings you here tonight?"

"Dinner."

She even *sounded* negative, angry, and disappointed. And a little hostile.

Apparently, Howard had told her about not going to Red Rock.

"Me too," he said quietly. "I didn't think it would be this crowded."

"It's a diner on a Friday night—of course it's crowded. Every restaurant is crowded on a Friday night in the city. It's when most people go out."

He wouldn't know. He was usually working, which is what he said just to prevent an awkward silence.

Brooke seemed to relax a little. "So why aren't you working tonight?"

"Um…I was caught up on everything. I don't have another class until Tuesday—and it's my last one for this semester."

Her eyes went a little wide. "And…and then what will you be doing?"

Nervously he looked over his shoulder again. Where the hell was the hostess?

"Owen?" Brooke prompted.

Looking back at her, he quickly stammered, "I'm supposed to leave to tour Red Rock." And he instantly regretted his words. To her credit, Brooke continued to look at him, not showing any reaction to his words.

"Brooke? Party of one! Brooke, party of one!" the hostess called out.

Brooke looked beyond him to the hostess, waved her hand, and then looked at Owen. "Well, it was…nice to see you. Enjoy your night."

"Thank you," he murmured but didn't look at her.

She hadn't gone two steps when she stopped beside him. "Would you like to join me? I asked for a small booth, so there's room for a second person."

Owen's head snapped up as he looked at her, completely surprised by her invitation. "Really?"

At first she didn't answer, but then she nodded.

"I…I'd like that very much. Thank you." Clearly, the new Owen was a glutton for punishment. Now that he had been the first to mention the trip to Red Rock, it was certain to come up, and he'd have to explain to her—face-to-face—why he didn't want to hire her. Well, he thought, not the *real* reason. There was no way he was going to admit how he was attracted to her. That would be…well, it might be some sort of discrimination issue, and he wasn't ready to deal with that either.

Brooke stepped past him, walked over to the hostess, and explained that Owen would be joining her, and then the two of them followed the hostess to a small booth in the far corner of the diner. They sat, and Owen thanked Brooke one more time for asking him to join her. She smiled at him, picked up her menu, and began to read it. He did the same.

The menu was like a large book, Owen thought. It was tall and thin, but it had about ten pages worth of options. Did he want breakfast for dinner? A sandwich? A burger? Pasta? Fish? Maybe there was such a thing as too many options because even with everything seemingly under the sun to choose from, he still couldn't decide.

"What are you thinking of having?" Brooke asked from behind her menu.

"I'm not sure. There's quite a lot to choose from."

"Mmm-hmm."

For another five minutes, Owen looked at his options. The waitress brought them glasses of water and took their drink orders, and Owen knew she'd be back any minute to get their food orders. Because he was a little overwhelmed and feeling the pressure to make a decision, the BLT seemed like a safe pick. Then one of the specials caught his eye—the brisket. His mother used to make one of the best briskets he had ever eaten, but maybe he'd give this one a try.

Satisfied, he closed the menu and put it down. A minute later, Brooke did the same. He was just about to ask what she was going to have when the waitress reappeared and put down their drinks. "You ready to order?" she asked.

Brooke and Owen looked at each other and nodded. He motioned for Brooke to order first.

"I am going to have…" She paused, picked up the menu again, and glanced at one of the pages. "The brisket."

"You got it," the waitress said with a smile. "Would you like a salad with that?"

"Um…yes, please. With ranch dressing."

"Okay." Writing down Brooke's order, she paused and then looked to Owen, still smiling. "And what can I get for you?"

He was a little dumbfounded for a moment. What were the odds of two people ordering the same thing out of a ten-page menu?

"Sir?"

Oh, right. His order. "I believe I'll have the same."

"And would you like the salad too?"

He nodded.

"Okay, great. Thanks!" Taking their menus, the waitress turned and walked away.

Owen gave Brooke a weak smile and immediately picked up his glass and took a long drink. It took all of five seconds before they were back to staring at one another. "So…"

"So…" she mimicked, a smile tugging at the corners of her lips.

Which were pink. And glossy. Owen almost groaned after noticing that.

Brooke was dressed similarly to the way she was the first time he'd met her—long, flowing skirt and lots of bracelets, but tonight, instead of a tank top, she had on a fitted white T-shirt and her hair was loose. And, as usual, she was carrying her sweater rather than wearing it.

And she smelled amazing.

Yeah, definitely had to stifle a groan.

"Where is Howard tonight?" he asked, searching for a somewhat safe topic.

"He's home. I'm going to a gallery tonight to look at a new artist's work. I would have taken him along, but he had a faculty meeting, and I know he tends to turn in early. I wanted to have some time to sort of walk around and experience a little of the nightlife in the city."

"By yourself?" Owen asked incredulously. "That's not particularly safe."

She chuckled. "Have you been speaking to my parents?"

He looked at her curiously. "I...I've never met your parents. How could I have talked to them?"

She shook her head, still laughing. "It was a joke, Owen. I was implying you sounded a lot like them. They're always very vocal about how I need to go out in groups rather than by myself. I get it. They're concerned. But I'm twenty-eight years old. Sometimes I enjoy going out and doing things on my own."

He nodded, looking down. "I can understand that." He paused and then looked back at her. "Doesn't it intimidate you at all?"

"What?" she asked curiously.

"The crowds? The city? I just wanted to grab something to eat and go back to the hotel, but I feel like I got picked up by the crowd, and the next thing I knew, I was here. It was a bit unnerving. I only intended to go a block or two and ended up a mile away."

She smiled sympathetically at him. "To be fair, a city block is very long. I don't think it's very hard to walk a mile here."

"Maybe."

Sitting there, Owen kept waiting for the other shoe to drop, for Brooke to call him out on not hiring her and using her uncle to tell her.

But she didn't.

Instead, she started talking about some of the shops she'd seen while walking around and how she'd ended up here at the diner—she was craving something that reminded her of her home on Long Island, and that meant going to a diner. By that time, their food had arrived, and they ate in companionable silence.

Owen couldn't help the pleasurable sound he made at the first taste of his dinner. It may had been more than twenty years since he'd tasted his mother's cooking, but the brisket he was having felt as if Lillian Shaughnessy had made it herself.

"It's quite good, isn't it?" Brooke commented.

He nodded. "My mother used to make the best brisket, and this reminded me of hers."

"You better not tell her that," Brooke teased and then looked crestfallen at the look on his face. "What? What did I say?"

Slowly Owen put his fork down and used his napkin to carefully wipe around his mouth. "My mother passed away when I was ten," he said quietly. "I ordered this for dinner tonight because when I saw it on the menu, it reminded me of her."

Brooke reached across the table and placed her hand on top of his. "Owen, I'm so sorry. I didn't know. I never would have—"

"I know," he quickly interrupted. "Sometimes something or someplace will remind me of her. I try not to let it make me sad, but sometimes…like now…I can't help it."

"I know what you mean," she replied softly. Squeezing his hand one more time, she pulled away and went back to eating. They ate the remainder of their meal in silence.

After the waitress cleared away their plates and left the check, Brooke tilted her head and looked at him. "So what are you plans for the rest of the evening?"

"I had planned on just doing some reading. I downloaded a mystery I've been wanting to read. Nothing exciting."

She nodded and reached for her purse.

"Dinner's on me," he said and stopped her before she could say anything. "You were very gracious to invite me to join you. From the looks of that line, I would have been waiting for a while, so…thank you."

"I didn't ask you to join me so you would pay for my dinner, Owen."

"I know. I just… Please let me do this." *Please let me clear my conscience a little.*

A slow smile crossed her face. "Okay. Thank you."

Together they stood, and Brooke led the way across the restaurant and out the door. Out on the sidewalk, they faced one another. "So this book you downloaded," she began, "have you started it yet?"

He shook his head.

"No. How come?"

"Well, I know once I start a book, I tend to want to get back to it quickly. Especially if it's a good one."

"I'm the same way." But he still wasn't quite sure why she had asked.

Brooke was studying her feet—or the ground, he couldn't be sure—and he could tell she had something else to say. Maybe she was trying to get the courage up to finally confront him. It was agony waiting for her to do it, and as much as he was dreading the confrontation, he was also hopeful she'd just yell at him and put him out of his misery.

But she was quiet.

Still.

Maybe he was going to have to be the one to own up to what he had done and apologize. He tucked his hands in his pocket, and just as he was about to say her name, she looked up at him.

"Would you like to go to the gallery with me?"

Chapter 5

THERE WERE A LOT OF THINGS BROOKE WANTED TO SAY to Owen.

Inviting him to join her on her night out wasn't one of them.

And yet it had been the first thing to fly out of her mouth.

"I'd like that," he said, smiling. "A lot. Thank you."

She couldn't help but smile at the look of relief on his face. Together they turned and began walking away from the diner, and Owen asked her about the artist they were going to see.

"I have to admit, I didn't do a lot of research on him. He's new to me, and really, I just wanted to go because I always enjoy going to galleries and experiencing new artists. It's kind of fun to see what other people are creating and then meet them and find out what inspires them."

"I can understand that. I would imagine you have a lot more opportunities to do that than someone in my field does. Most of the people I interact with have studied the same things I have and believe the same things I do, but it's always refreshing when I meet someone who has an opposing view or some new insight into what is going on in space and why."

They walked several blocks while making observations about the things they were seeing—like a running commentary on people-watching—and Brooke was enjoying it. She liked this side of Owen—when he was relaxed and out of his work environment. She had to wonder if he was even aware of how differently he behaved when no one was directly watching him.

"I don't understand the whole sandals-and-black-socks look," he was saying. Brooke followed the direction of his gaze and saw an older gentleman dressed in tan shorts, a red T-shirt, black socks, and sandals. "We broke my dad of that habit. I wonder if that guy has anyone willing to do the same for him."

And then she laughed. Out loud. To the point that Owen stopped and looked at her. "Are you all right?" he asked.

Brooke stopped walking and tried to contain her laughter. "I'm sorry, but…that was just funny!"

He looked confused. "What was?"

Shaking her head, she laughed a bit more. "The way you commented on that. For a second, all I could picture was you walking up to that man and explaining why his outfit didn't work!"

Owen started to chuckle. "I suppose that would be funny—and probably a little embarrassing for him to have a complete stranger walk up to him and critique his clothing choices."

"Definitely." Brooke was about to start walking again when she looked around and frowned.

"What's the matter?"

"When I left the house earlier, I parked by Navy Pier and just started walking from there. I ended up south of there, and the gallery is north of there. I suspect we're in for a long walk." She paused and looked around again. "Should we stop and get my car?"

Owen seemed to consider their options and then shrugged. "The weather tonight is pleasant, and I don't mind the walk if you don't."

She couldn't help the smile that crossed her face. Secretly, she had been hoping he'd want to walk. There was something to be said for exploring the city on foot, and the thought of doing it with Owen—even though she was still pissed at him—just felt right.

"I don't mind the walk either," she said and felt herself blush. "I have a sweater for later when it's cooler out."

"Well, then…shall we?" he asked, smiling at her.

And off they went through the crowds of people.

"That was…interesting."

"I never thought I'd see those two mediums used together."

"I may have to stab my own eyes out to make sure I never see it again," Brooke said and then shuddered. They had just left the art gallery, and she waited until they were at the corner before looking at Owen. "I am so sorry."

He looked taken aback by her apology. "Why?"

"That was horrible! Everything in there was offensive and tasteless and just…wrong! I can't believe an art professor would recommend that to anyone!"

"Maybe he didn't know exactly what kind of art was being displayed."

Brooke shook her head. "He had to know. He raved about the whole thing, like he was familiar with the kind of work this guy did!"

"Maybe he's into that kind of thing. There were a lot of people there who were praising pretty much everything they saw."

Even though she knew Owen was right, she was still horrified. All of the pictures featured nudes in cages—and then there was wire caging coming out of one picture to give it a 3-D effect. Splashes of color looked as if they were thrown onto the canvas, and all in all, the exhibit had been fairly horrific to her. Brooke didn't consider herself a prude, but these images were definitely not something she would have chosen to see.

Ever.

And now she was mortified because she had invited Owen along. To his credit, he didn't seem the least bit fazed by the whole thing. It was possible he was trying to be polite and didn't want to offend her in case she found the work interesting. But after the first five minutes of being there, Brooke had wanted to escape. Somehow, however, Owen had drawn her into conversation as they walked around the gallery and made several observations that had her wondering if he really didn't see what was so…bizarre about the entire thing.

And that had been eye-opening for her. They stayed much longer than she'd imagined they would, especially after seeing the art, but they had talked the entire time, and after a while, she didn't even notice their surroundings. She simply enjoyed the conversation, which turned to the architecture of the building rather than the show.

"So that was an art showing," Owen said conversationally.

She nodded. "I really wish it had been a better experience."

"Is this the sort of thing you want to do? Have your paintings displayed in one particular gallery?"

"I think so. That was one of the reasons I went to talk to Dr. Kennedy. I really wanted his input on ways to get my name out there to some of the local galleries. I was hoping he'd give me some insight into how to get started."

Without commenting, Owen simply nodded.

"I don't know about you," she began, "but the thought of walking back to the pier is just a little exhausting. Would you mind if we grabbed a cab?"

"Not at all." Walking to the curb, he quickly hailed one, and once they were inside, he instructed the driver where to take them.

"Thank you," Brooke said, resting her head back on the seat. "I know I could have made the walk, but I'm just worn out."

"It was a lot of walking," he agreed. "I'll have the driver drop you at your car and take me back to my hotel."

"Oh."

Turning his head toward her, he looked at her until she met his gaze. "What's wrong?"

She shrugged. It was silly to be disappointed. Looking at the clock on the dashboard, she knew it was late—almost midnight—but she wasn't ready for the night to end.

"I just thought I'd drive you back there, and maybe we could have a drink or something before we called it a night."

He studied her for a moment, and she was afraid

she had been too forward and he was going to turn her down.

"I'd like that," he said, surprising her yet again.

"Good," she said, smiling.

The ride to her car took only a few minutes, and Owen paid the driver and thanked him as they climbed out. Silently they walked to her car, and for the first time that night, she truly felt nervous. There wasn't anything she could put her finger on, but for some reason Brooke knew it was a big deal that they were out together tonight and they were both unwilling to let the night come to an end.

Or perhaps she was seeing only what she wanted to see.

They stopped next to her car, and she turned to him. "I don't think I know what hotel you're staying at."

"It would probably be easier for me to drive. That is…if you don't mind."

Brooke willingly handed him the keys, and they were on the move minutes later. Traffic was a bit lighter than it had been earlier in the evening but still heavier than she would have expected for this time of night. Everything was lit up, and the sidewalks were still crowded, and she loved the energy of it all. They turned off the main road, and Owen pulled into an underground garage and parked.

"I was so busy people-watching I didn't even notice where we are." There was a possibility that was the wrong thing to admit to, but…

"That's okay," he said, taking the keys out and handing them to her. Neither made a move to get out of the car though.

She watched him for a moment—noticed how he was staring at the steering wheel and how he seemed to be thinking about something, but she had no idea what. Turning in her seat, she faced him. "Owen—"

"I'd like to kiss you," he blurted out.

Her eyes went wide, and her heart beat madly in her chest. "You…you would?"

Owen looked at her, his dark eyes so full of emotion. He shook his head. "I'm sure there was a more eloquent way to say that, but…I'm not very eloquent," he added quietly.

Reaching out, Brooke took one of his hands in hers—relishing the warmth she found there—and marveled at how large it was. And there was strength there. He didn't have the hands of a man who sat behind a desk pushing papers around, and the skin-on-skin contact was far more arousing than she thought possible. "You're more eloquent than you think you are," she said softly.

The look he gave her said he didn't quite believe her. "I had a wonderful time with you tonight, Brooke, and I know we're going to go inside and have a drink, and we'll talk some more and…well…the longer we talk and the later it gets, it's going to make me want to kiss you even more. It's wrong for me to want to, but—"

"Why is it wrong?" she interrupted.

And there were those eyes that had her more than ready to crawl across the seat and into his lap. There was a vulnerability in his eyes that was almost her undoing.

"I hurt you. I know you didn't say anything about it, but I know Howard probably talked to you and told you about Red Rock." He looked away and shook his head.

"It was wrong of me to do it like that. I should have talked to you myself. I'm sorry."

"Owen, I'm not going to lie to you. I was hurt, and yes, I was pretty angry with you earlier. I know we haven't known each other very long, but I thought we were at least becoming friends. I hated hearing about your decision from my uncle, but…I kind of understand why you did it that way. I'm sure it wasn't an easy decision for you to make."

"None of this is easy," he murmured and then looked up at her again. "I'm not good at this sort of thing—playing it cool and pretending I'm not interested in you when in fact I am. So…I'd completely understand if you didn't want to stay and have that drink or talk like we'd planned. You're probably sitting there trying to figure out a nice way to tell me to get out of the car."

Brooke was about to correct him, but Owen kept talking.

"I thought about hiring you, but I couldn't. Not because I don't want you on the trip, but because I knew I couldn't handle working with you every day and having you close by while I'm attracted to you. And knowing you were only there because you wanted to paint and that you weren't interested in me."

Now she had to speak. Before he could get another word out, she squeezed his hand and got his attention. "But you're wrong."

He didn't seem to understand what she was talking about.

"I do want to go on this trip to paint—I'm not going to deny that—but…Owen, I'm attracted to you too. I've enjoyed getting to know you, and the more time we spend together, the more I want to spend with you. I was afraid maybe you didn't want me on the trip because I wasn't smart enough or—"

She never got to finish.

Owen closed the distance between them and cupped her face in his hands as his lips claimed hers.

———

Good Lord, she tasted sweeter than he had imagined.

Her lips were so soft, and when she sighed and leaned into him, Owen knew he had made the right decision. He skimmed her cheeks with the backs of his fingers and marveled at how she felt. Brooke's hand came up and rested on his chest before moving to his shoulders and around his neck.

They were pressed together chest to chest, and Owen cursed the fact that he had made his move in a parked car, like he was fifteen and on his first date.

Not that he'd dated at fifteen, but he knew boys who had.

Focus!

The woman in his arms was like a fantasy, a dream, and just knowing she was as attracted to him as he was to her was a very potent aphrodisiac. It wouldn't take much for him to sit here all night and continue to kiss and touch her, but it wasn't the right place for them.

And probably not the right time.

Slowly he broke the kiss and rested his forehead against hers, and they both caught their breath.

"Wow," she sighed.

No woman had ever reacted that way to his kisses, and before he knew it, he tilted his head and captured her lips again. Brooke kissed him back with equal fervor, and he shifted his arms the best he could, so she was almost cradled in them, and then marveled at how perfectly she fit there.

Images flashed in his head of taking her up to his hotel room. To his bed. The images were so vivid that he had to wonder if the two of them hadn't moved and were in fact there already. A car door slamming nearby told him they hadn't, and he reluctantly ended the kiss.

Again.

"I have a feeling if we don't stop now, we're going to start giving the people walking by quite a show," he said, placing one last kiss on her lips. They slowly broke apart and straightened in their seats. He was going to apologize but quickly dismissed the idea. He wasn't sorry. Kissing her had been the most impulsive thing he'd ever done, and he didn't regret it for one minute. He couldn't.

"I don't know about you," Brooke said, "but I can definitely use a little something to drink." She picked up her purse and opened the door. Looking over her shoulder at him, she smiled. "You ready?"

That was a loaded question. He was more than ready—for whatever she wanted. Rather than comment, he nodded, climbed out of the car, and walked around to meet her. Without conscious thought, he took her hand, and together they walked into the hotel. Owen paused in the lobby.

"The bar is closed, but we can grab something to drink from the store and sit if you'd like." He realized he should have remembered this before coming back to the hotel. He chose to stay here because it was clean and the rooms had kitchenettes, but it was far from being an upscale hotel. They could always go up to his room—it did have a comfortable living area—but after the kisses they'd just shared, he wasn't sure if that was a smart idea. He didn't want Brooke to feel like he was pressuring her in any way.

"That sounds fine," she said softly, her hand still in his.

Owen knew he wasn't going to be the one to break the contact. He was enjoying it. Probably more than he should. After purchasing a couple bottles of water, a bag of pretzels, and a candy bar—which Brooke had bashfully asked for—they walked back out to the lobby and sat down on one of the sofas. They sat in awkward silence as other hotel guests came and went—loudly—and Owen turned to Brooke and threw out a suggestion.

"It's completely okay if you say no to this, but… would you like to come upstairs with me? To my room?"

Her eyes went wide, and he felt an instant of panic.

"Just to talk—like we said," he added quickly. "It's very loud down here, and I just thought…but maybe it's late and you want to head home. It's fine. Really. Maybe we can see each other tomorrow. I was planning on touring some of the museums this weekend if you're interested. The weather is supposed to be fair, and we could walk around the city. And—"

"Owen?"

"Hmm?"

"You're rambling," she said with a small smile. "And in answer to your question…well, one of them, I would like to go upstairs with you. I agree. It's rather noisy, and every time someone comes in or goes out, the cool air comes in, and it's chilly."

He instantly stood and held out his hand. "You're sure it's not too late?"

Brooke shook her head. "I don't have a curfew, and I don't think it's too late. I'm a night owl. If I were home, or at my uncle's, I would be watching a movie or reading a book or playing Scrabble on my tablet."

They rode the elevator while talking about books — she told him about the latest Nora Roberts book she had just finished, and he told her the plot of the James Patterson book he had just downloaded.

"Uncle Howard's reading that one too," she told him.

And the conversation didn't stop there. They settled into his room with little more than a brief acknowledgment from Brooke that it was a nice space. Sitting on the sofa, they compared their interests not only in books but in movies, food, and hobbies. Owen already knew of her love of painting, but he found it fascinating when she shared her "mini-obsession" — her words — with word games and computer solitaire. He had to admit he occasionally played solitaire, but normally when he was on his computer or tablet, it was for work and research purposes.

But what he was finding most interesting about Brooke was the way she spoke so passionately about the things she did — whether it was something as big and profound as her art or as minute as playing a game of Scrabble. She found joy in it all, and it made him wish he were more like her. Science was his life, and it was fulfilling, but Owen couldn't say for certain if it gave him joy.

"You're frowning," Brooke said, interrupting his thoughts. "What are you thinking about?"

"I was sitting here thinking about you," he said, and

when her expression fell, he realized how what he said could have been interpreted. "I'm sorry! That…that didn't come out right." He chuckled. "What I meant was I was sitting here listening to you, and you're so…passionate about all of the things you do, and I realized that while I'm passionate about my work and the things I do in my spare time, it's not a joyful passion." He paused. "I'm not even sure I'd know what that felt like."

She studied him for a long moment—long enough that he started to squirm in his seat. "What makes you laugh?"

"Excuse me?"

She laughed softly. "Tell me something that makes you laugh—it can be a television show, a comedian, someone you know…just anything you know that makes you laugh."

It seemed like a simple question, but Owen was surprised when he couldn't recall anything right away. Panic started to set in because he realized how odd it was going to sound. After all, who had to think about what they found amusing?

Brooke put her hand on his thigh. "I am a sucker for romantic comedies. I don't like anything that goes for cheap gags or slapstick, but if I sit down to watch a movie, that's my go-to because I know it will make me laugh and feel good by the end of the movie."

Her logic made sense. "This shouldn't be so hard, right? I'm overthinking it."

She leaned back on the sofa, and Owen instantly missed the feel of her hand on him. "Maybe just a little," she teased. "How about something that makes you happy?"

"My family," he said without hesitation. His answer

must have pleased her because she was smiling again. "I guess they make me laugh too—sometimes at myself, but that's a given. When I go home to visit, there's always a lot of laughing, and sometimes I don't quite get the joke, but I laugh with them because…it feels good. And in the past couple of years, it seems like there's a lot more laughter in our family—probably because we've grown so much."

He didn't look over at her because he was remembering his visit home the previous month. Hugh and Aubrey's son, Connor, was a very active two-year-old who loved to climb, and Owen remembered watching Hugh running after him most of the time.

That had made him laugh.

Then there was sweet baby Lily—Aidan and Zoe's daughter. They had her dressed in a frilly outfit that almost seemed bigger than she was, and as she toddled around trying to learn how to walk, she would eventually fall in a big pouf of fabric. She was incredibly sweet and adorable, and she'd look at him with a big, wet grin and clap her hands whenever she fell.

That had made him laugh.

Soon Quinn and Anna's baby would be here, and the thought of his ultra-macho brother trying to handle a tiny baby had him laughing right then.

"Aha!" Brooke said with a chuckle. "I knew you'd think of something. Out with it! What's making you laugh?"

He told her about Quinn's personality and how he and his wife were expecting a baby. "It seemed natural for Hugh and Aidan to become fathers—they're both nurturing, and they did a lot to help raise the rest of us.

But Quinn?" He couldn't help but chuckle again. "Let's just say the entire family is going to get a kick out of watching him."

"He may surprise you all. This could be something to teach him a little humility."

That made Owen laugh even more. "I have to admit he has softened a bit since he and Anna finally got together. It's been a fascinating transformation. But I still think this baby is going to challenge him more than he thinks."

"Babies definitely can do that. It's hard to believe such a tiny being can wreak so much havoc on the adults around him." She laughed. "Or her."

Owen was about to comment on that when Brooke moved closer and put her head on his shoulder. He cleared his throat quietly and rested his head on hers. "Any babies in your family?"

She shook her head. "Nope. Although I think my parents would love that. They just recently started talking about it. Some of their friends have become grandparents in the past few years, and it's made them start campaigning for their own grandchildren." She started to reach for her snack, but Owen got it for her, handing her the water and the chocolate bar. "Thank you."

As they sat in silence, Owen wondered about her family. She didn't talk about them much, but then he figured maybe he just spoke about his more than the average person because he had such a large family. He looked down and saw a piece of chocolate being offered to him. Brooke's delicate hand was mere inches from his mouth. Was he supposed to take it from her hand with his or simply...bite it?

He opted for biting, and as he took the sweet chocolate into his mouth, his lips grazed her fingers, and he
heard her gasp softly beside him.

But not in a bad way.

His heart rate kicked up, and as he slowly finished
chewing, he reached up, took her hand, and brought her
fingers close to his lips. He swallowed and then kissed
her fingertips, licking the spot where there was still a bit
of chocolate, and heard Brooke moan.

Sexiest sound ever.

As if of one mind, they maneuvered until Brooke was
in his arms, and then he was kissing her again. His lips
claimed hers, and this time it was so much better, he
thought. Without having the car console between them,
he could feel her—every sweet curve, every delicate
inch of her was curled against him—and it was a heady
sensation. Owen had never considered himself to be
big or strong like his brothers, but with Brooke in his
arms, he did. He wrapped his arms around her as she
looped hers around his neck. If he died right now, he'd
die satisfied.

It was humbling to think that this beautiful and
amazing woman wanted him. Him. Nerdy Owen
Shaughnessy. And then all rational thought left him as
her hands raked into his hair, gently scratching his scalp,
and she moved to be almost fully in his lap.

There was no way for him to hide the effect she was
having on him. He didn't want to. And if it shocked her
or bothered her, she didn't let on.

Their kisses intensified, became more and more
urgent. His tongue teased and tangled with hers as he
pulled her closer—and yet he couldn't seem to get her

close enough. He needed to breathe—to get air into his lungs—but the thought of not kissing her was almost painful. When at last he couldn't take it, his lips left hers and trailed across her cheek, down the slender column of her throat. Owen's hand tangled in her long, silky hair as she arched back to give him better access to all the places he was trying to reach.

She whispered his name.

She begged for him to touch her.

And he knew there was a bed in the next room. It would take less than a minute to get them there.

But he couldn't move. Not now. Not yet. Instead, his hands began to move, skimming along her spine and around to her rib cage. He gently squeezed her waist and marveled at her curves. He stayed in that spot until he could control himself while his mouth nipped at the sensitive spot where her neck and shoulder met. He felt her shiver, heard her breath hiss, and he became almost obsessed with seeing and feeling all of her responses.

To him.

He'd never held such a responsive woman in his arms. Never felt as overwhelming a need for someone as he felt right now. It was hot… It was heady… It was erotic. It was…

Brooke moaned, took his hand in hers, and placed it on her breast, and they both seemed to gasp with a mixture of pleasure and pain. Unable to help himself, he lifted his head and looked at her—took in her flushed skin, her parted lips and closed eyes—and she made a very desirable picture. He almost wished he had the ability to paint because this…this woman in his arms…was the most exquisite piece of art he'd ever seen.

As if sensing his stare, Brooke opened her eyes and looked at him. Her eyes were bright, glazed, and she reached a hand around his nape and pulled him in for another kiss—deeper, hotter, and wetter than the last. She kissed him as if she needed him to breathe, needed him like she didn't need anything—or anyone—else. And it was enough of a confirmation that he knew what he had to do. Owen licked her lips one last time before raising his head and whispering her name on a sigh.

She looked at him as she caught her breath and he caressed her cheek.

"It's very late," he murmured.

She nodded.

"I don't want you to leave."

She licked her lips, and he had to stop himself before he groaned.

"I don't want to leave."

She was killing him.

He swallowed hard. "I can't believe I'm going to say this, but—"

"You always say what you mean, Owen." Her voice was a mere whisper.

"I want you to stay. I want to take you into the bedroom and take you to bed and make love to you."

"I want that too."

This time he did groan. And then he shook his head. "But we can't."

Her eyes widened a little. "Can't?"

Relaxing a little, he continued to caress her cheek. "I don't think we should. Not tonight."

Now she frowned slightly. "But you want me to stay." It wasn't a question.

"I do." He paused. "Even if we just curl up together and watch TV or talk. I just want to hold you. Maybe that's selfish of me, but…it's how I feel."

Slowly, Brooke pushed herself up from his lap and looked at him as if she was considering her options. For a minute, Owen wasn't sure what he was expecting her to say. Was she upset that he didn't want them to make love? Would she opt to leave and go home?

"Do I get a say in this?" she asked.

And all he could do was nod.

Without a word, she stood, but she didn't move away immediately, and again it left him to wonder at what it was that she wanted.

And then she held out her hand to him. "Is there a TV in the bedroom?"

Again, all he could do was nod. But he placed his hand in hers and stood.

And let her lead him to the other room.

—∽—

"Maybe this was a mistake."

"How can you say that? I think it's great."

"It's just so…crowded."

"What were you expecting? It's a Saturday."

They walked hand in hand through the Museum of Science and Industry, and while Brooke was having a great time, Owen clearly wasn't so sure. Pulling him into a small alcove, she faced him. "There is nothing wrong with it being crowded," she reminded him. "It's because this is an amazing place."

"There are a lot of kids. I didn't think of this as a kids' place."

"Owen, kids love science."

"Not when I was a kid."

"Yes, even when you were a kid, they loved it. They just didn't have the same level of appreciation that you did."

At first she thought he was going to argue with her, and she was pleasantly relieved when he didn't. "I guess I never looked at it that way."

"Stick with me, and I'll help you see that not everything is negative."

"There are still a lot of people here. I couldn't even get near that coal mine exhibit."

And she knew he was disappointed about that one because he'd mentioned it several times. "How about we go and catch the movie on the national parks?" she asked, hoping to distract him. "It's on an OMNIMAX screen, which is supposed to be pretty impressive. What do you say?"

It took him a minute, but he agreed, and they bought tickets. Waiting in line, Owen looked around, and she saw him frown again.

"We have tickets. We're going to get in."

"I know," he said a little distractedly. "I'm glad Howard opted to stay home."

They had woken up fairly early, having fallen asleep in each other's arms while watching *Silver Linings Playbook*. Brooke didn't believe for one minute it was a movie Owen would normally watch, but he had. And he'd held her. And it had been the most perfect night ever. And even though it should have been awkward this morning, it wasn't. She woke up to slow, sleepy kisses, and if given the chance, she would have opted for them to stay in bed like that all day.

The man certainly knew how to kiss.

And touch.

And…everything.

Unfortunately, she had been more than a little self-conscious about morning breath and how dreadful she looked after sleeping in her clothes all night. Owen had assured her she was beautiful, but she didn't quite believe him. So she had jumped up and offered to make coffee while Owen quickly showered and changed. He readily agreed, and once he was ready, they drove to her uncle's so she could do the same.

The look on her uncle's face when they'd walked in the door together had been priceless.

Shock. Then awkwardness. And then finally…pleasure.

Pretty much exactly how Brooke had felt and—she was fairly certain—Owen too.

She had excused herself so she could shower and change, and Owen hadn't mentioned what he and Howard had talked about in her absence. All she knew was that when she came back downstairs thirty minutes later, they were discussing the museum and Owen had issued the invitation.

Which Uncle Howard graciously declined.

And now as they waited in line, Brooke had to wonder why Owen was grateful for her uncle's absence. "How come?" she finally asked.

"I think he—like myself—would have enjoyed being able to see some of these exhibits at our leisure. This is the kind of place that is probably more enjoyable on a weekday when there's hardly anyone around."

Brooke leaned in close and whispered in his ear, "Then we'll just have to try again one day this week so you can take your time and see and touch and explore all you want."

She was only partially talking about the museum.

Owen must have understood her meaning because she saw him duck his head and blush a little.

She liked when he did that. He might not agree with her reasoning, but in her mind, seeing him blush and seeing that vulnerability made him seem stronger than any man she'd ever known. Someday she might even tell him that.

Stepping back, she smiled sweetly. "Won't that be fun?"

Swallowing hard, he nodded and squeezed her hand. He was saved from having to say anything by the movement of the line—they were being let into the theater. Curious to see where he'd lead them to sit, she kept her opinions and requests to herself. She figured him to be the kind of guy who would find a spot up close or at least in the center of the theater for optimum viewing.

She was intrigued when he led her to the top row and all the way into the corner. All sorts of thoughts went through her mind from "maybe this is the best viewing spot" and "it's probably quieter with less likely of a chance for other viewers to interrupt us with their chatter" to something a whole lot sexier when he turned and looked at her. There was heat and promise in those dark eyes that had her tingling.

Together they sat, hands still linked, and leaned in close to each other. Trying to keep them occupied until the lights went down, she pulled out the brochure they had been given with their tickets and began to read it out loud.

"For a hundred years, beautiful places like Yellowstone, Yosemite, the Everglades, the Redwoods, and Arches have been living monuments to the nation's vast and untamed wilderness," she began. "I don't think I've ever visited a national park. Have you?"

He nodded. "Yellowstone and Yosemite. Both were part of programs with the planetariums—similar to the one at Red Rock. It's always exciting to be in such a vast setting that is magnificent on its own and combine it with an astrological event."

It was on the tip of her tongue to question why it was that those events were different for him than the one at Red Rock, but she pretty much knew the answer. He was leading this one. At the others he was a bystander who could choose to participate when he wanted, and he could blend into the crowd when he didn't. It made her sad because the man she was getting to know was more dynamic and personable and clever and witty than he realized. But instead, she opened the brochure and continued her commentary.

"Celebrate the majesty of these treasured landscapes. Join world-class mountaineers and adventure photographers and artist as they bike, hike, and climb their way across America's most pristine parks, revealing a tapestry of natural wonders that will inspire the adventurer in us all." Refolding the brochure, she felt sad, and it must have shown on her face because Owen commented on it.

"I have a feeling I'm going to watch this movie and it's going to make me wish we could get on a plane tonight and just...go. I'm going to get inspired by the colors and the scenery, and it will be like sensory overload because it's on this big, giant screen, and I'm mad at myself for not bringing my sketch pad with me."

"Well, to be fair, you normally wouldn't need one for a day at a museum."

"Maybe," she murmured and leaned back in her seat.

The theater lights began to dim, and Brooke forced herself to push aside all thoughts of paints and brushes and colors and all of the longing inside of her to be a part of what was starting to show up on the screen.

But she was fooling herself. There was no way to ignore the colors or for her not to imagine how she would make them look on canvas. In the first two minutes, she could feel her fingers twitching with the need to pick up a brush. As if sensing it, Owen lifted her hand to his lips and kissed her. And when she turned her head he was right there. Waiting.

And all thoughts of painting, colors, and national parks vanished as Owen closed the distance between them and kissed her. Consumed her. Damn near devoured her.

Yes, the man had some skills.

She was thankful for the dark theater, the secluded corner, and the loud movie, so she was free to let out a moan of pleasure as his large hands cupped her face.

And that was another thing—his hands. She was getting addicted to them as well. For such large hands, they touched her as if she were delicate, and really, all Brooke was beginning to think about was how they would feel if they stopped touching her so softly, so delicately, and touched her the way she was aching for.

So not the place for *that* thought, but…there it was.

Owen abruptly ended the kiss, rested his forehead against hers, and gave her a lopsided grin. "Sorry," he said breathlessly, turning his head so he could murmur next to her ear. "I couldn't help myself."

She knew the feeling.

"That's okay," she replied softly and shivered when his tongue traced the shell of her ear. "I like it when you do that."

He nipped at her earlobe and then wrapped an arm around her and turned them so they could focus on the movie again. And for the next thirty minutes, Brooke was beyond content to savor the feel of the man beside her and take in nature at its finest.

———

The temperature had dropped a little by the time they left the museum. The mild weather of the day before was long gone. They huddled close together as they stood on the sidewalk and contemplated what they were going to do next.

"Are you hungry?" Owen asked, pulling her closer. "I know we had a late breakfast, but…"

"We did, but I'm not in a hurry to grab something."

He nodded. They had driven Brooke's car to the museum, and so they turned toward the parking garage and began walking. Owen was a little lost in his own thoughts. The movie had been extremely informative and enjoyable, and when it touched upon the Grand Canyon and Red Rock and specifically their brilliance for observing the night sky, he had felt like it was some kind of sign.

He wanted to smack himself in the back of the head. He didn't believe in signs. But as much as he kept saying that he didn't want to take on this project, there were far too many…signs, for lack of a better word, that were telling him to go. Why? He had no idea. All of the trips he had gone on in the past as an observer had been extremely enjoyable—almost life-changing in their beauty—and Owen knew part of the wonder was because of where and how he was seeing the event.

So why was he fighting this so much?

Because everyone's watching you...waiting for you to make a mistake and look foolish.

But Brooke can help you with that...

He looked down at her as they walked. Her expression was relaxed, her cheeks slightly rosy from the cool air, and just looking at her gave him a sense of peace. Having her with him on the trip would definitely help, but it was also going to be a distraction. A big one. In fact, he knew it would be hard to even remember to work or talk to his students when all he'd be able to think about was getting Brooke alone and touching her and kissing her and just being with her.

He stopped dead in his tracks.

Never before had anything distracted him from his work.

Ever.

"Are you okay?" Brooke asked, looking up at him with concern.

Nodding, he didn't say anything and started walking again. She didn't question him, and when they reached her car, she handed Owen the keys and walked to the passenger side. He liked how she let him drive. Of course, it was partially because he knew his way around the city better than she did, but still...

"Where should we go?" she asked softly, as if knowing his mind was still elsewhere.

Shrugging, he suggested, "You pick. The museum was all my idea. Where would you like to go?"

"Oh…that could be dangerous," she said playfully. "Look how disastrous my suggestion was last night. I don't think I can handle another awkward art exhibit."

That had him laughing. Yeah, they'd probably end up talking about all of the nude pictures they'd seen at some point, but for now he'd like to forget it too. "There's a simple solution to that—don't pick anything art related."

"Easy for you to say. That's like me asking you to pick something that isn't science related. It's just what we are naturally programmed to veer toward."

That was true. "Okay, so we're not ready to get something to eat, and we don't want to do anything science or art related."

"And we've already seen a movie."

"I don't think that counts. It wasn't a full-length movie."

Beside him, Brooke shrugged. "Still, it was moving pictures on a giant screen in a theater. Therefore, it was a movie."

Her logic was adorable, and he couldn't help but laugh again. "All we're doing is limiting our options exponentially." He pulled out of the parking lot and turned right—not because he had a place in mind, but because it was easier turning that way. "We could do something spontaneous. Something neither of us would ever typically do."

"That would require us thinking about it and planning it, and then it's not spontaneous." She paused. "We could walk around, but it's too cold. We could go shopping, but I'm not big on that."

"How is that possible? I thought it was genetic. All women love shopping."

She shook her head. "Not me. My mother killed my love of it after so many years on the pageant circuit. Every bit of free time was spent shopping for gowns and dresses and makeup." She shuddered. "I know she meant well, but it left me with an aversion to going to malls or getting glammed up for anything."

He glanced at her like she was crazy. She was wearing makeup, she was dressed in trendy clothes, and she looked amazing. In his eyes, she was glammed up. How much more…everything could she have been for these pageants? Which is what he asked her.

Sighing, she looked out the window as they drove around aimlessly. "My hair was never allowed to be straight—it always had to be curled. Which is why I wear it straight or clipped up now. So much damage was done to it from all the products and heat, and I'm done with that. Makeup could have been put on with a spackle knife—so heavy and garish. Don't get me wrong, I enjoy wearing makeup; it's just minimal now."

"I had no idea. But then again I never paid much attention to beauty pageants."

"There was so much pressure to be perfect all the time—to have my hair and makeup done perfectly, and my clothes always had to be designer and whatever was trendy. But the worst was the pressure to stay thin. I like food. I enjoy eating, and for so many years I had to exist on salads and water and go to the gym to stay fit." She gave a mirthless laugh. "Every minute of every day was scheduled for me based on what competition was coming up. I know it sounds crazy because some people had real struggles, but to me, it was brutal."

The pain in her voice spoke volumes, and he hated

that she had felt such anguish. He had no idea such a thing existed—not the pageants but the pressure. He took her hand in his and squeezed it and did his best to move on from that particular topic.

"If you could do anything you want right now, what would it be?" He paused before adding, "The first thing that comes to mind."

"Painting in a national park," she said quickly and then started to laugh. Turning her head, she looked at him. "I guess that movie got to me more than I wanted it to. All I could think about in the beginning was how jealous I was that I wasn't in one of those parks with a canvas and some paint."

An idea began to form in his mind, but it was very impulsive and totally out of character for him. It would require being so far out of his comfort zone that it threatened to paralyze him. But when he glanced over at Brooke and saw the serene smile on her face as she continued to chatter about the ideas she had gotten from watching the movie, Owen knew he couldn't just push his idea aside.

If nothing else, he had to at least mention it to her. Of course, there was a chance she'd think he was crazy and wouldn't agree to it anyway, but she could love it and want to go for it. Then what would he do?

"…I think of the layers in the rock, and it's just so amazing to see! Some of those lines are so incredibly straight that it shouldn't be possible, but it's the different colors that catch my eye. I would love to get close enough to touch them and smell them." She stopped and chuckled. "I know it sounds weird, but sometimes a scent will inspire me. That's why I love painting outdoors—the fresh air is never the same twice." Looking up at him, she added, "You think I'm weird, don't you?"

Owen shook his head. He would never think that about her. About anyone. He knew how hurtful it was when people labeled you as such. "No, I don't. I find what you're saying to be fascinating. I don't tend to see things the way you do—I'm a little more black and white. I would look at the layers in the rock and the colors from a scientific standpoint. I would reason why the colors are the way they are but without seeing them. You really see them."

Her smile broadened. "I do. And I know not everyone looks at things the same way, and that's what makes life interesting. We all don't have to see the same things the same way. It makes for great discussions and conversations. Can you imagine if everyone looked at, say, the Grand Canyon and went, 'Well…that's a big, brown canyon' and moved on?"

The simplistic example had him laughing. "That would definitely be—"

"Boring," she finished for him. "It would be boring. No two people should see it the same way. We all have different emotions, and I know if I ever went to see the Grand Canyon in person—and stood on the canyon platform—I'd probably be at a loss for words because I would be filled with awe!"

"How do you know that for sure? Maybe you'll be the one to go and say it's a big, brown canyon. You might be disappointed," he teased.

Brooke rolled her eyes. "A person would have to be an emotionless robot to have that kind of reaction," she countered. "Its size alone is enough to make you react with awe. So even if you didn't notice the colors, the pure scope of it would invoke some kind of reaction."

He hadn't thought of it that way.

Interesting.

"So you want to go and touch, paint, and smell the Grand Canyon?"

"Hell yes!" she laughed. "Why? You want to hop a plane and do that tonight?"

Without conscious thought, they had ended up back at Owen's hotel. Owen pulled into the underground garage and parked before turning toward Brooke. She was still chuckling, and it appeared she hadn't noticed where they were yet.

"Yes," he said firmly. "That's exactly what I'm saying. Let's get on a plane to Nevada tonight."

Chapter 6

SIX HOURS LATER, BROOKE STILL COULDN'T BELIEVE WHAT was going on.

She was in Nevada, currently checking into a hotel in Las Vegas because it was the easiest place for them to get reservations on such short notice. As Owen checked them in, she stood beside him, looking around at the massive lobby of the hotel. It was at the end of the Strip, and there wasn't a casino, and to her it was perfect.

The flight had taken less than four hours, but all of the rushing they'd done to get packed and to the airport on time had left her more than a little exhausted. Physically. Dealing with her family when she'd called to let them know where she was going had been mentally exhausting. Luckily, Uncle Howard had taken the phone from her hands and talked his sister out of her panic attack over her only daughter going off to Vegas for the weekend with a man she'd just met. A small giggle escaped as the reality of that statement hit her.

She was in Vegas.

With Owen.

It didn't seem real.

Looking over at him, she watched him sign for the room and accept their key cards. This was it. This was happening! He turned to her and smiled, and they walked in relative silence to the bank of elevators. Her mind was going a mile a minute, but she kept her thoughts to herself, unwilling to come off sounding like a babbling idiot.

They had talked the entire time on the plane about how unusual this impulsive behavior was for both of them and how Las Vegas wasn't someplace either would have chosen to go on a vacation, but then they rationalized how they weren't going for all of the bells and whistles of the Vegas Strip. It was merely a place to stay on short notice, and most of the time they'd be out at the Grand Canyon. Owen had reached out to his contacts at the Las Vegas Astronomical Society and let them know he was coming in early to tour the area at Red Rock.

And that call had made Brooke's heart beat a little faster because it meant he wasn't going to cancel the trip and there was still hope for them to work together. Although she had a feeling that even if she didn't go on the trip in a professional capacity, she might be able to convince him to let her come along as a friend...or a girlfriend. Just thinking of them on that level had her blushing. They had slept together—basically—but that didn't mean he was looking to have a serious relationship with her.

Did it?

Either way, he had reached out to the organization and inquired about the best way to go to the canyon that didn't require sitting on a bus for hours with a hundred other people. His contacts were very accommodating and told him he and Brooke would be able to take a helicopter to tour the area over Red Rock where Owen would be camping with his group. The helicopter would then take the two of them out to the canyon, where they would land and have a couple of hours to explore and take pictures. Brooke didn't have her paints and canvases with her, but if she had a few hours to explore and take pictures, it would be incredibly helpful for when she got home.

Owen opened the hotel room door, and Brooke walked in, feeling a twinge of nerves. Even though they had spent last night in Owen's room, the fact that this was their room—together—suddenly seemed huge.

And intimidating.

There was no place to hide. All of her...quirks...were going to be on display, and some of them she had hoped to keep to herself. At least for a while. There was no way she wanted to scare him off quite so soon—not when they were connecting. Swallowing hard, she walked farther into the room and put her bag down. She took a full minute to realize Owen was still standing by the door. She turned and looked at him. "Is everything okay? Do you not like the room?"

Shaking his head, he took a tentative step toward her. "The room is fine. After a while they all start to look the same."

"Then what's the matter?" She had a feeling she knew exactly what was going on in his mind—the exact same stuff she was just thinking of. Not everyone was meant to be impulsive, and maybe they should have booked separate rooms or at least a suite.

"I... It seems—"

"It's weird, right?" she finished for him and smiled when he seemed to completely relax.

"Exactly." He smiled back at her and finally walked into the room. "I know we talked about it, but now that we're here, I feel like I'm pressuring you or—"

"Owen," she quickly interrupted, "I said I was fine with us sharing a room. I know it doesn't have to…lead to anything. We slept in the same bed last night and survived, right?"

He nodded.

"And if we did it once, we can do it again. Right?"

He nodded again.

Damn. She was almost hoping he'd put up more of a fight—but for which argument, she couldn't say. There was no doubt that if he asked, she'd strip down and make love with him right then. But if he said he was uncomfortable and wanted to get another room, she'd be on board with that as well. So where did that leave her?

Confused. Utterly and completely confused.

"I wish you'd say something," she said with a nervous laugh.

Stepping in close, Owen cupped her face in his hands—she liked it when he did that. His gaze was intent as he looked at her. "You never have to worry about anything with me, Brooke," he said, his words quiet but fierce. "I will never ask anything of you that you aren't willing to give, and if anything about my being here with you makes you uncomfortable, I'll leave. Your peace of mind, your happiness, are all that matters. We're here right now for you. I want to see you paint in nature. I want to watch while you create, and I want to see the joy you get in creating art." He paused, his gaze scanning her face. "That's all I want from this weekend."

How was it possible that this man was still single? How could any woman who had ever met him or spoken to him not see how incredible he was? How selfless and kind? How incredibly handsome and sexy?

Her mouth went dry at the intensity of his gaze, and she licked her lips and watched as those dark eyes zeroed in on that action, and…good Lord she wanted to jump him right then and there. Leaning in a little closer, she was just about to reach up and kiss him when he placed a soft kiss on her forehead and stepped back.

"Why don't we grab some dinner and maybe do a little sightseeing?" he suggested, but Brooke heard the tremor in his voice. "Thanks to the time difference, it's still a bit early, and it's much warmer here than it was back in Chicago, so we can walk around for a while until we find something we want to see. What do you say?"

"I say give me five minutes to freshen up, and let's go!"

⁓⁓⁓

It was after eleven when they were walking back into the room. They had enjoyed dinner at the hotel and then taken a long walk down the Strip to people watch and check out what all the fuss was about.

Neither was overly impressed. After discussing gambling on their walk, they agreed that it held little to no appeal—not to mention that the smoke in the casinos was a major turnoff—and it was too late for a show. Brooke had been more fascinated by the artistry within the hotels, and Owen had gladly followed her around and listened to her talk about all of it. Hell, he could listen to her talk all night long.

He locked the door and watched as Brooke slipped off her shoes and began taking all of her many bangles from her wrist. Once she was done with them, she took off her hoop earrings. As if forgetting he was there, she stretched and then walked over to the wall of windows and looked out at the scenery for a minute before drawing the drapes.

They were alone, cocooned in this hotel room, and not for the first time, Owen had to wonder what he was supposed to do. Things like this didn't happen to him. She was the type of girl who used to make fun of him in school—the popular girl, the cheerleader, the beauty queen—and he learned fairly early on to just stay off of their radars. And yet…here she was.

In his room.

Sharing his bed.

It still hadn't fully sunk in that this was happening. She wasn't mocking him. This wasn't a joke, and no one had put her up to it. Brooke was here because she wanted to be here.

In his room.

Sharing his bed.

Yeah, that last one was still the hardest to wrap his brain around.

She turned away from the window, faced him, and smiled shyly. "Are you tired?" she asked, walking toward him.

"A little. It's been a long day, and we didn't get much sleep last night either."

Nodding, she stepped around him and went to grab her suitcase and put it on the luggage rack. "I know. I would have thought I'd be fast asleep by now, but…" She paused and looked at him, her toiletry bag in her hand. "I hope you don't mind, but…I need the TV on to help me sleep."

Relief swamped him. He wasn't sure what she'd been

about to say, but for a minute she had looked so serious
it had made him nervous. "I'm fine with that. Really."

"Okay," she said with a happy sigh. "Thanks." Then
she went into the bathroom to change.

Owen wasn't sure what to do as it hit him how he
hadn't given much thought to this aspect of the night.
Pajamas. He had grabbed a pair of sweatpants and a
T-shirt to sleep in—even though he preferred to sleep
in his boxers—but now he had to wonder what Brooke
slept in.

He almost prayed it was sweatpants and a T-shirt too.
Anything less than that was going to seriously test his
self-control. Shaking off the mental images of Brooke
in silk and lace, he went to work on sorting through his
own suitcase and getting out what he needed. When he
had everything ready and Brooke wasn't yet out of the
bathroom, he kicked off his shoes and walked over to
turn down the bed.

She still wasn't out.

Looking around the room, he found the remote,
turned on the TV, and began scanning the channels for
something to watch. He found the opening monologue
for *Saturday Night Live* and figured he'd leave it on
for now; if Brooke had another preference, she could
change the channel. He put the remote on the bed and
looked toward the bathroom.

She still wasn't out.

Now he was back to being nervous. Was she okay?
Was she avoiding him? Slowly he walked over to the
door and raised his hand to knock when the door opened.

And then he forgot how to breathe.

She wasn't wearing silk and lace, but she wasn't

wearing sweatpants and a T-shirt either. Thin, wispy straps covered slender shoulders and then came down to meet a modest neckline that gave him just a glimpse of what lie beneath. The light-blue cotton matched her eyes, and when he quickly scanned down, he saw the nightie hit her mid-thigh and showed long, tan legs.

Yeah, he was going to need oxygen. Soon.

"Sorry. All those years of beauty regimens on the pageant scene, and I can't seem to break the habit." She let out a nervous giggle, seemingly unaware that her appearance was close to giving him a heart attack. "But my pores look great, so I guess it's all worth it, right?"

Unable to help himself, Owen reached up and ran a finger along her cheek and marveled at its softness. Even without makeup on, she was stunning. He swallowed hard and forced himself to take a step back. "I'll um...I'll take my turn in there now," he stammered. "I turned on the television, but I wasn't sure what you'd want to watch. Feel free to change the channel."

"Okay. Thanks."

They switched places as Owen grabbed his clothes and went into the bathroom to change, making a mental note that tomorrow he wouldn't have to wait—he could change while she was in here doing her—what did she call it?—beauty regimen. Interesting. Either way, he was a lot faster, and five minutes later he stepped out into the room and noted that there was only one small lamp lit and Brooke was already under the blankets and flipping through the channels.

"Can't find anything you want to watch?" he asked, casually sliding under the blankets beside her.

She shook her head. "Different channels, different programming… I'll find something eventually. But if you want to go to sleep and the noise is too much, just let me know and I can read. I have my Kindle with me too. It helps me fall asleep when I can't find something good to watch."

"It's not going to be a problem. I grew up sharing a room with two brothers. Trust me, noise doesn't bother me."

Brooke put the remote on the nightstand and moved closer to Owen—there was no discussion, no awkwardness—she simply snuggled up beside him as he wrapped an arm around her. With her head resting on his shoulder and her hand over his heart, he felt complete.

"What are we watching?" he asked softly, placing a kiss on the top of her head.

A loud yawn was her first response before she said, "*50 First Dates*. I love this movie."

Looking at the TV, Owen vaguely remembered the movie—not that he'd seen it, but he remembered when it was out many years ago. He looked over at the light that was still lit on her side of the bed. "Do you want to turn out the light?"

She shook her head. "I'll do it later. After the movie."

He didn't give it another thought. He drew her closer and settled in to watch the movie.

―⁓―

Brooke woke up the next morning feeling slightly disoriented. She was wrapped in Owen's arms, their legs tangled together, and overall, it seemed like a great way to wake up. His body was such a warm and comforting presence around her that it took a minute for everything else to register.

The television was off, and so was the light. And suddenly...she couldn't breathe. The room was dark, and she had to start telling herself to relax, that everything was fine and there was no reason to panic.

Except she was.

Completely.

Struggling slightly against Owen, she quickly moved out of his arms and rolled over to turn on the light. A quick glance at the clock showed it was almost seven— their alarm was set for eight. She let out a shaky breath as she willed herself to calm down. Owen was still sound asleep, and she was thankful he wasn't awake to see her panic attack. God, when were they going to end? Five years and she couldn't overcome the irrational fear of the dark. Closing her eyes, she said a silent prayer—a plea—for it to end. To be able to move on. Just like she had countless times before.

It seemed odd how she didn't remember turning off the light or the television, nor did she remember Owen leaving the bed. When was the last time she had slept so soundly?

The previous night.

In Owen's arms.

With her heartbeat back to normal, she slid back down, curled up against him, and smiled when he hummed his approval in his sleep. Lifting her head, she studied him. His dark hair was mussed, he had stubble on his strong jaw, and his features were relaxed—more relaxed than she'd ever seen them—and he was just so handsome that she couldn't immediately look away. He fascinated her—everything about him. His mind, his wit, his humor. But it was his sensitivity that captured her heart. She understood his struggles—better than he would ever know—and yet even as he struggled with his own issues, he always sympathized with hers. And Brooke imagined he was the same with others—taking their feelings and fears into consideration before thinking of his own.

He was an amazing man.

Resting her head on his shoulder, she sighed and moved her leg against his, letting them tangle together once again. He pulled her in closer, and she went willingly, loving the feel of him from head to toe. It almost seemed a shame how they had to be up early, that the alarm would be going off in less than an hour. But still…it seemed like a nice amount of time to just lie in his arms and relax.

Closing her eyes, she moved a little so her head was on his chest and she could listen to his heartbeat. Slow and steady and exactly what she needed to erase her panic of moments ago. Unable to help herself, she kissed him there—on his muscled chest. The man certainly was full of surprises. He might dress like a nerdy professor—khakis and button-down shirts in drab colors—but she was coming to find he had the body of a *GQ* model.

It was almost enough to make her purr.

And she never purred. At least…she'd never wanted to. Until now.

Even though they had joked about it yesterday, being here like this still seemed a bit surreal. For far too long Brooke did what her family expected of her. She didn't take risks and didn't like to cause any worry. It was hard to be responsible all the damn time.

Not to mention it was boring as hell.

And up until she had gone to Chicago to stay with her uncle, she hadn't been tempted to toss all of the rules and expectations aside. And if anyone would have told her she would be doing just that and doing it with a man like Owen, she would have laughed.

But there was nothing funny about this. Her feelings for him were strong and serious and very real.

So much so that it scared her.

A light kiss on the top of her head told her Owen was waking up. One large hand slowly skimmed up her back and fisted in her hair, forcing her to tilt her head back to look at him. And when she did, all the breath left her. His expression—always so serious—was even more so right then. The intensity of those dark eyes had her tingling from head to toe.

"Hi," she said, her voice a breathy whisper.

He didn't answer—just continued to look at her until she wanted to squirm. With his hand fisted in her hair and the heated gaze, there wasn't a doubt in Brooke's mind he was fighting what he wanted to do.

What she wanted to do.

So why were they fighting it?

Without breaking eye contact, Brooke slid her leg over his and then moved up so she was straddling him. His other arm banded around her waist and pulled her close until their lips were mere inches apart. His words from yesterday came back to her.

You never have to worry about anything with me, Brooke. I will never ask anything of you that you aren't willing to give.

She was the one to move the last few inches, her lips

brushing his. Her tongue traced his bottom lip, and then she whispered his name again. For a second his grip on her hair tightened.

"You're sure?" he murmured, his voice a near growl against her lips.

She nodded.

And then they were done talking. Brooke wasn't sure who moved first, who initiated the kiss. They were of one mind as the kiss went from zero to sixty in less than a second. It was all hot and wet and deep and said everything she couldn't find the words for.

Owen's hand roamed down and cupped her bottom and squeezed, the move keeping her completely anchored to him—and oh my, did he feel good. Better than good. Amazing.

And hard. Everywhere.

Sex was something Brooke enjoyed. It was good. But this? This little bit of foreplay? It was hotter than anything she'd ever experienced. She wanted to touch him everywhere and feel his hands on her. Everywhere.

Owen deftly flipped them over so Brooke was now on her back beneath him. Her legs slowly wound around him as he settled over her. His mouth left hers and quickly traveled down to the neckline of her nightie. She wanted to rip the garment off and feel his mouth all over her heated skin.

Her hips lifted as she rubbed against him, silently begging him for more. Rather than acknowledge that movement, he cupped her breast as his mouth moved along all of her exposed skin.

He was killing her.

"Owen," she panted. "Please."

Lifting his head, his gaze met hers. "I dreamed of this," he said, his voice like gravel. "All night. Every night since I met you."

Oh...

"It's never been like this. I've never felt so...out of control. I've been trying to go slow. To be a gentleman..."

Brooke lifted a hand and raked it up into his hair and gripped it gently. "Right now...I don't want a gentleman."

His eyes widened for barely a second. "You're sure?"

She couldn't help the giggle that came out. "About not wanting a gentleman?" she teased. "Yes. I'm sure."

The sexy grin he gave her made her feel even achier than she had a minute before.

Her name came out like a plea right before he lowered his head and reclaimed her lips with his. The kiss went on and on, and as much as she wanted more—more stripping, more moving, more...everything—the way Owen kissed was its own brand of foreplay.

Delicious.

Then finally—*finally!*—his hands started to wander again, this time to the hem of her nightie. His hand slowly made its way under the fabric and rested on her hip, and she almost felt giddy at the touch. Silently she urged him to move, to stroke, to touch her where she so desperately wanted him to. She was so close to tearing her mouth from his and begging when...

Beep...beep...beep...

No. No, no, no, no, no!

Beep...beep...beep...

The sound must have finally registered with Owen because he lifted his head and looked around as if he couldn't remember where they were. With a muttered curse, he rolled off her and slapped the alarm clock. Then he was on his back beside her and breathing heavily.

As much as she knew she wasn't an overly emotional person, she wanted to be one right then and pitch a fit. Damn alarm clock. Why did it have to bring everything to a halt? They were awake already, so...why stop? She turned her head to look at him, saw the pained expression on his face, and knew she wasn't going to push him. Instead, she reached for his hand and slipped her hand against it until he clasped hers.

"You okay?" she asked softly.

He nodded.

"We...do we need to start getting ready, or do we... you know...have some time?"

Owen didn't look at her, but he opened his eyes and stared at the ceiling. "They're picking us up in an hour. I told Tom Donnelly how important it was for us to get as much time as possible in the canyon for you, and we need to do the flyover of Red Rock first." He muttered another curse, rolled off the bed, and stalked across the room until he was at the windows before he turned around. "I'm sorry."

Brooke sat up and looked at him as if he were crazy. "For what?"

Rather than answer, he raked a hand through his hair and turned back to open the drapes.

"Owen?"

"This weekend was supposed to be about you and your painting, and I..." He shook his head again. "I wasn't thinking clearly this morning."

She climbed from the bed, walked over, and wrapped

her arms around him, resting her head on his back. "But I was," she admitted. "I knew exactly what we were doing, and it was what I wanted. You don't owe me an apology, Owen."

He turned and looked down at her. "We have two days before we have to be back, and I want you to have all the time you need to explore and take pictures. I feel bad enough that I'm cutting into your time by meeting with the astronomical society at Red Rock."

"I don't mind it. I imagine I'll get some great pictures there too." She wanted to ask him about his intentions with Red Rock—if he was going to come back and do the trip—but now wasn't the time. And then the reality hit—they weren't going to finish what they started. They were going to be responsible and meet the people they needed to meet and be where they were supposed to be.

Dammit.

Seeing the struggle in his eyes, Brooke got up on her tiptoes and kissed him lightly on the cheek. "I'm going to go and take my shower and get ready. I promise not to hog the bathroom so you'll be able to get in there too. Why don't you order breakfast so we can eat a little something before we have to go?"

He nodded. "I can do that."

She smiled. "Thank you." Stepping away from him, she walked over to her suitcase and pulled out clean clothes and her makeup bag. Placing everything in the bathroom, she heard Owen moving around. Peeking her head out, she called out to him. "I would love some coffee and maybe some fruit and yogurt, please."

Looking up at her, he smiled and nodded again. "Anything else?"

"Do we need to bring our own lunches for later?"

"I'll call Tom and find out," he said, reaching for his phone.

When he started speaking, Brooke ducked into the bathroom and quietly shut the door. And braced herself for the cold shower she was definitely going to need to take.

—∿∿—

"Wait...what?"

"Camping. You should totally take advantage of the mild weather and the clear skies tonight and camp out. I've got tents and supplies you can use. You'll probably want to get your own sleeping bags, but we have everything else you'll need, including some telescopes. You interested?"

Was he? Owen wasn't so sure. It wasn't something he'd even considered for this particular trip. He'd camped out before, but he had no idea if Brooke ever had or if she'd even want to.

"Do you need to know right now, or can you give me a few minutes to talk to Brooke?"

"Let me know when I get there. If you want to do it, we'll stop at the Walmart and pick up sleeping bags. And just bring something warm to sleep in. It tends to cool down a bit at night."

"Thanks. I'll see you in a bit. And, Tom?"

"Yeah?"

"I appreciate everything you're doing."

"I'm looking forward to working with you, Owen. I've heard a lot of great stuff about you."

Great or embarrassing, Owen had to wonder. But he

refused to let his mind go there. He had things to do and decisions to make about the night. Fast. "Same here. We'll see you soon."

He hung up and paced the room, listening for the shower to turn off so he could talk to Brooke. He picked up the hotel phone and quickly called in their breakfast order. It was a good thing they weren't ordering anything big because they were already short on time. Room service assured him the order would be delivered in twenty minutes, and that helped him to relax. Walking over to his suitcase, he pulled out his clothes and jerked to a stop when he heard the water turn off and the shower curtain scrape against the rod.

Brooke, naked and wet, instantly popped into his head, and he groaned.

If they camped out tonight, there would be no repeat of this morning or even a continuation of it tonight. However, if they didn't camp out, they would miss out on an opportunity for her to experience the desert in a way that would benefit her work the most.

Which was why they were here in the first place.

For art, not for sex.

In his semi-aroused state, Owen couldn't help but wish he could have both.

Possibly at the same time.

The bathroom door opened, and Brooke stepped out—her hair was in a towel, but she was fully dressed in a pair of khaki shorts and a white T-shirt. Her face was still void of makeup, and she gave him a wide smile.

"I was fast this time, right? I know we don't have a lot of time, so I wanted to make sure you had plenty of time for your shower." She fluttered around, putting stuff in her suitcase and pulling out a pair of sneakers. "Is breakfast on its way?"

"It is," he said distractedly, too engrossed in watching the way she moved—so graceful. "I…um…I spoke to Tom, and he had a suggestion for us."

Brooke stopped what she was doing and looked at him expectantly.

"We can camp out tonight. At Red Rock. It would be like how we'll do it for the meteor shower except with just us." He looked at her, trying to gauge her reaction.

She didn't seem to have one.

He cleared his throat. "They have a tent, but we'd have to get sleeping bags—I imagine using someone else's sleeping bag is frowned upon—but we can stop and purchase some on the way out of town this morning."

Nothing.

"You'd have some time to paint. We could even pick up canvases and paints—probably not the quality you were looking for, but if you were anxious to create something while we were there, you could do it."

Still nothing.

Now he began to fidget and forced himself to look away and busy himself with going through his suitcase. "Of course, we don't have to do it. We can go on the helicopter tour today and see the sights, take a ton of pictures, and be done with it. It's not a big deal. I just thought—"

"Will there be any lights? Like streetlamps?" she asked.

It seemed like an odd question, and he looked at her in confusion. "Um…probably not. There are campfire circles, so we'll have light from those." He sighed and figured he'd better give her all of the facts up front, so there wouldn't be any surprises later on and she could make an informed decision.

"Okay, there are no electrical, water, or sewer hookups. There are public restrooms, but nothing at our site. There are no showers, but there are water faucets for drinking water that are located throughout the campground." He paused again and noticed her expression hadn't changed much. "It's pretty rustic. Basically, we'd be sleeping in a tent in the middle of the campground. What do you think?"

She pulled her cosmetics bag out of her suitcase and faced him again, her expression full of dismay. "I...I have some issues with—"

"Camping?" he finished for her, figuring it made the most logical sense. "I know it's not for everyone, and I will completely understand if you're not into it. I was just thinking about you getting the extra time to paint."

She shook her head, and her shoulders sagged. "Owen...remember last night I told you I need the television on to fall asleep?"

How could he have forgotten? Instantly he dropped the clothes he was holding, stepped forward, and wrapped her in his arms. "I'm sorry. I guess I had forgotten about that. With no electricity, it would be hard for you to fall asleep. I get it." He placed a small kiss on her temple and stepped back. "We'll just go ahead as planned."

"But—"

"I need to get in the shower before we're out of time. Breakfast should be here any minute. Charge it to the room." And he scooped his clothes up once again and went to take his shower.

And tried to keep telling himself it was all for the best—staying in the room tonight meant maybe, just maybe, they'd get to finish what they'd started.

———

It wasn't rational, and it was going to require an enormous leap of faith, but Brooke wasn't feeling particularly rational, and maybe this was the impetus she needed.

While Owen showered, she transferred a few things into the small carry-on bag she'd brought with her on the plane to carry her purse, Kindle, and some essentials to keep by her seat. She eyed Owen's luggage and thought better of rifling through it for him. He would be able to do it quickly on his own, she was sure.

With nothing left to do, she walked over to the mirror and put on some light makeup and then towel-dried her hair. By that time, Owen was coming out of the bathroom. He looked at her and smiled. Brooke walked over to him and took his hands in hers.

"I want to go camping," she blurted out.

His eyes went wide. "Really? Are…are you sure? You seemed pretty certain about—"

"I know. I know. But I think this could be the perfect solution to help me stop using the television as a crutch. Plus it's like you said, this is a perfect opportunity for me to get some extra time to paint. I'd be crazy to pass it up."

He studied her for a long moment. "We'll have to pack."

She motioned to her small bag. "I've already taken

care of that. At least my stuff. You can put yours in there too. We'll essentially be roughing it, so there isn't too much to bring. I'm guessing we'll get up fairly early and head back here, so we can shower before our flight home tomorrow night. So what do you say? Are we doing this?"

His gaze was serious—as it normally was—but for a minute she thought he was going to say no. With her breath held, she waited.

And then his features softened and he smiled. "Yes. We're going camping."

—∼∼∼—

"So…"

"Yeah…so…"

Tom stood up and wiped his hands on his jeans. "So the tent is done." He chuckled.

Owen gave him a lopsided grin. "I would have figured it out eventually."

Making the okay sign, Tom continued to chuckle. "I'm sure you would have, but I didn't want to risk you losing daylight before you were done."

Beside them, Owen heard Brooke laugh softly too.

"So I'm not great with mechanical stuff like this. It's not a bad thing."

"Except when you're camping and need to set a tent up," Tom teased and then picked his backpack up off the ground. "There's a Jeep in the parking lot for you if you need it. But I'll be back in the morning around eight to pick you up and get the tent and supplies. Is there anything else you need?"

Owen looked at Brooke, and they both shook their

heads. They had purchased food and supplies earlier in the day, and while Tom had been setting up the tent, Brooke had been setting up her art supplies. There weren't a lot of campers on-site, and for that Owen was grateful. Their campsite wasn't far from the restroom, and they had a spectacular view of the park.

"All right," he said with a smile. "Then you two have a great time, and I'll see you in the morning."

Owen and Brooke both thanked Tom, and once he was out of sight, Owen turned back toward the tent. Tom had explained it was the perfect tent for watching the night sky, and Owen could see why—it was big enough to sleep three, and it had a mesh roof that was perfect for stargazing. He walked over to their pile of supplies, took out the sleeping bags and pillows, set them up inside, and then went to work on getting the campfire set up as well.

"Let me help you with that," Brooke said, coming up beside him.

When they were all finished, Brooke pointed to a small box next to the tent. "What's that?"

Smiling, Owen walked over, picked up the box, and handed it to her. She looked at him curiously, and even after she looked inside, she still didn't seem to understand what she was looking at.

"It's a solar-powered battery pack," he said. "It means we can have a little light in the tent if you need it, and you can probably use your Kindle if you want to—at least for a little while."

Her response was to carefully put the box on the ground and then fling herself into his arms. And Owen wasn't complaining. His arms banded around her as he lifted her off her feet.

"You are the sweetest man in the world," she said against his neck. "Do you even realize that?"

Sweet? Owen had never thought of himself quite like that. He was just trying to be considerate of her needs. Which is what he said to her as he lowered her back to the ground.

Reaching up, Brooke cupped his cheek, and her smile was so full of gratitude that Owen didn't know how to respond.

"Who takes care of you?" she asked, her voice soft and full of concern.

"What do you mean?"

"You do so much for everyone, making sure people have what they need. Who does that for you?"

"I… No one's ever asked me that before," he replied honestly. Other than his family, there had never been anyone who looked out for him, and he never thought about needing anyone to do it.

Brooke was studying him, and the subject was making him uncomfortable, so he did his best to change it.

"I'm going to take the battery out and make sure it's fully charged. Tom thought it was, but it won't hurt to let it get some time in the sun. Why don't you see what you can get done while it's still light out?" He hoped he wasn't coming off like a jerk.

That morning they had spent an hour shopping for supplies and another hour touring Red Rock in the helicopter, and then it was easily four hours round-trip to the Grand Canyon, including their time in the canyon. By the time they'd landed at Red Rock, collected the camping supplies and tent, and made their way to the campground and set up, the day was almost over. Looking at his watch, Owen saw it was close to six. They maybe had another hour of decent daylight.

Brooke took a step back and nodded. "Okay. But what are you going to do with yourself?"

He shrugged. "I'll get the campfire going, and Tom also left me a telescope, so I'm going to see where the best place is to set it up. I'll be fine."

With another nod, she turned and walked over to her supplies and went to work. Owen was tempted to watch her but was keenly aware he had things of his own to do. Forcing himself to turn away, he went to work with the small telescope. For a portable, it was remarkably powerful, and soon he was lost in his own world.

The sky was starting to darken sometime later, and it wasn't until Brooke walked around him murmuring about needing the keys to the Jeep that he stepped away from his viewing through the telescope.

"Are you okay? Do you need to go someplace?"

Her panicked expression took him by surprise, but it vanished quickly as if she caught herself. "Um...I just want to put the paint supplies away. The tent is small enough without trying to cram all the paint and brushes and canvases in there. And besides, the materials don't smell great."

This all made sense, but Owen could tell there was something more to it—like she didn't want him to see what she painted. He could accept that—even understand it. Artists were temperamental that way. So rather than drag this out or question her, he reached into his pocket and took out the keys.

"Would you like me to go with you? It's a bit of a walk, and it's getting dark."

Brooke shook her head even as she was already walking away quickly. "I won't be long," she called over her shoulder, and Owen was half expecting her to sprint away.

She didn't.

She walked.

At a fast pace.

Rather than obsess on that, he moved around their campsite, taking out sandwiches and drinks and setting them up close to the fire. The temperature was going to cool once the sun went down, and though he couldn't speak for Brooke, he knew he would enjoy eating by the fire and waiting for the stars to come out.

"Stupid, stupid, stupid." The clipped words matched her pace as she hurried to the Jeep. Honestly, she wouldn't have minded Owen walking with her, but then he'd see what she was trying to hide.

Another painting of him.

What is wrong with me? she admonished herself. Twice in the past several weeks—and the only times she'd picked up a paintbrush—she'd ended up painting Owen. Today she painted him with the canyon as a backdrop as he looked through the telescope. She stopped, looked at the canvas, and sighed.

She'd captured him perfectly.

Again.

"Ugh...I have to *stop* doing this!" At the Jeep, she placed her supplies in the trunk, locked it, and quickly headed back toward the campsite. The sun was setting fast, and she wasn't up for walking alone in the dark. As she walked by the public restroom, she stopped in to use it before going back to their site, and when she got there, she smiled at the scene before her.

Owen had a fire going and had spread a blanket over the nearby bench and set their dinner up on it. All in all it looked very romantic, and if she pushed her unease aside, she could allow herself to enjoy the moment and the effort Owen had put into it.

"It looks like dinner is served," she said lightly as she walked over and sat down.

His smile was genuine, and Brooke was sorry she'd run off a few minutes before. Maybe he'd be flattered that she'd painted him... It was possible. The problem was that she was trying to wrap her own brain around why this man took her out of every comfort zone she had.

They ate in silence for a few minutes. It was just the two of them and the sounds of nature all around. The campground was relatively empty, and she wasn't sure if it was a blessing or a curse just yet.

"So are we going to see anything amazing in the sky tonight?" she asked.

"It's too early in the month for the Lyrids or any shower, but we should be able to spot some of the constellations. It's a perfect night for stargazing."

She looked over at the tent. "Tom said this tent was made for that specifically—we'll literally be sleeping under the stars. Do you think that's true?"

"Technically, we sleep under the stars every night," he began logically. "But with this particular tent, we'll be able to see them as we're lying down. It's got a seamless mesh roof, so there isn't anything to obstruct our view. Although...on a night like tonight, when there isn't much activity, I'm not sure we'll see anything impressive, but it's still going to be a nice view."

"What if it rains?"

He chuckled. "It's not in the forecast, and it's pretty rare to get rain in this part of the country. You know… the desert."

She hung her head and laughed at herself. "Right. Forgot about that. Sorry." And then she was embarrassed. At times like this she was extremely aware of the differences in their intellects. He was brilliant, a borderline genius, and she was just…Brooke. Nothing impressive about her at all. Average student. Average artist. Average woman.

"You're wrong," he murmured from beside her, his voice huskier than it had been a minute before.

Brooke looked up at him in confusion.

"There's nothing average about you."

Crap. Had she said that out loud? "I…I didn't mean to say that. At least not out loud," she admitted.

Taking her hand in his, he squeezed. "Why would you even think that about yourself?"

How could she even explain it? "For the most part, I'm okay with who I am. At least…now. I spent a lot of years struggling with it, but that was because my parents had groomed me to be someone I didn't want to be. I'm finally at a point where I'm comfortable in my own skin, but there's nothing…remarkable about me."

"I disagree," he said fiercely.

"It's okay. I don't think everyone has that…that certain something that makes them remarkable. You have a brilliant mind, Owen. That's remarkable. People want to come and listen to you speak and just…glean something from your wisdom." She shrugged. "I'm both intimidated by and in awe of that. And then I open my mouth and say something that is just completely…stupid." She groaned. "And I want to just kick myself."

"You didn't say anything stupid…"

She made a face as she looked at him. "Seriously? I just asked about rain in the desert. You don't think that's stupid?"

He didn't laugh or even crack a smile. "No, I don't."

"Owen…come on. You're not going to insult me. I need you to be honest with me, just like you always are."

"You want honest?" he asked, his voice gruff. He released her hand and cupped her cheek. "I love that you're not sitting here trying to come up with the kind of conversation that you think I want to have. I love listening to you talk about your art and your painting. And as for your comment about the rain, I think it's an honest concern considering we're going to sleep in a tent with a mesh roof. There's nothing stupid about it. And there is nothing average about you."

"Owen—"

He didn't stop there.

"I look at you, and I see an amazing woman—you're smart and witty. You make everyone around you feel at ease. You have an amazing laugh, and when you smile, it makes me want to smile." His thumb stroked her cheek as he spoke. "You move with the grace of a dancer, and no matter where we are or what we're doing, you embrace the moment. You're passionate and kind and giving."

Then he moved closer. Close enough that she could feel his breath on her cheek.

"And you're someone I feel very honored to know. And someone I want to know better." He swallowed hard. "And I want you very much."

Brooke let out a shaky breath. "I want you too. So much it scares me."

"I told you…you never have to be scared of me, Brooke. Ever."

"I can't help it," she whispered. "You're…you're so much more than I expected."

He rested his forehead against hers and brushed her lips with his. "And you're everything."

And then she was lost. Everything in her life seemed to lead her to this moment with this man. It was foolish to deny the attraction or the need for him that was close to consuming her. And she couldn't think of a more perfect time and place for them than right here and right now.

With a steadying breath, Brooke stood and held out her hand to him. Wordlessly, he took it. It wasn't smooth or graceful. In fact, it was a little bit awkward. But once they were inside the tent with the door zipped shut, it all changed. She raked a hand up into his thick hair and pulled him down on the padded floor with her. With his weight deliciously on top of her, her arms went around him, and all she could think was… *Perfect*.

This was them.

This was their moment.

Under a sky full of stars.

Chapter 7

OWEN WASN'T PRONE TO FANTASIES.

He was a realist through and through.

But this? The feel of Brooke wrapped around him was exactly what he'd fantasized about.

Only better.

Every touch of her hand, every sigh of her breath served to arouse him. He kissed her like a man who was starved and she was the feast. He touched her like a man who had been deprived of contact for too long. And he held her close—because she was the lifeline he needed to give him everything he'd ever wanted.

Knowing he had a tendency to stay too long in his head and overanalyze everything, he chose to focus on what he was feeling.

Warm, smooth skin.

Soft, wet mouth.

Yeah, that served to ratchet his arousal up a notch—or ten. The last thing he wanted to do was embarrass himself, so he moved on to focus on what he was hearing.

Soft sighs.

His name in a breathless whisper.

And the sound of nature after dark.

If anyone had ever asked him where the perfect place was to make love to a woman, he would have thought the correct response would be in a soft bed surrounded by candlelight. And he would have been wrong. Because this…this tent with the mesh roof in the middle of Red Rock Canyon was the perfect place for him to make love to this woman.

Brooke.

As if reading his thoughts, she opened her eyes and looked up at him, a slow smile blossoming on her face. Her every emotion was right there in her eyes, and what he saw there humbled him. The trust, the desire.

"Owen?" she whispered.

"Yes?"

Her smile grew as she arched her back and pressed more firmly against him. "I want to feel you…touch you—"

Rearing back, he tugged off his shirt and grinned when she took advantage of the space between them and did the same. And then she pulled him closer and they were finally skin to skin.

Perfect.

—————

"If you look over to your right, the constellation of Virgo, or Virgo the Maiden, can be seen."

"Are you sure? I don't see it."

Owen tucked her in close beside him. "Look just past the tip of my finger, and you can make it out. Or we can get the telescope and set it up—"

She shook her head. "No. I don't want to move from this spot." Then she snuggled even closer.

He was more than ready to say that he was wrong—that there wasn't anything in the sky for them to see—and make love to her again, but he didn't. This was something that felt right—looking up at the sky and talking about what they were seeing as their skin cooled and their heart rates returned to normal.

"Did you know Virgo is the second-largest constellation in the sky? Or that it looks a little bit like a sun lounger?"

"A sun lounger?" she repeated with a giggle. "Really?"

"Can you see it?" he asked softly, tracing the pattern in the sky.

"I think I see it. Is it near that bright star?" Pointing up at the sky, Brooke rested her hand on his and lowered them until they were both resting on his chest.

"Yes, it's by that bright star. Actually, Virgo can be easily located through its brightest star Spica—which is the fifteenth-brightest star in the night sky." Realistically, he could give a thirty-minute lecture on Virgo but didn't think it was the greatest postcoital conversation, so rather than keeping his focus on it, he opted to move on.

"Are you cold?" he asked.

She shook her head. "Nope. The temperature is perfect."

"Are you hungry? We never finished our dinner."

He could feel her smile against his shoulder. "I wouldn't say no to some chocolate, but I can wait."

"I have a bottle of water over here if you'd—"

"Owen?"

"Hmm?"

"Stop talking."

He smiled, kissed the top of her head, and listened to the sounds of the night that surrounded them. It was peaceful. Tranquil. And...too damn quiet. The quiet had never bothered Owen before, but right now it was making him uncomfortable. He wanted to talk to her or listen to her talk.

Or sigh.

Or purr his name as he kissed every inch of her again.

But he was afraid to do that. He wasn't sure if there was a required wait time between the act of making love and then making love again. Maybe it was too soon. Or maybe she might not want to because she was tired or— God forbid—she didn't enjoy it the first time.

Well, damn. That was a depressing thought. And how was he supposed to know for sure? It couldn't possibly be polite to just come right out and ask if she enjoyed it—or if he had performed all right.

Even though it was what he was dying to do.

Previous experience hadn't prepared him for such a scenario. One time and then…done. He'd never had the desire to catch his breath and dive back in for another round. And Owen knew if Brooke gave even the slightest of hints that she was interested, he'd be more than willing to go again.

And again and again.

With a quiet sigh, he focused on the sky again and saw a shooting star. It wasn't overly bright, but his eye was trained to see them. It was already fading, so he didn't mention it to Brooke, but he did notice that there were several bright stars in the sky tonight, not just Spica. It would probably be best for him to cool his libido by discussing the facts he knew about all of the stars and what made some brighter than others, what their names were and…

Wait. Did Brooke just shift? Were those her lips on his shoulder? He went still—almost to the point of not breathing—and waited. A slow grin tugged at his lips. She *was* kissing his shoulder…and one slim leg was rubbing against his until they were tangled together. One of her hands was roaming over his chest—so warm and smooth—and he held in a groan of pleasure.

The hell with that, he thought. Why withhold it? He wanted her. Wanted her to know how much he wanted her. And the last time, she had taken the initiative, leading him to the tent and pulling him down to the bedding. This time…well, this time he wanted—needed—to be the one to take the initiative.

In the blink of an eye, he rolled her over and had her pinned beneath him. She gasped and then let out a laugh of pure joy—the light from the moon was bright enough that he could see her smile and the gleam of pleasure in her eyes.

"I've been mentally talking to myself about the stars in the sky," he murmured.

"Is that what you wanted to talk about?" she asked sweetly.

Owen shook his head. "No. It's not."

"What did you want to talk about?"

Rather than answer, he dipped his head, nipped at the swell of her breast, and smiled when she gasped again. He soothed the spot with his tongue and breathed in the scent of her. She said his name, and he remembered she'd asked him a question.

"I want to talk about how you taste," he murmured against her skin, surprising himself with this kind of sexy talk. She purred at his admission. Encouraged, he tried again. "And how soft you are…all over." Another purr, and her hips began to move beneath him.

Fascinating.

"But most of all, I want to talk about how much I crave you again," he growled and then Brooke fisted his hair in her hands and pulled him down for a kiss that was just this side of brutal.

Which was fine.

He was done talking anyway.

———————

It wasn't easy, but Brooke managed to keep her painting hidden from Owen, and when they got back to the hotel the next morning, she made arrangements to ship it home. Then they returned to the hotel room to pack up.

"It's still kind of early," she said as she put the last of her things in her suitcase. "Did you have anything planned for the day? Did you need to look over anything else with Tom?"

Owen was standing by the window and looking out at the scenery. He shook his head. "I think the helicopter tour and camping last night gave me sufficient data on what to expect."

He didn't turn to look at her as he spoke, and his voice was slightly stilted. It was very unlike him, and yet it was how he'd sounded all morning. Quiet. Detached. And it made her heart sink. Was he regretting making love with her? Was he uncomfortable with the turn in their relationship and how he was stuck spending the day with her and traveling with her tonight? And now that she thought about it, he hadn't touched her or even tried to since they woke up. She'd imagined they'd come back to the room and shower together and maybe make love in the bed. But once she'd returned from shipping the canvas, she'd found Owen had already showered and dressed.

Oh God, she thought. How in the world could she possibly get herself out of this?

Swallowing the panic, she zipped her bag closed and forced a smile onto her face. If he needed time alone, she'd let him have it. "I'm going to check my bag downstairs at bell services and go tour the Bellagio. That was one of the hotels I was really curious about." She turned quickly to grab her bag.

She never heard him approach.

"Wait… What… Are you upset with me?" he asked, his brows drawn together. His hand had gently grasped her arm, and his appearance right in front of her took her by surprise.

Brooke shook her head. "No!" She paused and forced herself to calm down. "Of course not. You just seemed like…" She shrugged. "You seemed like you wanted to be alone, so I was giving you a bit of a break from me. We've been together for two days straight." Then she chuckled. "More than that actually. I just figured I'd go out and play tourist so you could have some time to yourself."

He stepped closer, and her heart skipped a beat. "I don't want time to myself."

"Then…then what's wrong?" she asked softly and then wanted to kick herself. The last thing she wanted was to pressure him—he did that enough to himself.

When he didn't answer right away—when he turned his head and looked toward the window—Brooke was fairly certain she had been right. He was just trying to be polite because that's who he was. Slowly, she pulled out of his grasp and turned to pick up her purse. "I'll meet you back here in the lobby around five so we can maybe grab a bite to eat before we have to head to the airport."

Owen didn't say a word.

Exhaling slowly, Brooke picked up her suitcase and looked at him one more time before walking to the door. It shouldn't have surprised her—after all, Owen was a shy and quiet man, and last night he had been anything but. So rather than push him further, she knew the right thing to do was leave. For now. Even though it was the last thing she wanted to do.

Reaching for the doorknob, she jumped when Owen's hand slammed on the door just above her shoulder. Her heart beat madly, and every inch of her tingled with awareness. It was like this every time he was close to her.

But she didn't turn around.

And she didn't say a word.

She waited.

Slowly Owen moved in closer until they were barely touching from head to toe. He nuzzled her hair and breathed in deeply. "Don't go."

She was torn. The last thing she wanted was for Owen to ask her to stay out of some sense of obligation. But when she shifted slightly and felt his body behind her—so hard and strong and warm—she did her best to stifle a smile.

Dipping his head, Owen placed his mouth on her throat where her pulse was thundering, and the contact made her tremble. She whispered his name.

Hands moved from her shoulders down her arms, until he had her dropping her purse and suitcase on the floor. Then they traveled back up and held her firmly against him. His mouth kept moving against her—each kiss, each nip hungrier than the last.

"Owen—"

"I'm a selfish bastard," he said gruffly. "I told myself last night was enough. That I would keep my hands to myself today, but I can't. God help me, Brooke, I can't."

His hold on her was almost brutal, and she wanted to turn in his arms, to kiss him like she was aching to, but he didn't let her. "I don't want you to keep your hands to yourself," she sighed, moving against him. "I... I thought you were having regrets...that you were sorry that we—"

He spun her around and silenced her words as he kissed her. Her arms instantly went around him, and she wanted to climb him like a tree. The transformation of this man from quiet scientist to lover was breathtaking, and she loved it. He fascinated her, intrigued her, and turned her on so much she thought she'd combust.

Wordlessly, he lifted her up and carried her over to the bed. She felt boneless, completely awash in the sensations his hands and mouth were creating, and when he lowered himself onto her, Brooke realized maybe this was the man he was always meant to be.

—⁓—

"I wish we could have timed it better to see the fountain show at night," Brooke said as they walked up to the entrance of the Bellagio hotel. "I've seen it in movies, but it would have been very cool to see it live and in person."

Owen wasn't all that impressed with the whole fountain ballet concept, but he would have watched it with

Brooke. They held hands, fingers entwined, as they walked. Honestly, he could have used about ten hours of sleep, but the thought of missing out on any time with her was beyond unappealing. He wanted to stay awake and talk with her, be with her, and sleeping would mean he was missing out.

So now he was stuck touring a hotel and casino.

His mind wandered to the past few hours. After he'd carried Brooke to bed, he'd felt like a completely different person. And if he were honest, it had been the same last night. Owen prided himself on being level-headed and in control at all times. He didn't do emotional, and he'd never understood people who claimed to get carried away by their emotions.

Except now he did.

Completely.

It was more than a little scary to him—this feeling of being out of control. And the sex? He had a sneaking suspicion he was some sort of perv or closet sex fiend because never had he been so…aggressive during the act. There were times when he'd almost apologized because he thought he'd hurt her with his…enthusiasm. His only saving grace was that Brooke seemed to enjoy it.

Imagine that!

And he felt completely ridiculous because one of his first thoughts this morning was how he needed to call Riley and make sure he was…normal. Not Riley but himself. Was sex like this for other people, or was he some sort of freak? Like that would be anything new. He almost snorted at the thought. He was already a freak in just about every aspect of his life, and he'd kind of hoped to limit his weirdness. If he had to add sex to the list, Owen wasn't sure what he'd do.

"Look at this," Brooke said with awe as they stepped into the lobby. "It's magnificent, isn't it?"

He nodded, but his mind was still back on the whole freak thing.

Brooke must not have noticed because they kept walking and she kept talking. He looked at her—her long hair flowing, her curvy body clad in a pair of black capris and a white tank top. It was the most basic attire, and yet on her it made her look like a model.

He had it bad.

They wandered around for almost an hour—taking in the artwork and the architecture and people-watching—when Brooke stopped them in the casino. "What do you say, Owen? We have to play the slots at least once." Her entire face was flush with excitement.

"Why?"

She rolled her eyes and playfully swatted at his arm. "We've been in Vegas for a couple of days. We have to gamble at least once."

"But we said we didn't like to gamble," he argued gently.

"Have you ever gambled?" she countered.

"No."

"Neither have I. So how do we know for certain we don't like it?"

Owen considered her question for a moment and realized he had no comeback. She was watching him anxiously, and he knew if it would make her happy, he'd do it. "Okay, let's give it a shot." As they made their way farther into the casino, his rational brain kicked in.

"You know," he began, "Every spin has identical chances as the previous spin. Like a coin flip. The computer program picks a random symbol on the first reel, then the next, and so on. The probability of lining up the winning combinations, combined with the payout for those combos, is what determines the payback of the machine. Nothing influences the outcome of the symbols, not how long it's been since the last jackpot hit, not whether your slot card is inserted, not whether the machine has been running hot or cold. Are we sure that's the way we want to gamble our money?"

Brooke stopped in her tracks and faced him. "Owen?"

"Yes?"

"Sometimes it's not about winning the money; it's just for the fun of it. I'm not suggesting we gamble with large sums of money. I'm thinking the nickel or quarter slots. Nothing major." She studied him. "Okay?"

He supposed losing a dollar or two wouldn't be the worst thing in the world.

An hour and fifty dollars later, Brooke was gently pulling him away from the machine. "Okay, okay…I think we've lost enough," she said with a laugh. "Boy, they really suck you in, don't they?"

Raking a hand through his hair, Owen agreed. "It was slightly addictive. I just kept…waiting! I was so sure I was going to hit that winning spin!"

The next thing he knew, she was hugging him—completely wrapped around him. He put his arms around her and held her close, unsure of why she was having this reaction but certainly glad that she was.

"Thank you," she said, and he loved the feel of her warm breath on his skin.

"For what?"

"That was a lot of fun! It was pointless and a little bit silly, but now I can officially say that I've gambled."

"But we lost."

She shrugged. "So? It wasn't about winning!" She pulled back and looked around. "Now, I don't know about you, but I'm pretty hungry. Maybe we can have an early dinner here and then go back to the hotel to get our bags. What do you think?"

He was about to answer, but there was a ruckus on the other side of the slot machines. The raised voices were loud enough to be heard over the noise level of the casino and the music that was piped in.

"Well, that doesn't sound good," Brooke murmured. "And to do it in the middle of a casino? That's embarrassing."

And yet neither of them moved.

The voices grew louder. "I don't see what the big deal is, babe! Why are you so bent out of shape over this?" the male voice yelled.

Owen looked at Brooke. "Bent out of shape?" he whispered. "Do people still say that?"

She giggled but then hushed them both when the female voice started to yell again.

"Why? Why do you think?" she screamed. "I catch you with another woman, and you honestly can't understand *why* I'm upset? What is wrong with you?"

"I would think it was obvious," Owen whispered, unable to believe they were both still standing here listening to this faceless couple arguing. "Maybe we should—"

"Darcy!" the male yelled. "What the hell? It's not a big deal. She didn't mean anything!"

Darcy? Owen thought. It wasn't a particularly common name, but still…what were the odds of it being his sister?

"And neither do you!" the female yelled back, and Owen couldn't help but notice the similarities between this Darcy's loud voice and his sister's.

Acoustics. That's what he was attributing it to. All of the noises combined together were making this random woman sound like…

"I have five brothers who would love to kick your ass!" she screamed. "We're through!"

"Oh thank God," Brooke murmured. "That poor girl. I can't imagine having to deal with such an awful situation with an audience. Come on. Let's go get something to eat."

They turned and Owen was nearly plowed down by someone coming from the opposite direction.

"*Darcy?*"

"*Owen?*"

Well…crap.

Brooke looked between the two of them, and it took a minute for everything to start to make sense. "Um… Owen?"

He turned and looked at Brooke, quickly schooling his expression to go neutral. "Brooke…this is my sister, Darcy. Darcy, this is Brooke."

The young woman turned and looked at Brooke as if she were an alien and muttered a distracted "hi" before turning back to Owen. "What are you doing in Vegas? And in a casino? Isn't there a planetarium somewhere around here you should be at?"

It took a lot of self-control for Brooke not to step between them and tell Darcy how rude she was being!

"Amazingly enough," Owen said smoothly, his focus back on his sister, "they let me get out and socialize with you mere mortals once in a while. Lucky that you got to witness it."

Darcy stared at him in wide-eyed disbelief for a moment before she broke out in laughter and launched herself into his arms. "I knew you had a sense of humor in there somewhere, brainiac!" She squeezed him tight before stepping back. "But, seriously, what are you doing here?"

Owen explained about the project in Red Rock and then about Brooke's painting and how they decided to take the impromptu trip. Which had Darcy's dark eyes going wide again right before she looked at Brooke.

"Wow! I can't believe you got my brother out of the lab! And to Vegas, no less! Yeah, you!" Then she stepped closer and sort of pushed Owen out of the way. "What did you say your name was again?"

Brooke nervously looked at Owen before focusing on Darcy again. "Um...Brooke. Brooke Matthews."

Darcy smiled wide. "Seriously? Like the actress? That is *so* cool!" She turned and looked at Owen. "Admit it, you had no idea she shared her name with a famous model-slash-actress, right?"

He looked away briefly and sighed. When he faced her again, his expression was stern. "What are you doing here, brat? I thought you had that internship back in LA. You were talking about it nonstop when you were home last month. Does your boss know you're off gallivanting in Vegas instead of working?"

To her credit, Darcy seemed genuinely taken aback by Owen's stern words and tone. "I...I..." She paused and huffed. "I'm an adult, Owen. I took a three-day weekend. It's not a big deal."

"It seemed like a big deal," he countered. "And who was the guy you were fighting with? You didn't mention that you were dating anyone."

She rolled her eyes. "Gee, I wonder why?" she deadpanned. "I learned a long time ago to not bring up my dating life when I'm around you guys. You all freak out and for no good reason."

"Again, it seemed like there's a good reason. You catch this guy cheating on you, and you're okay with screaming at him in the middle of a casino but not with your brothers wanting to protect you? That seems a little off, don't you think?"

With a huff, Darcy paced a few feet away and then back again. "Look...it's not a big deal, okay? It was just—"

"Are you going to stand here and seriously say that to me after I—along with everyone else in the casino—heard you tell that guy how his cheating on you was a big deal?"

"That's not... It wasn't..." She let out a little shriek of frustration. "I handled it, didn't I? I don't need you or Aidan or Hugh or Quinn or Riley to fight my battles for me!"

Owen was about to answer when a big, burly-looking guy walked over, his gaze keenly focused on Darcy.

"Okay, Darce, you had your fit. I get it, and I'm sorry. It won't happen again. Can we go now? I thought we were going to try to see Britney's show tonight."

For a minute, they all seemed to just stop and stare.

Was this guy for real? Seriously, did he not understand all the ways he was a jackass?

"I'm not going anywhere with you, Jimmy," Darcy said, crossing her arms over her chest. "Why don't you find your kissing partner and go see Britney with her?"

Jimmy looked at Brooke and then at Owen before returning his attention to Darcy. "Who's this dork? Is this who you're trying to make me jealous with? Be serious, babe."

Owen went to take a step toward him, but Brooke reached out and placed a hand on his arm to stop him.

"That's one of my brothers," Darcy said defiantly.

Jimmy laughed. "If the other four are like him, I'm pretty sure I'm okay. Now, c'mon, Darcy. It's getting late. Let's go."

"She's not going with you," Owen said, his voice deep and menacing, and both Brooke and Darcy looked at one another with surprise. "I suggest you respect her wishes and leave."

Jimmy stepped in close. He was only a couple of inches taller than Owen, but he was built like a linebacker. Owen didn't back down. "Really? You're telling me to leave?" Jimmy asked.

Owen nodded. "I am."

"Jimmy!" Darcy cried and jumped between the two men. "Just go! We're done! Deal with it!"

But Jimmy didn't take his eyes off of Owen. "I'm not ready to deal with it. We came to Vegas together, we're sharing a room, and we're flying home together tomorrow."

"No, we're not," she countered. "Not as far as I'm concerned."

"Is there a problem here?" Everyone turned as a uniformed officer approached.

"Yes," Darcy said quickly. "This man is bothering me." She pointed at Jimmy. "He's made threats toward me, and I'm afraid to leave with him."

"Damn it, Darcy!" Jimmy yelled.

She gave him a smug look.

Brooke reached out for Owen's hand and gently tugged to get him to turn around. When he faced her, she could see how tense he was. "Are you okay?"

He shook his head but didn't speak.

"What do you want to do?" she asked softly.

He was saved from answering as Jimmy cursed and the officer led him away. For a minute, Brooke thought it was all over—crisis averted. But Darcy spun around and faced Owen with a furious look.

"What is wrong with you?" she demanded. "Did you think you were going to take him? What would you have done if he'd hit you?"

"I imagine I would have hit him back," Owen snapped.

Darcy snorted with disgust. "Right. Because besides taking impromptu trips to Vegas, now you're a fighter. Damn it, Owen—"

"What was I supposed to do?" he yelled. "Was I supposed to just stand here and let him talk to you like that?" He suddenly stopped talking at the sound of his phone beeping with an incoming text. But he didn't bother reaching for it. "Tell me, what did you expect me to do?"

"I would have thought you of all people would..." She stopped when her phone dinged with a text message too.

A small crowd was still milling around them, attracted by the yelling and arguing, and Brooke stepped between Darcy and Owen and spoke in her most diplomatic tone. "Why don't we stop giving everyone a show and go find someplace else to talk? And it seems to me if you're both getting texts, there's a chance they could be related. So take out the phones and see what's going on."

Both Darcy and Owen agreed, and they walked all of two steps when Darcy gasped and Owen stopped dead in his tracks.

"What?" Brooke asked. "What's going on?"

"Anna's having the baby!" Darcy cried, smiling broadly.

There was never a doubt in Owen's mind about going home to be with his family to celebrate the birth of its newest member. However, all of that was currently complicated by logistics.

They had gone with Darcy to get her bags—just in case Jimmy decided to come around and make trouble—and then quickly took a cab back to the hotel to grab their own. Beside him, Brooke was quiet. As a matter of fact, she hadn't said much since Darcy's announcement about the baby.

"C'mon, you guys!" Darcy said excitedly. "The cab is waiting to get us to the airport. I've already checked flights, and we can get on the seven fifteen to North Carolina. It's direct, but we'll get in late. Once we confirm, we can call Dad to let him know, and hopefully someone will come and meet us, so we won't have to rent a car."

Bell services brought their luggage, and then they were all piling back into the cab and heading the short distance to the airport.

And still, Brooke was silent. But to be fair, Darcy had been talking nonstop about how this time she was finally going to be there when a Shaughnessy baby was born and how her bosses would have to deal with it because she wasn't going to miss out. Owen held Brooke's hand and silently willed her to look at him and say something, but she didn't hear it over his sister's incessant chatter.

At the airport, they started to walk toward the ticket counter when Owen had finally had enough. "Darce, give us a minute, okay?"

She nodded and pulled her phone back out to see if there were any updates on Anna.

"Hey," he said softly, cupping Brooke's chin. "You've been quiet. Are you okay?"

She nodded. "I...I didn't want to interfere. You know...family stuff. You and Darcy seemed to have a lot to figure out, so I didn't want to complicate things with my two cents."

He couldn't help but smile. "And what's your two cents?"

"Well... I was going to say you didn't have to worry about me. Our flights will be leaving around the same time, and I hoped you'd call me when the baby arrived." She smiled, but Owen could tell there was something else bothering her.

Rather than question her or pressure her to answer, he leaned in and kissed her softly on the lips. When he raised his head, he did what he always did—he said exactly what was on his mind. "Come with me."

"What?"

He nodded. "Come with me. Come meet my family. We're big and loud and overwhelming—especially when we're celebrating something like this—but…it would mean a lot to me if you were there."

"Owen…this is a family thing. I'm not so sure this is the right time…or maybe it's too soon for me to meet everyone."

With a chuckle, he motioned over his shoulder to where his sister stood. "She's the scariest of the bunch, and you've already hit it off with her. Compared to Darcy, my father and brothers are like a day at the beach."

"She's not so bad," Brooke said. "I think we just caught her at an awkward moment."

"No," he said, shaking his head. "She's scary and intimidating. And even though she's the baby of the family, we're all a little scared of her, and she knows it."

Brooke didn't look like she believed him. "But… she's…she's—"

"Exactly," Owen said and chuckled again. "Trust me. She's had to put up with five overprotective brothers. She's learned how to stand up for herself, but we—well, mostly my brothers—still find her to be scary at times."

"Not you?"

He shrugged. "She was different with me. I didn't bother her, and she stayed out of my way. I guess I was lucky."

"Hey, you guys!" Darcy called out. "We need to get moving if we hope to get on this flight!"

Owen looked back at Brooke with hope. "So? What do you say? Will you come home with me?"

Her shoulders sagged slightly. "Owen, we've already

been gone for several days. I'm out of clean clothes, and—"

"We're about the same size," Darcy said as she popped up beside them. "Sorry. I was eavesdropping."

"Um—"

"Plus, you know…we will have access to a washer and dryer at Dad's," she added helpfully. "But I totally have clothes you can borrow. And with Zoe living close by, I'm sure she has stuff for you too."

"Um—"

"Darce?" Owen said.

"Yeah?"

"Go get in line at the ticket counter. We'll be right there."

She gave them a thumbs-up and happily walked away.

"Problem solved." He grinned.

"You know that wasn't the only thing I mentioned."

And then it hit him. He was pressuring her. Damn. Ducking his head, he shook it. "You're right. I'm sorry." Looking up at her, he gave her a lopsided grin. "I'm just not ready to say good-bye."

Her expression softened. "It's not good-bye…not really. It's just for a few days."

"Still not ready for it." He took both her hands in his and tugged her close before resting his forehead against hers. "I'll respect your wishes. If you want to head back to Chicago, I'll promise to call you when the baby arrives."

Then he kissed her.

Seriously kissed her.

He kissed her until it was bordering on X-rated.

When he raised his head, he liked the way Brooke's eyes were glazed over, how breathless she was, and how wet her lips still looked. It was almost enough to make him pound on his chest with pride as he claimed, "I did that!"

Squeezing her hands one last time, he stepped back. "So...I'll call you."

She blinked several times, and then her gaze seemed to focus. She nibbled on her bottom lip, and he knew he had her thinking... She was considering it. He looked over at Darcy, who was almost to the front of the line.

"I better go," he said. "Text me when you land so I know you're home safe, okay?" Another step back, and he let go of her hands, instantly missing the contact.

"Owen?"

"Yeah?"

She let out a loud sigh. "Are you sure it's okay for me to go with you? I don't want to impose on a family event."

His only response was to smile and grab her hand so they could join Darcy in line.

―――

The flight was fairly uneventful, but they arrived late due to the time difference. Luckily for them, so far Anna's labor had been slow, so they hadn't missed the birth. It had been decided they would take a cab from the airport to Owen's family home, due to the late hour. When they arrived, everything was dark, and Ian Shaughnessy had already texted that he was staying at the hospital to await the arrival of his third grandchild.

"See you guys in a couple of hours," Darcy said as she walked to her room with a tired wave.

"It's been a long day," Brooke said, yawning. It was a little comforting to know that she wouldn't have to meet any of Owen's family until the morning. For now, she just wanted to crawl into bed and sleep.

"Dad said Hugh, Aubrey, and Connor will be here in the morning and Riley and Savannah are planning on arriving later in the morning too. So, for tonight, it's just us and Darcy in the house."

Relief washed over her again, and instead of saying anything, she nodded. Owen took her by the hand and led her up the stairs to one of the guest rooms.

"It still feels weird coming home sometimes."

"How come?"

"Dad did a major renovation on the house a few years ago, and it's completely transformed. This isn't anything like the house I grew up in even though it is the same one."

"It's beautiful."

Flipping the light switch revealed a queen-size bed and a room that was done in earth tones with a beach decor. All in all, it was very inviting. Brooke immediately kicked off her shoes and sat on the bed. She looked over at Owen and noted that he was still standing by the door looking as if he wasn't sure what to do.

Which was crazy—it seemed like the man knew exactly what to do and he did it well. And even though she was beyond exhausted, if he even hinted at wanting to make love, she would be completely on board.

She stood and made fast work of turning the bed down. Then she looked at her suitcase and frowned. "I should have asked Darcy for something to sleep in."

Owen walked over to the dresser, pulled out a T-shirt,

and handed it to her. "I keep some extra stuff here. It'll be big on you, but…it's something."

Brooke closed the distance between them, wrapped her arms around him, and hugged him. "Thank you." Then she moved away and undressed, sliding the T-shirt over her head. When she turned around, she noted that Owen was watching her intently. Reaching out her hand to him, she whispered, "Come to bed, Owen."

Within minutes, he had stripped down to his boxers, turned out the overhead light, and turned on the small bedside lamp before sliding into the bed beside her and pulling her close. Limbs tangled together, her head rested on his shoulder, and in no time, they fell asleep.

———

Hours later Darcy banging on the door woke them up.

"Did you get the text? Are you up? We need to go!"

Owen opened his eyes and tried to sit up, but Brooke was wrapped all around him, and he wasn't ready to move just yet. He cleared his throat. "I…I didn't hear the phone. What's up?"

"She's finally at nine centimeters. Dad thinks the baby will be here within the hour, so come on!" she whined. "I'm going to make coffee!"

Just then Brooke lifted her head and gave him a sleepy smile. "What time is it?"

He looked over at the bedside clock. "It's just after seven. Sorry."

Sitting up, she yawned and stretched. "Do I have time to grab a quick shower?"

He nodded. "You do that, and I'll go ask Darcy for something for you to wear, okay?"

Within minutes they were on the move to get ready. Owen placed the outfit his sister gave him on the bed and then went to use the bathroom downstairs to get ready. Every time he looked at Darcy, she was practically bouncing on her toes with excitement, and he couldn't help but smile each time.

"Aren't you missing work?" she asked him.

"I was scheduled to give my last lecture today, but I let the university know there was a family emergency, and they had someone cover for me."

She smirked as she studied him.

"What? What's so funny?"

Darcy shook her head. "I'm not laughing." But she was definitely amused.

Owen sighed loudly. "Darcy—"

"All I'm saying is that Brooke is good for you." It was said lightly and with a shrug—she was stating a fact.

"Tell me why."

Her grin grew. "Well, it seems like this is a relatively new relationship, and yet she got you to hop on a plane to Vegas for a spur-of-the-moment trip, you gambled, and now you're blowing off work. I love it!" She hugged him quickly and took a step back. "You're turning into one of us—you know, normal."

It was on the tip of his tongue to argue with her—he hated when people implied that he wasn't normal—but he understood what she was saying, and it wasn't an insult. So he just gave her a smile of his own and shrugged. "It's not so bad, I guess."

"That's the spirit!" Darcy said. "I wish we'd get an update. The wait is killing me!"

"I'm sure as soon as they know something, they'll text. All we can do is wait."

Brooke came down the stairs just as Owen received another text. "They're finally letting her push," he read, and the next thing he knew, they were all rushing out the door and climbing in the car his father had left for them. "I don't think I know whose car this even is," he commented as they pulled out of the driveway.

"It's Aidan's," Darcy said. "Dad mentioned it last night. He has his work truck if he needs to go anywhere, and Zoe has the SUV, so this is just a spare."

The entire drive to the hospital was spent listening to Darcy talk about how excited she was and how she couldn't wait to see Quinn have to change a diaper, and while Owen laughed and even made his own observations, he couldn't help but notice Brooke had gone quiet again. It was possible she was just tired, but he had a feeling she was once again feeling overwhelmed about meeting his family.

As they pulled into the parking lot, he decided to cut his sister's chatter short. "You're going to love meeting everyone," he said to Brooke. He parked the car and shut it off before turning in his seat to face her. "There are a lot of us—"

"You're gonna meet Dad and Martha, his lady-friend," Darcy said with a giggle, "and Aidan's here with Zoe. I think Lily is with a sitter this morning. And Anna's parents are here along with her brother, Bobby, and at some point you'll meet Hugh and Aubrey and Connor—who is the cutest boy ever—and then Riley and Savannah, and of course Quinn and Anna, so that's—"

"Fourteen people," Owen finished for her. "But don't let the number scare you."

"The sheer loudness will probably scare you more than anything, but hopefully the fact that we're in a hospital will make us keep it to a low roar," Darcy countered and then laughed. "I'm heading in! So excited!" And then she hopped from the car and all but sprinted to the hospital entrance.

Brooke took a steadying breath and looked at him, still looking a little overwhelmed. "I still feel like I'm intruding."

"And I'm telling you you're not. They're all going to love you. And if I know my family, they're going to hug you and treat you like you're one of us. Don't worry."

This must be what animals in the zoo feel like, Brooke mused to herself.

For the first time possibly ever, it would appear that Owen Shaughnessy was wrong. There was something to worry about—namely, his family.

There were no hugs; there weren't even real smiles. There was just a whole lot of…wide-eyed curiosity.

Good thing she'd showered at least.

Brooke couldn't ever remember a time when she'd felt this uncomfortable, and just when she was about to excuse herself to grab a cup of coffee from the cafeteria, all heads turned and then everybody stood up.

"We have a girl!"

Chaos ensued for at least fifteen minutes as everyone listened to Quinn—at least she assumed it was Quinn— talk about how amazing his wife was and how beautiful his daughter was. And even though she had never met them before, Brooke felt herself get a little emotional just listening to him talk.

Quinn ran a hand through his hair and let out a long breath. "I'm telling you, I don't know how she did it. I mean, I always knew Anna was strong, but...damn. I was practically on my knees with exhaustion and..." He stopped talking when he caught sight of Brooke. Everyone turned to look at her, and she wished the floor would open up and swallow her whole.

"Oh, Quinn," Owen said after a moment, "this is Brooke. Brooke, this is my brother Quinn."

She reached out and shook Quinn's hand and offered congratulations on the new baby, and he smiled and thanked her before everyone started talking again and asking when they were going to be able to see the newest Shaughnessy.

"The nurse told me that in about thirty minutes you'll be able to come up and see her in the nursery. Anna may need a bit longer before she's ready for everyone— besides her folks." He smiled over at his in-laws.

"And does my granddaughter have a name yet?" Ian asked.

Quinn smiled broadly. "Kaitlyn Marie Shaughnessy."

Everyone awwed and smiled. "That's beautiful," Ian said, his voice thick with emotion. "Absolutely beautiful."

Clapping his hands together, Quinn got ready to leave. "Okay, in about thirty minutes, you can start coming up. We've made friends with the nurses on the floor, and they're prepared for all of you. Just...behave."

There was laughter and teasing, and Quinn waved as he went back to be with his wife and new baby girl.

What must that feel like? Brooke thought. *To create a new life and to hold it in your hands for the first time?* She hadn't seen Kaitlyn, and really, Brooke didn't know Quinn and Anna. But in that moment, she was incredibly envious of them and felt a little overwhelmed with the entire thing.

Owen's arm came around her waist, and he tucked her in close beside him, kissing the top of her head. "You okay?"

All she could do was nod.

As if sensing her mood, he took her by the hand and gently led her to a sofa in the corner, away from his family. When they sat down, he didn't speak. He waited until she was ready to.

Sometimes she hated how considerate he was while being so in tune with her.

Dammit.

With a sigh, she looked at him. "I shouldn't be here," she said softly. "From what I can tell, Darcy is the only one who seems even remotely friendly." She shook her head. "I'm sorry. I… Maybe there was another way to say that—"

Owen shook his head. "No. I understand. Everyone seemed a little…off, so I'm sorry. I guess I thought they'd at least be nice to you."

"They have been nice," she countered. "But…they're looking at me like I'm some sort of… I don't know. I'm getting a bit of a complex." She looked around the waiting room and realized most of the Shaughnessys were looking their way. "Would it be completely rude if I went to the cafeteria to get a cup of coffee? I'll be back before you go in to see Anna and the baby."

He nodded but didn't speak. Kissing him on the cheek, Brooke stood and walked away, thankful the cafeteria was straight ahead of her and she wouldn't have to turn and see everyone watching her.

She hadn't gone ten steps when a thought hit her—was this what it was like? For Neal? People looking at him like he was a freak? No doubt Owen had been on the receiving end of the same thing—not from his family but from schoolmates or colleagues. A sick feeling settled in the pit of her stomach, and she placed a hand there and quickly ducked into the nearby ladies' room.

How many times had she looked at her brother like that? Like he was weird just because he was different from her? From everyone? How did he handle constantly being an outcast when, after one morning of it, Brooke was practically in tears?

And maybe the bigger question was: How was she supposed to stay with Owen while dealing with such intense scrutiny?

Chapter 8

"DID WE GET HERE IN TIME?"

Owen looked up to see his brother Hugh and his wife, Aubrey, striding into the waiting area hand in hand. He stood and walked over to join his family even though his mind was spinning and his heart ached for Brooke. The look of defeat on her face as she'd walked away had devastated him.

The woman with the beautiful smile wasn't smiling.

And those eyes that always shone so brightly were now dimmed.

And it was because of all the people standing in front of him…the people he loved.

"Owen!" Hugh cried as he walked over to greet him. "Glad you're here! How are you?"

Owen shook his brother's hand and then embraced him as they always did, but Owen was in too much turmoil to do more than nod. Hugh looked at him and then turned to look at the group.

"What's going on?"

"It's nothing," Owen forced himself to say and went to accept a hug from Aubrey. "Where's Connor?"

"We're sharing a babysitter with Aidan and Zoe, so we stopped and dropped Connor off on our way here," Aubrey replied and then looked around excitedly. "So? Do we have a new baby?"

Everyone started talking at once, and Owen took a

step back and looked over at the sofa in the corner long-
ingly. He was just about to turn and walk over to it when
he was flanked by Hugh and Aidan, and together the
three of them sat down.

"Okay, what's going on?" Hugh asked. "You look
depressed. More so than usual."

Owen frowned at him. "When do I look depressed?
I'm never depressed."

Hugh rolled his eyes. "Okay, you look far more…
serious than you usually do. Is that more accurate?"

Before he could say anything, Aidan spoke up. "I'm
going to take a guess and say he's pissed at us."

"Us?" Hugh parroted. "I just got here. Why's he
pissed at me?"

"The rest of us," Aidan clarified. "When he showed
up here this morning with Brooke, we were kind of…
surprised."

Hugh looked around. "Brooke? Who's Brooke?"

"She's probably climbing out a window or hailing a
cab to the airport right now," Owen murmured.

"I didn't ask *where* she was," Hugh said. "I'm asking
who she is."

"From the looks of it, she's Owen's girlfriend."

It sounded so juvenile, Owen realized. *Girlfriend.*
Unfortunately, he wasn't sure what else to call her, so
he nodded and said, "She is."

"So what's the problem?" Hugh asked, confused.
"Was she mean? Disrespectful?"

This time, Owen spoke before Aidan could. "She was
perfectly polite to everyone. She came here because I
asked her to and assured her that my family would love
her—after all, everyone loved Zoe, Anna, Aubrey, and

Savannah!" he snapped, realizing just how annoyed he truly was.

"Oh," Hugh said quietly and then seemed to consider his next words. "So she's like…a serious girlfriend."

"I hate that word," Owen murmured.

"I'm sure she's very nice," Aidan said diplomatically—as he was prone to do at times like this—"but I think we're all just a little out of sorts. It's been a long night, we're functioning on minimal sleep, and to be honest, no one knew you were dating anyone."

"And that matters…why?" Owen asked in confusion. "I didn't know you were dating Zoe, and yet when you brought her home for dinner for the first time, I was polite."

"We were polite," Aidan corrected, "but we were also…surprised." He raked a hand through his hair. "And you have to believe me on the lack of sleep. I already don't get enough because of Lily's schedule, and last night we all stayed here late because we thought Anna was going to have the baby. We didn't mean to upset you, Bro. And we certainly didn't mean to upset Brooke."

"Well, you did," Owen said and hated that he was actually pouting. He was better than that, but…this bothered him. "She didn't want to come. We were in Vegas, and she was going to fly home—"

"Wait, wait, wait," Hugh interrupted with a grin. "What were you doing in Vegas?"

Owen explained about the Red Rock project and Brooke's painting and the general reasons why they went—but not what happened between them while they were there.

Both Aidan and Hugh clapped him on the back with big smiles on their faces. "That's awesome!" Aidan said. "Good for you!"

"So you flew in directly from Vegas?" Hugh asked.

"We did. We were supposed to fly back to Chicago last night but had some time to kill, so we went and gambled awhile—just the slots," he said for clarification, "and then we ran into Darcy fighting with her boyfriend—"

"What?" Both his brothers jumped to their feet, all good-natured ribbing over.

"What the hell was Darcy doing in Vegas?" Hugh demanded.

"And who was the guy?" Aidan asked.

Uh-oh…

Thinking quickly on his feet was never Owen's strength, but for some reason, it came naturally today. "Can we please focus on how rude you were to Brooke?" he snapped. "Geez, way to try and throw everyone's attention elsewhere." He snorted with disgust. "Typical."

"Hey…wait a minute," Aidan said, sitting back down. "I told you why I behaved the way I did. And if you must know, Zoe already called me out on it."

"Yeah, well…she wasn't particularly friendly either," Owen said, looking away.

"Damn," Aidan sighed, slouching in his seat.

"What the hell did you do?" Hugh asked Aidan as he motioned toward Owen. "He's never like this. Ever. You must have been beyond rude to upset Owen like this. And where's Brooke? Do you think she's left the hospital?"

"Owen, I'm sorry. You have to believe me. If she left…I…I'll take you to the airport myself to go after her."

"I hope it doesn't come to that," Owen said with a weary sigh, kind of enjoying how much his brothers were almost groveling to him. Then, out of the corner of his eye, he saw Brooke. He immediately stood and wondered if he should go to her.

"Holy shit," Hugh whispered.

"Maybe now you understand our earlier reaction?" Aidan quietly replied.

"I can hear you both," Owen said without looking at either of them. His heart pounded in his chest until he swore everyone could see and hear it as he watched Brooke's approach. She looked at his brothers, her expression guarded, and then her focus returned to Owen. She handed him a cup of coffee. "Thanks."

"We ran out the door too fast this morning to drink ours, so I thought you might want one," she said softly.

Taking a sip of his, he motioned for her to join him on the sofa. "Brooke, this is my brother Hugh. Hugh Shaughnessy, Brooke Matthews."

Hugh's eyes went wide as he shook her hand. "Wow! Like the actress? Awesome!"

How was it that *everyone* was aware of this fact except him?

Brooke blushed and settled in beside Owen. "Yeah, my mom was a big fan of hers and had high hopes of me being a model, so—"

"Who's a model?" Aubrey asked as she joined them, instantly introducing herself to Brooke.

"Oh...um...I was just saying how my mom had hoped I'd be one," Brooke replied sheepishly.

"So what do you do?" Aubrey asked, and Owen almost kissed her. Other than Darcy, Aubrey was the only one to give Brooke a genuine smile along with a friendly greeting.

"Right now I'm teaching art part-time. I'm trying to find work at a gallery back in Chicago. I'm staying with my uncle while I look."

"So you're a…you're like one of those…" Aidan began, trying to find the right word.

"She's an artist," Owen finished for him through gritted teeth.

No one mentioned her work again.

"Hey, you guys!" Darcy called out. "Quinn just texted that we can come up now to the nursery and see Kaitlyn!"

Owen was never more relieved to go and look at a baby in his entire life.

The Shaughnessy family seemed to fill the hospital cafeteria, and for the life of her, Brooke wasn't sure what to make of the whole thing. They'd gone up to see baby Kaitlyn—who was beyond perfect—and they had all visited with Anna. Why were they still here, other than having something to eat? Why didn't everyone go home and get on with their lives? It seemed…strange.

Although she had to admit, watching the way they all interacted with one another was a bit fascinating. Their dynamics were amazing. They all laughed and joked, and even after all the tension earlier, she could see that this was how they normally behaved toward one another. It was something she never experienced with her own family.

Still, at least now she was a little more at ease with

everyone. And if she had the opportunity, she would thank Anna for that. It wasn't until they were all crowded into the poor woman's hospital room that everything seemed to turn around.

"Oh my God!" Anna had cried when Owen had introduced her. "I am so glad you're here! Quinn told me about you—not just from when he met you in the waiting room but from hearing about you from Owen!"

"Oh...um—"

"And you're an artist?" Anna asked. "That is so amazing! We have a *ton* of blank walls in our house, and I would love to put some paintings up. Do you have a portfolio? I mean, I know you don't have one with you, but maybe you can send me some pictures via email of what you have?"

"I...I mean...sure," Brooke had said nervously, desperately aware that all eyes were on her.

"I'm just so glad you're here." Anna beamed, and Brooke could tell that she meant it.

Until she started to cry.

"Damn hormones," Anna muttered as she wiped at her eyes. Quinn had quickly settled beside her, put his arms around her, and kissed her gently on the top of her head while telling her how amazing she was.

After that, everyone seemed to relax a bit, and even though Brooke had no idea what they were talking about half the time, they weren't completely ostracizing her either.

Baby steps.

So now they were all in the cafeteria because Anna had fallen asleep, and Brooke was back to her original question: *Why?* She turned to face Owen, ready to ask,

"Owen...Brooke...can you hang back for a minute?" The request came from Ian. Brooke noticed he was standing alone—everyone else had gone—and her stomach sank. He motioned for them to sit at a corner table, a much smaller one than they had just vacated.

"What's up, Dad?"

Ian smiled at them both as he sat down. "I think I owe you both an apology."

Color her surprised.

"For what?" Owen asked, but Brooke had a sneaking suspicion he knew exactly the reason behind it.

"I'm afraid you caught us at our worst this morning," Ian began and gave them both an apologetic smile. "It was a long night, and everyone was out of sorts. Aidan and Zoe had argued because she wanted to be here for Anna but Aidan insisted she go home and sleep. She eventually did, but she was back here first thing, and there was still some lingering tension from that."

"I don't see where—"

He sighed. "Then there was an awkward...discussion...when Martha commented on the baby calling her grandma."

Silence.

Brooke didn't know much about the Shaughnessys, but she was aware that Owen's mother had passed away a long time ago and that Ian and Martha weren't married. So no doubt the woman implying that she'd be the baby's grandmother probably did not go over well at all.

Ian cleared his throat and shifted in his seat. "As you can imagine, it caused quite a stir. Aidan firmly reminded Martha that she was not the baby's grandmother, and if that weren't awkward enough, Anna's parents readily agreed with him." He looked over at Brooke and said, "Robert and Mary Hannigan have been our friends since the kids were little. Mary was my wife Lillian's best friend. So you can see why things got tense."

"And this happened…?" Owen prompted.

"Pretty much right before the two of you arrived with Darcy this morning. We were all reeling a bit from the argument, and then you showed up, and…" He paused with a nervous chuckle. "We were all a little surprised to meet Brooke. You hadn't mentioned you had a girlfriend."

Beside her, Owen sagged a little in his seat. "To be honest, we—"

"It's okay, Owen," Ian quickly interrupted. "I know you hadn't planned on bringing Brooke home to meet the family quite like this, and you're more of a private person than your siblings, so…no one's blaming you for not telling us. I'm just sorry it all happened the way it did this morning." Again, he looked over at Brooke. "And I'm so sorry this was your first impression of our family. We're normally much nicer than this."

Relief swamped her because at least she knew the cold shoulder she'd received wasn't anything personal against her. "Thank you, Mr. Shaughnessy. I was a little self-conscious about joining Owen. This was a private family event."

"Nonsense," Ian said, rising to his feet. "The birth of a baby should be celebrated by everyone, and I hope you won't hold this morning against us."

Ian's grin was infectious, and Brooke couldn't help smiling in return. "I won't, and again…thank you."

"I'm sorry the lodgings are getting all tossed around," Ian said, looking back at his son. "It didn't occur to me last night to mention any of it. You were all texting me to tell me when you were coming, and I lost track of it all. I figured it would work itself out."

"It's not a big deal," Owen said softly. "Not really. I guess I'm just used to always staying at the house—like Darcy. But this has been the first time we've all been home at the same time in a long time, so—"

"You'll like Aidan and Zoe's place. I think you're the only one other than Darcy who hasn't stayed there. And Zoe's an excellent hostess—the place will be stocked with everything you'll ever need or want."

"As long as I can do some laundry, I'll be fine," Brooke said. "I don't want to bother Darcy for any more of her clothes."

"She said she didn't mind," Owen commented.

They all walked out of the cafeteria to join the rest of the family, who were all waiting in the lobby for Riley and Savannah to come back down. This time, Brooke was able to view them all through different eyes and with more understanding.

Maybe the decision to come here with Owen hadn't been such a bad one after all.

———

"I swear I didn't intend for things to be this way."

"It's not a big deal."

"But…it is. Technically we were just supposed to go and take some pictures in the desert, and now—"

"Owen?"

"Hmm?"

"Stop worrying."

He wished he could. Zoe had just left after showing

them around the apartment. She apologized at least a dozen times to Brooke for the way they'd all behaved earlier in the day, and now they seemed like they would be friends. That made Owen smile. It was very important to him that his family love Brooke as much as he did.

Love.

A slow smile spread across his face. Yeah, just the thought of that emotion wasn't enough to send him into a state of panic. But the current situation? Well…that was a different story.

"All I'm saying is what started out as you being nice and inviting me to sit with you at dinner has had you in my bed every night for five nights in a row. I swear this wasn't what I had in mind when I accepted your invitation in the diner."

She chuckled. "Are you sure?"

He didn't get the fact that she was teasing at first, but when he saw the twinkle in her eye, he understood. Unable to resist, he walked over to her and wrapped her in his arms. "Well…maybe I was a little bit hopeful," he teased and kissed her softly on the lips. "Okay, maybe more than a little bit.."

And then he kissed her again—deeper. Brooke wrapped herself around him, and as much as he didn't want to move—because kissing her was becoming a serious addiction—the thought of having them continue this on a soft bed was too great to deny. Slowly he maneuvered them so they clumsily made their way to the bedroom. Every time one of them stumbled or knocked into something, they merely laughed and met up again for another kiss. Owen had no idea kissing could be so playful and fun!

They collapsed on the bed in a tangle of limbs and laughter, and if anything, it was the happiest Owen had felt in a long time. Hearing Brooke laugh? Feeling her in his arms? It all had him realizing just how boring and staid his life had been, and more than anything, he didn't want to let this feeling go. If anything, he wanted to hold on to it with both hands and say a prayer of thanks for it.

In the back of his mind, Owen knew he wanted what his brothers had found, but he couldn't imagine any of them having something that felt quite like this. It was special, and it was just for him and Brooke.

Lifting his head, he looked down at Brooke and nearly groaned when she licked her lips and gave him a flirty smile.

He loved her.

It was fast and crazy and something that he didn't want to deny—didn't feel he could keep to himself any longer.

"Make love to me, Owen," she whispered huskily.

It was on the tip of his tongue to tell her what he was feeling, but today had been an emotional day, and he didn't want to overwhelm her any more than she already was. So he showed her how he felt, putting all of his love into every kiss, every touch, every move. And when they finally settled in each other's arms, breathless and exhausted, he promised himself that when they got back to Chicago, he'd tell her.

And said another prayer that she felt the same.

———

Kaitlyn Marie Shaughnessy came home to a houseful of loud people, and she was not too happy about it.

When Quinn and Anna arrived at their home, everyone was already there with enough food to feed a small army. The new parents thanked everyone and let them all get a peek at the baby but didn't waste too much time getting her up the stairs and settled into her nursery.

"Maybe we should have waited a little bit before coming over," Ian said worriedly. "I didn't think about the possibility of Kaitlyn getting upset by all the noise."

"Nonsense," Zoe said, kissing her father-in-law on the cheek. "She'll get used to it. And we won't stay long. We'll all have lunch together and clean up and then leave them to enjoy their first day home, just the three of them."

Conversation flowed over how Hugh and Aubrey dealt with their first day home with Connor and how they were thrilled to have everyone around to share in the big occasion. Darcy reminded them how she wasn't there, so it didn't count. After the laughter and teasing died down, Zoe recalled her and Aidan's first day home with Lily and how terrified they were every time she cried.

"That's what babies do," Ian said. "It's their job. They've been snug and secure for nine months, and then all of a sudden, there's a houseful of loud people disrupting them. I'd probably cry too!"

They all laughed again, and as Owen looked around the room, he noticed that Martha wasn't there. Had the argument yesterday caused hurt feelings, or was it something more? His father looked and sounded okay, but Owen wasn't so sure. He made a mental note to ask his brothers if anyone knew what was going on.

For the next hour, they gathered around the large

dining room table and enjoyed their potluck lunch. There was fried chicken and sandwiches, a variety of salads, and a mountain of cookies and desserts. Everyone had contributed to the meal, and there was more than enough left over for Quinn and Anna to enjoy for several days.

"I know I'm supposed to take advantage of the time Kaitlyn's sleeping to get some sleep myself," Anna said at the end of the meal, "but I would just love a little time to sit and talk with the girls." She looked around the table excitedly. "What do you say, ladies? How about we let the guys do the cleanup and we go into the living room and relax?"

"Hey, wait a minute," Quinn said with a bit of a pout. "What if I want to nap while she's sleeping? I was awake just as much as you over the past few days."

Anna stood and gave him a look that spoke volumes. "Tell you what, the next time you push a human being out of your body, you get to take a nap. How about that?"

Raising his hands in surrender, Quinn immediately made a zipping motion across his lips and waved her—and the girls—on their way.

Owen was actually relieved things were playing out this way, and it made him smile that Brooke readily went along with Anna, Darcy, Zoe, and Aubrey. When it was just the Shaughnessy men around the table, it hit him how they were all quiet.

Which was extremely uncommon.

"It's times like this," Ian said softly, "when I miss your mom the most."

All around him, Owen noticed his brothers nodding—just like him. And although he understood his father's sentiment, it was a little bit different for him personally.

Holidays or special occasions didn't make him miss his mother the most; just the quiet of an ordinary day did. Sometimes when he was alone with his thoughts and feeling overwhelmed by them, he missed having his mother to talk to. He remembered her sitting patiently beside him so many times when he was younger— encouraging him, helping him feel less overwhelmed by his thoughts and see the positive side of things.

That's what he missed.

Every. Single. Day.

"I know I say it often," Ian continued, "but as much as she loved you boys, she was over the moon to finally have a girl. And I think if she were here today, we'd have to pry Kaitlyn—and Lily—out of her arms." He chuckled. "That's not to say she wouldn't be wild about Connor. But your mother loved the thought of dressing up a little girl in frilly dresses and bonnets."

They all smiled at the image—and if they were like Owen, they remembered some of the getups Darcy was dressed in when she was a baby. Darcy looked more like a doll at times than a real baby, but Owen could remember how excited his mother was every time she got to show off her baby girl to friends and family.

Aidan cleared his throat. "Zoe is always buying dresses for Lily. Then she gets upset when something gets spilled on them or she gets messed up." He chuckled and shook his head. "I'll never understand it."

"Connor's a tough little guy through and through, and I have to tell you," Hugh said with a grin, "he makes a hell of a mess, and we've learned to buy clothes that are more durable than fashionable."

Quinn groaned and slouched in his seat. "You think

Anna would hate it if I put Kaitlyn in jeans and T-shirts instead of dresses?"

"Oh stop," Ian said with a touch of humor. "You have a long time before you have to worry about that, and there's nothing wrong with letting her wear both. No one needs to be in dresses every day."

For the next few minutes, his brothers talked about the wonders of parenthood, and Owen caught Riley's eye, wondering if he'd mentioned the fact that he and Savannah were expecting yet. It seemed odd how no one was mentioning it, and Owen did not want to be the one to let the cat out of the bag.

As if sensing his question, Riley gave his head a slight shake. Owen knew there was a story there, and more than ever, he wanted a few minutes alone with his twin to talk. He wasn't sure if there was a polite way for them to excuse themselves to have a private conversation without their brothers having something snarky to say. So he'd wait. Eventually, they'd have to get up, and maybe then he'd be able to pull Riley aside.

Rather than obsess about Riley, he let his mind wander to Brooke and how she was handling getting grilled by his sisters-in-law.

———∿∿∿———

Girl talk.

Brooke loved girl talk!

She was the queen of it, and this group of girls—now that they were all a little more relaxed—seemed like they would be awesome to hang out with. Anna was talking about her labor and how funny Quinn was. That led to both Zoe and Aubrey sharing their stories.

Brooke and Darcy looked at each other with amusement and shook their heads.

"Not for nothing," Darcy interrupted, "but I feel like it's wrong for me to get such a kick out of hearing how my big, strong brothers get reduced to such doofuses in times of crisis." She laughed. "I hope you all use that to your advantage."

"Every day," Zoe said, and Aubrey and Anna quickly agreed.

"So what were you doing in Vegas, Darce?" Aubrey asked, grinning.

Darcy rolled her eyes. "Who blabbed?"

"Owen mentioned it when he was arguing with Aidan and Hugh at the hospital," Aubrey said and shifted on the sofa to get comfortable. "And don't change the subject. What were you doing in Vegas, and who were you with?"

"Ugh," Darcy groaned. "I cannot believe I ran into Owen in a casino. I mean, what are the odds?"

"He was probably your safest bet," Zoe commented. "If it had been any of your other brothers, we'd be bailing someone out of jail right now."

"Owen was pretty fierce about it," Brooke said, coming to his defense. Not that what Zoe said was a put-down against Owen, but she wanted these women to know that he could go up against his brothers—or anyone—if he needed to.

"Oh, really?" Zoe asked with a big smile. "Do tell."

Brooke was about to answer her, but Darcy relayed the story—and did justice to just how fierce Owen actually was.

"I'm telling you, I wasn't sure if I should be impressed or scared for him. Jimmy's a pretty big guy, and I think if the fight had come to blows, he would have hurt Owen. But not before Owen put up one hell of a fight." She grinned over at Brooke. "It's obvious that Brooke has done wonders for the quietest Shaughnessy."

"So this Jimmy person, was it serious?" Savannah asked.

"Nah. It was all pretty casual. Honestly, it's like there are no good guys out there. I keep going on these dates and getting fixed up, and they're all jerks. How is that possible? Where do you go to meet decent guys?"

"Don't look at us. The decent guys we're all with are your brothers," Anna joked.

Darcy sighed. "There's got to be a decent, non-Shaughnessy man out there for me."

"You're young, Darce," Anna said. "When the time is right, you'll meet someone." She paused. "How's the job going?"

"It's going," she replied wearily. "I don't know... I'm just not impressed with anything right now. Job. Men. Life. For so long I wanted to get away from this town and from everyone and have an adventure, and it's not at all like I thought it would be."

"Sometimes it takes a while to find what you want to do," Aubrey said. "Look at me. I spent so many years doing what my father wanted me to do that I had no idea what my dreams were. If it weren't for your brother and Bordeaux Bill, I don't know what I'd be doing right now."

"And even though I knew what I wanted to do," Zoe added, "it took a long time for me to find the balance I needed. Back in Arizona, I was my own boss, and it wasn't all that great. Then I came here and worked for Martha and...well—"

"Aidan sort of ruined that for you," Anna interrupted. "Granted, he did rectify it in the end, but he made you miserable in the beginning."

"Well, you were no better," Zoe chuckled. "Not that you made me miserable, but you struggled with your own career choices too." She shook her head. "I still don't know what you were thinking with the whole real estate thing. You were born to run the pub."

Anna shrugged. "Like Darcy, I was at a point where I wasn't impressed with anything anymore and thought I needed to try something new." She looked over at Brooke. "What about you? I know you're an artist, but…is that your career?"

Four pairs of eyes turned and stared at her. "Oh… um…I'm hoping it might be, but—"

"Her stuff is amazing!" Darcy chimed in. "She showed me some pictures of it while we were on the plane. I mean…even for pictures on a phone they looked great, so you can imagine how awesome they look in person. Take out your phone! Show them the one that looks like a Van Gogh!"

Brooke smiled but waved her off, not wanting everyone gawking at her artwork. Not now anyway.

"It can't be easy," Savannah said. "I've known quite a few artists in my line of work, and it's not easy to get noticed and make a living out of it."

"I teach art part-time at a community college in Chicago."

"Is that where you're from?" Zoe asked.

Brooke shook her head. "Long Island. My parents are still there. But I needed a change of scenery, and my uncle invited me to stay with him and see if Chicago had anything to offer. I lucked out with the position teaching art—but it's a night school sort of thing that's more for recreation than for a degree."

"So how did you meet Owen?" Aubrey asked.

For a minute, Brooke was waiting for the spotlight to shine in her eyes. "My uncle works at the university where Owen's been lecturing. They've known each other for years. When Uncle Howard found out Owen was going to be leading a group out in Red Rock, he thought I might be a good fit as his assistant."

The four women looked at each other and then back at Brooke as if she were crazy.

"Owen's not comfortable leading the group, and my uncle thought maybe with an assistant to help him, he might be more at ease." She paused when Riley walked into the room and sat down next to his wife. Brooke cleared her throat and continued. "So...um...he also knew one of my dreams was to paint in the desert, but it upset my folks too much to think of me going on my own. It seemed like a win-win—Owen would get an assistant, and I'd get to paint."

"I'm confused," Anna said. "And maybe it's because of lack of sleep. But if you're Owen's assistant, when did that change to you and him being...you know. You and him."

Awkward. Normally Brooke didn't mind sharing her personal life with people, but she was a little protective of her and Owen's new relationship. She could feel herself flush.

"He refused to hire me," she said, looking at each of them in turn. "He's pretty much against the trip as a whole—although I think he's still going to do it. But he wants to do it on his own terms. Without an assistant."

"So how'd you end up dating?" Savannah asked, a kind smile on her face. Unlike the one on her husband's. Riley was studying Brooke rather intently, and she almost wanted to squirm under his scrutiny.

"He was pretty much avoiding me, even though I had thought we were starting to become friends, and we ran into each other Friday night while out to dinner. I was going to a gallery to see an artist's debut that was recommended to me, and I stopped at a diner to get something to eat. Owen showed up, and the line was out the door, so I invited him to join me. He came with me to the gallery, and then we stayed up all night talking."

"Aww," Anna sighed. "I love that!"

Her reaction made Brooke smile. "Then we spent part of the next day touring a museum that Owen had wanted to go to, and then we decided to do something crazy." She shrugged and smiled. "So we hopped a plane to Vegas. Owen toured Red Rock, and I was able to paint a bit."

"Are you disappointed that you're not going on the real trip with him?" Aubrey asked.

"A little," Brooke admitted. "I think I could have helped him with the group and with the overall preparation. But Owen knows what he's doing. If he believes he can handle it on his own, then he can."

"And what about your painting?" This came from Riley, and his tone wasn't nearly as light as the girls'. "Are you disappointed to miss out on a longer trip to do *your* thing?"

It was the way he emphasized the word *your* that clued her in on his deal. Looking him square in the eye, she replied, "Of course I'm disappointed. Red Rock is beautiful, and the meteor shower is supposed to be spectacular. The opportunity to paint that—which is my real area of interest—would have been amazing. I primarily paint the night sky, which is why I thought painting in the desert would be so exciting—the large expanse of sky." She shrugged. "I took a lot of pictures this weekend, and I'll work off of those."

Without a word, Riley kissed Savannah on the head and left the room, leaving Brooke to wonder if her answer pleased him or pissed him off. She honestly couldn't tell.

"Don't mind him," Savannah said, as if reading Brooke's mind. "He's protective of Owen—he says it's a twin thing. The two of them often joke about their bond. Riley swears he can sense when things are wrong with Owen, but Owen refuses to buy into it. It's kind of funny at times."

"Growing up it was hard to remember that they were twins," Darcy said. "They really are so different. Add that to the fact that they don't look alike, and you can almost believe they're not twins."

Conversation flowed back to all of the brothers and their similarities and differences. Brooke did her best to follow along, but her mind kept wandering to Riley and the way he'd watched her and questioned her. And all of her insecurities from earlier in the day came flooding back.

———

"You got a minute?"

Owen looked up and smiled at Riley. "Yeah. Sure."

Together they walked out to the backyard and sat down at the table next to the pool. "You haven't told anyone about Savannah's pregnancy," he said quickly. "Why?"

Riley sighed. "After I talked to you, Savannah and I decided to wait until after Quinn and Anna had the baby. We didn't want to take away from their big day."

Owen chuckled. "Really? Didn't they horn in on your wedding?"

Riley laughed with him. "Yeah, but...that just made it all the more fun. They deserved to have the attention all to themselves with Kaitlyn. We'll wait another week or two, and then we'll tell everyone."

Nodding, Owen waited a moment before speaking again. "Did Dad and Martha break up?"

"What are you talking about?"

"The argument yesterday at the hospital. I'm sure you heard about it. Then Martha wasn't here today, so—"

"I think it was agreed upon that today would just be about us." He paused and laughed. "I think they were going for being politically correct or something. But part of me thinks she was a little embarrassed by the whole thing yesterday."

"What do you think about that?"

"What?" Riley asked, confusion on his face.

"About her wanting to be called *Grandma*. It's a little presumptuous, don't you think?"

Riley shook his head. "They've been dating for two years. Dad brings her to everything, and honestly, she treats all of us like her own, along with Lily and Connor. I guess she's either pushing for a commitment from Dad or for a clear definition of her place in the family."

Owen could understand that.

"You know," Riley began, "we haven't talked since I called to tell you about the baby."

"I know."

"And it would seem like you've been quite busy." Riley's expression was serious—just like his tone. "I can't believe you'd do something big like hop on a damn plane for Vegas with a woman you barely know, but have a serious crush on. And you didn't even call and tell me."

Shit. "I know."

Riley leaned forward in his seat, his hands clasped tightly in front of him. "What are you doing, Owen? What do you know about this woman that makes you comfortable flying across the country with her and bringing her home to meet the family?"

"To be fair, I did try calling you. Not before Vegas," he quickly amended, "but a couple of weeks before that. I needed some advice, and you didn't answer the phone. And might I remind you, you haven't called me either. For all your talk about this twin telepathy thing—"

"What did you need advice on?"

"Brooke was meeting me for coffee—like coming to my office to have coffee with me. I was having a bit of a panic attack about it."

"So what did you do?"

"I called Quinn."

Riley sat back against his seat and sighed loudly. "Seriously? Quinn? You couldn't have tried to reach me through Savannah or something?"

"I just said I was having a panic attack. I needed to talk to someone right away, and tracking you down wasn't my top priority," he snapped and then sighed. "Look, I needed to talk to someone right away, and I did."

"Okay, so you had coffee with her. That's enough to bring her home here?"

"It's more than that," Owen said defensively. "What is your problem with her?"

"Who said I have a problem?" Riley asked, one dark brow arched.

"You're asking me that? We're practically like one person, Riley. And for all your spouting about the whole twin connection, you're choosing now to pretend it doesn't exist?"

"Okay, fine. I have a problem with her."

Rather than ask him again, Owen glared and waited for Riley to explain himself.

"From everything you told me about her on the phone, she's not for you."

Owen's eyes went wide. "Need I remind you how I barely knew her that day? I had just met her! And," he added quickly, "at the time, you were the one encouraging me to pursue her!"

"Not pursue her. Not exactly."

"Yes, exactly," Owen corrected. "You told me she was the key to me getting more comfortable around people. And now all of a sudden you're outraged over it? Why?"

"She's not quite what I expected," Riley said carefully. "And to be honest, I find it odd that she got you to do all these crazy things you never would have done— and that you didn't even bother to tell me about! We tell each other everything!"

"Everyone in this family is constantly harping on me

about not being so rigid and trying new things, and now that I do them, it's wrong," Owen said with exasperation.

"Not wrong…just…" Riley sighed with frustration. "She's an out-of-work artist looking for a job! And you are her ticket to getting what she needs—a job, a chance to paint, and an all-expenses paid trip to do it. Seems like it's all pretty one-sided, Bro. Did she even pay her way on your jaunt to Vegas, or did you play the sap and take care of that too? Is she sleeping with you? Is that how she conned you into doing these things?"

In his entire life, Owen had never felt rage toward one of his siblings.

Until now.

He gripped the arms of his chair and took a minute to collect his thoughts before he said something he might regret. Riley didn't look the least bit sorry for his harsh words. "I may not be as worldly as you," he began with a deadly calm he didn't quite feel, "but I'm far from being a sap. You may think you know everything there is to know about women, but you don't. And apparently, you don't know me very well either. I have never—*ever*—been someone who trusts people blindly. I weigh everything out—almost to the point of obsession."

"Owen—"

"I spent a fair amount of time getting to know Brooke. And on top of that, I know her uncle. He's a mentor and a good friend. I trust him. He didn't have a problem with my taking Brooke to Vegas. Why? Because he trusts me as well. He believes in me, and more than that, he looks out for me." He stood and stared down at his twin. "Which is more than I can say about you."

"That's what I'm trying to do here," Riley snapped.

"A girl like her...Owen, you're my brother, my twin brother, and I love you, but Brooke is way out of your league!"

For a minute, all Owen could do was stare. "Out of my league?" He paused. "You know, when I did talk to you about her, you did everything you could to encourage me to get to know her! And now that I have..."

Riley sighed. "The way you described her and the way she is...let's just say I didn't envision her to be this...this—"

"This what?" Owen asked, teeth clenched.

"She reminds me of those girls in school—all cool attitude with a hint of bitchiness. Do you remember how girls like her used to torment the shit out of you in school? Why—*why!*—would you even want to associate with someone like her?"

"She's nothing like that," he replied defensively. "Have you witnessed her being bitchy at all? And believe me, the way this weekend has gone, she'd have every right."

Riley shook his head dismissively. "She's just going to mess with you and break your heart."

It wasn't as if the same thing hadn't gone through Owen's mind since meeting Brooke, but hearing his brother say it stung more than he thought possible. "And what if she does?" he yelled and immediately hated how loud he was being, how out of control he felt.

"I'm just looking out for you," Riley said, doing his best to remain calm.

Owen shook his head and then looked down at his brother, who was still sitting. "My whole life I never once asked you to fight my battles," he began with a tremor in his voice. "But you always stepped up and defended me. For years I've lived on my own and taken damn good care of myself. I've been in relationships before—not as many as you, but I have dated enough women that I know how I feel. All of the women who came before Brooke? Some of them weren't very nice. Some of them were out-and-out boring. And you know what? You met most of them and didn't say a damn word. If you're looking out for me, why didn't you see the negative in them, huh? Or do you have such little faith in me that you don't think I deserve to date a beautiful woman?"

"That's not what I'm saying."

"It's exactly what you're saying. Nobody questioned any of you about the beautiful women you dated. Only me," he added sadly. "And you know what? Maybe Brooke will break my heart. Everyone gets their heart broken at one time or another. And if she does, I can tell you right now I wouldn't regret or change a damn thing."

And with that, he turned and strode back into Quinn and Anna's house.

He didn't look at or talk to his father or brothers, all of whom he passed on his way through the house. His sole purpose was to find Brooke and leave. When he found her in the living room with the women, he walked over and held out his hand. "We're leaving."

She stood and looked at him warily. "Are you okay?"

"No. We just...we need to go," he said quickly. Then he turned toward Anna. "I'm sorry to leave like this. Congratulations. Your daughter is beautiful." And before Brooke could do more than wave, he led her across the room and out of the house.

"Owen!" Brooke cried once they were outside. "What's going on?"

He didn't speak until they were in the car and pulling out of the driveway. "I had… Riley…" He paused and let out a heavy breath. "We had an argument. And rather than stay and make a scene, I thought it best if we leave."

"Oh…okay. So…we're just going back to Aidan and Zoe's?"

"I'd like to see if we can get a flight out tonight."

"We have flights booked for tomorrow morning," she reminded him. "I don't think we need to—"

"I'd rather leave tonight," he said curtly. "I…I just don't want to be here anymore."

"Owen—"

With a huff, he glared at her. "Look, I know you don't understand it, and quite honestly, this is something new for me as well. I've never felt like this! And I know what's going to happen if we stay. Aidan's going to come over and try to calm me down, and you know what? Right now I don't want to calm down. Right now I'm entitled to be angry. I'm sorry if you don't agree."

"That's not what I'm saying."

They pulled into Aidan and Zoe's driveway and parked. Without looking at her—Owen was studying his hands on the steering wheel—he sighed. "Can we please see if we can fly back to Chicago tonight?"

Nodding, Brooke softly replied, "Okay."

Together they walked up to the apartment over the garage, and Brooke immediately pulled out her tablet and began researching flights to Chicago. There were some, but…

Owen was packing—and not slowly and methodically

like he normally did, but pretty much tossing everything he had with him into his bag. Within minutes he was done. "Have you found any flights?"

Brooke walked over to him and gave him a sad smile. "There are two I think we can make. But neither is a direct flight, and both carry some hefty fees for changing." She studied him for a moment. "Are you sure you don't want to stay? We can go to a hotel if you don't want to be here. If you're that certain you don't want to see your family right now, we can call a cab and leave the car here with the keys and just…go." She grabbed his hands and squeezed. "I hate to see you this upset."

Yeah, well…he wasn't so thrilled to be feeling this way either.

Five minutes ago he was certain he wanted to get on a plane and leave. But now? Brooke's thumbs were caressing his wrists, and it felt…good. Really good. And if he wasn't imagining it, she had moved a little bit closer. He could smell her perfume, feel the heat coming from her body. Owen refused to believe for even a minute that Riley was right. Brooke wasn't using him. What they had shared in the past week? No one was that good of an actress.

"What can I do?" she asked softly. And then, yes, she definitely moved closer. They were chest to chest, and looking down, he could see her nipples had hardened.

And damn if *that* didn't affect him.

Maybe now wasn't the right time. He knew his emotions were too close to the surface, and yet…

As if reading his mind, Brooke took a step back, pulled her shirt up over her head, and gave him a sexy smile. It was all the encouragement he needed. And for the first time in his life, Owen was a little bit selfish.

He took.

And he wasn't gentle.

And damn if it didn't feel good.

Chapter 9

No one came to talk to him.

Not really.

Aidan came to the door that morning as planned and drove them to the airport. Brooke didn't know enough about the Shaughnessys to say for certain whether it was normal or not, but she certainly felt the tension all the way to the airport and on the flight home.

Back in Chicago they took a cab to her uncle's place. She had told Owen he didn't have to come with her, that he should just go back to his own place, but he reminded her that his place was a hotel room and no one was waiting for him there. It was easy to forget that little fact about him not living there, when it hit her: she didn't know where exactly he did live.

"Where's home for you?" she asked, her hand wrapped in his.

Owen looked at her like he didn't quite understand the question. "We were just there. North Carolina."

She shook her head. "I know that's where you're from, but you don't live there anymore. Otherwise we would have stayed at your place rather than staying at your dad's and then at Aidan's. When you're done here in Chicago, where do you go home to?"

For a minute, he went quiet, and then he shrugged. "I have a place back near DC. It's as close to a home as I have right now."

"Just right now?"

Owen nodded. "When I took on this promotion that had me traveling all over the country, it seemed a little pointless to have a home I'd be paying bills on when I wasn't living there. So I have a small loft close to the Albert Einstein Planetarium, which is part of the Smithsonian. That's where I'm hoping to stay once the lecture series is done."

"When does it end?"

"Red Rock is the official end of it," he said quietly. "I know we haven't talked about it…not really, but—"

Brooke quickly cut him off. "Let's not talk about it right now." She put her head on his shoulder. "We can talk about it later. You don't owe me an explanation, Owen, and I certainly respect your wishes. Uncle Howard never should have interfered."

He kissed the top of her head. "But then we wouldn't have met."

She couldn't help but smile. "Probably not." Straightening, she looked at him. "But I'd like to think it was still possible. That maybe while I was visiting Uncle Howard at work, our paths would have crossed."

Owen rested his forehead against hers. "I probably would have mumbled something lame and walked away."

She chuckled. "And I would have thought you were very endearing and found a way to get to know you. I'm persistent like that."

"I enjoyed when you were texting me," he admitted. "I know I didn't respond, but…they were the highlight of my day."

"Then I'll have to remember to text you now that we're back and you'll be on the road." And for a minute, her heart squeezed hard in her chest. Their relationship certainly wasn't traditional, and they had gone from barely knowing one another to lovers rather quickly, but the thought of not seeing him every day was a little hard to deal with right now.

The cab pulled up in front of Howard's town house, and Owen paid the driver as they stepped out and collected their bags. Hand in hand, they walked up the front steps and inside. "We're home!" Brooke called out.

"Are you sure he said he was going to be home? I thought he had classes today."

"When I spoke to him last night, I told him when we'd be home, and he said he'd be here." She put her suitcase down and walked down the hall toward the kitchen. Then went to the living room. And then to Howard's office. She turned and looked at Owen. "I guess you're right. Maybe he wasn't fully awake when we talked. He did sound tired."

"That's probably it."

Brooke took Owen by the hand and led him back to the kitchen. "It's almost lunchtime. Do you want to go and grab something?" She looked in the refrigerator and didn't see anything she could put together for a decent meal, and she made a mental note to go food shopping that afternoon. "There's a good deli around the corner. We can grab some sandwiches and come back here if that works for you."

Owen nodded, but she could tell he was distracted. "Hey," she said softly, touching his arm. "You okay?"

"Something's off," he said cryptically. "Howard is as sharp as a tack. I find it rather odd that he said he'd be home and then isn't."

Brooke waved him off with a soft chuckle. "You've never been around him when he's relaxing at home. He's easily distracted. Like I said, it was a little late when I called him with our travel plans, and he was probably half-asleep." She looked down at herself briefly and then back to Owen. "I'm going up to change. I feel like I've been in the same clothes for days, and even though everything's clean, I would love to put on something different. I'll be down in five minutes." She gave him a quick kiss on the cheek and then stepped around him to go up the stairs.

There was a spring in her step, and Brooke realized that even with the negative way their trip to North Carolina ended—and even though Owen still wouldn't tell her what he fought with Riley about—she was happy. Genuinely happy.

Owen was like a breath of fresh air for her. For so long, she'd dated men who were just…wrong for her. They were dating her for the wrong reasons. Back in high school, it was because she was popular and pretty and a pageant queen. As she had grown older, her relationships still seemed to be pretty superficial. Men didn't take her seriously. She was arm candy—expected to look pretty but not have too much to say and certainly not have an opinion. Especially those men who were encouraged by her parents.

How archaic was that?

She slipped into her bedroom, quickly stripped off her capris and T-shirt, and found a pair of jeans and a light sweater to put on. The temperature outside was quite a bit cooler than what they'd left back on the Carolina coast, but the day was still beautiful and mild. Looking in the full-length mirror, she smiled. Casual and comfortable was such a blessing, and living with her uncle meant she could dress this way without any snarky comments from her mother about her unfortunate appearance.

Just thinking about it made her giggle, and she decided to complete her look with a pair of tennis shoes.

Just because she could.

A quick glance around the room showed that everything was in its place. She threw her dirty clothes into the laundry hamper and then left the room. Howard's bedroom door was slightly ajar, she noticed. She paused and realized he always left the door wide open. Maybe he had been in a hurry. Stepping closer she went to push it open and froze.

And then screamed.

———— ᜰᜰ ————

Everything in Owen froze for a second at the sound of Brooke's scream. Then he sprang into action and dashed up the stairs. There were half a dozen doorways, and he quickly found her—hovering over Howard.

"Holy shit," he hissed as he came into the room and dropped to his knees beside her, pulling his phone out and calling 911. Beside him, Brooke was administering CPR and talking to Howard to try to wake him. Owen wasn't a doctor, but he knew his friend did not look well. If they hadn't come home now…

Brooke started to cry. "You need to wake up," she was sobbing. "Please, Uncle Howard! Wake up for me!"

As gently as he could, Owen moved her aside and took over the CPR. "Go downstairs and open the door for the paramedics. They should be here any minute."

"I don't want to leave him," she cried. "Owen, I can't... I can't lose him!"

He knew she needed comforting, and he also knew he wasn't the best at that. Right now they needed to be calm and in control—he'd console her after the paramedics arrived. Until then... "I'm here with him, and I need to keep this going. Please open the front door and direct them when they get here." His tone was firm, and Brooke seemed to sober up. With a quick nod, she ran down the stairs.

Owen knew the basics of what he was doing, but without knowing why Howard was unconscious, he was afraid of doing more harm than good. He looked around the room distractedly and didn't see anything out of place. Once they had his friend stabilized, Owen knew he should call the university and see the last time anyone had seen Howard. He only wished he knew that information now.

A few minutes later, there was a loud ruckus downstairs, and he knew the paramedics had arrived. As soon as they entered the room to take over, Owen jumped out of their way. Brooke had come back up and answered as many questions as she could while Owen held her close. He could feel her trembling, and he had no idea how to make her feel better.

They followed the paramedics down the stairs, and Brooke asked if she could ride in the ambulance. They explained why she couldn't, and Owen assured her that he'd get her there as fast as possible. As soon as the ambulance pulled away, they locked up the house and ran to Brooke's car. Owen was a little more familiar with driving in the city, and although they couldn't keep up with the emergency vehicle, he knew they'd arrive not far behind.

Brooke was silent for the entire drive, and when he pulled up in front of the hospital, he let her out before parking the car. When he joined her several minutes later, she was pacing in the waiting room.

"Any news?" he asked.

She shook her head. "It's too soon. They said someone would come out and talk to us when they knew something." She wrapped her arms around him and held on tight. "I should have been here. How long was he lying there like that? Oh God…what am I going to do?" Then she pulled back. "I need to call my parents. They have to know."

Howard and Brooke's mother were siblings, and from what little Owen knew about the family, they weren't overly close. At least that was what he had come to understand from his relationship with Howard, not directly from Brooke. Now that he thought about it, she hadn't shared a whole lot about her family. How was that possible?

When he looked up, she was sitting in the corner on one of the sofas, with the phone to her ear, and he hated that she had to be the one to call her family with bad news. He remembered when he had to do that when he'd found Aubrey unconscious a few years back. It had terrified him—not just finding her, but being the one to have to make the call. Luckily he had a strong family; he had no idea what Brooke was dealing with on the other end of the phone.

Was he supposed to go over and sit with her? Should he give her privacy? He cursed his own awkwardness. His gut was telling him to go and sit with her, but somehow he wasn't sure if she wanted an audience.

His own phone vibrated in his pocket, and he pulled it out and saw his father's name on the screen.

"Hi, Dad."

"I take it you made it home all right," Ian Shaughnessy said as a greeting.

Owen gave him a quick run-down of what was going on. "So now we're just waiting and…and I don't know what it is I'm supposed to do."

"What do you mean?"

"Brooke's on the phone with her parents. Should I be sitting with her? Giving her space? Should I have made the call? I already know I'm going to take care of calling the university and seeing what I can find out there, but… this is her family, and I'm not her family."

Ian was silent for a moment. That wasn't unusual, especially when the two of them talked. Out of his entire family, Owen had always felt he was the most like his father. They were both quiet and kept to themselves. Ian had finally broken out of that in the past several years, but Owen was just learning how. And as much as Owen would say it was his mother who understood him, he and his father shared the same temperament.

"I think you should be nearby," Ian finally said. "She's going to need you."

"I know," Owen replied softly.

"How about you? Are you okay? I know you and Howard are very close."

"I honestly don't know, Dad. I didn't have time to think. I just sprang into action. And then I had to focus on getting us here to the hospital. It hasn't sunk in yet that something could go terribly wrong."

"Try not to think like that."

"What if he'd been lying there for days?" Owen asked as he became slightly overwhelmed at the thought. "What if—"

"What if it had just happened and you got there in time?" Ian countered.

"I hope so, Dad. I do." He looked over at Brooke and saw she was still talking.

"I have to admit, I was calling to make sure you were all right. We didn't get a chance to talk after you left Quinn and Anna's yesterday. I wanted to give you some space, but—"

"And I appreciate it. I...I don't think I've ever felt like that before."

"You kind of took us all by surprise," Ian said with a low chuckle. "You're the most mild-mannered out of the bunch. Riley didn't get into it—and I didn't ask—but for you to storm off like that, I know you were upset."

"Dad—"

"But now's not the time. I just wanted to make sure you were okay. I had no idea you were dealing with this emergency with Howard." He paused. "Go and be with Brooke, and call me later if you can, okay?"

"Thanks."

Owen disconnected the call and looked at Brooke again, and rather than join her, he called the department head at the university. When he got the information he needed, he tucked his phone away with the ringer off and walked over to sit beside Brooke.

"I'll call you as soon as I know something," she was saying softly. "Okay. Bye."

She looked...sad. Defeated.

Without a word, he took the phone from her hand, placed it on the seat beside him, wrapped his arms around her, and held her.

———

Two hours later, Brooke was holding her uncle's hand.

"I'm sorry to worry you like that," he said, squeezing her hand.

"I'm so relieved we came home when we did. When I think about what could have happened—"

"Don't," he said, interrupting her. "I'm thankful to you. To you both." Looking over at Owen, he smiled. "So tell me about your trip."

Brooke chuckled. "We don't need to talk about that right now. You need to rest. The doctor said he was going to come in and check on you, and I don't want to get in trouble for keeping you up."

Howard waved her off. "Nonsense. It will be a good distraction. Did you take a lot of pictures?"

For the next several minutes, Brooke told her uncle all about the helicopter tour and her impressions of the Grand Canyon and then how they camped out at Red Rock. "I did a little bit of painting there—we bought some supplies—and really, it was wonderful."

Owen chimed in and told Howard about his meeting with Tom Donnelly and the astronomical society.

"So does this mean you're definitely going to do the trip?" Howard asked and then smiled when Owen nodded. "I'm glad, Owen. I am. I think you're going to do an amazing job."

"I'm not so sure about that. But I'm willing to try." He reached out, grabbed Brooke's free hand, and gently

A SKY FULL OF STARS

squeezed it. "And as long as Brooke is with me, I'm sure I'll be fine."

She couldn't help the small gasp that came out at his words. "Really?"

Owen smiled and nodded. "I probably could have picked a better time to ask you, but—"

"Of course I want to go!" she said softly but excitedly, squeezing his hand back. But her excitement quickly faded as she turned back toward her uncle. "Maybe I shouldn't go. You're going to need someone here to—"

Howard waved her off. "Nonsense. I have plenty of friends who can come and stay with me."

"I don't know," she began hesitantly.

"I promise that I won't be alone," Howard said firmly. "I'm perfectly capable of finding someone to stay at the house to help out."

"If you're sure…"

"I am."

She relaxed again and smiled. "Okay. Good."

"I'm so glad the two of you are going to do this," Howard said. "I think it's going to be a wonderful experience. And being that you've already camped out at Red Rock, you'll be a little bit more prepared."

"I had never gone camping before," Brooke said with a chuckle, "but this was kind of fun. Not that I'm looking to do it a whole lot, but now that I know what to expect, it will make the trip more pleasurable."

Howard chuckled. "Your mother would have a fit if she knew you went camping. Somehow I doubt she's ever considered taking a camping trip."

Brooke shook her head. "Never. You know she

doesn't like to get messed up, and she enjoys modern conveniences far too much."

"Her loss," Howard said. "Maybe we'll leave that part out when you tell her about the trip. Both of the trips."

She nodded and smiled sadly. "I know we're going for distraction here, but...I'm worried about you. Your doctor wouldn't tell us anything. Do they... Do you know why you passed out? What caused you to stop breathing?"

Raising her hand to his lips, Howard kissed it. "I'm a little tired now, Brookie. Would you be terribly upset if I just rested my eyes for a bit?"

Sighing, she took her hand from his and forced herself to smile. "Of course not. It's important for you to take it easy. Do you want us to leave?"

"Why don't the two of you go and grab something to eat?" he suggested. "We'll talk after the doctor comes back. Okay?"

It felt like he was avoiding the issue, but she let him. For now.

Standing, she placed a gentle kiss on his head. "We'll be back soon."

Later that afternoon, Owen stood quietly beside Howard's bed. Brooke had stepped out to talk to the doctor, to get a better understanding of the news they'd just received.

"How long have you known?" Owen finally asked.

"I found out about six months ago."

Nodding, he pulled up a chair closer to the bed and sat down. "Why didn't you say anything?"

Howard sighed softly as he looked over at Owen. "Denial mainly. After all, I don't know many people who would be anxious to share the news that they have cancer."

"Did they know then that it was this advanced?"

He nodded. "You may not believe this, but…the opportunity to extend my life by a couple of months with treatment wasn't appealing."

Owen looked at him with confusion. "I…I don't understand."

"The quality of life I would have isn't what I want. I've watched several people take that route, and the pain and the sickness from the treatment are sometimes worse than the illness itself." He paused. "I've lived a good life. I've experienced great love—the kind that only comes around once in a lifetime—and I'm ready to see her again."

It took a moment for Howard's words to sink in. Owen swallowed the lump of emotion in his throat. "What about your family? Brooke—"

And then Howard surprised him by smiling. "All of my affairs are in order. I've taken care of everything, so no one will be burdened when I'm gone. But Brooke? Well, I have to admit I was torn about asking her to come and stay with me for these few months. It was a little selfish on my part. I've always had a soft spot for her. After she lost her brother five years ago, I've watched my sister and brother-in-law put a lot of pressure on her. I guess I wanted to step in and give her a reprieve for a bit while I still could."

"Lost her brother?" Owen forced the question out. Why hadn't Brooke told him about that? After all the things they'd shared, why would she leave something that important out?

Howard's smile turned sad as he gave a small nod. "Neal. He was three years older than her. Brilliant young man, like you, but his specialty was math. The way his mind worked was amazing."

"How did he die?" Owen asked quietly.

"Suicide."

"I...I didn't know. She never—"

"She doesn't talk about it. It's too hard. Time doesn't make it any easier. Sometimes I wish she would. I think it would be good for her. Give her some closure."

Everything in him ached for Brooke. For her family. For Howard. Owen couldn't even imagine what a loss like that would feel like. Losing his own mother had been beyond devastating. It had been quick and senseless and not of her own doing. He knew, given the chance, Lillian Shaughnessy would still be here with her family. To know that someone decided to end his own life was beyond comprehension.

"Needless to say," Howard went on after Owen's silence, "we were all devastated. How had we missed the signs?"

"Was he living at home?" Owen asked. "Was he in constant contact with his parents?"

Howard shook his head. "He had been going to MIT, but he had just come home for the summer break. Looking back, we all said he seemed quiet and a little withdrawn, but he was always that way. Neal wasn't social and outgoing like Brooke, and I guess it was hard for any of us to notice a difference. I thought it was the extra pressure of going for his PhD. But Neal always put more pressure on himself than he should have." He gave Owen a pointed look. "I blame his father for that one."

"You don't like your brother-in-law?"

"Never cared for the man. And I never cared for the way they raised their children. Over the years, I brought it up to my sister, but…it was too late. The damage was done."

"What do you mean?"

"Brooke and Neal were never allowed to be close. Neal was the brain; Brooke was the beauty. That's what they were groomed for." He sighed. "I was so relieved when Brooke finally spoke up and started to take control of her life. Although she's still searching for what she wants, at least I know she's doing it for herself and not to please her parents."

"She doesn't talk about them a lot."

Howard chuckled softly. "That doesn't surprise me. Her coming to stay with me was sort of an escape. After Neal died, her parents became overprotective of her. Which is natural. But the poor girl couldn't go anywhere or do anything without them hovering. It wasn't healthy for any of them."

"That's why you didn't want her going to the desert alone to paint," Owen commented.

"No. That just wasn't safe no matter what. But I want her to paint—or be out in the world doing what she loves! She's young and talented, and even if she doesn't figure out what she wants as a career until she's forty, it's still okay!"

"But—"

"Brooke needed this time to gain some confidence and try to find herself. She was never allowed to choose. I know she has a lot of regrets about her relationship with her brother."

"Why?"

"They were so opposite. But I think it would have still been the case without their parent's interference."

"Siblings do tend to be different and have their differences," Owen observed.

"Not like this," Howard said, his tone going serious. "Brooke was…well…she was a brat. There's no other way to put it. She was a bit of a spoiled brat who took great pleasure in teasing her brother. Normally it's the older sibling teasing the younger one, but that was just one of the ways the two of them were so different." He shifted in his bed to get more comfortable. "I think once she went away to college, she grew up a lot and realized she had been a bit hard on Neal. I'd like to think that had he lived, they'd have learned to like each other and maybe even become friends."

Owen couldn't imagine what it would be like to not get along with his siblings. As it was, he was completely at his wit's end over his argument with Riley. He'd never *not* talked to one of his brothers. Or Darcy. And even though they weren't all always in constant contact, there was never such animosity that would make them enemies.

"After…well…*after*," Howard said solemnly, "Brooke spent a lot of time volunteering at different schools and reached out, through her art, to a lot of the kids who were like Neal. Quiet. Shy. She wanted to do her part to show these kids that it was okay to be different and to show the ones who were being mean, the bullies, that they were wrong. It was a project she felt very strongly about. I think she'll always take the side of the underdog because she's witnessed firsthand the effects of what can happen."

And then something hit him—was that what she was doing? Was he… Did she view him as the underdog? Was he a project for her? A way of assuaging her guilt over her brother? The thought had him feeling sick to his stomach, and then Riley's words came back almost to taunt him.

Brooke is way out of your league.

She's just going to mess with you and break your heart.

"Do you think she can make it as an artist?" Howard asked, snapping Owen out of his thoughts.

"Yes," he replied, his voice confident and firm.

His answer seemed to please Howard. "I do too." Reaching out, Howard patted Owen's hand. "That's why I knew the two of you would work well together."

Guilt settled over him. Owen was many things, but he wasn't a liar, and there was no way he could sit here and lie to his good friend now. "I care about Brooke a great deal, Howard," he said softly.

"I know."

Owen looked up at him and saw a serene smile back on his friend's face. "It's more than that. I…I'm in love with her."

Howard arched a brow at him. "Is that so?"

Owen nodded. "I have to admit, this is all completely new to me. I've never… I mean… I know this is fast. We just met."

"I've told you my story probably a dozen times before, Owen," Howard said. His eyes were starting to droop, and he yawned. "I'm the last person you need to explain yourself to."

With a shrug, Owen said, "Maybe. Or maybe I need to talk it out because this is completely new to me. Things like this don't happen to me. And…" He stopped. As much as he wanted to share the revelation he was just agonizing about, this was still Brooke's uncle and therefore not the most objective person he could talk to.

"I can see the wheels in your head spinning, Owen. We've known each other long enough, and we're more than just colleagues. I consider you a true friend. What's troubling you about this?"

And then as if his mouth suddenly had a mind of his own, Owen spilled the whole story about how his family had reacted to meeting Brooke and his subsequent argument with Riley.

"You don't argue with your brother," Howard said simply.

All Owen could do was nod.

"I think perhaps you're looking at this the wrong way."

"How is that possible? Riley told me exactly what his issue was with Brooke, and it was insulting."

Rolling onto his side to face Owen better, Howard spoke, his voice stronger than it had been a moment ago. "Your brother may write songs for a living, but that doesn't mean he's good with words."

Frowning, Owen replied, "I'm not following you."

"Do you think it's possible that Riley was more upset about you not coming to him first and not telling him about all of the things you were doing than about Brooke herself?"

"I…I don't know."

"Seems to me that you and Riley always talk about everything and he's always been the one out living life and experiencing things. Your roles have reversed a little. Maybe he's not comfortable with the switch."

It made sense, Owen thought, but still…

"But that's not the only thing bothering you," Howard said as if reading Owen's mind.

It was possible that, other than confronting Brooke herself on the subject, Howard was his best bet.

"The story you just told me—about Brooke and her project after her brother died?" he began. "What if…" Owen paused and took a steadying breath. "What if *I'm* a project? What if I'm here believing that we're building a relationship, and she's looking at me as some shy and awkward guy she's trying to save?"

Howard studied him for a long moment—long enough that Owen started to feel uncomfortable. He was just about to speak again when Brooke came back into the room with the doctor.

Owen could tell immediately that she was stressed. She had a smile on her face, but it was forced. She was worried for her uncle, and he could sympathize with her. On the other hand, he wished she had been out of the room for another five minutes. Maybe Howard would have set him straight.

Or confirmed what was fast becoming his worst fear.

"Well, Mr. Shields, it looks like you'll be staying with us for a few days," his doctor began.

Owen stood, and Brooke immediately came to his side and clasped his hand in hers, and they both listened to the doctor describe what the coming weeks were going to be like for Howard.

——⁂——

"Do you want to stay here or go back to your hotel?" Brooke asked as they finished dinner back at Howard's home.

"I need to go over and get some things. Like you, I'm out of clean clothes."

She gave him a small smile. "Mind if I tag along?"

"Not at all."

It was silly that she was relieved that he wanted her to. Ever since they had left the hospital, she had been getting a weird vibe from him, and for the life of her, she couldn't figure out why. It could be that he—like she—was worried about her uncle. Either way, she certainly didn't want to be alone here in the house, and as crazy as it sounded, the thought of sleeping alone was completely unappealing.

Wow. Funny how fast she got used to that.

She rose from the table, cleared away their dinner dishes, and loaded them in the dishwasher. The silence seemed to drag, but she wasn't sure what to say to break it without having it sound forced or awkward.

"Do you want to stay there tonight or come back here?" Owen asked softly, tentatively.

"Would you be terribly upset if I wanted to stay here?" Brooke watched him shake his head and noticed the look of disappointment on his face. "We don't have to," she said quickly. "I'm fine with staying at the hotel too. I just thought maybe we should stay here and watch the house for Uncle Howard."

"Oh," he said with a sheepish grin.

"What? What's that look for?"

"I thought you were saying you wanted to stay here. By yourself. That you didn't want us to stay here together."

Ah, she thought. They probably did need to talk about this. Walking over to him, Brooke took Owen's hand

and led him to the living room where they sat down on the sofa. She took a steadying breath and prepared to put her heart on the line.

"Okay, maybe this is going to freak you out, but here it is—I like being with you, Owen. A lot. And right now, with everything going on with my uncle, I don't want to be alone. It's selfish of me, I know, but there it is. I've...I've enjoyed sleeping beside you, and I know I'm a little bit quirky about my sleeping habits and all, but..." She looked at him pleadingly. "Will you stay with me tonight?"

Owen reached out and caressed her cheek. "Of course." Then he studied her. Really studied her. She could tell he had something he wanted to say, and she figured she'd just wait him out. "Can I ask you something?" he asked, his voice barely a whisper.

Brooke nodded.

"Will you tell me why you need to sleep with the light on?"

Her eyes went wide as a soft gasp escaped her lips. "How... I mean... I don't—"

His hand stopped caressing and instead gently cupped her face. "Brooke, you slept fine without a television when we camped and when we spent the night at my father's. It was more about the light." He continued to watch her. "I just..." He stopped and sighed. "I just want to know everything about you, and this seems to be a big thing for you."

Oh God. Even though she knew this was going to come up eventually, Brooke wasn't sure she could handle it right now. It had been an emotional day, to say the least, on top of what had been an emotional weekend.

On so many levels.

His hand skimmed down to cup her jaw. "You don't have to," he finally said.

"I know," she said quietly and then moved out of his grasp. Sitting stiffly, her hands clasped in her lap, Brooke stared at the floor when she began to speak.

"You're right. It's not the television that I need; it's the light."

Beside her, Owen nodded but said nothing, waiting for her to continue.

"Believe it or not, it's not something that's plagued me my whole life. It didn't start until a few years ago. Five, to be exact. I feel so foolish every time I think about it. I mean, how many grown-ups are afraid of the dark?"

"I would imagine more than you think," he said. But he didn't move to touch her, and he didn't try to give her any statistics or facts like he was prone to do.

"I was home for my summer break. Technically I should have graduated that spring, but I couldn't seem to find a major and was well on my way to becoming a professional student." She gave a mirthless laugh. "I was so happy to be home. I needed the break, and for so long I had been feeling like I was wasting my time and my tuition. Honestly, I wanted to quit—or at least take some time off. So I was determined to talk to my parents about it."

"And did you?"

She nodded. "I got a lecture on why it was important to finish my education. They didn't care what the degree was in, just that I get one. That was their deal. They claimed it would make me look better on paper." Saying it out loud brought back all the same sick feelings she'd had that night so long ago.

"I argued my case and then just said I was overwhelmed. The pressure was too much, and once I figured out what it was I wanted to do, I'd go back and get a degree."

"What did they say?"

"My father told me he didn't believe I'd ever finish and it was a rotten way for me to waste his money. He spouted all kinds of figures at me—tuition, living expenses, textbooks, dorms… Ugh. It went on and on and on." She paused, a small smile playing at her lips. "And then my brother stepped in."

Without a word, she stood and went to the kitchen to grab something to drink, needing a minute to get herself together. When she went back to the living room, Owen was still sitting where she'd left him, his expression neutral.

Sitting down, she took a long drink from her glass of water before speaking again. "Neal and I were very different. We rarely spoke to one another—not like the way you would talk to one of your siblings," she corrected. "So I was surprised he would not only get involved in this argument I was having with our parents but that he would take my side."

Beside her, Owen nodded, and Brooke wasn't sure if she was grateful or annoyed by his silence.

"He defended me. He told them how much pressure there is at school and how there were benefits to taking a break before finishing. Personally, I thought he was a little crazy—like I couldn't believe he understood my struggle. After all, he had been through college and graduate school and didn't have any issues. And after I'd done nothing but pick on him for being such a brainiac for so many years, this would have been the perfect opportunity to rub it in my face about how he was superior to me or put me down for being a quitter or a slacker."

"He understood," Owen said, and Brooke realized he was speaking from experience.

She nodded. "He did," she said with a sigh. "Our parents were getting ready to go out with some friends. They were going into Manhattan for dinner and to see a show, and they weren't interested in continuing the conversation. They left without us resolving anything."

"That must have been upsetting for you."

Again, she nodded. "It was. But I was used to keeping that sort of thing to myself. I had plans to go out with friends later that night, so I allowed myself to focus on that after my parents left."

Taking another drink, she looked at Owen. "Would you like some water?" she asked.

"I'm good."

"So there I was getting ready to go out, and Neal came into my room and asked if I was all right. I don't know which part of that freaked me out more—the fact that he had come into my room or that he was concerned about me." She laughed softly.

Owen chuckled with her.

"He sat down on my bed, and we talked. Really, really talked. I told him about how I was struggling, about how I wasn't enjoying college and how the only classes I did enjoy were the art ones. We laughed about how many pointless classes you're forced to take, and why was I taking biology when I wanted to be an art major? Or why do they require health if you're a math major?" She laughed again. "For the first time in my entire life, I felt like we were connecting."

"That was how I felt the other day with Darcy," Owen said and then immediately apologized for inter- rupting her story.

"No...don't apologize," she said quickly. "I like learning more about you too." Reaching out, she squeezed his hand, and then they just sat in silence for several minutes. "It started raining—storming really. Thunder, lightning... It was so loud. I just remember thinking that it was so damn loud." Her heart began to beat wildly in her chest just then, as if she were back in her childhood home listening to the rain beat on the roof.

Owen squeezed her hand, and it brought her back to the present.

"My friend Kate called and wanted to know if we were still going out. Neal excused himself and said he had some studying to do. I thought it was odd since he was off for the summer just like I was, but I didn't say anything." Emotion clogged her throat as tears welled in her eyes. "If I had just said something...kept him with me...kept talking to him instead of worrying about my stupid plans," she sobbed as the tears rolled down her face.

"Brooke," he murmured and moved closer, putting his arms around her and cradling her close. "Don't. We don't have to talk about this anymore."

But she wasn't listening. She'd come this far, and Owen deserved to know everything. "Kate and I talked for a long time, probably another half hour, trying to figure out what we should do. I was getting ready to hang up with Kate when there was a loud boom of thunder and I remember seeing the entire block light up from the lightning. Then the lights went out. I screamed," she said with another small laugh. "I don't even know why, but the lights went out, and I screamed. Kate yelled at me for screaming in her ear, and we decided we were going to just stay in and meet up for lunch the next day."

Swallowing hard, she pushed on. "I put the phone down and tried to remember if I had any candles or a flashlight, not remembering I could use the light on my phone. So I left my room and made my way down to the kitchen, certain I'd find a flashlight or something to use down there. The thunder… It just seemed to keep going and going and going, and it vibrated off the walls to the point where I thought I'd go mad!" She paused. "And then it stopped. And everything was quiet for a minute. I called out to Neal to see if he knew where the flashlight was, but he didn't answer."

Her voice began to fade on the last word, and Owen continued to hold her. Brooke felt him place a kiss on her temple, and she realized she was clutching his shirt. He was murmuring to her, but his voice was so soft that she wasn't sure she understood him.

"I went back up the stairs to knock on Neal's door. I knocked, I called out, I banged on the door. Part of me thought he was just being funny because he'd heard me scream like a baby. Then I thought that maybe he had headphones on with his iPod or something. I opened the door to his room, and it was so dark—besides the power being out, all of his curtains were closed. I started to walk across the room, and I tripped over something. I thought it was maybe one of his duffel bags he'd brought home from school."

Her tears started again, and if she didn't cling to Owen, she'd try to reach out and touch her brother.

"Cursing, I stood up and called him a jerk for not putting his stuff away. I walked over to his desk and realized he wasn't sitting there. So I turned around, and there was another flash of lightning—bright enough that it lit up his room even through the drawn curtains. And that's when I saw him."

"Brooke—"

"He was on the floor," she cried. "I had tripped over him. It didn't occur to me what I was seeing. I dropped to my knees thinking he was asleep or...or maybe just hurt. But when I rested my hand on the floor, I felt it. It was wet. Sticky." She was openly crying now, hiccupping as she tried to explain to Owen why...what she had gone through.

"It's okay," he murmured. "No more. You don't have to say any more."

But she shook her head. "I ran from the room. Ran to get my cell phone and called 911. I had to sit there in the dark until the paramedics came. I sat there holding my brother, begging him not to go, not to leave me! Not now. Not now that we had finally talked to each other! I apologized to him over and over and over again. Begging him to forgive me!" She swiped at her eyes and took a moment to compose herself. "The storm meant that it took a little bit longer for the ambulance to get to the house. Not that it would have mattered. Neal was gone."

"I'm so sorry," Owen whispered over and over again. "I'm just so sorry."

"Sometimes I'm thankful for the dark. I couldn't see... I don't want that to be how I remember him. The last time I saw him, he smiled at me. Really smiled. So the blackout? It saved me. But now? Now I can't stand it. When I'm alone in the dark, I panic. I start to think about what I'm not seeing, and it feels like I'm suffocating." She shook her head. "You must think I'm completely insane, right? I mean, I'm twenty-eight years old. I should be over this, right?"

Owen rested his head on hers. "After my mother died, I wouldn't get in a car if it was raining," he said slowly. "My father never questioned it. I wouldn't get in a car, I wouldn't ride the bus, I just…refused. I missed a lot of school that year, but everyone understood. Eventually, I was able to do it, but it was so hard. And I know I was lucky."

"Why?" she whispered.

"Not only did my father understand, but so did my siblings. I was always more…sensitive than my brothers. And if anything, they could have had a field day on me about it. But it was like they understood it too. Everyone thought I outgrew it. Sometimes, though, if I can, I still avoid it, and it's been more than twenty years. I think about her—out in the rain and…" He paused. "She died on a rainy Tuesday in her car due to a drunk driver." He stopped and stroked Brooke's back, her hair. "You're the only one I ever admitted that to—that I still struggle with it."

And that's when she felt it.

Tears that weren't her own.

And together, they sat and held each other until there were no more tears left.

―∾―

They never went back to Owen's hotel.

He had lost track of the time, and when he felt Brooke sag against him and heard her even breathing, he picked her up in his arms and carried her up to her bed. With the small bedside lamp on, Owen went back downstairs, locked up the house, and called the hospital to check on Howard one more time.

He felt gutted. Emotionally drained. Even though Howard had told him part of the story, he had no idea how horrific it all was. Especially for Brooke. It was surprising that her fear of the dark was the only scar she carried.

Well, the only visible one.

No doubt she still struggled with a lot internally. How could she not? He felt bad for pushing her to talk, but how could he have known her fear was related to the story Howard started to tell him earlier?

Listening to her talk about her brother—about how detached they were from each other—was almost beyond Owen's comprehension. And Owen excelled at comprehension. No, for all of his issues with his siblings, they were all always there for one another. He might not have understood the things that Quinn did, didn't understand his brother's thought pattern or his interests, but that didn't stop Owen from cheering him on in his endeavors or listening to him—or any brother—talk about the things he was passionate about. And it was no different for them. His siblings never understood what Owen was passionate about, but they would listen and do their best to encourage him.

It made him sad how Brooke never got to experience that.

Looking at the clock, he saw it was just after nine.

Fairly early. He walked over to where he'd put his cell phone down and took it with him into the living room— looked out to Howard's small yard, his chess set. How many times had the two of them shared a game? Never here at the house but at different places, wherever they were. And it wasn't until just now that he remembered all of the times Howard had referred to his nephew while they played. Why hadn't he made the connection sooner?

If he learned one thing tonight, it was that life was sometimes too short, and holding grudges—no matter how much you feel you've been wronged—didn't benefit anyone.

Quickly scanning through his contacts, he pulled up Riley's number and stared at the screen for a long moment. The contact picture was of the two of them when they were five. Savannah had found the picture and programmed it into both of their phones because she thought they were adorable. He smiled as he looked at the picture. Owen was dressed as a cowboy, and Riley was an Indian. They were facing each other and laughing.

Yeah, it was a great picture.

And he missed his brother.

Hitting the call button, he got comfortable on the sofa and listened as the phone rang. And rang. And rang.

"Hey, this is Riley. Probably making music or sitting in awe of my beautiful wife. Leave a message, and I'll get back to ya. Later!"

Owen mentally cursed. The last time he had heard that recording, he hadn't left a message. He wasn't going to make the mistake again.

"Hey," he said. "It's me. Call me. I miss talking to you."

Chapter 10

FOR THREE WEEKS, THINGS WENT SMOOTHLY. IT WAS AS IF the planets had aligned and things were going their way. Owen laughed at the metaphor because he knew the odds of that happening were slim to none, and he didn't think it would affect whether he and Brooke had good fortune. But still, he'd heard the saying and felt like it fit.

Howard was home from the hospital, but he'd had to retire from the university. The entire astronomy department had thrown a big party for him, and Owen and Brooke had celebrated his career along with him. It was bittersweet.

This was a phase of life that Owen wasn't sure how to deal with—waiting for someone to die. Just thinking it seemed bizarre, but it was exactly what they were doing. Sort of. The doctors gave him three more months. And that was being optimistic. The pancreatic cancer was extremely aggressive, and although Owen admired Howard's stance on not taking treatment because of the quality of life it would cost him, he wasn't sure he'd make the same decision if it were him.

In the meantime, they were trying to carry on with life as usual. Owen had spoken to numerous members of his family—Darcy being the most frequent caller. Not to talk to him but to Brooke. He finally just gave her Brooke's number, and from what he could tell, they'd spoken several times. Darcy was suddenly interested in art and had all kinds of questions about it. Brooke loved talking to her and enjoyed sharing her knowledge with his sister. Owen found that he liked how his sister was reaching out—or that any member of his family was reaching out. Especially after the debacle on the day Kaitlyn was born.

He and Riley, however, had yet to have a conversation. They'd played phone tag, and it just seemed like there wasn't enough time in the day to do all of the things he was trying to do. Same for Riley.

Looking at the calendar, Owen saw that he had five days before he left for Red Rock. He and Brooke hadn't talked about it since that day in Howard's hospital room, but he had a feeling that, if given the choice, she'd opt to stay home and look after her uncle. Riley was traveling a bit to try to nail down some plans for the reunion of his band. Owen hadn't followed the drama too much, but it seemed now it was their drummer, Julian, who was holding out. Eventually, he knew they'd work it out, but the entertainment world was so foreign to him that he didn't even try to understand it anymore.

Behind him, he heard the front door open and smiled when he turned and saw Brooke walking in with groceries. After the first night that Howard spent in the hospital, Owen had spent the majority of his time at Howard's house with the two of them. At first, he had felt awkward about it, but once Howard was home, he expressed how grateful he was for Owen's presence there. Howard didn't want to be a burden to Brooke and thought Owen being there would be a great help to them all.

"Hey, beautiful," Owen said, taking some of the bags

from Brooke's hands. "Why didn't you tell me you were going shopping? I would have gone with you."

She smiled and swatted him away playfully. "Oh, stop. I can easily do the food shopping. It was more important for you to be here with Uncle Howard."

"We had some tea. Played some chess. The usual." And that had been part of their daily routine. While Brooke ran errands or painted, he and Howard would play chess and talk—about life, science, and even death.

"Did we hear from hospice yet?"

Nodding, he told her all about the phone call and how someone would be visiting the next day. She looked relieved.

"Okay, good. That's good." Turning, she began putting groceries away. "So, um…I talked to my mother earlier today, and it looks like she's going to come and spend a few days while we're in Red Rock."

He froze where he stood. "Really?"

Looking over her shoulder at him, Brooke nodded. "I didn't want to say anything until I knew for certain that she was coming."

For a minute, he didn't know what to say. He had automatically assumed she wasn't going to be with him—not that he didn't want her with him. He did! But he had mentally prepared himself—sort of—to go alone.

"What's wrong?" she said, turning to face him. "You don't look happy. Do you want me to stay home?"

"No!" he said quickly and walked over to touch her. Reassure her. "That's not it. I guess I just figured you wouldn't go, and I didn't want to push you about it. I resigned myself to going without you."

Standing on her tiptoes, she kissed him quickly on the

lips. "Well, now you don't have to accept it because I'll be there with you to help."

They worked together to put the food away while Brooke talked about all of her plans to help him with his group and the ways they could have some social time to help put everyone at ease.

"After Neal died, I learned to excel at that interaction. I worked at some of the local schools, volunteering with their art departments to reach out to kids who were having a tough time in school because they were quiet or shy or different. Some were victims of bullying or just had other social issues. I thought maybe we could do something artsy if that's okay with you, perhaps during the day, before the shower starts."

Owen couldn't imagine what exactly would constitute *artsy*, but he nodded anyway. She was talking—he knew she was—and yet he couldn't quite focus on what she was saying. Mainly because he couldn't help but feel like this was all wrong. That what he believed about the two of them wasn't true.

That she was out of his league.

And he was just one of her projects.

Damn it.

He knew he nodded when he should and even smiled when she did, but he wasn't feeling it. He wasn't…hell, he wasn't feeling as confident about them as he should, and he hated how old insecurities were creeping back in.

Call Riley.

Maybe that was the issue. Maybe Owen needed to prove not only to himself but also to his twin that things were right. That they were okay. But he knew he couldn't call Riley while he was here with Brooke. He needed some time to mentally prepare himself and this time, he would track his brother down—no matter how long it took—and they'd finally have the conversation they'd been needing to have for weeks.

"…I don't know how easy it would be to have everyone bring canvas and paint, but maybe some sketch pads or something—"

"I have to go," he interrupted her and immediately realized how awkward he sounded. "Sorry."

Brooke looked at him oddly. "Are you sure you're all right?"

He nodded. "I have some calls to make. Things I've been putting off, and…it would probably be better for me to do them back at the hotel."

Her shoulders sagged, and her expression turned sad, and for the life of him, Owen wasn't sure why. He wasn't particularly good at reading situations like this, and right now, he was more focused on his own emotions than hers.

Probably not a good sign.

But rather than say what she was thinking, she looked up at him with a small smile. "Okay. Will you be back for dinner?"

Would he?

Clearing his throat, he said, "Probably not. Besides the calls, I have some work to do for the trip, and a night in alone will go a long way to getting it all done."

She looked at the ground. "Oh."

There were many thoughts swirling in his head of things he could say, but instead he went with "I'll talk to you tomorrow." Then he kissed the top of her head and left.

Maybe it was the coward's way out, but it was what it was.

Better they both acknowledge what he was and what he wasn't.

It might make her "project" a little bit clearer.

———

"Everything all right, Brookie?" Howard asked as he walked slowly into the kitchen.

Brooke forced a smile onto her face and noted how much her uncle had changed in the past several weeks. It was hard to believe she was looking at the same man. His gait was slower, and he looked like he had aged considerably. But still...she was glad she was here with him.

"I'm fine," she said brightly. "I bought us some salmon to make for dinner. The one you like, with the pesto-dill butter." She busied herself straightening the already-clean kitchen. "I'm thinking rice with it. What do you think?"

Before she knew it, he was beside her, and she recognized the look on his face—he wasn't buying her cheery routine any more than she was.

"Owen just left."

Howard nodded. "It's all right, you know."

Leaning against the granite countertop, she sighed. "I know. But...he just seemed... Something's bothering him."

"He's getting ready for a trip he doesn't want to go on, and he still hasn't cleared the air with his brother. That's a lot for anyone to deal with. Did he say where he was going?"

"Back to the hotel to do…well…all the things you just mentioned."

Howard chuckled. "Don't look for trouble, Brooke. The two of you have been inseparable for weeks. It's not a bad thing to take a night off."

"I know, I know, but…" She paused and looked at him. "I'm telling you, there's something else wrong. He won't tell me, but…it's there. I can see it when we're talking sometimes. He gets this look on his face, and it reminds me of how he looked when we first met. Like he's uncomfortable with me or something."

"I hardly think he's uncomfortable with you. Not anymore."

She wanted to believe him, she did. Unfortunately, she had spent so much time around Owen that she knew him better than he thought.

"I told him about my mom coming to stay with you while we're in Red Rock, and he completely paled."

That made Howard laugh again. "Your mother has that effect on people."

Brooke laughed too. "Yes, on people who know her. Owen's never met her, and it wasn't so much the fact that Mom was coming here but that I was still going on the trip with him."

"Have the two of you talked about it?"

"The trip?"

Howard nodded.

She shrugged. "Not so much. We've sort of been—"

"You've both been so wrapped up in worry about me that you're not communicating," Howard said and then frowned. "Okay, do you want some advice?"

She nodded. "Please."

"Leave him be for tonight. Let him go and clear the air with Riley and get his work done. You should do the same."

"I should clear the air with Riley?" she teased and then smiled when her uncle gave her a hearty laugh.

"Not exactly," he said vaguely, pausing. But he didn't expand on his thinking. "And then tomorrow I want you out of the house for the day. Go with Owen to a museum or lunch and then dinner and just… I don't want to see you back here tomorrow night either."

"Uncle Howard!" she cried. "I can't do that! You shouldn't be alone!"

He waved her off and walked to the refrigerator to grab something to drink. "I won't be. A few of my buddies from the university are coming over tomorrow night for a game of poker and some pizza. I'll ask one of them to come early and another to stay the night."

"Pizza isn't very healthy for you right now," she reminded him.

Howard turned and gave her a sad smile before cupping her cheek in his hand. "All the healthy eating in the world isn't going to change what is, sweetheart. I might as well indulge without the guilt."

And for the second time in less than an hour, she was kissed on the head and had to watch a man she loved walk away from her.

"I was just getting ready to call you."

Riley laughed out loud. "Because we're twins! I told you, it's totally a thing! We're completely in tune with one another."

Owen rolled his eyes and settled in. "I'm not doing this with you right now."

"Oh, lighten up. You're just upset because you can't disprove this. We're freakishly in sync with one another."

"Then how come it's been three weeks and we haven't synced up? Explain that."

"Simple. We both *wanted* to talk. We both *tried* to get in touch with the other, but sometimes things get in the way. I can't explain how the universe works—that's your deal."

"Being busy has nothing to do with the universe," Owen argued, but his heart wasn't into it, and he let the rest of his argument go unsaid.

Riley was silent for a moment too. "I did want to talk to you before now, you know."

"I know."

"You never did that before."

"Did what?"

"Stood up to me and then walked away. It felt... I didn't like it."

Owen smirked. "Yeah, it wasn't quite as satisfying as I thought it would be."

"Then let's not do that again."

"Riley—"

"Okay, look. I get it. I was...I was a complete ass and completely out of line. I was a little bent out of shape, and...I took it out on you."

"What were you... What did you call it? *Bent out of shape?* Why?"

"You and I talk all the time. All. The. Time. Even when I was on tour or you were traveling and lecturing, we made the time. We tell each other everything. And then you didn't."

Damn. Owen didn't need his brother to clarify. He knew exactly what he was referring to. "It wasn't intentional."

"I know. I get that now. But at the time, it wasn't quite so clear."

There were so many questions in Owen's mind that he wanted to ask, things he needed to know, but all that came out was "You hurt me, Riley."

Silence, then, "I know. I'm sorry. I don't have an excuse—I wish I did."

"Do you think so little of me that it's inconceivable that a beautiful woman would want to date me?"

"That's not what I said."

"It kind of is. You said she was out of my league."

Riley muttered a curse. "Dude, she's...she was... You've never dated anyone like her. I was just surprised."

"No, you were rude and insulting," Owen corrected. "Not that it matters."

"Why? What happened? Are you still dating?"

"For now."

"Okay, it's a good thing I have the rest of the day free because we're not getting off the phone until you tell me everything. And I'm serious. I have nothing else to do. Savannah's out shopping with her parents, and I've got a fully stocked refrigerator to keep me going. The ball's in your court."

"Well, damn."

Riley burst out laughing. "Did you just curse?"

"I do that from time to time."

"Maybe Brooke isn't so wrong for you."

And then it was as if the dam broke. Owen started talking, and no matter how much he wanted to stop—to let Riley comment or say something—he couldn't. He shared about her brother's suicide, her fear of the dark, and her "projects" with helping socially awkward kids and how he was feeling like he was now one of those projects.

When Owen finally finished, he was breathless. He rested his head on the back of the sofa and closed his eyes, feeling like he'd run a marathon.

"Wow."

Owen couldn't muster a response.

"Am I allowed to say something now?"

"Sure," Owen replied quietly.

"First off, you're an idiot."

That had him sitting straight up. "Excuse me?"

"You heard me. You're an idiot. For a guy with such a high IQ, it's a bit shocking how your brain works sometimes."

Raking a hand through his hair, Owen struggled for a quick comeback. But he wasn't fast enough because Riley started talking again.

"So this beautiful woman who, according to you and the girls, is also incredibly sweet and humble—"

"Wait. What girls?"

"Our girls," Riley said. "Zoe, Aubrey, Anna, Darcy, and Savannah. I got an earful from all of them after you left Quinn's that day."

"Oh."

"As I was saying…you think the way she deals with her grief over losing her brother is somehow related to her relationship with you. Do I have that right?"

"Maybe…" When worded like that, Owen was no longer sure.

"Can I say something without coming off as being a complete womanizing jackass?"

"I don't know, can you?"

"Ha-ha. Very funny. You're getting a bit of a snarky sense of humor," Riley quipped. "I like it."

"Riley…"

"Okay, here's the thing. I've met a lot of women in my life. I've been involved with a lot of women in my life."

"Yeah, yeah, yeah. I get it," Owen murmured.

"No, you don't," Riley quickly corrected. "I've met all kinds of women, Bro. I've dated women who were with me because they liked me and ones who liked the persona and the fame of who I am. They're fairly easy to spot—especially to the people around you. I'll admit that I got hurt a time or two because I didn't want to see the signs, and believe me, everyone was pointing them out to me."

"So…"

Riley growled a little with frustration. "Look, maybe I'm not making sense here, but…bottom line? Brooke's clearly not that kind of woman. The girls all figured that out, and the more I thought about it, I knew they were right. And after everything you just told me, it all fits."

"What fits?"

"Dude, you're seriously not this clueless, are you?"

"I don't—"

"I can't say with any great certainty because I'm not there and I don't know Brooke like you do. But here's the thing—maybe her heart was in that place when her uncle mentioned working with you. Maybe she did see it as a chance to do something helpful for someone who shared some common traits with her brother. But as for her turning that into a romantic relationship—a sexual one—for the sake of being a good Samaritan? No way. You're wrong."

"But what if—"

"You're wrong," Riley said firmly. "Have you tried talking to her about it?"

"And say what? That I hope I'm not just one of her projects? That I applaud her dedication to the cause of helping socially awkward nerds everywhere?"

"*Nerds*? Did you just use that word? What are you, twelve?"

"What else would you call me?"

"Um…brilliant. Genius. Loyal. Amazing. Talented. Gifted." Riley paused. "Was that enough, or do you want more?"

"Be serious."

"I *am* serious, and you've got to get over this complex you have."

"It's not a complex. Not really."

"Okay, then you need to get over this insecurity. You're not that shy kid anymore. You're a successful and well-respected scientist. It's time you owned it."

Own it? Owen wasn't even sure what that meant. "I know who I am, Riley."

"I don't think you do."

Owen sighed wearily. Sometimes talking to his brother was beyond frustrating. "Believe me, I do. I know my strengths, and I know my shortcomings. There are far more shortcomings."

"Then you don't know who you are," Riley stated.

"Because from where I'm sitting, you're pretty freaking impressive. You speak to students all over the country."

"So? You perform in front of tens of thousands of people."

"It's not the same thing. I stand on a stage, and I have the band right up there with me. I'm not engaging one-on-one. I'm singing to the masses. I'm playing a part. But what you do? You go up and stand in front of these classes—sometimes a hundred or more students at a time, right?—and you engage them. Sometimes one-on-one. You make a difference in their lives."

"So do you, Ry. Everyone knows who you are. Everyone sings along with you."

"You know what, yes. People know me, and they sing my songs, but you? You change lives. What you do every single day helps the next generation of scientists. Right now some kid is looking through his telescope and wondering about why the stars are shining in the sky, and it's because of you he'll be able to learn that."

"Not exactly."

"The research you do and the lectures you give? That helps, Owen. Don't second-guess yourself. And don't second-guess yourself with Brooke. Talk to her about what you're feeling. Communication is key in any relationship but especially in a romantic one. I chose to walk away from Savannah rather than talk to her if you remember correctly. And what good did it do? We were both miserable, and it was time together that we lost."

"Even if I talk to her, knowing Brooke she'll downplay the whole thing. And then I'll let it go because I won't want to argue with her about it. But in the back of my mind, it's always going to be there. I'm always going to wonder if…"

"If you're nothing more to her than a project?"

"Exactly."

"Then don't be one."

"What?"

Riley sighed loudly and spoke more succinctly. "You don't want to be a project, then stop. Acting. Like. One."

"Okay, repeating the words louder and slower isn't helping. And I'm not acting like a project."

"You kind of are. You're insecure about this trip, and that tells people you lack confidence and therefore need help."

"That's not what I'm—"

"It's exactly what you're doing. You can deny it all you want, but it's how people see it. I don't agree with it, and I don't like it for you, but…it is what it is."

"So what am I supposed to do? Just stop being insecure?"

"Yup."

Owen jumped to his feet and began to pace. "Don't you think if it was that easy I would have done it already? Do you think I enjoy being like this?"

"You must, or you would have made some attempt at changing," Riley said.

"I have!" Owen cried out. "I went to Vegas, rode in a helicopter, camped out, and made love in a tent under the stars! I gambled, and I stood up for Darcy against this giant of a man who could have snapped me like a twig! Believe me, I have made more than my share of attempts to change! And you know what? Why should I? For my entire life, you've all told me there's nothing wrong with me. And yet now you're sitting here telling me I need to change? Which is it, Riley? What the hell am I supposed to do? Which guy am I supposed to be?"

"You're supposed to be you. Just…you with some confidence. Believe in who you are. You're a rock star, Bro. No different than me—just in a different field."

Owen gave a mirthless laugh and collapsed back down on the couch. "Hardly."

"It's true. Or don't you remember what Mom used to call us?"

The quick squeeze of his heart almost made him gasp as he began to smile. "Superman and Clark Kent," he replied.

"We're the same, Owen. You're just my mild-mannered alter ego."

"I wouldn't have minded wearing the cape a time or two."

Riley laughed. "Nah…too much pressure. Trust me. It's not so great to have the eyes of the world on you. I'd love to be behind the scenes and just be able to live my life. Especially now, with a baby on the way."

And just like that, the subject changed, and Owen felt good about it. This was who they were and how it was supposed to be. They talked about anything and every-thing, and it was always comforting when his mega-famous brother was able to show his more human and down-to-earth side. It was special to him mainly because it was something Riley didn't show to many people.

They talked so long that Owen had room service bring up his dinner while Riley prepared his own, and then they switched to Skype and ate dinner together. They talked about their family and all of the babies and how their brothers were all handling fatherhood. Conversation flowed from one topic to another, and through it all, they laughed and encouraged, and more importantly…they forgave.

———

It was after eleven when they finally hung up, and Owen felt completely at peace. He knew what he had to do, and although it didn't make him happy, he knew it was the only way he could move forward.

Standing, he collected his dinner tray, put it outside in the hall for housekeeping to pick up, and then quietly closed the door. There was paperwork he needed to do, but he was too relaxed to do it. He moved around the room—closing the curtains, turning down the bed—and then stripped down to his boxers and turned off all but one light before grabbing his iPad and sitting on the bed.

He contemplated calling Brooke, but it was late, and even though he knew she would be awake, he had been talking for hours and was relishing the quiet.

It was probably better for them not to talk. Not tonight. Besides being completely talked out, he felt… raw. His emotions had been put through the ringer during his conversation with Riley. Not that it was a bad thing—they had cleared the air, and Owen felt good about it. All of the other topics—especially their family and specifically their mother—were doing Owen in at the moment.

He swiped the tablet screen, tapped on the photo app, and immediately pulled up a picture of Lillian Shaughnessy. So young. So happy. So beautiful. Closing his eyes, Owen inhaled deeply and swore he could smell her perfume. Leaning back against the pillows, he swallowed hard, telling himself not to cry.

"It's not fair."

"What's not fair, sweetheart?"

"Just once I want to wear the cape," Owen said with a pout. "All the time Riley gets to wear it, and he doesn't share. You always tell us to share."

Lillian looked at her far-too-serious child and smiled, smoothing a hand over his hair. "Why do you want to wear the cape so bad?"

"Because that would make me Superman. I want to be Superman! Why can't Riley be Clark Kent for once?"

She stood, walked over to the pantry, pulled out a plastic container, and placed it on the kitchen table in front of Owen before taking the lid off. Oatmeal raisin cookies. Then she poured him a glass of milk and placed it next to him before taking her seat.

"Do you know why Superman is so great?" she asked, taking a cookie and breaking it in half. She handed one half to Owen and then took a small bite of her own half.

"Of course," Owen replied, examining the cookie in his hand. "His superpowers. He has superhuman strength and speed, X-ray vision, superhuman hearing, heat vision, he can fly, and he has superbreath! Did you know that? It's like freeze breath!"

With a smile, Lillian said, "Wow! That is a lot!"

Owen put the cookie down and rested his face in his hand. "Exactly. And Riley gets to do all of it."

"Does he?" Lillian asked lightly. "I don't see him

flying around the house, and he certainly doesn't have superhuman hearing or he'd be in here trying to get some of these cookies."

He looked at her and seemed to consider her words. At age seven, he knew he put a lot of pressure on himself to think things through before acting on them. No one else did, but it made him feel better. "But he has the cape—"

"It's just part of the costume. You and I both know Riley can't fly. He can sing like an angel, but he can't fly, baby." She gently ruffled his hair. "Now you, my sweet boy, you have superpowers that no one else has and you don't need a costume to bring out."

His eyes went wide as he turned in his seat to look at her. "I do?"

She nodded. "You sure do!"

"What? What is it? What's my superpower?"

She studied him for a moment. "You have the ability to see into the sky and talk to the stars," she said softly. "They twinkle just for you, you know."

He blushed but couldn't help but smile. "Mom—"

Lillian nodded, and her expression sobered. "It's true. You are the smartest boy I know, and when you put your mind to something, you can make it happen. I wouldn't be surprised if one day, the planets all lined up just because you told them to."

"I don't think so. But I wouldn't mind seeing a bunch of shooting stars or a meteor shower," he said with wonder. "That would be cool."

"Ooh…I would like that too. We'll have to do some research and find out where and when we can see them."

"You can't get a schedule for shooting stars, Mom," he said with a giggle and then picked up his cookie and *took a bite. "But maybe we can see about a meteor shower." He paused. "We'd probably have to stay up all night and camp out."*

"Then that's what we'll do."

"Really? You promise?"

She nodded. "And I'll tell you what, not only will we stay up all night and camp out, but I'll get you your very own superhero cape."

"You will?"

She nodded again. "Even though I think you are the perfect Clark Kent, especially when you wear your glasses. You're very handsome."

He blushed again. "Mom—"

"Come on," she whispered, leaning in close and kissing his cheek. "Let's sneak a few more cookies before anyone else realizes we have them."

No one made oatmeal raisin cookies like his mom.

And they never did get to camp out and see a meteor shower. Life had always gotten in the way, and there'd never been the time.

Slowly, reverently, he touched the screen, as if touching her face. "I miss you, Mom," he said quietly. "Every day."

So many times he wondered what she would think of him now—had he grown into the kind of adult she would be proud of? Would she be tired of listening to him spout scientific facts and statistics? Or would she feel sad to see how he was still struggling with being social? Or disappointed because he was so different from his siblings?

He knew the answer to all of those questions.

She'd be proud of him. She'd love listening to him, and she'd encourage him every chance she got and tell him that she would never be disappointed in him.

Because she loved him and accepted him. Always.

And at that moment, he wished there was another woman who would do the same.

———◇◇◇———

"I...I don't understand," Brooke said, staring at Owen with wide eyes.

"I think it would be best if you didn't go to Red Rock with me."

"But...why?" She was completely confused. They had been having an amazing day—they'd gone to the museum in the morning and enjoyed the smaller crowds since it was a Thursday, and then they'd gone out for lunch. Afterward they had gone to the planetarium, and Brooke was enjoying the cosmic wonder show they were watching.

Until now.

"I just feel it's something I need to do on my own," he said, but his eyes were on the screen.

She wanted to scream and demand to know why and why he had chosen right now—in the middle of a movie!—to tell her this. Her first instinct was to get up and storm out, but she wouldn't. For starters, she hated to make a scene. And second, she wasn't going to let him ignore her input. She'd make him explain himself—to her face—when the film was over.

So she sat and silently fumed. No matter how hard she tried, Brooke couldn't get back into the movie, and her mind raced trying to come up with why he was doing this. What had changed? What had she done wrong to make him want to push her away?

Was she too clingy because of her uncle's illness?

Was she making too many demands on his time?

Or pushing him for more of a commitment?

Hell no, to all of them! If anything, he had been the one pushing for their time together! Okay, maybe that wasn't entirely true, but in the beginning it had all been him. He had wanted her to go home to meet his family, and he was the one who insisted on staying with her when her uncle had gotten out of the hospital. So then why turn her away now?

She looked around and wondered when the hell this movie was going to end, glaring at Owen out of the corner of her eye. He seemed completely unfazed. Like he hadn't just dropped a bombshell on her.

When the lights finally came on, Brooke calmly picked up her purse and walked out of the theater a few feet ahead of Owen. They walked in silence until they were outside the planetarium, and then she quickly made her way to one of the benches before she turned and faced him.

"What the hell, Owen?" she demanded and felt a kick of satisfaction when he paled slightly. "What's going on with you? Why would you say something like that to me in the middle of a movie?"

"I…um…" He began to nervously look around. "Can we… Let's find someplace else to talk."

"Like another movie theater? No, thank you."

"Look, you know I tend to say exactly what I'm think-ing. I'm sorry I did it the way I did. That was wrong."

Well…at least he knows it, she thought.

"Can we go someplace where it's more private?" he asked, taking her hands in his.

And there it was again—something in his eyes, and she heard it in his voice. Something was going on, and she wanted to deny it. Ignore it. Pretend she didn't notice. Without answering, she tugged him toward the sidewalk and quickly hailed a cab. Once inside, she gave the driver the name of Owen's hotel.

Owen looked at her quizzically but said nothing. Their fingers were still entwined, and she gave him a sexy smile. And that seemed to confuse him even more.

They drove in silence.

They walked through the hotel lobby in silence.

They rode up in the elevator in silence.

When they were in Owen's room, he said her name, but she quickly put her finger over his lips to silence him.

"I don't want to talk," she said, leaning in close so when she moved her fingers, their lips were almost touching. "I missed you last night. And right now, I need you."

Maybe it was wrong. Maybe it was a little manipulative. But it was also the truth. She had missed him—missed the warmth of him sleeping beside her, the feel of his arms around her. And she had a feeling that if they started talking, she wasn't going to like what he had to say. So she was stalling. Avoiding. But that didn't for one minute minimize that she truly needed this right now.

Him.

Owen swallowed hard, his gaze dark and serious. "Brooke—"

"Please," she whispered. "Just…please."

All hell broke loose after that. She loved this about him—loved to make him lose control. While she loved it when he was tender and sweet with her—when their lovemaking was tender and sweet—she loved unleashing the beast in him even more.

His hand fisted in her hair, and he tugged, her head falling back to expose the slender column of her neck. Then his mouth was there, and she couldn't help but moan. When Owen's other arm banded around her waist and she was pressed up against him from head to toe, she knew she'd made the right decision.

This wouldn't solve anything.

It certainly didn't mean she had forgotten what he'd said earlier.

But right now it was everything she wanted.

He was everything she wanted.

Owen held her close as they both tried to catch their breath.

Brooke was exhausted and sweaty, her heart was racing, and she felt completely boneless. And she couldn't help the smile on her face.

He kissed the top of her head before he rolled away from her and sat up. She was about to question what he was doing, but she watched as he stood, walked over to the mini-fridge, and pulled out two bottles of water. Handing one to her, he climbed back onto the bed and under the sheet with her—but he didn't touch her.

They drank in silence, and Brooke knew—she just knew—this was it.

She hadn't changed anything.

She had simply delayed the inevitable.

"Brooke…"

Straightening, she took a steadying breath and braced herself for whatever it was he had to say.

"How do you feel about me?" he asked, but he wasn't looking at her, he was studying the bottle of water in his hands.

"Seriously? After what we just shared, you have to ask?" she said teasingly.

But he didn't laugh.

Didn't even crack a smile.

"I'm serious. How do you feel about me? Us? This relationship?"

Reaching over, Brooke took one of his hands in hers and kissed it. "I'm crazy about you, Owen. I love being with you and I miss you when we're not together. What's going on? What's this all about?"

She wanted to tell him she was in love with him—had been practically since the beginning—but she didn't want to scare him off. She had a feeling he was a flight risk at this point.

Turning his head, he looked at her. His expression was sad. "When you were doing your volunteer work in the schools, did you ever meet anyone like me?"

That was an unexpected turn. "Like you?"

He nodded. "You know…quiet. Shy. Socially awkward."

She made a face at him. "You keep using that phrase, and I don't believe it applies to you. Shy, yes. Awkward, no. You do just fine in social situations, Owen."

He slowly pulled his hand away. "So…did you?"

As much as she couldn't understand why, she knew he wasn't going to let this go. "Of course. That was my goal—I told you that. I worked with the kids who were quiet and having trouble fitting in. They were all great kids who just needed a little encouragement."

"And what did you do to encourage them?" he asked quietly.

Her back stiffened a little. What exactly was he implying? "I taught them how to draw and paint. I encouraged them to use their creativity to speak to others."

Owen nodded. "Did you date any of them?"

Ah… Now she got it.

And it pissed her off.

Jumping from the bed, Brooke stalked naked across the room and began getting dressed. As soon as her panties were on and her bra was in place, she looked at him. "Most of them were under the age of fifteen," she snapped. "I was twenty-three. So no, Owen, I didn't date any of them."

She quickly finished dressing and noticed he hadn't moved from the bed. And it just angered her more.

"Is that what this is all about? You think I'm looking at you as a way to ease my guilt over how I treated my brother? That's just sick, Owen. You know that, right?" she cried, and when he didn't answer, she wanted to scream. "For your information, I haven't done volunteer work in a couple of years. It was very emotional for me, and the hoops I had to jump through with the school systems made it nearly impossible to do any good. And it occurred to me I was doing it for the wrong reasons. As much as I knew I wanted to do it to show these kids that they were special and it didn't matter if the popular kids liked them or if they had a ton of friends, the truth was I was doing it to try to redeem myself! I was the mean girl! I was that bitch everyone looks back on and says how much they hated! And no matter how many kids I taught to draw and like themselves, I couldn't change what I'd done, and I couldn't bring my brother back!"

She scooped up her purse and slid on her shoes before she faced him again.

"I never saw you as anything except a man I wanted to know, a man I wanted to spend time with. You were never a scientist to me or a project or a way to assuage my guilt—you were always Owen. I love that you're shy! I love that you blush when I smile at you! Damn it, Owen, I love *you*!" Then she snorted with disgust. "But the joke's on me because it was all one-sided. Talk about reverse snobbery."

"Brooke," he began, but there was little behind his voice.

"No," she interrupted. "It's true. You can sit here in judgment of me for who I am—or who I was. And I get it because I still do it to myself all the damn time. But at the same time that you're judging me, you're doing the exact same thing you claim others did to you." She took a step toward the bed, her hand over her rapidly beating heart. "I know the things I did, and I have to live with them every day for the rest of my life. I don't need you sitting here waiting for me to do it to you."

Owen went to stand, but she put a hand out to stop him.

"Don't!" she snapped and willed her tears that were

starting to blind her not to fall. "Just…don't. You don't have to worry, Owen. I won't be at Red Rock. I won't bother you. You don't have to worry about me trying to *fix* you." Then she turned and walked toward the door. With her hand on the doorknob, she looked at him one last time. "There was never anything wrong with you that needed to be fixed."

Chapter 11

TWO DAYS LATER, OWEN LOOKED UP AS HIS FATHER WALKED into the room carrying a large, dusty box.

"What's that?" he asked.

Ian Shaughnessy smiled as he placed the box down on the living room floor. "I decided to go into the attic and see what we might have up there for the kids. I'm all for buying new toys, but I thought it might be fun to see if your favorites were packed away."

Owen had decided to check out of his hotel in Chicago early and come to North Carolina to see his family before heading to Red Rock. It seemed like a good time to get away—and it was a good distraction to help take his mind off of Brooke.

Except…she was all he could think about.

Maybe his father's trek up to the attic would help.

"So what did you find?"

Sitting beside him, Ian clapped his hands and rubbed them together. "I have no idea, but it says *Toys* on the side in your mom's handwriting, so I'm hoping we'll find some good stuff in here."

Ian opened the box, and Owen looked on in wonder. Here was something tangible—something his mother had touched, put her hands on—that no one had touched since. "I thought you went through the attic after Connor was born?"

"I did. But it was for baby furniture for the nursery.

That attic is like a black hole. It's big and dark and holds all kinds of treasures. But it's a lot to do on my own. So I'll admit, I didn't look for anything other than furniture."

Owen nodded and then watched as his father began to pull out items.

Toy trucks, trains, and cars. A jack-in-the box, a plastic baseball bat…

"Connor will love all of those," he said, imagining his nephew playing with the toys. "It will be nice for him to have a collection of toys here so Hugh and Aubrey don't have to bring so much with them every time."

Ian looked over at him and smiled. "My thoughts exactly." Then he turned and went back to pulling items out of the box. "I was hoping there'd be some stuff in here for Lily, but this box is from you and your brothers. Unless…" He fished around and smiled as he pulled out a crown and held it up victoriously.

"You think Lily will like it?"

Placing the crown on the table, Ian reached into the box again. "Not just the crown, but…" He pulled out a felt cowboy hat and then a sword, placing them all on the coffee table. "Costumes! I was hoping to make them a treasure chest filled with costumes the kids could use for dress-up."

Owen chuckled. "That would be nice. You'll have to go back up to the attic and see if you can find a box of Darcy's things. I'm sure you'll find plenty of costumes up in there. Seems like I remember her always wearing something."

Ian laughed with him. "You all went through that phase. Sports uniforms, cowboys, Indians, superheroes…you kids dressed like them all."

Owen smiled at the memory. "Riley and I were just talking about that the other night."

"Really?"

He nodded. "We talked about how Mom used to call us—"

"Superman and Clark Kent," Ian interrupted, smiling at the memory. "You two fit the bill on that. Riley in his cape, jumping around on the furniture, and you studiously reading a book with your glasses on." He laughed softly and shook his head. "I believe there's a photo album somewhere with the pictures from the Halloween your mom dressed the two of you like that. Everyone thought it was so clever."

Looking back now, Owen could see why. But at the time... "I always wanted to be Superman."

Ian looked at his son. "You did?"

He nodded. "Riley always took the cape." It sounded ridiculous to keep saying that as a grown man. Then he shrugged. "It was who we were destined to be, I guess." He hoped he sounded humorous, but when he looked up at his father, Ian's expression was serious.

"Do you believe that?"

"Dad, I know Riley isn't Superman—"

"Pretty damn close sometimes," he countered. "But... do you think we—your mother and I—do you think we pushed you into those roles? Those stereotypes?"

"Like I said, it was who we were destined to be. I was always studious. I never wanted to do the things Riley or Aidan or Hugh or Quinn wanted to do. I wasn't athletic or social. I didn't like the spotlight on me."

Ian reached over and patted him on the knee. "I'm afraid you get that from me."

"I know."

Pushing the box aside, Ian shifted on the sofa until he was fully facing Owen. "Your mother was the one with the big personality." He shook his head. "I never understood what she saw in me. I was serious and studious...always wanted to do what was practical rather than what was fun."

"There's nothing wrong with that, Dad. You were responsible. You had to be. You had six kids to take care of."

"No...I understand that. But we didn't start out with six kids. I was like that even before we got married."

That was surprising, Owen thought. He'd never much thought about his parents before they were parents. "Really?"

Ian nodded. "I was never quite as smart as you," he said with a chuckle. "I was always in awe of your intellect. But I always had my nose in a book. While my friends were out on Friday and Saturday nights, I was home reading."

"You had to leave sometimes," Owen commented. "Otherwise you never would have met mom."

A slow smile crossed Ian's face. "I went to visit my grandparents the week after I graduated high school. She was visiting her grandparents who lived on the same block." When he looked at Owen again, his eyes were a bit misty. "I took one look at her...and I knew. I just knew she was the girl for me."

"How could you know? You...you hadn't even talked to her." There was an urgency to his question because he'd felt a similar reaction the first time he'd seen Brooke.

"Owen, you and I are not men who believe in whimsy

or things we can't prove. We're practical and realistic. But I can tell you this—that day when I first laid eyes on your mother, I believed that dreams come true. I believed in love at first sight. And I believed in the power of wishing on a star and the possibility of fairy tales." He paused for a moment. "Your mom made me believe in all of those things."

Owen thought for a moment, and it didn't take long for him to conclude that he understood 100 percent—Brooke had made him feel those things as well. "Can I ask you something?"

"Of course."

"How..." Owen paused for a minute to collect his thoughts. "If Mom was so different from you, how did... I mean... What did you say when you first talked to her?"

Ian ran a hand over his graying hair, his smile still in place. "She came and talked to me first," he began. "I was sitting on the front steps of my grandparents' house reading, and she was walking by." He smiled at the memory. "She stopped on the sidewalk and looked at me and asked what I was reading. It took me a minute to realize she was talking to me."

"What were you reading?"

"*The Adventures of Sherlock Holmes*," Ian replied. "I used to love those stories."

"I remember you reading them to us when we were kids."

"You were the only one who was listening," his father replied with a quiet laugh. "Quinn and Riley were reading comic books while Aidan and Hugh were arguing over sports."

"I used to love hearing you read them," Owen admitted and then he stopped and thought. "Did Mom like those books? Is that why she came over and talked to you?"

"I don't think she liked Sherlock Holmes per se, but she enjoyed reading. She came and sat next to me, and we talked about books."

"It's nice that you had that in common."

Ian shook his head. "Not really. We had very different views on books. Your mother was more interested in reading magazines—particularly the entertainment ones or the ones that were for women." His smile grew. "She told me about all she had learned about makeup and clothes from reading magazines. I thought she was crazy. Beautiful…but crazy. I knew right away we had very little in common."

"So what did you do?"

"We sat on the front porch for hours talking—mainly your mom," he chuckled, "and her grandmother called for her to come in the house. I knew I had to do something— say something—to guarantee I'd see her again."

Owen leaned forward as if he were anxiously awaiting the meaning of life. "And?"

"And I couldn't think of a damn thing to say. She sat there smiling at me expectantly, and my mind was blank."

Again, Owen knew the feeling. "Well, you must have thought of something because you got married and had six kids," he stated, hoping to move his father along in the story.

"She was going to a party with her grandparents. Some sort of retirement party for one of their friends.

She told me how much she didn't want to go—how there weren't going to be people there her age or that she knew—and she stood up and asked me to go with her."

"Wow. She asked you out first?"

Ian nodded. "In my mind, she wasn't asking me out on a date. She was asking me to go with her because she didn't want to be the only young person there."

"Did you go?"

"No."

Eyes wide, Owen sat there in stunned silence. "Why? Why wouldn't you go?"

"Because pretty girls didn't ask boys like me out," he said and then sighed. "At least it had been my experience up to that point. So she waved good-bye and said she'd see me around, and I watched her walk away."

"What were you thinking as you watched her?"

"I thought…there goes…everything."

"Wow," Owen said with a sigh, leaning back against the sofa.

"Exactly. I felt sick to my stomach. I had laughed more in those few hours than I had in my entire senior year of high school. When she got to the front door of her grandmother's house, she turned and waved to me again, but her smile was sad. Disappointed. And it made me feel even worse. Actually, I knew exactly how she felt because so many times I had been the one to get turned down. So I knew that sad smile well."

"Me too."

Ian reached over again and patted his son on the knee. "I'm sorry that you do. I know we all experience rejection, but for men like us who already lack confidence, it's pretty devastating. I watched all your brothers deal with breakups and heartbreak, but…I never felt like they knew it at the same level that I did." He shook his head. "Not that I wished it on them—or on you. I wouldn't wish it on anyone. And yet…there I was rejecting a beautiful girl because of my own insecurities."

"Did you talk to her the next day?"

"Nope."

Now Owen knew the frustration his siblings felt when their dad told a story because right now, his father was killing him with this snail's pace. "Dad—"

"I got up off my duff and walked down the street right then and there," Ian said with a grin. "She stood there in the doorway watching me—wary at first, and then she began to smile. Oh, she had the most beautiful smile!" He looked at Owen. "Right?"

Owen agreed.

"I walked right up to her and asked her to have dinner with me—to skip the party and go out with me instead."

"Please tell me she said yes."

"She did," Ian said happily.

"Wait…but you said you didn't talk to her the next day."

"We couldn't. Her grandmother grounded her for staying out all night with me, so we had to wait a few days before seeing each other again."

"All night? You and Mom stayed out all night? You were eighteen! How could she get grounded?"

"Your mom was a year younger than me—but not really. She would turn eighteen the following month, but her grandmother was a bit old-fashioned, and it upset her that we stayed out all night. I think she used your mother's age as an excuse." Then he laughed. "Your great-grandmother never liked me much—particularly after that. But in the end, it all worked out."

"I never knew that about you two."

"Who? Me and your mother or me and your great-grandmother?" Ian teased, and when Owen rolled his eyes, he just laughed more. "Anyway, I am thankful every day that I chose to come out of my shell and take a chance. We didn't get our happily ever after…but what we had during our time together was better than any fairy tale." His voice became thick with emotion. "I sit here and watch all you kids finding your ways, finding your forever people, and it makes me so happy. You may think I'm crazy, but I talk to your mom about all of you all the time."

Tears stung Owen's eyes. "You do?"

"Absolutely. I know it probably seems crazy—after all, it's not like she's going to answer me—but it makes me feel good to talk to Lillian about how her kids are doing." He turned his head away for a moment and then looked at Owen, his expression serious. "You were the one we worried about the most."

"Why?"

"Because you're like me."

"I think it's my greatest trait," Owen said, meaning it. "You're the best man I know, Dad. I only hope someday I'm half the man you are."

"Son, you are more than twice the man I am," Ian countered. "You're brilliant and successful in your career, and you don't shy away from things that make you uncomfortable."

What? Was he serious? "Dad…yes, I do. All the time! It's why I'm here right now—because I'm hiding out!" Owen stood and paced the room, stepping around the pile of toys. "I may be willing to take on things with my job that I don't love or that take me out of my comfort zone, but in my personal life? I'm a coward."

Ian studied his youngest son for a moment and then stood. "I'm thirsty. You want a beer?"

The only time Owen drank beer was when he was home with his family. He followed Ian to the kitchen. "Sure."

Taking his time, Ian pulled out two bottles, opened them, and handed one to his son. Then he took a long pull of his before he spoke again. "What are you afraid of?"

"You mean in general or with women specifically?"

Ian leveled him with a glare.

"Dad… She's… Brooke is—"

And right then Ian held up a hand to stop him. "She brings light into your world. She makes you smile and makes you stop taking yourself so seriously. She challenges you, and you see the world differently when you're with her."

Owen nodded. "How did you know?"

"Because that's what your mother did for me." He placed his beer down on the kitchen counter. "Every relationship comes with challenges, Owen. No two people are alike, and really, you shouldn't be. When you're with the right person, you make each other better. You…you enhance one another. Does that make sense?"

"I don't know."

"Owen, look at our family. I mean look at the dynamics of all the relationships. I was shy; your mother was outgoing. Aidan hated changes of any kind, while Zoe's entire life was about making changes. Quinn was a bit of a charismatic womanizer, while Anna was a homebody. Riley could charm the entire world except for Savannah. And your brother Hugh was the worst. That boy was so steeped in the routines he'd set up for himself that he had no idea how to handle someone like Aubrey! The yin and yang. The balance."

"You've seen Brooke, Dad. I mean…look at her. And then look at me. Are you honestly saying you see us working?"

"What's wrong with you?"

Ugh. Why did he keep setting himself up for these conversations? "Dad, I'm a fairly nerdy guy. She used to compete in beauty pageants."

"Wow," Ian murmured, reaching for his beer. Then he turned to walk out of the room.

"*Wow*," Owen repeated. "What do you mean…*wow*?"

"I mean when did you become such a snob?"

Owen's eyes went wide. "*Snob?* I'm not… I've never… Why would you even say that?"

"Because that's exactly what you're being! A snob! All those years you complained about people judging you by how you looked or how you talked or the subjects you studied, and yet here you are doing the exact same thing to Brooke." He paused and took a drink. "I'm a little disappointed in you."

"I'm not—"

"You are!" Ian cried out with exasperation. "You think because Brooke is a beautiful woman, she can't be genuinely interested in you! What do looks have to do with it?"

"I told you about her life…about her brother… Don't you get it?"

"I do, Owen. I think you're the one who doesn't. And for such a smart man, that makes you foolish."

"Hey!" Hadn't Riley said something similar just days before?

"That's what I'm saying," Ian snapped. "Hey!" And then he turned and walked from the room.

"So what am I supposed to do?" Owen yelled after him. "Am I supposed to just pretend that I'm not concerned? Just…just forget what I know? I can't do that!"

Ian turned and looked at him. "You're supposed to believe in yourself! For crying out loud, Owen, we've been telling you that for your entire life! The only one doubting you is you!"

It was a tense and quiet few minutes as they both made their way back to the sofa to sit down. Owen's mind was reeling. He was tired—exhausted really. His father—hell, everyone—was right. The only one with a problem with him…was him.

And he had thrown away his…everything.

When he looked over at his father, he saw him going through the box of toys again.

"How do I get her back?" he asked quietly.

Ian turned his head and looked at Owen, his smile growing. He reached into the box and pulled out one last thing. "I think this would probably do the trick to give you the confidence you need."

It was Superman's cape.

——— ∿ ———

Brooke stared at the reminder on her phone.

Leave for Red Rock.

Yeah, that was supposed to be the plan. Her airfare

had already been paid for, as well as a three-night hotel stay. All of it was going to waste.

Dammit.

The alert was telling her that her flight was in six hours. She wished she had thought to go through her phone and cancel everything on her calendar about this trip. It was hard enough dealing with her breakup with Owen—she didn't need her phone rubbing it in.

Brooke sat on the bed, leaned against the pillows, and sighed. How the hell had things gone so wrong? It didn't matter how many times she replayed her argument with Owen over and over in her head, she still couldn't believe he could doubt her feelings for him.

And surprisingly, he never came out and told her how he felt either.

She had told him she loved him—and it hadn't changed anything. Granted, she'd done it while screaming at him in the middle of an argument, but...still. For what it was worth, Brooke was glad she'd said it.

Even if it was in anger.

"Why would you even think someone as good as Owen would want you?" she muttered to herself. "There's no way to shake this stupid perception people have of you, no matter what you do."

Her phone rang, and for a second, she thought it was Owen calling to tell her he was sorry and beg her forgiveness. She quickly reached over and grabbed the phone.

Darcy.

The last thing she wanted right now was to talk to any member of the Shaughnessy family, but she knew how persistent Darcy could be—she would only keep calling. Better to get it over with now.

"Hey, Darcy!" she said, forcing the cheeriness into her tone.

"Oh my God! Where are you? Is he okay?"

"Um…what?" Brooke asked, instantly concerned.

"Owen!" Darcy cried. "I swear I can't get anyone on the line. I had a lousy connection with my dad, and none of my brothers are answering. Dad said Owen was sick at the hotel. Is he okay? Have you taken him to the doctor?"

"I—"

"I know he's stubborn—it's always the quiet ones, you know?—but tell him he has to go to the doctor. Especially with this big meteor shower thing going on."

"Darcy, I…I don't know what you're talking about. I'm not with Owen."

"You're not?" Darcy asked, her tone going up in surprise.

"Uh…no. I don't even know where he is."

"He's in Nevada. Dad said he left yesterday. I just assumed you'd be with him. Have you talked to him?"

"Not in a few days," Brooke said quietly, although her heart was racing. Owen was sick and alone? What was he doing in Nevada already? They were supposed to fly out today! The obvious answer was that he'd changed his flight, but it didn't explain why he'd left earlier than he'd scheduled.

"Are you guys okay? Did you have a fight?"

Brooke sighed. This was definitely not a conversation she wanted to have. With anyone. "We broke up."

"Shut. Up."

That almost made her smile. "It's the truth. Unfortunately."

"Wow... I'm sorry. Was it because he's weird? It's okay, you can tell me. We all think it at one time or another. Owen's very intense and scary smart, and sometimes it comes off as weird."

"No!" Brooke cried, suddenly angry that a member of his own family would describe him that way. "He's *not* weird! He's never *been* weird! He's brilliant and sweet and kind and...I love his intensity and the way his mind works! His intellect challenges me, and I hate how no one else seems to get that about him!" Then she muttered a curse and forced herself to calm down.

"Damn, Brooke. Relax. I wasn't saying it like it was a bad thing," Darcy said. "So...if you think he's so awesome, why'd you break up?"

She gave Darcy the abbreviated version of their fight. "The thing is, just like you and everyone else will always look at Owen and think he's a little weird, people are always going to look at me and think *mean girl*. I hate it. I hate it as much as he hates the label that's stuck on him. But I can't force him to see me differently. I can't do anything more than I already have to prove I'm not that girl anymore or that I don't see him as some sort of project."

"I know exactly how you feel."

"You do?"

"Unfortunately, yes."

This was new information to Brooke. Not that she knew a whole lot about Darcy Shaughnessy, but everything she'd heard had been about how she was intimidating to her brothers, not to anyone else.

"I know everyone teases me about being small and scary," she began with a laugh. "But that's just because

I was the only girl in a houseful of men. I used to think it was fun getting bossy with them and saying things to freak them out to get my way. I guess I didn't realize I was doing it at school and with my friends too."

"It sort of takes on a life of its own," Brooke said.

"Exactly! Anyway, part of the reason I wanted to go to school out of state when I graduated was because… well…I wanted a clean slate. I wanted to go someplace where nobody knew me. Where I wasn't one of the Shaughnessys or where people didn't know I had five older brothers or that I had a big mouth."

"Darce, to be fair, everyone's kind of a jerk in high school—"

"It didn't matter. I was mean to a lot of people. I would use the threat of my brothers to get my way with people, while at home I was pushing them all away for always being in my business." She paused for a moment. "So besides being a mean girl in school, I was a complete brat at home."

"Oh yeah…been there. Done that. Except without the five older brothers. But I was horrible to Neal just the same. You at least still have all your brothers and they didn't take your actions to heart. I'll never…" She couldn't finish the statement. It didn't matter how much time had gone by, the pain was never going to lessen.

"Hey," Darcy said softly, "I'm sorry. I can't even imagine what you're feeling. I know I'm lucky my brothers all care and that they love me but…the thing is…I'm not very close with any of them either. We all joke and laugh, and we're happy when we're together, but…I'm still an outcast in a lot of ways."

"It's probably because you're so much younger."

"That has a lot to do with it, but at the same time…I haven't got anything in common with them. It kind of sucks."

"I'm sorry, Darce. I really am. I'm sure in time—"

"I know," Darcy quickly interrupted. "I know. I'm glad they're all married and they married great women who *do* get me. They're all so perfect for my brothers… You are too, you know."

Brooke sighed. "I thought so too. But it just wasn't meant to be."

"Well…I hope you and I can still be friends."

"I'd like that. A lot."

"I should go. I want to try to get Owen on the phone and make sure he's okay. I kind of feel like he and I bonded after the whole fiasco in Vegas. I hate that he's sick and alone in some hotel room."

So did Brooke.

"You said the connection with your dad wasn't good. Are you sure he said Owen was sick?"

"Yes! We were talking and he was saying how he was going to try to get a flight out because Owen was sick and he was worried and—"

"Okay, okay… I still have my ticket, and it's a direct flight. It won't get me there soon, but it will get me there today," Brooke said, worry for Owen overwhelming her. "Is Riley still in LA? He could get there faster."

"He's in London this week for a performance or something," Darcy replied anxiously. "Are you serious, Brooke? You would do that? Even though…you know…you guys aren't dating anymore?"

"Darcy, the breakup wasn't my idea. I hate it, actually.

But I couldn't stay with him knowing he thought the things he did. I told him I loved him, and—"

"*You did?* Oh my God, that's *awesome*! You have to go! You have to go and make sure he's okay, and then maybe—"

What can of worms had Brooke just opened? "One thing at a time, Darce…one thing at a time."

"Okay, you're right. Sorry. I just… Owen's the best, you know? I mean, out of all of my brothers— and I know they're all great—Owen's special. He's got the biggest heart, and I hate knowing he's alone so much. That's why I thought it was so great that the two of you had found each other. I knew you'd take care of him."

Brooke's heart actually hurt. "I wanted to…"

"Then go! Please!" Darcy begged. "Go to him. He's already a mess over this trip. I know that can't be helping him with whatever's going on right now."

Could she do this? Could she get on the plane and go to Owen? What if…

"What if he doesn't want me there?"

"Oh please. How could he not?"

Now her heart felt as if it would pound right out of her chest. Maybe this was exactly what she needed to do—to see him and make him see reason. To convince him to give them another chance!

Jumping up from the bed, she said, "I've gotta go, Darcy. I have to pack!"

"Yeah! I totally love that you're going! Promise me you'll call and tell me what's up! And I'm going to want to know everything! Like every word he says when you barge in there and demand that he take you back!

Only…wait until he's not sick anymore. You know… show him a little sympathy. And then—"

"Darcy!"

"Yeah?"

"I have to go!"

"Okay, okay! Sheesh!"

―⁓―

Twenty minutes later Brooke walked outside and found her uncle sitting alone at the chess table. "You got a minute?"

"For you," he replied, smiling, "I've got as many as you need. What's up?"

"First…how are you feeling?"

He shrugged. "Not so bad today. Your mother texted that she'll be here at five, so I'm hoping to still be feeling that way when she gets here."

"You'll have to give her my love."

Howard's brows shot up. "Excuse me?"

"I'm going to Red Rock."

And then Howard's entire face transformed from confusion to pleasure. He was positively glowing. "Really?"

Brooke nodded. "I have to. I have to go to him."

Slowly, Howard came to his feet and walked over and hugged her. "Thank God."

She pulled back and looked at him. "What does that mean?"

"Brookie, you've been moping around, and when I spoke to Owen yesterday, he sounded positively morose. It's obvious you're both miserable. So go. I'll handle your mother for you."

"I hate to just leave like this."

"Nonsense. You were always going to be leaving on this trip. You just forgot about it for a while."

Brooke couldn't help but smile. Leaning in, she kissed him on the cheek and gave him another hug. "Thank you. For everything."

"Promise me something," he said, his tone serious, solemn.

"Anything."

"Stop looking at the past. Both of you. It's time to start looking toward the future."

"I know," she said softly. "I'm going to try."

Howard shook his head. "That's not enough. You need to move forward now, but to do that, you need to say good-bye—to the past. To your guilt. To everything."

Her throat tightened. "How... I don't know—"

"This little green space I have out here is a sanctuary to me. I come out here sometimes and...talk."

Seriously, now? Now he was choosing to go back into this speaking-in-riddles mode?

"I love when we come out here and talk," she said, hoping to prompt him along. She still had to call a cab.

Howard shook his head. "Although I enjoy that too, that wasn't what I was talking about." He paused. "I come out here and talk to your aunt. And Neal."

She took a small step back and looked at him as if he were crazy. "You mean when we were younger. When—"

"No. I mean now. In the present. Hell, I sat out here talking to your aunt just last night. She'll be thrilled that you're going after Owen."

Maybe his illness was making him hallucinate, she thought. "Uncle Howard...you can't—"

He didn't let her finish. "Brooke, you can talk to those who are no longer with us anywhere you want. It doesn't have to be at a cemetery or while you're in church. This garden, your aunt and I used to sit out here a lot—have a glass of wine, talk about our day. When you and your brother would come to visit, we'd sit out here, play chess, and talk." He paused, laughed softly. "That boy was a whiz at chess, but I had figured out his strategy."

"His strategy?"

Nodding, Howard said, "He favored the bishop. Always." Then he pointed to the corner of the yard. "I had that made for him—as my own little memorial to him. I think he would have liked it."

And there in the corner of the yard was a three-foot-tall statue of a bishop. Why hadn't she noticed that before? "When did you do that?" she asked, even as she walked over to it.

"About a year after he died. I keep it there—it's always in my line of vision when I play—and it makes me feel like he's here with me." He shrugged. "But maybe that's just the wishful thinking of an old man."

She turned to him, tears in her eyes. "It's lovely. And it's perfect." Her heart hurt, her throat constricted.

Howard put a hand on her shoulder, squeezed. "Talk to him. Before you go. Just…talk to him."

Before she could form a protest, he was in the house, the door closed. Brooke stood there for a long moment, not knowing what to do or say. It seemed…weird. When Neal had died, he'd been cremated. There was no cemetery plot to go to, no markers anywhere. He had loved the ocean, and his ashes had been scattered there. Now,

as she looked down at the bishop, she smiled because...
Neal had a marker.

The spot was shaded, and she slowly sank to the grass
and sat facing the garden. A small, self-conscious laugh
came out before she could stop it. "Am I crazy?" she
murmured and then waited to see if someone would
answer. After a long moment of silence, she swallowed
hard and took a steadying breath. With her eyes closed,
she slowly breathed out and then focused on the bishop.

"I know it's too late," she began, her voice trembling,
"too late for this to really matter or make a difference,
but...I'm sorry. I'm so, so sorry." She paused, swiped
at the tears that were already blinding her. "That night—
that horrible night...I know I said that to you, screamed
it, begged you to hear me, but you were already gone.
Maybe you did hear me, but...it was too late." Her voice
cracked, and she took a minute to compose herself.

"If I could, I'd take every mean thing I ever said to
you, every indifferent shrug, every snarky comment—
I'd take it all back. I'd listen to you. Learn from you."
Then she stopped and chuckled. "Not that I would have
been successful. You know I was never very good
with academics."

A small breeze blew by, and Brooke did her best to
tame her hair, move it out of her face.

"I never understood why...why we were so different.
I look back, and it's easy to blame Mom and Dad. But
we weren't children. Not at the end. We knew better. We
could have tried harder." And then it hit her. "We both
could have tried harder, Neal. I know I wasn't perfect,
but neither were you. You were the smart one—I'm sure
you figured it out long before I did that we could have

changed our relationship. Maybe...maybe if you had talked to me like a sister rather than a nuisance..." Then she stopped, knew she was kidding herself. "I probably wouldn't have listened."

Swiping away more tears, she let out a long breath. "Why'd you do it like that? Was that my punishment? Was that your way of finally getting even with me for being such a bitch?" Her voice grew stronger, her heart beat harder. "Well...you win! It was horrible! And it was mean and cruel—far more than anything I ever did to you!" She jumped to her feet, suddenly filled with rage. "Do you have any idea what that did? What your actions did to me? To Mom? To Dad? If you weren't happy, why didn't you talk to someone? Uncle Howard or a counselor or...anyone! Damn it, Neal, there... What you did wasn't the answer!"

Another breeze blew, and Brooke cursed the fact that her hair was loose.

"You've missed so much," she said after a long, quiet moment. After she'd gotten herself a little more under control, she continued. "That night...it was so wonderful to talk to you! I learned more about you in that one hour of conversation than I had ever known before then. I felt like... I thought you enjoyed it too. That maybe you actually liked me—as a person. It made me feel good that my successful and supersmart brother saw some value in me beyond a pageant title." She paused. "And then you left. And you left me to find you. Why? Why, damn it?"

Another pause. Another moment to calm her breathing, her thoughts. She knew she wasn't going to get an answer. "You would have liked Owen. He's scary smart like you. But he's so much more than that. He's kind and sweet and gentle and compassionate. I look at him, and I'm in awe—not just of all he's accomplished but because he sees me in a way that no one else ever has. I think about how amazing it would have been for us to all have dinner together, for me to have to sit there and listen to the two of you talking about things that I didn't understand." She chuckled. "And I probably would have griped about it, and ultimately we would have laughed and found a topic we could all talk about. At least… that's how I like to think it would have been."

Somewhere off in the distance a horn honked, and she could hear a car door closing—life beyond the fence was moving on.

Just as she needed to.

"I miss you. Every single day…I miss you. I wish I had known you—really known you. And I'm so sorry that you thought that leaving this world was better than staying here." She stood and waited—hoped—for… something. Anything. Some sort of sign that he'd heard her. Did her uncle ever get that?

She wiped away her tears and sighed, looking down at the bishop. "What I wouldn't give to just talk to you one more time." Reaching out, she touched the statue, knowing full well it wasn't Neal, but it seemed…fitting. "I love you." Her voice was no more than a whisper.

Turning, she walked toward the house and felt… better. A little emotionally drained but better. If she could, she'd talk for hours, and maybe at another time, she would. But for now—for today—it was good. The wind picked up, and she looked at the chess table and saw that her uncle had left the pieces out. They started to wobble in the wind, and she hurried forward to catch any that fell. Amazingly, only one did. Crouching down, she picked it up. As she stood, Brooke studied the piece in her hand and smiled.

The bishop.

Her hand closed tightly around it, and she smiled and looked up at the sky.

"Thank you."

Placing the piece in her pocket, Brooke walked back into the house and found her uncle sitting on the sofa reading. She walked over and kissed him on the forehead. "Thank you."

He didn't ask for her to clarify. He smiled at her because he knew.

"You were absolutely right," she said.

He nodded.

Looking at her watch, she knew it was time to go. "I need to... I still have to call—"

"Go," Howard said, his smile serene. "Have a safe trip."

"Wish me luck!"

"Always, Brookie. Always."

She was about to leave the room when she turned to him. "I owe you a chess piece."

Chuckling, Howard waved her off. "No worries. I have a spare set of pieces."

Relief swamped her. "I love you, Uncle Howard."

"Love you too, my sweet girl. Now go or you'll miss your flight!"

She ran up to her room and grabbed her luggage, purse, and phone and then quickly ran back down. She had ordered an Uber to take her to the airport, and the car was due any minute. Rather than wait for a text, Brooke headed for the curb.

It was silly to go to the airport so early, but if there was a chance she could get on an earlier flight, she was going to take it.

The car pulled up, and she tossed her bags in and climbed in beside them. The driver confirmed which terminal she was going to, and then they were on their way. She contemplated calling Owen—to alert him she was coming and to check on him—but decided against it. She didn't know if she'd be able to handle him telling her not to come. No, she'd rather take the chance and show up and deal with him face-to-face.

The airport was only ten miles away, but with traffic it took almost thirty minutes to get there, and she was practically bouncing in her seat the entire time. She quickly paid the driver, collected her belongings, and ran to the ticket counter. Unfortunately, there were no seats available on flights that would get her to Nevada any sooner—the only ones that left sooner had layovers and wouldn't save her any time, so she opted to stick with her original flight.

To pass the time, she ate lunch, bought some magazines, and pretty much cursed the clock, which didn't seem to be moving at all. When her flight was finally called, she almost jumped up and cheered. And although it felt like it took forever, she knew it wasn't long before she boarded and the plane was ready for takeoff.

She fidgeted almost the entire flight. To the point that she was getting angry looks from the woman sitting beside her. But Brooke didn't care. Her mind was racing with trying to come up with what she was going to say to Owen when she saw him and…

Wait a minute.

Where was she going to be seeing him? Damn it! In all of her rushing around, she never thought to confirm he was staying at the hotel where they had originally planned to! What if—because of his change in travel plans—he had changed his hotel too? There wasn't anything she could do about that now. Once she was off the plane, she'd have to text Darcy to see if she could find out. If not, she was stuck taking a shuttle to the hotel and hoping for the best.

Sure enough, it looked like she was going to hope for the best. When the plane landed, Darcy wasn't answering her calls or texts, so with no other choice, Brooke took the shuttle she and Owen had originally booked and headed for their hotel.

Once Brooke arrived, she went to the front desk and asked for Owen's room. Part of her was afraid they wouldn't tell her, but luckily, both of their names were on the reservation.

"Yes, ma'am. Mr. Shaughnessy checked in early. He is in room 1010. If you walk to the far left side of the lobby and turn right, you'll find the elevators there." The clerk handed her a key and wished her a pleasant stay.

"Thank you," she said, relief flooding her. It was all she could do to keep from running across the lobby, but that's not to say there wasn't a whole lot of pep in her step! At the elevators, she was back to being nervous as she hit the button and waited, and she was thankful that when the elevator arrived and the doors opened, she was the only one boarding.

"Don't be nervous, don't be nervous, don't be nervous," she chanted. "If nothing else, you know he's polite and won't throw you out." That was little comfort actually. She didn't want Owen to be polite; she wanted him to be happy to see her. Thrilled to see her. Hell, she wanted him to be so relieved that she was there that he would fall to his knees in gratitude.

Wishful—and ridiculous—thinking, she knew.

The elevator dinged as it stopped on the tenth floor, and Brooke stepped out and got her bearings. With the sign pointing her in the right direction, she took a steadying breath, turned to the right, and made her way down the hall.

At room 1010, she stopped. Looking down at herself, she straightened her top and smoothed down her skirt before quickly running her fingers through her hair. She almost reached into her purse for her lip gloss but knew she was just stalling for time.

"Just do it. Just knock. It's not hard."

And yet...she didn't.

For a solid minute, Brooke stood there and wondered if she had made the wrong decision. Maybe this wasn't the time to act rashly and do something so out of the—

Then she remembered the last time she had done something impulsive—when she and Owen had hopped a plane to Vegas together.

And it was the best decision she'd ever made.

Lifting her hand, she knocked on the door and said a silent prayer that this impulsive trip would turn out even better than the last one.

She swallowed when she heard the doorknob rattle. The door opened, and her smile and greeting fell when she got a look at Owen. He was pale and shirtless. His dark hair was in complete disarray, and he had a large bandage covering the right upper part of his chest.

"Oh my God," she whispered, her hand already reaching out to him. "What happened to you?"

Chapter 12

OWEN WAS PRETTY SURE HE WAS HALLUCINATING. THAT WAS the only explanation he could come up with for seeing Brooke at his door. Before he could say a word, she was carefully backing him into the room and closing the door.

Her hands were gently touching his head, his cheeks, before raking through his hair. It all felt so good, so right...

"Come on," she said, "you need to be sitting down." They walked across the room to the bed, and Owen willingly sat and rested against the stack of pillows. "What do you need?" she asked. "What can I get you?"

His head finally cleared enough to realize that he wasn't hallucinating. She was here. She was real. "What are you doing here?"

Brooke kicked off her sandals and smiled at him before walking over to the mini-fridge and getting two bottles of water. She handed one to him. "I heard you were sick, and I was worried about you."

Sick? How...? Who...?

"Darcy called me. She didn't know... She hadn't heard..." She stopped and sighed. "Don't be upset with her. She was just concerned about you and thought I was here with you. After we talked for a little bit, I knew I couldn't stay away. Now what's going on? Have you seen a doctor?"

"Doctor? I'm not—"

"You look very pale," she said, sitting on the edge of the bed beside him, feeling his forehead again. "But you don't have a fever." Then her eyes went to the bandage. "What happened? Did you get hurt?"

He shook his head.

"Owen, please. What's going on?"

Sitting up a little straighter, he grimaced with pain and cursed under his breath. Why had he thought this was a good idea? He reached up, gingerly found the edges of the bandage, and slowly pulled it away from his skin.

Beside him, Brooke gasped. "Owen! What did you…?" She reached out, but he immediately stopped her.

"Don't touch it. Not yet."

"Why…? When…?"

The cool air on his skin actually felt good. He reached over to the nightstand, found the ointment he was supposed to use, and gently applied it. When he was done, he looked at Brooke with a lopsided grin. "I thought it would be cool."

A shy smile played at her lips. "It's a tattoo."

He nodded. "I know."

"You got a tattoo," she said as her smile blossomed.

"I did."

"It's very—"

"Painful," he interjected. "In case you were wondering, the word is *painful*. Tattoos hurt like hell. I was completely misinformed on this."

She laughed, and it was the sweetest sound in the world. "Who told you that? Everyone knows tattoos hurt!"

"Riley. I'm totally going to get even with him for this. He told me it would hurt a little, but this feels like my skin is on fire!"

"Oh no! Are you sure it's not infected?" she asked, concern lacing her voice.

Owen shook his head. "It's normal. I just have a low threshold for pain. I talked to the artist and Riley and went online and did some research, and it's all normal. It should start to feel better by tomorrow."

"So what can you do in the meantime?"

"The ointment, letting it breathe, and ibuprofen are about it." He shrugged and then winced. "I'll live."

"That's good," she said, still smiling. "I'm very glad to hear that." One of her hands came to rest on his stomach. "I can't believe how much I want to touch it. It's amazing, Owen. Truly amazing. What made you decide to do it? You never mentioned anything like this before."

"I had a lot of heart-to-heart talks in the past week, first with Riley and then with my dad. And in each of those conversations, this topic kept coming up."

"Tattoos?"

He chuckled. "No. Not tattoos but…" He pointed to the art.

"Superman?" she asked with amusement.

He nodded and then told her the story of how Superman played an important part in his life and his perception of himself. At first, he felt a little bit foolish, but the look on her face was one of wonder and understanding.

Because she understood him.

Probably better than he understood himself.

"This is to remind me that I'm stronger than I think I am. And that I don't need the cape," he added with a quiet laugh.

"I don't know about that," Brooke said, laughing with him. "It could be a good look on you."

"If you think it is, then I'll gladly go and get one," he said, his hands twitching with the need to reach out and touch her.

But he couldn't.

Not yet.

"Careful… I may take you up on that!" They were laughing, and then they weren't. Things grew quiet, and Brooke lowered her gaze.

"I'm sorry," he said gruffly. "I hurt you. It was never my intention."

She looked up at him then. "I didn't give you any reason to think any differently. I don't have a very good track record, and if I were you—"

He pressed a finger against her lips to stop her words. "No. I knew. Deep down, I knew I was wrong in what I was thinking. All along I kept second-guessing myself and wondering how an amazing woman like you could ever want to be with a man like me. I was looking for excuses to back up my crazy logic. It was wrong of me, and I'm so sorry, Brooke."

Her blue eyes were glazed with unshed tears as she looked at him. "I want to hug you, but I don't want to hurt you!"

In that moment, he cursed the placement of the tattoo. Why hadn't he gone for the arm? Why had he listened to Riley about the chest being the best spot? But his need to touch her, to hold her, was stronger than his need to not be in pain. Wrapping his arms around her, he gently pulled her in close and claimed her lips with his.

After several minutes, they broke apart, breathless.

"I missed you," she said, their foreheads resting against each other. "I missed you so much. I know it was only five days, but—"

"I missed you too. That's why I left and went to visit my dad. I knew if I was in Chicago I wouldn't be able to stay away. But I was so ashamed of myself that I didn't know what else to do."

"This morning my phone beeped to remind me of our flight. I was so sad because I wasn't going to be here with you. I wanted to be—even though I was mad at you, I still wanted to be here with you. And it has nothing to do with the meteor shower or your group of students, Owen. I just wanted to be with you."

He smiled and kissed her gently one more time. "This is where I want you to be. Right beside me. In my arms. Always."

She shifted on the bed so she was lying on the side opposite his tattoo and rested her head on his shoulder. "I like the sound of that."

"I love you," he said, his voice deep and confident. "I should have said it to you the other day. Hell, I should have said it weeks ago." Owen moved so he could look in her eyes. "I love you."

And then she smiled—the smile that had turned him upside down from the very first day. "I love you too."

And just like that, everything was right with his world.

—∿—

They talked for hours.

Owen wasn't even sure of the time.

All he knew was Brooke was lying beside him and it was wonderful.

Across the room, her phone was beeping with what sounded like a ton of incoming texts. She finally excused herself to make sure everything was all right. When she fished her phone out of her bag and looked at it, she started laughing.

"Everything okay?"

She nodded, walked back over, and climbed onto the bed. "They're all from Darcy. She wants to know if you're all right and if we're all right, and then she wants a picture of the tattoo."

He couldn't help but laugh. Leave it to his sister to make so many requests.

"And she said to tell you that since you got one, it totally clears the way for her to get one too."

Owen reached over, took the phone from Brooke's hand, and immediately texted Darcy that he wanted to be left out of that discussion. There was no way he wanted to be held responsible for his sister getting a tattoo.

He let Brooke take a picture of his Superman emblem and grinned when she looked at him and told him how sexy it was.

Best. Idea. Ever.

Sort of. If it wasn't for the pain.

After sending a few more messages to Owen's sister, Brooke stood up, turned off her phone, and placed it back in her bag. Then she walked over to the wall of windows and sighed happily. "Quite the view, Dr. Shaughnessy."

"I'll say."

She looked over her shoulder at him and rolled her eyes even as she laughed. "I was talking about the view from the window—of Red Rock? It's spectacular."

Owen rose, walked over, and stood behind her,

wrapping his arms around her waist. "It was either the canyon or the Strip. I opted for the canyon for obvious reasons."

"It's a great view—not as great as the one we had in our tent the last time, but this way we have a lot more comfort."

He smiled and kissed the top of her head. "Air-conditioning and a king-size bed are definite perks, but I kind of enjoyed our pallet on the ground in our mesh tent. It was cozy, and it meant you had to be close to me the whole time."

"I don't think you'll ever have to worry about that. I find I like being close to you when we sleep."

He hugged her, and even though it made him wince briefly as her shoulder hit his freshly inked skin, it was worth it.

"I could look at this view all night," she said.

"Me too." But he wasn't looking at the canyon. He was looking at her.

As if sensing his gaze, she turned and looked at him. "Why don't we order dinner and watch the sunset from here?"

"I like the sound of that."

Within minutes they'd called in their order, and Brooke made sure Owen sat and rested while she unpacked. When she muttered a mild curse, Owen asked her what was wrong. "I didn't call to check on Uncle Howard or to make sure my mom got in okay. It's kind of late there, but—"

"Call your mom's phone then. That way if Howard's sleeping you won't wake him up."

She agreed, immediately taking out her phone and

sitting on the small sofa across the room to make the call. While she did that, Owen walked over to the desk and picked up his own phone. He pulled up Darcy's name and started a text to her.

Hey, brat
Hey, brainiac
Thank you
For what?
eye roll Seriously?
So you guys are good? Brooke is still there?
Yes
Good. Then my work here is done
You're a little bit of an evil genius
I know
I had planned on going to her after the trip
Too long
I agree. This way is much better
Cool tattoo btw
Glad you approve
Does it hurt?
More than you could ever imagine. I wouldn't wish this pain on my worst enemy
Nice try. I still want one
Talk to Dad
eye roll
I'm serious.
We'll see. I don't even know what I'd get
In trouble. You'd get in trouble
Lol! I love that you're finally getting a sense of humor
You can thank Brooke for that

> *I knew she was good for you*
> She's the best
> *Then why are you wasting time texting with*
> *me? Go and catch up on lost time!*
> I think I will. Night, brat
> *Night, brainiac*

He finished the exchange with a smiley face emoticon, and Darcy replied with a smiley face sticking its tongue out.

Which was no less than what he expected.

Putting his phone away, he looked over and saw Brooke smiling as she spoke softly, and Owen felt... happy. At peace. And if it weren't for the stinging pain on his chest, he would say everything was perfect.

Soon.

Within minutes, their dinner was delivered, and Brooke hung up her phone and put it away again.

"Everyone okay? Did your mom make it in all right?"

"She's there and settling in and a little disappointed that I wasn't there, but when I told her why, she was very happy. She said Uncle Howard has been singing your praises, and now she wants to meet you even more."

That made him feel a little sick to his stomach, but it was a problem for another day. He wasn't going to let anything ruin this night.

Together they sat next to the window and watched the sun setting as they ate and talked about their plans for while they were there. Their original plans allowed them a full day of sightseeing before the rest of the group arrived, and Brooke mentioned the possibility of going shopping the next day for art supplies.

"I know I should have planned better, but I didn't bring anything with me again. I can make do with the same kind of stuff I purchased the last time."

"You know," he began, putting his utensils down, "you never showed me what you painted the last time. I was so curious, but I figured you'd show me if you wanted to."

Then he noticed her blush. "I'm sorry... I don't mean to pressure you. I just thought—"

"I painted you," she admitted shyly.

"What?"

Brooke nodded. "I did. I finally had the opportunity to paint in the desert, and I painted you."

Owen wasn't sure what to say to that. He was... stunned. But flattered. "Really?"

She nodded again. "You were looking through the telescope, and you just looked so...intense and at peace at the same time. The canyon made for a beautiful backdrop, but the majority of the painting was you. I was so embarrassed. I didn't want you to think I was weird or anything. That's why I quickly put it in the Jeep."

"I had no idea," he replied, feeling somewhat pleased and honored by her admission. "When we go home, can I see it?"

"Sure."

But she didn't sound sure; she sounded hesitant.

"Brooke, really...if you'd rather not—"

"I painted another picture of you," she blurted out.

His eyes went wide. "You did?"

"Uh-huh."

"When?"

"Right after we met. My uncle had set up a room for

me to paint in, but I hadn't felt any inspiration. For two weeks, I felt so guilty because he went through all the trouble of setting it up and buying me supplies, and I wasn't using them. Then the day after I met you, I went into the studio and thought I'd paint what I pictured in my mind—what we'd talked about with the desert—and I ended up painting you."

"I…I don't know what to say."

"Say you don't think I'm a weirdo," she joked, but he sensed there was a hint of vulnerability there.

"I certainly don't think that. I'm flattered, Brooke. I think your work is amazing, and to know you considered me to be a worthy subject is just…well…it's humbling."

"You haven't seen them. You may hate them."

He laughed. "More than the nudes in the cages?"

She laughed out loud with him. "Please don't ever compare my work to those! If it ever comes to that, I swear I'll give up art forever!"

Reaching across the table, he took her hand in his. "Don't ever do that. You have such a gift, it would be a crime to give it up and not share it with the world. Promise me you never will."

"Owen," she said with a sigh.

"I know. I get it… I know we're just joking around, but I meant what I said. You have such an amazing gift, and I want to see you get the attention for it that you deserve."

She smiled but shook her head. "I wish it was easy to make happen, but I haven't really been trying all that hard. Maybe someday… I'm not in a rush. Not really. I'll be teaching this summer, and I plan on making my way around all the galleries in Chicago and the surrounding areas and seeing if I can get some of my work displayed."

Pulling his hand back, Owen took another bite of his dinner as he thought for a minute. "I know I don't know a whole lot about art—not like you—but…is Chicago the right place for you to be doing this? Wouldn't someplace like New York be more to your advantage?"

She shook her head again. "Too much competition there. Besides, the timing is right for me to stay in Chicago. With the way my uncle is feeling and with his prognosis, I want to be there. Maybe after…" she began and then stopped, and Owen knew exactly what she was thinking.

"I know," he said.

Brooke looked up at him and wiped away the tears that began to fall. "I want to be close to him. It's important. I don't see myself staying in Chicago, but I don't particularly see myself heading back to Long Island either. It's weird not knowing where I belong."

Very carefully, Owen put down his utensils. This was it. This was the exact opening he'd been hoping for.

"With me," he said, his tone and expression serious. "You belong with me."

A slow smile played at her lips. "I like that."

"Of course, I'm not sure where I belong yet either. Maybe we can take some time and figure that out together."

Her smile grew. "I like that even more."

Everything in him relaxed, and once again, he reached for Brooke's hand. "I had planned on going back to DC for a little while. I have a place there, but…I don't want to have a place there anymore. I'm tired of simply having a spot to keep my things. I want a home to go to every night and someone there waiting for me." He squeezed her hand. "Will you make a home with me?"

And now her smile was positively dazzling. "Yes. I want to make a home with you too."

"Would it be wrong to ask your mother to stay a little bit longer with Howard—maybe an extra week?—so we can have some time to ourselves?"

"I think that's a great idea! Would we stay here in Vegas or go someplace else?"

"Wherever you want to go. We could be spontaneous again," he suggested. "I think it worked well for us the last time."

"I totally agree."

They finished their dinner and worked together to put their trays out in the hallway before locking the door and facing each other. Owen reached up and gently caressed her cheek. "You are so beautiful."

She blushed at his compliment and placed a hand over his, pressing his palm to her skin. "I was afraid you wouldn't want me here," she confessed quietly.

Owen shook his head. "Never. You never have to be afraid of that." Then he took her by the hand and led her across the room to the windows. He slowly closed the curtains and then led her over to the bed.

And then he was kissing her. Her face cupped in his hands, Owen was unable to wait another minute to touch her. Brooke sighed and melted against him, and he waited for her to wrap her arms around him.

But she didn't.

And then she broke the kiss and took a step back. He was just about to question her—ask what she was doing—but he saw the sexy grin on her face. First she peeled her shirt up and over her head and tossed it aside. Then she shimmied out of her skirt. The light blue scraps of silk and lace she wore matched her eyes. He swallowed hard and went to reach for her again, but she stepped out of his grasp.

"Just one more minute," she said huskily as she walked across the room.

The view of her from behind was almost as spectacular as from the front. He was momentarily confused about where she was going, and then the main lights in the room went off. A lamp next to the bed was still lit, so he knew she'd be okay.

Brooke turned and walked back toward him, and when they were toe to toe, she reached up, raked her hands through his hair, and pulled him down for another deep, wet kiss. He loved kissing her almost as much as he loved touching her; right then, his hands wanted in on the action and immediately cupped her bottom, pulling her snugly against him.

He lost track of time again—something that was becoming fairly common when she was near—and he was just about to make the move to lower her to the bed when she broke the kiss.

"Lay down," she whispered to him.

Owen discovered he liked it when she took control. Wordlessly, he complied. Positioning himself in the middle of the bed against the pillows, he watched as she gave him a mischievous look.

Then she peeled off her bra.

Yes.

Her panties went next.

Even better.

Then she stood there for a moment and let him look his fill. Owen slowly rolled onto his side, feeling himself trembling with need for her. Her name came out as a plea, but she didn't move right away.

Gracefully, she leaned forward and kissed him. It went from light and sweet to deep and wet in the blink of an eye, and Owen growled with impatience. He wanted her. Needed her. He reached out and placed a hand on her hip, gently guiding her toward him, and he thought he had succeeded when Brooke placed a knee on the bed.

She pulled away again, and he was almost ready to cry.

She was torturing him. Teasing him. And he was on the verge of begging.

Opening his eyes, he looked at her and saw she had her hand on the bedside lamp. Was it still too dark in here? Was she hoping for a setting to make it brighter? He was about to roll over and offer to turn on the other lamp when she did something that completely surprised him.

She turned out the light.

And that was completely all right with him because he was pretty sure they created enough fireworks to light up the entire night sky.

─w─

Two days later, Owen looked at the group of people and smiled. Everyone was talking and asking questions, and for the first time in his life, he felt like the most confident one in the crowd.

And that was saying something.

It was just after two in the afternoon, and Brooke was

leading his group in a painting session. While she was explaining about colors and techniques, several of his students were trying to explain to her why the layers in the canyon were colored the way that they were. And rather than getting flustered by their disruptive comments—as he certainly would have—she went with the flow and managed to turn them back toward looking at the colors on their palettes.

It was an amazing gift that she had.

Even Owen was standing with a canvas in front of him and a variety of colors of paint on his palette. Not that he was comfortable with painting, but Brooke had put so much work into learning about his work and about the meteor shower they were going to witness tonight that he thought it was only fair that he tried to learn about her work.

He had a feeling he was going to embarrass himself way more than she ever could, but that was all right with him. Owen knew that no matter what he managed to put down on the canvas, she was going to be encouraging and praise him in one way or another.

That took a lot of the pressure off.

For a few hours, they all worked on their artwork, but as soon as the sun started to shift and changed their lighting, Brooke encouraged everyone to start cleaning up. Owen moved along with his students, and when he was almost done, he searched for Brooke and found her over by the campfire, setting up preparations for dinner. They had made arrangements for food to be delivered, and she was talking with the food vendor and setting up enough seating for everyone.

Yeah, she was a definite blessing to this trip.

And his life.

And as soon as this trip was over, he was anxious for their life together to begin.

———～～～———

Brooke couldn't help but be excited. The energy of the group had transformed since they'd finished eating, and everyone was getting their gear together to find an optimum spot to view the meteor shower. She couldn't understand quite why they were looking for a specific spot—they were in this big, open space. To her, it was all premium space.

And she was going to be watching it all with Owen.

It didn't get better than that.

As the sky darkened and everyone was milling around and talking, it would have been easy to feel like an outcast—after all, she didn't know even one-tenth of what these people knew about the cosmos. However, she didn't. Besides having the opportunity to interact with everyone one-on-one earlier while they'd been painting and eating, she found it didn't matter if they were scientists and she was an artist. They were all people who were here to observe one of the greatest shows in the sky.

It made them all equal in her book.

She was looking up at the sky to see if she noticed anything on her own without anyone pointing it out when she felt Owen move in close behind her, his arms going around her waist. Brooke immediately rested her body against his and smiled.

"I haven't missed anything yet, have I?" she asked quietly.

Behind her, Owen chuckled. "Nope. No activity in the sky yet. You're safe."

She laughed softly. "I was just giving myself this inner pep talk about how it didn't matter if I didn't know as much as everyone here, but at the same time, I'm excited about what we're going to see. This is my first meteor shower."

"Sometimes they are spectacular. If the conditions are just right and the sky is clear, you can witness a phenomenal show."

"The sky looks pretty clear to me," she observed. "Does that mean…?"

He shrugged. "There are no guarantees, but we're going to be up all night watching, so I'm sure we'll see at least some."

That took a little of the wind out of her sails. "So it's not an ongoing event?"

"Unfortunately no. Sometimes it can be as few as three per hour, but it can go as high as sixty for this particular event."

"That's quite the range."

Owen nodded. "We go by the zenithal hourly rate—it standardizes the shower rate to optimum observing conditions. Think of it as an accurate scale for how many meteors we can expect to see. It's not foolproof, but it's a pretty good standard to follow. The shower rates are usually corrected for fully dark skies, and the meteor radiant point has been artificially located at the zenith, directly overhead. The actual rate of meteors seen by most observers, however, is normally a little bit lower."

"Which means nothing can accurately predict how many we'll see, but it's like a guideline." She looked over her shoulder at him and noted the smile on his face. "What? What are you smiling about?"

"Normally when I start spouting scientific facts like this to my family, they don't comment on it or they try to change the subject."

"Why would I change the subject? I brought it up."

He placed a kiss on her temple. "I like how you engage in the geek talk."

That had her laughing out loud, and she immediately turned in his arms. "*Geek talk?*"

Chuckling, he pulled her closer. "It just came to me."

This was something she'd noticed over the past few weeks with him—he was more relaxed and more comfortable with just being himself.

"I love you," she said softly.

Owen looked at her, brows furrowed for a moment. "Because of the geek talk?"

Brooke shook her head. "No. I love you because of all that you are."

"Even with the geek talk?" he teased.

"That's just a perk." On her tiptoes, she gave him a quick kiss. "Okay, where are we going to position ourselves? Have you picked out our spot yet?"

"Is it wrong that I'd rather be in our tent than out here?"

That pleased her. Her sexy, quiet scientist would rather be with her than observing one of the biggest meteor events of the year. How cool was that?

"Maybe we can sneak off a bit later. What are the ideal viewing times?"

"The peak time is actually right before dawn. So we'll all stay up as late as we want, catch a couple of hours of sleep, and then get up around 4 a.m. and watch some more."

"Is everyone doing that?"

Owen shrugged. "It's a matter of personal preference. Most people want to stay up all night and watch it all—which is what I should be doing."

"But…?"

He hugged her close again. "But that was before I had a reason to hide out in my tent for a couple of hours."

Swatting playfully at him, she casually stepped out of his embrace. "The last thing I want to be is a bad influence on the teacher."

"Ugh…I'm not the teacher. I'm just the one facilitating—"

"Oh, stop. You're the teacher, and everyone's waiting for you to lead them and talk to them about this cosmic phenomenon."

"I wouldn't call it a phenomenon—"

"Owen!"

"What?" he asked, choosing to ignore her exasperation.

"Go lead!"

"Come with me?" He held out his hand to her, and of course she took it. Hand in hand, they rejoined the group, and soon all eyes were on Owen as he began to talk about the history of the Eta Aquarid showers.

———ᴖᴖᴖ———

"It's beautiful."

"No. You're beautiful."

Brooke snuggled closer to him as they pulled their sleeping bag around them. The sun was just starting to come up as the last meteor made its way across the sky. "That was amazing. Thank you."

"For what?"

"For sharing it with me," she said, her head resting on his shoulder. "I know I sort of dozed off in the middle of it all, but—"

"Not everyone can stay up all night. You got back up for the best part."

"Mmm."

"I think everyone's going to be heading back to their hotels soon, and then we're going to meet up tonight for dinner and to discuss what we saw and compare notes. I know I wouldn't mind a couple of hours of sleep."

"In a bed," she said sleepily, followed by a loud yawn.

"As long as you're there, I don't care where we sleep."

"Mmm."

Sure enough, within an hour, everyone was packed up and driving back to their hotels. Brooke and Owen had chosen a nicer resort than most of the students, and while Owen had felt bad about it when they had made their initial reservations, right now he was glad for the privacy. He had talked to people all day yesterday and all through the night. Right now all he wanted was a little peace and quiet and to be able to hold Brooke in his arms while they slept.

Once they were back in their own room, neither said a word as they moved around closing the curtains, pulling down the blankets, and stripping off yesterday's clothes. Once they were in the bed and under the blankets, they automatically curled toward one another and tangled their limbs together until they were pressed together from head to toe.

"This is nice," she murmured.

"Mm-hmm."

"Owen?"

"Yes?"

"We never decided where we were going to go once we're done here."

He lifted his head and looked down at her. The room was fairly dark, with only a sliver of light coming from behind the curtains. "You want to talk about this now? I thought you were tired."

She shrugged. "I thought I was too, but now that we're here, my mind is just sort of refusing to cooperate."

Yawning, he shifted to get more comfortable. "And do you know where you want to go?"

"I do."

He waited a minute and then asked with a hint of amusement, "Well?"

"Well...our last spontaneous trip brought us here, and we got to combine business and pleasure."

"Right."

"I think our next spontaneous trip shouldn't include business at all. It should be all about having fun and doing stuff we wouldn't normally do."

"Okay."

"Like...hiking or fishing or—"

"I grew up fishing all the time. We lived by the ocean." He yawned again.

"I'm sorry... You're exhausted. I, at least, got a nap last night. Go to sleep, and we'll talk about this later."

"It's okay. It's on your mind, so we should talk about it now," he said, but his voice was soft and slurring just a bit.

Brooke turned and placed a kiss on his chest. "Sleep, my sexy scientist. And if we have to close our eyes and point to a spot on a map to decide where we'll go, that's fine too."

Beside her, Owen murmured something, but she couldn't understand it, and just before she gave in to sleep herself, she heard him say, "I love you."

And she had the sweetest dreams after that.

"This wasn't quite what I had in mind."

"It wasn't? Are you sure?"

"Brooke—"

She smiled and scampered away, laughing the entire time. They had ended up back in North Carolina and were staying at Aidan and Zoe's—although they were currently at Quinn and Anna's to swim in their massive pool.

When they had woken up that afternoon three days ago, Brooke had said what she wanted most was to go back and meet his family all over again. It seemed like an odd request, but she had been so earnest about it that he readily agreed. He'd made the calls, and before he knew it, everyone was on board for another family get-together.

Riley and Savannah were coming in from London on their way back to LA, and Darcy even said she'd be coming home—mainly because she'd quit her job and lost the lease on her apartment and it seemed like a good time to come back to North Carolina for an extended stay.

No matter what the reason, Owen looked around

the yard and knew that within a few hours, his entire family—all the people he loved—would be together.

Looking over his shoulder, he saw Brooke climbing from the pool and held in a groan. Good Lord, the woman was so damn sexy in her bikini. It was a shame they were around his family, or he'd—

"I know that look."

Owen turned and saw Quinn swimming his way. "Excuse me?"

"That look. The way you were just eyeing Brooke. I know that expression well."

"You were…?"

"No, doofus," Quinn said with a laugh, splashing Owen in the face. "I mean, it's the way I look at Anna when she's walking around in a bikini. Hell, the first time I saw her in one, I almost swallowed my own tongue!"

"And that's how I was just looking at Brooke?"

Quinn's smile was big and goofy. "Hell yeah, you were! Good for you, Bro!"

The old Owen would have felt awkward having this conversation—or at the very least embarrassed. But now, he was too happy and too relaxed. "You're right—good for me."

"She's awesome, Owen. Really. I'm glad the two of you worked things out." Then he looked at his younger brother and nodded toward the bandage on his chest. "You know you're not supposed to be swimming with that thing yet, right?"

Nodding, he said, "I know. That's why I've got it covered and I'm staying in the shallow end."

Quinn shook his head and laughed. "So you're only being a partial rebel. Nice!"

360

He shrugged. "So when's everyone getting in? Do you have the official schedule?"

Relaxing against the side of the pool, Quinn took a minute to think. "Dad's picking up Darcy at two. He's going to bring her home first before coming here for dinner. Riley said they were getting in at four, but they're renting a car. Dinner will be a little late, but I don't think it will be too bad. Hugh and Aubrey should be here any minute, and Aidan and Zoe are trying to convince Lily to take a nap. So they should be out here soon."

"What about Martha?"

"What about her?"

"Are she and Dad…?"

Quinn shrugged. "Dad hasn't said much, and to be honest, I haven't asked. We're all in a bit of a sleep-deprived haze around here—at least Anna and I are. Darcy's news took everyone by surprise, but I think Dad's glad to have her back home for a while."

"It will be good for her."

"What about you, Bro? Where are you going to be now?"

He looked over at Brooke and saw her holding Kaitlyn while she talked to Anna, and it made his heart swell. That was what he wanted—he wanted to see Brooke holding their baby, to have what his brothers had.

"We're going back to Chicago for a while to take care of Howard. And then—"

"Man, that's gotta suck. I mean, you're just hanging out there with him while…"

Owen nodded. "It's hard. I hate it. I hate it more than anything. It's hard when you lose someone unexpectedly. But this? It's like you get the time to prepare yourself, but it's never enough. I know she's struggling with it, and I almost feel bad that we're here, but we talked about it and thought it would be good. Not just for us but for Brooke's mom and Howard."

"That's good. That's great. I'm just sorry you're both having to deal with it."

"Howard's been a great friend and mentor to me. And I'll never forget him. Not just because of the things he taught me or the time we spent together but because he brought Brooke into my life."

Quinn smiled and patted Owen on the back. "You're a lucky man."

"Thanks."

"Not as lucky as me, of course," he teased. "But lucky nonetheless." Then he swam away.

Owen was done in the pool. He made his way to the steps and climbed out. He grabbed a towel and walked over to where Brooke and Anna were sitting and talking, but his eyes were locked on the baby in Brooke's arms. Anna quietly excused herself as Owen crouched down beside Brooke.

"She's so tiny," Brooke said, stroking the baby's cheek. "And so soft."

"She looks good in your arms," he said, wanting to reach out and touch them both, but his skin was cold and wet.

"And she smells so good." Holding Kaitlyn close, she inhaled deeply. "Why do babies smell so good?"

"I'm sure it's not like that all the time."

"It doesn't even matter. She smells wonderful right now." She looked at Owen and smiled. "This is a good trip."

"How can you tell? We just arrived."

"We landed yesterday, and it's all been good. Your whole family is coming, and everyone's happy."

"Except Darcy."

Brooke shrugged. "I think this is going to be a good thing for her too."

"Why do you say that?"

"That job wasn't for her. She's interested in art right now and trying to figure out what she wants to do. Maybe some time with her family will help her get focused and figure it all out. It worked for me."

He chuckled. "You were living with your family and had to leave them to figure your stuff out."

"Uncle Howard is still family, and he helped me a lot." She paused, and her smile faded a little. "I'm resigning from the teaching job at the community college."

He looked at her with surprise. "You are? Why?"

She shook her head. "I don't want any distractions. Howard's got so little time left, and I want to spend it with him. I don't want to be held down to a teaching schedule. He told me how happy it makes him to see me paint. So…that's what I'm going to do."

Leaning in, Owen kissed her on the cheek. "You're an amazing woman. You know that, right?"

"I'm glad you think so."

"I do," he said, his tone deep and serious. "I always have, and I always will."

"That's good because I think you're pretty amazing too—always have and always will. We make a good pair."

He nodded but couldn't speak. Instead, he rose and went to grab them something to drink. Before he knew it, the yard was filling up with his family. Aidan and Zoe finally came out to join them, each looking somewhat exhausted after trying to convince their daughter to go to sleep. Hugh and Aubrey arrived a few minutes later and immediately had to chase Connor down before he jumped in the pool.

Anna brought out trays of snacks, and as they all sat around the large table, Owen realized that, for the first time in his life, he felt like he was surrounded by his peers. He was part of a couple, and as they all talked and laughed, it hit him how it was a good feeling to be this comfortable around all of them. He reached over and took Brooke's hand in his. She had to relinquish her hold on Kaitlyn so Aubrey could get her turn, and all he could think of was the time when it would be their baby getting spoiled by the Shaughnessy siblings.

It seemed weird to be thinking such things, but at the same time, it felt right. He caught Brooke watching him, and he suddenly wished they were alone, so he could tell her how he felt. But there would be time for that later.

Time flew as they continued to talk and eat. Everyone was in and out of the pool and goofing around, and it was the most fun Owen had had in a long time. Soon his father and Darcy showed up and Quinn began putting steaks on the grill.

"What about Riley and Savannah?" Ian asked. "Shouldn't we wait for them?"

"Riley texted about twenty minutes ago. They got an earlier flight, so they should be here by the time we're sitting down to eat."

Anna turned on the outdoor lights as the sun was starting to go down. They were all crowded around the table, and there seemed to be more plates of food than people, but that's how a dinner with the Shaughnessys normally went.

As if they'd planned it that way, Quinn put the platter of steaks on the table just as Riley and Savannah came walking through the door. Greetings were called out, and everyone hugged and kissed and moved in their seats to make room for the new arrivals.

Owen always marveled at how conversations were had in such chaos. From what he could tell, there were about four different ones going on right now. Each of them was loud and boisterous, and it was all music to his ears. Beside him, Brooke was talking with Darcy, and he loved watching the two of them—they each spoke so animatedly and with such passion—and he realized, again, how well Brooke fit in with his family. When he looked across the table and caught his father's eye, Owen smiled. His father raised his glass in a mock salute to him, and Owen responded in kind.

They finished eating and everyone helped with the cleanup before gathering to sit on the deck around the fire pit. Things were a little quieter, a little more subdued. Brooke was resting her head on his shoulder, and for a moment, the conversation had died down. Owen looked up at the sky, spotted the brightest star, and smiled.

Sirius.

His heart squeezed as he remembered being a child and thinking that Sirius was his mom smiling down on him.

And now he could say with great certainty that it was

possible. Because if ever there was a night for Lillian Shaughnessy to be smiling down on her family, it was this night.

Epilogue

Three months later…

"Is this the last of it?"

She nodded. "I think so." Then she paused. "I hope so."

Owen came and stood beside her, putting his arms around her and holding her close. They were closing up Howard's house. All of his things were packed up and were either being donated or going into storage until Brooke's parents came to get them. Brooke and Owen had already taken the things that Howard specifically wanted them to have—including the chess set—and shipped them to the house they were renting in North Carolina.

Movers came in and took the last stack of boxes out. The room was empty. The house was now empty. Brooke stood in Owen's arms, and he could feel the slight trembling of her body. "You going to be okay?"

She nodded, but he heard her sniffle. "It all…it was just so much faster than I thought it would be."

"I know." And he did. When they had gotten back to Chicago after the visit with his family, his friend's health had deteriorated quickly. Six weeks after their return, Howard was gone. He'd had his affairs in order—there was very little for them to do other than sell the house. His estate was to be split between Brooke and her mother. There had been no one else. No other family.

"I think…I kept hoping—"

"I know," he said softly. They'd had this conversation before. Multiple times. And it still wasn't any easier.

Then Brooke seemed to pull herself together as she stepped out of his embrace. "I'm just going to look around one more time."

Rather than argue about how she'd already gone through the house four times, he nodded. "I'll wait for you outside." She nodded and went up the stairs. But Owen didn't leave. He went into the room that had been Howard's study and looked at the walls that had once been lined with books and degrees. They were all packed away now.

This was another new aspect—new feeling for him. When his mother had died, nothing around their home had changed. It wasn't until a few years ago that they had even attempted to change the house that his mother had loved. He had been too young to remember packing up her clothes, her belongings. He and Brooke had spent the past two weeks doing just that with Howard's things—laughing one minute and crying the next. He was emotionally drained. That's why he knew the move was going to be good for them. A fresh start—a chance to make new memories.

Stepping outside he watched as the last boxes were loaded onto the truck. He thanked the movers and stood back as they closed and locked the doors. Within minutes, the truck was gone and Owen was alone on the sidewalk. Part of him wondered if he should go inside and see if Brooke was all right, but he thought better of it. This was her final good-bye to her uncle, and she deserved some privacy.

Ten minutes later, when she came out, he saw the telltale signs that she'd been crying. He opened his arms, she stepped into them, and he held her.

"Thank you," she whispered a few minutes later.

"Are you ready to go?"

Brooke's eyes swam with tears again. "Not really. But I know it's time."

Slowly Owen led her away from the house and to her car. He held the door for her as she climbed in and then he walked around to the driver's side. They made their way across town to the hotel Owen always stayed at— they were going to be there for one more night before driving to the Carolina coast.

"Do you think he knew?" she asked as she looked out the window. "Do you think at the end he knew what was going on?"

Owen knew exactly what she was referring to. "He was extremely alert right up until the end. We'd been talking a lot, late at night. He wasn't afraid. All he kept talking about was how he was going to finally be with his wife again."

Brooke smiled sadly. "I'm glad. I'm glad it gave him peace."

"He had peace about it all. Having the time with you and your mom meant a lot to him. He just wanted to know you were both happy and that you were going to be okay."

Turning her head, she looked at him. "I told him our news. He wasn't awake, and…it was right at the end. But I'm glad I got to share that with him. I hope he heard me." She paused. "Do you think he did?"

Owen had no way of knowing for sure, but he knew

what Brooke needed to hear. So he nodded. "I do. I think he heard everything, and if he could have, he would have told you how thrilled he was." That seemed to please her because she turned and looked out the window again and she was smiling.

They arrived at the hotel, and he took her by the hand. "Are you hungry? I know it's a little early for dinner, but we could order something now and have it sent up, or we could walk and get something?"

"Let's get room service. It's a little too hot to be walking around." She placed her hand on her belly as they walked through the front entrance of the hotel.

"Are you okay? Are you feeling all right?"

Brooke rolled her eyes and smiled. "Owen, you are going to have to relax a bit. We've got seven more months of this to get through. You can't worry every time I touch my stomach."

They were having a baby. The first Shaughnessy to get pregnant before being married. Him. The safe one in the family was suddenly the rebel—a tattoo and a baby. It was quite the wild time in Owen's life.

They were going to be married next weekend, when they were back home with his family. Brooke's parents were flying down to be with them, and they were having a sunset wedding on the beach. While they were trying to plan where they would have the ceremony, the idea had come to Brooke—mainly because she wanted to paint the sunset on the beach. And he figured it was the perfect way to give her what she wanted.

His life had taken a completely different path than he'd ever thought possible, but as he held her hand and they rode up the elevator to his room, Owen realized that even though it was different, it was perfect.

And he wouldn't trade it for the world.

Darcy Shaughnessy gets more than she bargained for
when what was supposed to be a lively, rejuvenating
Christmas with family turns into a snowbound weekend
with a brooding—and devastatingly handsome—stranger.

Don't miss the conclusion of
The Shaughnessy Brothers series
by Samantha Chase.
Read on for a sneak peek!

HOLIDAY *Spice*

Chapter 1

THERE HAD BEEN A LIGHT DUSTING OF SNOW OVERNIGHT, and as Benjamin Tanner watched the sunrise, he realized how this scene never got old. This was where he was meant to be—to live and breathe—in the mountains of Washington.

That didn't mean he didn't want to travel or see some of the rest of the world, but this was always going to be where he called home. His brothers had both moved away once they'd finished college, and while it meant he didn't see them very much, Ben understood the need to forge your own path.

The forests, the mountains, and working with wood had never appealed to either Jack or Henry. For as long as Ben could remember, his brothers had been athletes and intellectuals—and neither had any interest in anything remotely artistic that required working with their hands. And he was fine with it. Really. Growing up, it had meant Ben got to spend a lot of quality time with his grandfather that his brothers never got to experience. It meant that all of his grandfather's hard work had led to something—to leaving a legacy that was now Ben's to pass on someday.

Some. Day.

Maybe.

If he didn't start getting his priorities in order, there wouldn't be anyone to leave this legacy to, and that made him sad. Turning away from the window, Ben looked at the open floor plan of the home's main floor. At one time, this had been a simple three-room cabin his grandfather had built. Over the years, he'd expanded, and when Ben's grandparents died and left the house to him, he always knew he'd make improvements on it. And he had. Some were out of necessity, and others were... well...everyone should live in a space they enjoyed.

The property was magnificent, and his grandfather's workshop was still standing. There was a lot of new equipment and upgrades out there too, but for the most part, Ben preferred working with the same tools his grandfather had used. Of course, over the years, so many of them had needed to be replaced, but he did his best to stick to the basics and stay away from the newer power tools.

Anyone could work with those.

It took time and patience and skill to do it all by hand.

Speaking of...He took a minute and flexed his left hand. It still hurt like a son of a bitch, and he knew it would continue to feel that way for a couple of days— not enough to make him stop working, but it was going to slow him down. And right now that wasn't necessarily a bad thing. There was nothing worse than the sting of a sharp metal blade cutting through skin—no matter how many times it happened.

Looking over at the kitchen table, he saw the letter that had turned his perfectly peaceful world upside down. He'd committed to doing a book on his artwork and he was supposed to do a fair amount of writing— including a very lengthy foreword and introduction— and he hadn't done jack shit to get it done.

And now he was out of time.

As much as it pained him to admit it, he needed help. Fast. He needed to find someone who was organized and had a basic knowledge and appreciation for art—specifically the kind of art that he did. On top of that, they needed to be able to write about it in a way that would make readers both intrigued and excited about his work. There was only one person he could think of to fit the bill and that had been Savannah Daly—well, Savannah Shaughnessy now. She'd interviewed him about three years ago, and even though he'd been vehemently against it at the time, she'd been fairly easy to work with—not intrusive, and she didn't waste time. She came and got on with the interview and was gone without it being too incredibly awkward. And in the end, she'd done a kick-ass article on him that had garnered him enough new clients to keep him working well into the next decade.

She'd kept in touch since then, sending him cards or notes when she'd seen or read something about his work. Honestly, if he had to have someone in his house for a couple of days to get this whole book thing off his plate, he couldn't think of anyone else he'd want to do it. He considered her a friend.

And he didn't consider many people that.

So he'd called her, and after talking to Savannah, he had reluctantly agreed to her version of helping him out. She couldn't come personally, but she was sending someone to him—someone she trusted and assured him would be an asset. Right now he wasn't so sure. It was no different from his publisher sending someone, but at least this way he had a personal reference from a friend.

Darcy Shaughnessy. Over the last several years, Ben had heard Savannah mention her sister-in-law, but he'd never had the opportunity to meet her himself. Now he was going to. Soon. But he still wasn't sure she was going to be of much help to him. After all, she wasn't a writer like Savannah, and that was what Ben had wanted. Ultimately he had accepted the offer because Savannah had assured him that Darcy had brilliant office skills and a creative mind—all of the things combined she swore would help him finish this project.

With a stretch, he walked into the kitchen and poured himself a second cup of coffee and contemplated his day. There wasn't any reason to be up this early—it was just the way his internal body clock worked. And with his hand still throbbing, he knew going to the workshop right now wasn't wise.

"Looks like a paperwork day," he murmured and then realized the paperwork was everywhere. A muttered curse was his first reaction and then a more vicious one when he raked his bad hand through his hair and rubbed it the wrong way.

"Okay, so clearly it's going to be *that* kind of day. Great."

Yeah. Things weren't looking too good for him to make much progress on anything right now. Darcy was due to arrive this evening, and he'd already invited her to join him for dinner, so he was going to have to attempt to clean up. Not that the house was dirty, but there was stuff everywhere. Like paperwork. Newspapers. Tool catalogs. The first thing to do would be to do a quick sweep of it all and throw away the junk he didn't need.

It took over two hours because there were a lot of tool catalogs he'd forgotten about and now he had a list of items he wanted to order for some projects he wanted to do in the spring.

"Still progress," he told himself as he began—in earnest again—to weed through the junk mail and minimize the piles.

By the time lunch time rolled around, Ben was beginning to wonder if maybe he should have offered to go
to LA and work with Savannah there. It probably would
have been a whole lot less stressful and aggravating than
this nightmare. But on the upside, the living area looked
good. Small piles of magazines and catalogs were fanned
out on the coffee table and he could totally live with
that. He dusted off the newly uncovered surfaces and
then ran the vacuum and felt a sense of accomplishment.

Maybe it wouldn't be so bad after all…

Six hours later, the steaks were ready to go on the grill.

The salad just needed to be dressed.

The potatoes au gratin were in the oven.

And there was a platter of assorted cheeses and
crackers on the counter along with a bottle of wine and
glasses. He might not entertain much, but he hadn't forgotten how to be a good host.

Off in the distance, he heard a car door close and
smiled. It seemed weird that he was actually looking forward to this night. It was possible that Darcy would want
to wait until morning to get started, but hopefully—with
a few strategically placed hints—she'd see there was
no time like the present. After all, the sooner they got
started, the sooner they'd be done. And if she felt half as
awkward about this unconventional situation as he did,
she'd see his thinking was right.

He opened the front door and was heading down the
steps and about to call out a greeting, but words simply
escaped him.

Dark chestnut hair that seemed to caress her shoulders.

Fair, flawless skin that had a hint of rose from the cold. And wide green eyes that seemed to sparkle as she looked over at him with a smile. Ben noticed how she moved with grace and ease and confidence. Medium build with trim legs encased in well-worn denim and…He had a feeling he was staring and forced himself to stop.

Stepping forward, he closed the distance between them and held out his hand. "Darcy? Hi, I'm Ben."

Darcy smiled brightly at him as she shook his hand. "Hi! It's a pleasure to meet you. Savannah's told me a lot about you."

Ben took her hand and forced himself to keep his eyes on hers and not to look as shaken as he felt. She had a firm handshake—one that in a professional meeting he'd appreciate—but right now he found it hard to ignore how small her hand felt in his or how soft her skin was. He noticed the odd expression on her face and realized he hadn't responded to her.

Part of him wanted to ask if it was good or bad stuff she'd heard, but he figured it would sound too corny. "Likewise," he said instead. "How was the trip?"

"My flight was great, but I had a little trouble getting here from the airport," she said, but it didn't come off like a complaint. "You're certainly not close to any major cities. I was beginning to think I'd never get here."

He chuckled. "Sorry. I guess I should have warned you."

She laughed with him. "Savannah mentioned it, but I thought she was exaggerating." She paused. "The scenery was amazing. Seriously, with the little bit of snow on the trees, it felt like I was driving into a Christmas card scene or something."

They stood there for a moment and Ben realized he

still had her hand in his. It would seem weird just to drop it so he kind of casually slid his palm against hers until he could simply put his own hand in his pocket.

"Thank you so much for doing this," he said as they pulled apart. "I don't know how much you know about this project. Savannah said you were there visiting and on vacation so…"

"Well, you caught me at a good time. I think I would have gone broke if I stayed much longer."

"Broke?"

"Savannah and I did a lot of shopping," she said. "With Halloween coming up, I bought Aislynn a couple of costumes…"

"Does she need more than one? She's a baby, right?" he asked with mild amusement.

She nodded. "She is, but all the more reason for her to need multiple. Babies are messy."

"Makes sense."

"Then I started Christmas shopping…"

"It's October," he stated, figuring she might need the reminder.

"I know. But the stores already had Christmas stuff out—I swear it gets earlier and earlier every year—and that got me all excited because it's Aislynn's first Christmas."

"Do babies know it's Christmas?"

She giggled, and just the sound of it made him smile.

"She may not, but I bought her the cutest little elf costume." She stopped and blushed. "Sorry. Here we are standing out in the cold and I'm yammering on about my niece."

"It's quite all right," he said, enjoying the color in her cheeks. "But now I kind of feel worse about taking you